RUINED REIGN

SABRINA LOZIER

THE SAINTS & THEIR POWERS

Uri the Bright – Healing
Briar the Cunning – Plants
Inerys the Terrifying – Poison
Amari the Eternal – Appearance
Zillah the Vengeful – Spiders
Kieran the Unbreakable – Shadows
Torryn the Gentle – Animals
Jin the Resilient – Metal
Cairn the Strong – Stone
Nadia the Peacemaker – Song
Felix the Trickster – Illusion
Moroz the Unyielding – Ice

ERINYA
SKARSDEN BAY
CONVENT OF THE SAINTS
THE CITADEL
OHAN TERRI
THE RAVAGED WOOD
THE NORTH PLAINS
LAUGHING DOG INN
SOUTHERN MARSHES
ASIF VILLA
ARMY CAMP
GREA
CART

ARAN
SEA
BOREADS GLACIER
SIREN'S
WAIL
FENRIC'S
KEEP
THE DEADWOOD
WHITESAW
MT RANGE
OSE RIVER
GRASSLANDS
ENCHANTED
WOOD
HARROW FOREST
ER
S I A

RUINED REIGN

1

JACK

The lion and the unicorn
Were fighting for the crown
The lion beat the unicorn
All around the town.

The shadows swarming Jack's mind cleared as a path opened before him in the mist. He moved with purpose though his mind couldn't recall how he'd come to be here. The click of his shoes rang off the cobblestones, violently discordant against the stillness of night. Slowly, his memories returned. He'd come out for fresh air, to feel the cold in his lungs and the wind rustle his hair.

His father had punished him again. His back still bore the fresh puckered skin from the lashes. Always his back. Never a mark where anyone could see, where anyone might suspect the king mistreated his own son and heir.

The sting had slowly subsided, but as the wildwinds pushed through the dark alley, they slipped under his cloak, searing his skin again. Jack hissed. He wanted to feel angry, sad, disgusted, but he found no word for the overwhelming tightness in his chest that plagued him day after day. His only reprieve came from visits to his sister. Or from Anna. And after laying in the dark for the last several days, it was all he could do to stand.

His father refused to believe his son had been blinded and bedridden, choosing to believe Jack was being defiant instead. Hence the lashes to his back.

A building appeared before him in the mist. The waning moonlight cut a jagged path before him, leading to the stables that sat at the edge of the palace grounds. His sister was often there these days, though he wasn't sure why. She'd never been fond of horses before.

Another cursed wind blew into his face as he stepped through the threshold of the stables, where a flickering lantern illuminated the space with faint light. Horses nickered quietly at him as he let in a draft. These were the king's finest steeds, reserved for himself, his children, and the paladins. Stable hands worked tirelessly to keep them in excellent shape.

A shuffle up ahead caught his attention: the creaking of a saddle's leather and clinking of its stirrups. A sharp inhale of breath resonated, and the clinking stopped abruptly, as if the person did not want to be heard.

Who would be saddling a horse in the middle of the night?

Jack stilled, listening closely as he inched forward. He peered around a corner, his brow pulling in confusion. It was one of the stable hands, a tall boy with blond hair and a short-cropped beard. Next to him stood two horses, one already saddled.

His sister's horse.

Jack took another step forward and the young man spun toward him, a second saddle slung over his shoulder.

The boy froze, his eyes going wide.

"Your Highness," he said, swallowing. "What are you doing here so late at night?" It was a rude, panicked question considering who he spoke to.

Jack said nothing but stared at his sister's steed. Saddle bags hung across the back of the saddle and several other bags sat on the floor.

On instinct Jack reached for his knife, though he didn't draw it. "What are you doing? Are you stealing my sister's horse? Is this how you repay your king?"

"It's not what you think." The boy raised a hand while setting the saddle down with care.

"Really? Because it looks like you're running off with two of my father's prized horses."

The boy swallowed again, both hands raised in defense now. "I promise. It's not what it looks like. Jill and I—" he stopped himself, realizing his mistake. "The princess, Her Highness—"

Jack stepped back. "Why did you call her Jill? She isn't your equal." The words lashed out of Jack's mouth and struck the boy like he'd been slapped.

"Please. You're her brother. You should know her better than anyone. You know she'd be forced to marry a stranger for an alliance—"

"She's running away." Jack's insides turned to ice. He was reminded of another night he'd come here, a night when he'd heard tender, whispered words. He had never suspected anything. Not from Jill.

His sister, his confidant, his only friend was leaving him.

Leaving him for some stable hand. She was leaving him to face the wrath of his father all alone. Did she not understand what their father would do to him if she left?

The young man stiffened but gave a slow nod. "We're leaving. Tonight."

Tonight. The word was like acid on a wound. The final blow in a battle of betrayal.

Did she even plan to say goodbye?

She'd told him nothing. She would have disappeared into the night, never to be seen again. Would she marry this boy? Would they have a family? He never would have known either way.

Fiery rage exploded through him, like a dam bursting, like a spark igniting. Like something shattering between them forever.

I feel your rage, my prince.

That voice was the last thing he heard before his memory dimmed. A shadow swept across his vision. He could not hear, nor see, nor touch. Only anger and pain pulsed through his body.

When his vision returned, he stood in the stable once more, his knife held aloft and dripping crimson blood. The boy collapsed in front of him, clutching his neck. He looked up at Jack, features contorted in pain as blood seeped through his fingers. But he didn't speak a single word.

The boy shuddered, released a final breath, and then went still.

Jack dropped the knife, staring at his bloodied hands.

How? Why?

The stable door creaked open, and another young man entered, tall with dark skin. The boy froze as he took in the scene in front of him. His gaze shifted between the corpse and the prince and his knife.

Jack marched forward and pressed his knife to the boy's throat. "You tell a soul who did this, and I will end your life and the lives of everyone you love."

The stable hand nodded, silent.

Before he could say another word, Jack stormed out, tossing the bloodied knife in the bushes and rinsing his hands in a trough of water.

As he rounded a corner he heard it. A wail of sheer pain and fury.

Jill.

He must have missed her by mere seconds. He ran and stood in the dark corner of the palace walls, listening to her pitiful wails. Despite his wrath, tears streamed down his cheeks.

She will be better off without him, my prince.

Jack started, swinging his head around.

"Who said that?" His whisper echoed into the silent night.

Who I am doesn't matter. Yet. But I can tell this is just the beginning of a very beautiful friendship.

Jack bolted upright in bed. Sweat dripped down his neck and back despite the chill of his room, the fire in the hearth having burned to smoldering embers. He rubbed his aching forehead, thankful he was in control of his own body for the moment. He didn't know how long it would last though.

He never did.

After Jack had drunk the water from the well, his memories had become murky, like recalling a night of partying after one too many drinks. Only one thing he knew for sure.

Malum had taken control of him.

It was Malum who'd threatened his sister, Malum who'd ordered Millie's brother be tortured for her betrayal, Malum who always seethed and raged within him. Or perhaps it was Jack who seethed and raged as he watched helplessly, a prisoner in his own body. The words he said, the things he did —they were rarely his own doing anymore.

But the night you killed your sister's love?

Shut it.

Night after night it was the same dream, the same sequence. And still he wasn't certain whether he'd been the one to slay the stable hand, Will, or if Malum had forced his hand.

He wasn't sure if he wanted to know. If it had been him and him alone, what did that make him?

A murderer, Malum whispered.

Bile rose in the back of his throat, and Jack squeezed his eyes shut to banish the dizziness that came over him. It was no use.

Throwing off his bedsheets, he grabbed a shirt and coat and headed for the door, ignoring his messy black hair in the polished mirror as he passed. Ignoring the faint scars that crossed his back like spiderwebs.

He needed to see her while he still could. While it was still him.

Malum chuckled in his mind. The Black King was always amused whenever Jack tried to do something on his own and it infuriated him to no end.

Jack slinked down the marble corridor, avoiding the guards' gazes as he passed. They gave no reaction to his presence.

Millie's room wasn't far from his and intentionally so.

Whether it was for his protection or hers, he still hadn't decided.

You know what people will think of you visiting the girl in the middle of the night?

Jack gritted his teeth. *And why should I care what people think? You've done more to damage my reputation than I ever could have.*

If you say so.

Jack turned another corner and the double doors to Millie's quarters stood in front of him. He wondered what Jill would think of Millie staying in her old rooms. Once upon a time, he could have answered that question easily. She'd have been livid. Now, he wasn't sure of anything when it came to his sister.

It seemed she was destined to abandon him no matter what, either to his father's devices or to Malum's. The thought only irritated him more as he knocked on Millie's door.

Silence greeted him. He stood there a minute before knocking again. Was she even in there? Or was she truly such a deep sleeper?

He knocked again, panic pressing into his chest. He needed to see her, to hear her voice, to know she was okay before Malum stole him away again.

"Millie?" he called. "Are you in there?"

At last, shuffling rose from the other side of the door. The steps were slow and tentative, and Jack wasn't sure whether it was from sleepiness or because she knew it was him at the door.

The corner of his vision dimmed.

Another burst of panic shot through him. He was fading. His mind was slipping back into the murky depths, like the tide lapping at the shore.

He knocked on the door again, louder this time. "Millie, please!"

His vision had gone completely dark now.

Please, Jack begged.

I'm sorry, my prince. Your time is up.

The door swung open, but Jack was already gone.

2

JILL

*J*ill would never get used to the massive city within the Whitesaw Mountains. The day she'd arrived —nearly two months ago now—trailing behind Grimzy, the view was magnificent enough to make her forget about her fight with Jack, if only for a moment.

Today, she followed Asif and Lyra as they wandered the main road within the city, twice as wide as any road Jill had ever seen. She supposed it was because the mountain men were twice as large as other races. Everything here was on a larger scale. The buildings were taller, the roads wider, and the homes bigger.

Homes and shops were carved into the interior of the mountain. The red-tinged rock revealed intricate designs of creatures and animals both familiar and otherworldly. Through the center of the city ran a large underground river from which everyone drew their water and fished. It rushed past them, sparkling and splashing over the banks. At the head of the underground city was the humble, albeit large, home of the Whitesaw tribe chief, its structure a dazzling mix of smooth red and white rock. Its domed rooftops reminded Jill of her own home, yet she preferred the simplicity of the mountain men's taste.

From the ceiling of the cavern high above, stalactites hung with glowing orbs of varying colors. Firegems—a type of gemstone varied in shades of red, orange, and amber—bathed the entire city in warm light, making Jill feel less like she was underground. The warm light had been an unforeseen blessing when all the refugees arrived, making them feel a little more at home. And more refugees arrived each day seeking shelter, protection, and supplies.

They sought a place of sanctuary and safety.

Humans, felines, boarmen, gazelles, inkwells, and more filled the underground sanctuary. It seemed no one was safe from Malum's terrible monsters. So far, the Whitesaw people had been able to accommodate the refugees, but Jill worried for the day when they could take in no one else. When would they stop allowing refugees? When would they have to stop for lack of space and resources?

Jill recalled a story she'd heard from her tutor of a siege on the Citadel fifty years before she was born. The king had harbored as many of his people in the upper district as he could, but eventually, they had no more room. No more food or water. He'd shut the gates on his people leaving them to fend for themselves.

The story still haunted Jill.

A small hand grabbed hers, dispelling the dark thoughts.

"Are you all right?" Lyra's sweet voice asked. Even at seven years old, she was a beauty. Her green cat eyes were a stark contrast to her golden skin and dark hair.

Jill forced a smile. "Of course."

"Asif says you talk in your sleep."

Jill glared at the boy, who gave her a sheepish grin.

Since she'd arrived in the Whitesaw Mountains, they had all been staying in the chief's home, sharing one of its rooms. Jill didn't mind. She preferred not to be alone. Apparently, that came with a cost.

"Is that so?" Jill asked.

"Well, I can't understand most of it," Asif drawled, rolling his eyes. "Just when you say David's name."

A sharp pain pierced Jill's chest. *David.*

"Well at least I don't pass gas in my sleep," Jill retorted.

Lyra giggled as Asif blushed. Jill smiled as he shook away the blush and rolled his eyes again.

"I'm surprised you could hear anything over Lyra's snoring," Asif teased.

"I don't snore!" Lyra swatted her older brother.

"Yes, you do."

"Do not!" she said, shoving Asif toward the river.

"Enough, you two. I don't need to fish either one of you out of the river today."

Asif laughed, as if the thought of Lyra pushing him into the icy river was amusing.

The young feline girl grabbed Jill's hand again, her features sobering. "I miss him too," she whispered.

Again, Jill's heart squeezed. She spent most of her days avoiding thoughts of David. Or her brother. Or the promise she'd made to take the throne from him. Here in Grimzy's home, it almost seemed like she could escape the memories, the weight of everything on her shoulders.

Almost.

They rounded a bend in the street coming to where the refugees currently resided. Compared to the Lost Tribe, the accommodations provided by the Whitesaw people seemed luxurious. People still slept in tents, but they were made from durable canvas rather than tattered rags. They had fresh water too, thanks to the underground river. The Whitesaw Tribe provided the refuges with as many supplies and as much food that could be spared.

Yet it still wasn't enough.

The Whitesaw people sacrificed so much to help them. Jill suspected they would have done so even if Grimzy weren't the chief's son. The mountain men and women may have been bigger and taller than any other race, but their people lived with a kindness and gentleness that surprised Jill. She didn't doubt they would keep accepting people until the mountains could not physically hold anymore.

"Your Highness," a deep voice rumbled.

Jill turned to see a familiar face staring down at her. "Grimzy." The mountain man wore traditional Whitesaw robes of red and orange belted at the waist and wrapped up and over one of his shoulders, exemplifying his twisting red tattoos. The outfit took getting used to after he'd worn a traditional loin cloth for so long. But he was the Chief's son, so he was expected to dress accordingly.

"*Paladin* Grimzy," the man said, his dark eyes sparkled with amusement, and he smirked before turning and leading her through the tents. They were to meet with the representatives of the Lost Tribe today to formulate a more long-term plan for the refugees.

Jill's stomach twisted at the thought. She didn't want any of this to become long term. She wanted to see these people restored to their homes and villages and livelihoods. But so long as Malum's monsters ran loose, no place was safe.

Grimzy led them toward the largest tent, where the representatives held meetings. While she was glad the people had found others to represent them, she didn't like that it was necessary in the first place. It seemed too permanent a thing for something she hoped would be temporary.

It also didn't help that the representatives hated her.

Pushing aside the tent flap, Grimzy entered while she shooed Asif and Lyra away. Asif groaned and his shoulders slumped, but he shuffled off after his sister.

Turning back to the tent, Jill counted to five, attempting to slow her racing heart before she pasted on a smile and shoved her way inside.

Several firegems lit the tent from stands raised several feet off the ground. A large table sat at the center, covered in maps and candles and wooden cups. Around the table sat the representatives, and at the head, a gazelle woman with a special hatred for Jill. She had been the one to humiliate Jill several months back when the princess had attempted, and failed, to rally the people of the Lost Tribe. In the end, it was David who'd convinced the woman and others to help.

She also held Jill personally responsible for the fire that burned the Lost Tribe to the ground, even though it had been the work of a Carthesian assassin who'd killed himself before he could be interrogated.

Unfortunately, Jill also held herself responsible. The assassin had decided to attack everyone in the Lost Tribe, and many had lost their lives.

"Welcome, *Your Highness*," the woman said curtly.

"The pleasure is all mine, Elisha." Jill forced another smile, unwilling to let the woman see how her tone irritated Jill.

Beside Elisha, the self-proclaimed head of the representatives, was a boarman named Seamus, an inkwell woman named Javyn, and a feline man named Nadeem.

"Thank you for your invitation," Grimzy said in his calming voice. "We are honored."

"As are we, Paladin Grimzy. Though you did not inform us the princess would be joining you." Elisha said the word *princess* like she was talking about a slug.

"The princess wishes to know the state of her people and how she can serve them." Grimzy's deep voice was a warning.

"The princess is the reason we are here to begin with," Javyn piped in with a high-pitched voice.

"The princess—" Grimzy started.

"Can speak for herself." Jill eyed Grimzy and then turned her attention to the representatives. "Do you truly think I don't care what happens to these people?" She looked at each of the representatives in turn. They each glanced away, except for Elisha.

Stubborn woman.

"If you cared about your people as deeply as you say, then why do you do nothing day after day? You hole up in the chief's home, far away from the discomforts of this camp. If you cared for your people, why didn't you stop your brother sooner?" Elisha's words were ice grating on stone.

"Enough," Grimzy said, his voice a deep rumble that tore the gazelle woman's gaze away from Jill. The two stared at each other, Elisha's jaw flexing before she let out a disgusted sound. Grimzy continued, "The princess is my personal guest. As for the situation regarding the king, that is between her and her brother."

Each person in the tent wore their tension openly. On instinct, Jill reached for her sword, forgetting she'd been instructed to leave it behind so as not to appear a threat.

Little good that did.

Now, Jill felt naked and exposed. These people didn't care in the slightest who she was or what she'd done. In their eyes, she had caused the destruction of their homes, failed to stop her brother from gaining control of the monsters, and was now in the way of their personal goals to establish control over the people.

"We don't have time to discuss the princess's sleeping

arrangements, Elisha," Nadeem spoke, his voice soft but stern. Red and black locks tumbled to his shoulders, barely hiding his pointed ears with tufts of orange fur on the tips.

"Agreed," said Grimzy. "Now, should we discuss what we came to?"

Elisha glared at Jill again but relented. "Yes. It seems the number of arriving refugees is growing each day. And each day our supplies dwindle. We need more—"

"The Whitesaw people have already given so much. You would do well to thank them for their hospitality," Jill interrupted, her temper flaring.

"Do not suppose you know what I was about to say." The gazelle woman sneered. "We need more supplies beyond what the Whitesaw people can provide." She looked at Grimzy. "I know full well how generous your people have been to us already." She shot the princess a smirk.

Jill immediately recognized her mistake. She'd been tactless and quick to jump to conclusions about Elisha and her mistake had been twisted, making her look like a fool in front of everyone. She resisted the blush fighting up her neck.

Some queen you'd make.

"What Elisha means to say, Your Highness, is that it may be time to consider looking outside these walls for additional supplies," Nadeem said.

Grimzy nodded and Jill too, though reluctantly. They were right. Sooner or later the mountain men and women's generosity would run out. She pictured again that horrible siege from history and shivered. She'd do anything to avoid that.

"What do you suggest?" Jill asked, stepping closer to the table. She examined the maps, each depicted different regions of Erinya on different scales. At the center was a map of the Whitesaw Mountains and the nearby towns and villages.

Seamus, a boarman with a wispy beard, traced a calloused finger across the nearby towns. "Reports from the newest refugees, as well as some of our informants, have told us that all the nearest towns are nearly empty. The crops have been destroyed and picked over by wild animals. Venturing further away, however, puts us at risk of running into one of the king's monsters."

"So, there's nothing?" Jill's chest constricted as her mind started spinning with the horrifying prospect. Their choices were few. They could risk exploring further outside of the caverns but who knew when or where the vulgan—as Malum's monsters had been named from historical records—might appear. They could turn people away, but the notion made her sick to her stomach.

"Not nothing, actually." Elisha crossed her arms as she cast a sideways glance to Javyn.

The inkwell woman pursed her lips but finally spoke. "I know of someone who can help us. A smuggler. He has relations with Welynn, the Ohans—" she hesitated. "And Carthesia."

Jill's shock must have been evident because Elisha rolled her eyes again. Jill ground her teeth, frustrated at her inability to hide her emotions.

"Did you think your perfect little kingdom was devoid of criminals?"

"No," Jill shot back, "Just criminals with such a wide range that Carthesia would be among his allies."

Grimzy raised a hand, his own jaw flexing. "Why do you think he would help us?"

Javyn wrung her hands then cleared her throat. "We don't know. Not for sure anyway, but he's clever. No doubt a kingdom in ruin is bad for business plus—" she looked back at

Elisha and then the princess, "Your Highness may be able to offer him a bribe he can't refuse."

Jill could have laughed. Their entire plan hinged on her being able to bribe this smuggler, yet they didn't want her anywhere near the rest of their plans.

"That's awfully convenient," Jill said, crossing her arms. Her own pettiness told her to turn on her heels and walk out of the tent right then and there. Only fear kept her from doing it. Fear for her people and what might happen if she didn't swallow her pride.

"We will consider it," Grimzy said, "How do we find this smuggler?"

"It's actually quite easy. These days he runs the operation from afar," Javyn explained.

"His name. We need his name," Jill ground out.

"It's Peter. He runs a little tavern called Peter's Pumpkin Alehouse. And it's not too far from here."

3

———

DAVID

What am I doing with these people?

The thought plagued David endlessly as he rubbed his forehead, missing the days when the only person jabbering on was Asif. At least then he'd had Grimzy. How he missed the gargantuan man.

Now he sat trapped in a tiny hut in an abandoned feline village with near strangers, waiting for Kylian to make up his mind.

Kylian Doyle, self-appointed leader of this operation, currently sat cross-legged on a cushion, studying maps and documents with tools David didn't understand. The inkwell girl, Zyla, tended the fire while humming a song he'd never heard before.

And then there was Bo. She was quite possibly the only person who loathed their current situation more than he did. She lay in a corner, scraping a stick against the walls, carving figures into the wood. Her back faced the rest of the group, yet she seemed to take pains to scrape as loudly as she could.

David leaned his head back against the wall, pressing his

eyes closed, wishing for the thousandth time he hadn't abandoned Jill in that wood.

I would have died with her.

At this point, he might have preferred death to their current circumstances. Nearly two months had passed since the incident at the well, and the darkness that started there had only spread. The vulgan which had once stuck to the shadows now roamed freely, like a pack of hunting dogs let loose by their master. The prince had been crowned king and his rule had taken an oppressive turn.

More soldiers roamed the land, given free rein to do whatever they pleased. Taxes were raised. Food grew scarce as farmers, fishermen, and hunters abandoned their homes in search of better places to live.

And all because of that *thing* inside Jack.

Bo had tried to explain it to them—how this Voice, Malum, came from a realm beyond life or death and how the vulgan were truly his, though Bo controlled them for a time.

None of it made sense.

"I've been having a thought." Kylian broke the silence without looking up from his work. He was always working on something, though he never deigned to tell them what was so important.

"Yes?" David prompted, knowing by now that Kylian liked the drama of having a captive audience.

"We've been here, what, two weeks now? And we've seen almost no one." Kylian tapped his quill to his chin. He didn't bother to look at any of them, but David could tell he still relished the hold he had on their attention.

"Is that your entire thought or is there more?" David asked.

Kylian finally looked up, casting a withering glare in David's direction. "No, *David*, it's not." Kylian said his name like he was speaking to a child. "I've been thinking that since we've seen almost no one, people must be hiding somewhere."

"You should get an award for that astute observation," Bo said from her corner. David fought back a laugh.

Kylian sighed heavily, as if they were the annoying ones and not him for never getting to his point in a simple way. "I think it's time to move on. There's nothing here. I had hoped, given the records I have access to, that we might find one of the Saints' Heirs among the feline clan but obviously, they've moved elsewhere."

David bit his tongue. Kylian spoke endlessly of the Saints' Heirs, how they were the only hope for Erinya, and that finding them and freeing the Convent was the only way to bring down King Jack and his monsters.

"Well, I could have told you long ago there was no one here," David said. For the last several months, they'd traveled from village to village, hiding out where they could from the vulgan and King Jack's soldiers. Now they were back in the same village where he and Grimzy found Asif so long ago, staying in the very hut where they'd also sought refuge.

"Yes, but you see, I had another reason for wanting to come see the feline village. You have seen the hieroglyphs on their homes, have you not?"

"Of course I have. They depict the families and their birth prophecies."

"Precisely. I wanted to see them for myself if any predicted the rise of a new Saint."

David's brow furrowed. "And what have you found?"

"Nothing, I'm afraid."

"Shocker." Bo didn't even turn as she spoke.

"You needn't be so bitter, Bo. You are one of the Heirs yourself. Have you come any closer to discerning what your power may be?" Kylian watched her carefully, like he was examining a newly discovered specimen rather than looking at a young girl.

"No, I haven't Kylian. So just drop it, okay?" Bo ground out the words, still scratching away at the wall.

"There's no reason to snap, Bo," Zyla said. "I think we're all just growing restless."

That was the greatest understatement David had ever heard. He'd always hated being cooped up for too long, even as a boy. It was why he'd taken up hunting in the first place. He enjoyed the quiet company of the forest—the rustling of the trees, the gurgling of creeks and springs, the chitter of small animals scurrying through the undergrowth. He'd never been particularly at ease around people.

You were at ease with Jill.

The thought surprised David and turned his stomach. He didn't want to think about the princess, who was no doubt still in her palace, watching as her brother tore the kingdom apart. She'd done her best, but she could have done more. She could have rallied the people before it came to this. She could have helped him get the cure so he wouldn't be stuck with this Saints-forsaken curse. Instead, she'd insisted on trying to save her father, and it hadn't mattered in the end anyway. The supposed cure had severed any remaining link Jack had to his humanity.

"So, what do you propose we do?" David asked, pulling his hunting knife from his belt. He'd been trying to make new arrows for days but had few supplies, so he'd settled for sharpening his knife. He could've left any time he wanted, and yet he didn't want to be alone. Even if he didn't particularly enjoy their company at times.

Something else compelled him though. He knew he could go to Grimzy's people in the mountains, but he wasn't sure he could face his friend after everything that had happened. After leaving Jill. David wasn't sure Grimzy would forgive him. David wasn't entirely sure he deserved forgiveness.

"Well, I think it's time for us to leave."

"And go where, Kylian?" Bo's voice dripped with disdain. "It's a nightmare outside."

"Would you rather stay here? Carving stick figures into the wall while you wallow in self-pity?"

At that, Bo sat up, a snarl on her dirty face. "Shut up, Kylian. You don't know anything about me or what I've been through." Her gaze dropped to the floor, her features hardening as she curled herself into a ball. David's eyes flicked to her feet. Until he looked at them, he sometimes forgot about the girl's club foot.

"Kylian." Zyla's soothing voice was quiet but clear.

Kylian heaved another sigh, rubbing his eyes. "I say we go back to the Convent. Find some way to rescue those captured by the Ohans."

"And what if they're dead?" Bo asked, her voice uncharacteristically quiet.

David glanced between the pair, struck by a strange sense of familiarity. There was something odd about these two that he couldn't put his finger on.

Kylian shook his head with a confidence that never faltered. "No. Ohan-Jin wouldn't kill the Saints' Heirs. He would use them. And, if we're lucky, others may have escaped. Hasani, Ymira, and Aaira fled with us before we split up to find Bo."

"So why aren't we looking for them?" David asked. It seemed foolish to be chasing down ghosts and shadows if already-known Saints' Heirs had escaped.

"We need to find all the Saints' Heirs before Jack does, or the Ohans for that matter. If Jack, or rather the Black King, learns of them, he will try to entice them to his side. Or worse.

The Heirs we know now would die before defecting to his side. But the Heirs we haven't found might not be so lucky."

David disliked his logic but didn't argue. Personally, he wasn't overly fond of placing any of his hopes in the Saints' Heirs. While he'd heard the legends of the Saints who'd first defeated the Black King in the Battle of Shadows long ago, they still felt like an otherworldly force. In his mind, they were unreliable at best. Frauds at the worst. Kylian claimed Bo herself was one of these heirs, but David had not seen an ounce of power come from her.

What about Paladin Millie?

The thought disturbed him. He didn't know what to make of the girl from the little time they'd spent together at the well. But Jill had told him of her power, of how she'd used it against the princess during the tournament. Then he'd seen her power firsthand.

A soft crunch outside dragged David from his thoughts, far too quiet to be an animal. He wouldn't have heard it had he not been listening for threats. He stilled, holding up a hand to the rest of the group as he grabbed his bow and crept toward the door.

The group fell silent.

The fire popped and cracked in the hearth. *Saints, we shouldn't have lit a fire.*

A knock came at the door.

David inhaled, calming his speeding heart and raising his bow. He inched toward the door, grabbing the handle and throwing it open.

He nearly dropped his weapon. Standing there with a smirk on his face was the last person David had expected to see.

"Luca?"

4

———

MILLIE

Sweat dripped down Millie's neck, pooling at the small of her back. Though her thick hair was tied back into a braid, dark tendrils had escaped their confines to hang in front of her face. She gave them no heed as she raised her sword to block the strike aimed at her head.

Her arms trembled beneath the weight bearing down on her. She glanced up at Master Ravala, hoping he would go easy on her today.

His piercing glare told her otherwise.

"You need to transform," he said without losing his breath. He was going easy on her and still she struggled.

"I can't," she hissed through gritted teeth. Her heart pounded in her chest, from both exhaustion and fear. If she didn't transform fast enough, Ravala could still slice her.

"You must." He pressed down harder on his own blade, breaking Millie's stance. "Or I will crush you."

Millie's vision blurred, perspiration dripping into her eyelashes. Inhaling once, twice, she let her mind succumb to the darkness.

A clang rang out through the training grounds as she dropped her sword and, when Millie opened her eyes, she looked up at the inkwell man from more angles than should have been possible. Somehow, her mind made sense of all the information coming at her.

She had transformed into fifty large spiders, each one the size of a man's hand. Surging forward, she sent her swarm toward Master Ravala, climbing up his legs and torso. The man had grown accustomed to Millie's tactics and hardly reacted, whipping around in a circle to fling off several of her spiders.

She sent the spiders that landed on the ground after her fallen sword, combining their strength to lift the weapon before she called the creatures back to herself, reforming with the blade in hand.

She stood behind the man now and swung awkwardly at his legs. He turned and blocked in time, their steel blades ringing through the rotunda.

Millie smiled as one spider that had not returned to her bit down on Ravala's wrist. The man cried out, dropping the sword in surprise.

Inhaling, Millie called the last spider into herself. It melted at her feet, specks of darkness returning to her body. With the last spider returned, some of her strength did as well. She'd been working on letting a few spiders remain when she reformed, if only so she could maintain the element of surprise.

"Well done, Paladin." Master Ravala's deep, gravelly voice sounded the tiniest bit breathless.

Millie beamed, a flush rising to her cheeks. She was drenched in sweat and ached all over, but the man's praise sent a flicker of joy down into her toes. She was beginning to understand why the princess had looked up to him so much.

Nausea hit her gut. It always did when she thought of Jill, but she wasn't sure if it was out of fear or respect for her former mistress.

"Thank you, Master." Millie bowed low.

After Jill fled the palace, Millie began training with Master Ravala almost immediately.

After Malum tortured Doon, that is.

Another wave of nausea had Millie buckling at the knees. She gritted her teeth and forced her eyes shut, hoping the sensation would pass.

"How are you feeling these days?" Ravala's gaze flickered toward the guards surrounding the training grounds.

Each day more guards showed up, though Millie didn't understand where they were coming from. Something about them wasn't quite right, their eyes glazed over. They never spoke beyond giving basic commands to people and stood as still as statues. Unnaturally still.

Millie risked a glance at the guards as well. None of them moved or reacted to the conversation—they never did—but she knew they were listening. Always.

"All right, I suppose. The king has kept me busy these days with training and investigating the princess's whereabouts." No longer did she think of Jack in any way other than her king. It was easier that way. Easier to pretend that everything between them had been nothing more than a dream. Or a horrifying nightmare.

She rubbed the scar across her neck. He'd traded his soul to bring her back from the dead, and she still didn't know how to feel about it. She felt gratitude, of course, but guilt as well. If she had died that day, he might have had a fighting chance against Malum. Instead, he'd saved her and doomed the kingdom.

"And your brother?" Ravala eyed the guards again, taking her weapon from her.

Millie swallowed. "Getting stronger every day, thanks to the king's magic."

It was true, though she didn't understand it. After Millie had helped Jill escape, King Jack had brought in her brother from the dungeons. Millie was surprised he was still breathing.

When he'd appeared before them, Doon had looked far paler than she'd ever seen him, his sunken eyes yellow and bloodshot. His bones showed through his waxen skin, giving him the look of a skeleton brought to life.

Millie shivered at the memory. She couldn't think about the number of times the king had her brother whipped in front of her. Then she'd been forced to watch as Jack—no, Malum—carved out one of his eyes. Doon's screams still echoed in her ears. She doubted they'd ever leave her.

"Paladin Millie?" A small voice pierced her dark thoughts.

She turned. A young errand boy inched toward her, toying with the buttons on his vest.

"Yes?" Her lungs contracted. She knew what he'd say before he even opened his mouth.

"The king would like to speak with you." The boy refused to meet her eyes and instead stared at the ground, still fiddling with his vest.

Millie glanced back at Ravala, who gave her a grim nod. Turning back to the boy she said, "Thank you. I'll be there in a moment. Why don't you go down to the kitchens and grab one of the sticky buns cook always makes?"

The boy looked up at her with wide blue eyes before nodding a quick thanks and running off.

"You may get the boy in trouble if he should be doing other things, you know?"

Millie's jaw clenched. She knew. She knew better than anyone. But she wouldn't let this boy live in the same fear she had as a child.

"Thank you for today's training session, Master. I must be going." Without looking back, she exited the training grounds and slipped inside the marble halls.

MILLIE WAITED outside the king's quarters, preparing herself for the oncoming conversation. She was reminded of Malum knocking on her door just a few nights earlier. She'd known it was him before she'd even opened her door. He hadn't said much, only smiled at her and told her Jack sent his regards. It was torture, knowing Jack was still in there and she was powerless to help him. Sometimes, just briefly, she caught glimpses of Jack in the king. The mischievous smirk. The bright green eyes. The warm smile. She lived for those precious moments, and she wondered who would speak to her today.

The door opened and there the king stood wearing a cold smile that didn't reach his eyes.

So, it was Malum then.

"Welcome Millie." The sound of his voice was Jack's, but the cadence was off. Jack's voice oozed warmth and playfulness. Malum's tone was slippery, like a snake with smooth words.

"Your Majesty." She dipped her head, unwilling to meet his eyes. After all this time, she still wasn't used to seeing Jack in this state. Seeing someone else in Jack's body.

"Come in." Malum turned without waiting for her, making his way to the large desk by the windows. The chair faced the door, a distinctly un-Jack-like thing to do. Somehow Millie knew Jack would have had the desk pressed up against the windows, his chair facing the gray-green ocean.

"You summoned me?" Millie hated spending any time alone with Malum, but her fear was particularly sharp within his quarters.

"I did. Come, sit down." He gestured to the seat on the other side of the desk.

"I'll stand, thank you." In truth, Millie's feet and legs ached from training and she would've loved nothing more than to collapse into the plush velvet chair. But she knew Jill would never do such a thing. To place yourself in a seat lower than your opponent was to ask them to gain the upper hand.

Malum smiled with Jack's face. It was an eerie sight to see his lips pull and his eyes grow dark.

"Suit yourself. I thought you might be more comfortable is all."

"I'm used to discomfort."

Malum released a breathy laugh. "I suppose you would be, having been a maid all your life." Millie wasn't sure what he hoped the jibe would accomplish, but she wouldn't give him the satisfaction of seeing her annoyance.

"Can I be of service to you, Your Majesty? Or should I return to the training grounds?" She wanted to make it clear that she was following his command to train with Ravala and that he'd interrupted.

"Straight to the point, I see." Malum steepled his fingers together, looking down at his desk. "As a matter of fact, you can be of service to me." He paused, letting the uncertainty of his request dangle like bait on a hook. Only Millie was the bait, waiting to be devoured. "I have reason to believe my sister is hiding out near the border of Welynn."

"You mean Jack's sister." Millie couldn't resist correcting

him. It felt like an insult to both royal twins for Malum to suggest Jill was his sister.

Malum threw back his head and barked out a laugh. "You have quite the sharp tongue today, *Millie.*"

Millie's heart sank, her entire body stilling at the way he'd said her name. Jack had spoken to her, even if only for a moment.

"He won't be coming out to play today." Malum glowered.

He did it on purpose. He wants me to stay and listen to him, and he knows just how to make me.

Millie looked away, gripping the knife at her waist. What was it that Ravala always told her? Don't let your feelings control you or something? Yet here she was, fury boiling under her skin and hope dying like the embers of a smoldering fire.

"As I was saying, I believe *the princess* is hiding somewhere near the border of Welynn." Malum resumed speaking as if the brief interlude had not taken place at all. "Perhaps in the Whitesaw Mountains or with one of the animal clans. I hear many of my people are traveling that way these days." Something flicked across Malum's face, like the beginnings of a sneer, then it disappeared as if nothing had happened.

He's angry. He doesn't like the people rejecting his rule. And if Jill is there, what would stop them from following her instead of him? Millie watched him carefully, waiting for another slipup, but his mask was firmly in place once more.

"I tire of waiting for my pets to apprehend the princess. I want you to find her and capture her. Bring her back to me for execution."

The temperature of the room dropped, ice sliding down Millie's spine.

"What?" She gaped at the man in Jack's body. Malum had picked up a quill to jot something down on a document as if the command were as casual as asking her to fetch supper.

"You heard me," he said without looking up.

"But—but she's your sister, *Jack*." She said the word with emphasis, begging him to stop Malum. Jack would never do this.

Malum's body faded suddenly then materialized on the other side of his desk. He grabbed Millie's chin and wrenched it up to look at him. Millie stood helpless, like a mouse transfixed by the snake about to consume it. He didn't choke her or hurt her, but his meaning was clear.

He leaned closer, his lips brushing against her ear. She suppressed a shiver as he said, "I gave you your life back. I gave you your brother's life back. I can take it all away in an instant."

He released his grip on her and was back in his chair in an instant. Millie trembled.

I will never be able to hide my fear like Jill could.

"As you said, Jill is not my sister. She's Jack's sister. But she's also a traitor and a threat to this kingdom. You will hunt her down and bring her back to me. I will see her executed for her crimes. And if you do not," he paused, flashing her another cruel smile, "I will end your brother's life for good this time."

Millie's mouth was parched, and she dared not breathe. What could she say? How could she change his mind?

I can't.

Jack was truly gone.

5

BO

"Who's Luca?" Bo asked, her mouth sour. She wasn't overly fond of unknown characters showing up out of nowhere.

Before anyone could object, David escorted a feline man into their hut. David's eyes were wide, but he was smiling. She didn't think she'd seen the hunter smile once since they'd met. Bo glanced at Kylian, whose narrowed gaze told her he was equally suspicious of the newcomer. Only Zyla walked over to greet the pair.

David turned to the rest of them, oblivious to their suspicions. "This is my comrade, Luca. We served in the army together."

Luca bowed his head to each of them in turn, a sign of respect among the Feline Clan. With some reluctance, Bo bowed her head back, but she refused to trust the man. Who just shows up out of the blue, knowing exactly where their friend is? It didn't make any sense.

Luca turned back to David, who instructed him to sit by

the fire. Once the two men were settled, David offered him a cup of the tea Zyla had made.

"I don't understand. How are you here? I thought you were dead." David shook his head, brow furrowed.

"I was badly wounded. Woke up a week after the explosion to find you guys had left." The man glanced between the others, his gaze landing on Bo.

Bo glared at him before picking at her fingernails. She wanted to make it abundantly clear what she thought of his mysterious appearance.

"You and Grimzy didn't even bother to check if I was still alive, did you?" Luca sounded annoyed, but there was a smirk on his face. "You two just took off."

"Well to be fair, I didn't think anyone could survive that explosion. And the commander sent us off to hunt down the vulgan the very next day."

Bo's attention snapped back to the two men. Luca's smile had fallen, his expression turning dark. She wondered if it had been the same commander who'd kidnapped her and sent her off to the Ohans.

"Yes, I'm aware. In fact, that's one of the reasons I'm here. You never returned after your hunt." Luca quirked a brow.

David glanced at Bo as if looking for her help, but she just shrugged. He had a very good reason for not returning to the army. Between the vulgan and King Jack's coronation, Bo suspected David feared what that evil commander might ask him to do.

"Clearly, I didn't." David clenched his jaw.

Luca considered David, then nodded as if he understood the hunter though David hadn't explained himself. "Much has changed since you've been gone. And I fear it's only going to get worse from here."

Silence filled the hut, punctuated by the pops and cracks

of the fire, but even those quieted at Luca's words. The coals and embers shuddered like the flame within Bo. As much as she tried to ignore it, fear stalked her constantly these days.

The men continued talking in hushed whispers, but Bo stopped listening. She didn't want to know what was going on outside. These monsters were ruining the land, ruining the kingdom. And it was all her fault.

Bo leaned her head back against the wall, wondering where it had all gone wrong. Was it when she'd agreed to help the Ohans? When she'd betrayed the Order? Or had it all started when she'd lost the vulgan in the first place?

Or maybe it started with my mother.

She hated the resentment that welled up inside her. Her mother had stolen her as an infant. Her mother had torn the veil between life and death. Her mother had freed the Black King and his vulgan.

The woman wasn't even her real mother. So why did Bo still love her?

If Bo had been stronger, she could still be in the mountains with them. She'd be living in the dark all alone, but at least other people would be safe. The thought made her want to snarl.

Instead, a soft voice interrupted her dark thoughts. "Are you all right, Bo?"

Kylian had come to sit beside her in the corner, having put away the maps and documents. Zyla perched beside David and his friend, listening intently.

"How on earth could I be all right, *Kylian?*" She clenched her fists until her nails bit into the palms of her hands. "I lost the vulgan, and now they're ravaging the kingdom. I'm supposed to be a Saints' Heir, some sort of hero, but I couldn't even stop Jack from drinking the blasted water." She let out an irritated huff. The last thing she wanted was to have this conversation with Kylian. His pompous attitude had done nothing but irritate her from the moment they'd first met.

And yet, he'd been nothing but kind to her, far kinder than he was to anyone else, even when she was acting like a nightmare. He tolerated others at his best. At his worst, he was arrogant. Or so Bo thought.

"Have you made any progress in determining your gift?" Kylian asked, changing the topic as he raised an eyebrow at her. Bo had the distinct sense that he was looking for something specific, examining her like she was an oddity rather than an actual person. She hated the feeling of it, so she looked away.

"No." Bo hadn't given it much effort though. What was the point?

"You know the vulgan were never yours."

Bo shook her head, confused, before looking over at Kylian. "Of course I know that."

"Do you, though? You seem to place a lot of responsibility on yourself that was never yours to bear."

Bo swallowed, looking back at the fire. How else was she supposed to feel exactly? How was she *not* supposed to blame herself for everything?

"Those creatures always belonged to the Black King. They only imprinted on you because you were one of the Saints' Heirs. They sensed your power. And I suspect that even if none of this had happened, eventually your hold on them would have slipped, and they would have returned to their true master."

"You have a way with words, Kylian," Bo said dryly.

"I'm serious."

"So am I. If you're trying to make me feel better, you're not doing a great job."

It was Kylian's turn to let out a huff of frustration. "What

I'm trying to say is that you can't blame yourself for what's happened. None of this was your choice."

Bo had no response for that. She was tired of trying to figure out whose fault it was. In some ways, it was easier to blame herself. At least that way there was someone to direct her anger at. Where would all the anger go otherwise?

"Yeah, well. That's easier said than done." Bo picked up the little stick she'd had earlier and started scrawling on the wall again, making it clear she was done talking.

Kylian pursed his lips but stood and strode away, returning to his documents while eyeing David and Luca.

Bo laid back down and turned into the corner. Somehow, she would make this right. Somehow, she would fix everything she'd broken, even if it broke her.

6

MALUM

alum was disturbed by the growing connection between him and Jack. Jack should have stayed in the back of his mind, venturing out only when Malum allowed. But Jack was stronger than he'd anticipated, fighting for control.

No matter though. If Malum excelled at anything, it was being in control.

He'd nearly gotten used to the prince's body. Jack was much shorter than Malum had been. His skin was lighter and his muscles were weaker too. Malum, while technically human, had come from the long line of the Jarundi in the Distant Lands. A tall, willowy people who inhabited jungles and mountaintops, their exceptional breeding gave them physical advantages over others. The humans here were pitiful by comparison. How they'd come to rule this land when stronger races existed, he would never understand.

Nevertheless, the prince's body was preferable to others he might have inhabited. What stroke of fate had landed him in this position he couldn't say, but he was delighted all the same.

Why do you torture Millie? Jack asked in Malum's mind.

Oh, how their roles had switched. Malum smiled, his reflection faint in the window he stared out of. Since he'd come to inhabit Jack's body, he had a peculiar habit of staring at the sea, lost in thought. Another disturbing connection. He'd always loathed the sea, yet now he felt unable to look away.

"I'm not torturing her. I'm threatening her," he said aloud. "There's a difference."

You're cruel, Jack said.

"And you've never been cruel? You've never murdered your sister's love in rage even though you yourself were in a secret relationship with a mere servant girl?"

Jack recoiled, silent but brooding.

"That's what I thought." Malum smirked, more than satisfied with this outcome. Better that the boy learned his place now before he became problematic.

A knock sounded at the door.

"Just a moment," Malum said, strolling over to where his coat hung off the back of his chair.

Since becoming king—again—he'd started wearing all black, black coats and vests and shirts all embroidered with gold details and accents. They were not Erinyan colors, but he didn't care. He was the Black King whether anyone knew it or not. He would own his dark magic.

At the door stood Paladin Salazar and General Jakhar. The two men looked grave but bowed before him.

"I take it you've made the announcement?" Malum said, picking a piece of lint off the cuff of his sleeve.

"Yes, Your Majesty," said Paladin Salazar, "But I fear the people won't be happy with these changes. There is already great unrest in the lower towns."

Malum looked between the two men. The general, a stout gazelle man with short horns protruding from his head, wouldn't meet his eyes. Paladin Salazar didn't seem to have any issue leveling him with a piercing glare. Malum was indifferent though. They thought they were dealing with a pompous prince turned king much too young. They had no idea who truly stood before them.

"The people will always be unhappy with something. But please, let us not have this discussion here. Come in."

Malum held the door open wide, gesturing for them to join him inside. They stepped over the threshold but remained standing. Malum shut the door, taking care to use both locks as well as the spelled lock to keep any eavesdroppers from overhearing their conversation.

His magic was slowly returning, different from that of the Saints, more powerful than theirs too. For now, all he could manage were smaller spells. Silencing spells, protection wards, simple illusions. But soon . . .

"I fear the situation may be more dire than you understand, Your Majesty." Paladin Salazar stood tall before the king, undaunted by his presence.

Malum's eye twitched. He would have to do something about the paladin's lack of respect before it got it out of hand.

"What is the issue then?"

"The taxes you've demanded are far too steep for anyone to pay. People simply cannot afford to give any more, not without risking their own livelihoods."

"And?"

Paladin Salazar's gaze widened, a flush rising up his neck. "Winter is coming. People are struggling to simply prepare for the season ahead and you demand more of them? Some may not make it through the winter because of these taxes."

"And how, then, are we to pay for our soldiers at the border? We know the Ohans plot against us, rallying an unknown number to their cause. We fight a battle on two fronts. And then, of course, we seek my sister." Another disturbing question mark. He disliked the fact that his vulgan had yet to find the princess. He disliked having her out of sight at all. Who knew what she planned, what revenge she might seek.

"Your Majesty, with all due respect, if we demand these taxes from people, we may find ourselves waging war on more than two fronts." Paladin Salazar stepped forward, the pleading in his voice obvious. The general remained silent, fidgeting with the tassels on his belt.

"Fine then."

Paladin Salazar breathed a sigh of relief just before Malum added, "If the taxes cannot be paid, then a son or daughter of age can be taken to serve in the army instead."

"What? You can't be serious?" Salazar's tone became defiant. "The people won't let it happen."

Malum raised a brow, stepping closer to the man whose face had turned a violent shade of red.

"What will the people do, exactly? Will they fight? With what weapons?" Malum paused. "Tell me, Paladin Salazar, how old is your own boy? What's his name, Renlow?"

The paladin grew deathly still. "Yes. He's fourteen."

"And he is your only child, correct?"

Paladin Salazar's breathing quickened, and his chest visibly quaked. Ah, there was that respect he'd been looking for. "Yes, Your Majesty."

"Lower the conscription age to fourteen. If the people cannot pay the tax, a son or daughter of at least fourteen shall be taken into the army."

Silence resounded through the room. The general stood slack-jawed.

"Like you mentioned, Paladin, if they find themselves unable to pay the tax, then at least they won't have to pay for another mouth to feed. The people should thank us. We will give their children food and a place to live." Malum smiled at the look of fury on the paladin's face.

"What happened to you, Jack?" the paladin whispered.

Heat bubbled up in Malum's chest, and he stepped forward, grabbing the man by the throat. "Jack is gone." Malum shoved the man away, relishing the look of fear on his face. "Give my regards to your son."

7

JILL

Peter, Peter, pumpkin eater,
Had a wife but couldn't keep her;
He put her in a pumpkin shell
And there he kept her very well.

Jill was struck by a sense of déjà vu as she approached the smuggler's tavern. Was it only a few months ago now that she'd met David in a similar tavern as they fought off her father's brutish soldiers and a vile innkeeper?

A bitter wind whipped in front of her, blowing back her hood. The frosts were coming, and with them snow and ice. The Whitesaw Mountains were warm within but treacherous outside. They had to work quickly if they wanted to secure enough supplies to last through the winter.

Jill marched forward, pushing open the doors to Peter's Pumpkin Alehouse. Grimzy had refused to let her go alone but stayed with her horse and watched the tavern from outside.

As Jill stepped into the warmth of the tavern, she was struck by its elegance. She'd expected sticky bar stools, drunk patrons, and wind whistling through the slats of the walls. Instead, she was met with a space that bordered on luxurious. Green velvet chairs lined up neatly under round tables. Instead of burning candles, vases filled with glowing firegems served as the tables' centerpieces. Patrons drank from gold and silver goblets, large rings adorning their fingers. Why they were here despite the chaos befalling Erinya she had no idea, yet scattered around the room were patrons dressed in clothing as fine as any she'd owned as a princess.

This was no ordinary tavern.

For the first time in her entire life, Jill felt underdressed. She had gone from being a princess who owned hundreds of gowns to a rebel who kept only two simple outfits. Instead of daily baths after long training sessions, she was lucky to scrub herself with a washrag every few days. Dirt and blood were permanently crusted under her fingernails, and her auburn hair was pulled up in a tangled knot most days.

A few people turned to look at her, sneers and arched brows met her gaze before she looked to the floor. Sweat coated her palms as she sidled up to the bar. She sensed the judgmental gazes even with her back to the room.

Had she ever been like that? Had she ever looked down on others for what they wore? For how filthy or clean they were? She bit her lip. The thought made her uncomfortable. She'd done all those things at some point.

A young woman walked out of the kitchen door, pasting a smile on her face as she looked Jill over. The woman's long black hair hung in hundreds of braids filled with red and gold beads; two horns swirled at her crown. A gold nose ring highlighted her dark bronze skin and Jill's stomach clenched with jealousy. She seemed far too beautiful to be working as a barmaid, even at an upscale inn like this.

She looked Jill up and down with a scornful tilt to her lips. "Are you lost dear?"

Heat spread across Jill's face. Never had she felt so exposed, so below her station. Once, she would have reprimanded the young woman, revealing her identity and lording it over her. Now, Jill felt small and insignificant. Even if she could reveal her identity, she doubted the girl would believe her.

"No. I—um—I came to speak with Peter. About . . ." Jill wracked her brain. "A business venture." It sounded far too obvious to her, and she realized she had no idea how illegal smuggling bargains took place. Royalty hadn't exactly prepared her for that.

The girl's smile fell, and her tone turned icy. "Peter is not interested in any *business ventures* at the moment. And I doubt you could offer him much anyway." The girl looked Jill up and down again, making her meaning clear.

"Please," Jill said through gritted teeth. "I need to speak with him. It's important."

The young woman crossed her arms, drawing attention to her ample curves and fine gown. Far too fine a gown for a barmaid. "Sweetie, you need to go."

Chairs shifted and scuffed along the floor behind her. She was drawing too much attention. But what could she say? How could she convince the girl of her situation?

Jill dropped her voice low, leaning across the bar. "Listen, I know about Peter's dealings. And I know he has a connection with the Ohans among. . . Other important clientele. I also know the king's monsters are likely impacting every aspect of his trade. Sooner or later, the king will catch Peter and sentence him to Murderer's Row. But—" Jill stopped. The girl's nose had started twitching. "I know how to deal with the vulgan."

The quiet between the young women was profound, like all sound had been sucked away and held only the next few breaths. Jill needed this girl to listen. She could not walk away from this empty handed.

"You're bluffing."

"I killed one of them."

The girl blinked as if dazed but then her expression returned to its icy glare. "Peter won't see you. Return to whatever little hole you crawled out of and don't come back."

Jill felt like someone had dunked her in frigid water. She had never been so callously refused. Never.

A strong hand gripped Jill's arm. "Miss, it's time for you to leave." Jill looked up at the man holding her arm. He was dressed in a blue petticoat with curled hair pulled back in a low ponytail. Although his clothes were refined, the size of his muscles had her following his lead without argument. She felt numb from head to toe.

Then she was outside, pulling her cloak tighter to shield her against the bitter cold.

Grimzy approached, his footsteps light despite his towering size. He frowned down at her then knelt on one knee so they were face-to-face.

"What happened?"

"He wouldn't see me," she breathed. "Well, the barmaid wouldn't let me see him." She blinked away a tear. "Grimzy, how can I keep doing this? I've already failed once, and everyone expects me to fail again. In the mountains, people assume I'm a spoiled princess. But here, they think I'm trash that stumbled in off the street."

She looked back at Grimzy, meeting his stern gaze.

Another tear slipped down her cheek. She wasn't a princess anymore. She wasn't anything. How could she ever expect to take back her kingdom when she couldn't even convince a barmaid to let her see someone?

Grimzy's large hand wiped the tear from her cheek, the touch almost fatherly despite the mere decade separating them. A strange rumbling rolled through the ground beneath her feet as the mountain man stood, balled his fists, and approached the tavern behind her.

She watched him duck through the doorway. The doors here were a little higher to accommodate the nearby mountain men, but Grimzy resembled a giant even among his own people.

She shuffled in behind him, still dazed and numb. Is this what Millie felt like as a maid all those years? Is this why she cowered before Jill every second they were together? Saints, she'd been awful to Millie. What she wouldn't give to go back and change all that.

Grimzy approached the bar and loomed over the barmaid. He'd traded in his robes for a pair of pants and a light vest but opted to remain shirtless, revealing his muscled torso.

The barmaid looked up at the mountain man and then caught a glance of Jill at the doorway. Her lips pursed as her gaze traveled back up to meet Grimzy's.

"Can I help you, sir?"

"Yes, you can. You will let this young woman see Peter, or I will report you both to the king himself." Grimzy's voice sharpened with an edge Jill had never heard before.

"I'm sorry, sir, but Peter—"

Grimzy slammed a hand on the bar top, making the entire room shake. Then he pulled his hand away to reveal a golden pendant. It was the paladin's seal, which served as a clasp on the cloaks most of them wore.

"It's Paladin Grimzy." His words were sharp with fury, and Jill's pulse skittered in her chest.

The young woman blanched then stuttered, at a loss for words.

"What is all the bleeding commotion out here? Josie what in the Saints—" A young man barged out another door adjacent to the kitchen, freezing as he looked at the angry mountain man.

"These two want to speak with you, Peter," Josie said.

Jill took a slow step forward, examining Peter. He was far younger than Jill had expected, early twenties at most. His red hair and beard were cropped short but in a fashionable style. Smudges of black ink covered his hands.

Peter glanced between her and Grimzy, narrowed eyes alight with curiosity. "Come into my office. I would love to hear this story."

Josie glared as Jill and Grimzy followed Peter. Like everything else in the tavern, his office was plush and organized. A roaring fire blazed in the hearth. Stacks of papers were arranged in tidy piles on a large desk nestled into the corner. Bookcases lined the room, though none of their shelves held books. Instead, they held trinkets from all over the five kingdoms. Some Jill recognized, like the small cylinder that clicked and produced a flame. Others she did not. Spheres of various colors and sizes, a metal tool that looked like two blades that clashed against each other, and bottles of a strange black powder all lined the shelves.

Peter walked to a small table beside the hearth, pouring dark amber liquid into a glass. "Drink?" He raised the glass in question.

Jill shook her head while Grimzy simply stared.

To Peter's credit, he did not cower beneath the mountain

man's gaze. Whether he was foolish or brave, Jill had yet to determine.

Peter smiled, leaning back against the table, shoving a hand in his pocket. He lifted the glass to his lips, a playful smirk twisting his features.

"So, what brings one of the king's paladins to my part of the countryside?"

"I'm with her."

Peter looked at Jill again as if seeing her for the first time. He took another sip. "Am I supposed to know who she is? I'm good at reading people, but I don't actually read minds."

Jill released a harsh breath and stepped forward. "My name is Jill. Princess Jillianna of Erinya."

Peter gave a humorless laugh before rolling his eyes. "Well, this is my lucky day. A princess and a paladin dropping in on my front doorstep." He set the glass down, crossing his arms.

Jill was stunned. She'd finally revealed her identity, a great risk considering Jack was after her, and this man seemed unimpressed.

"We need your help." She rushed forward despite the doubts rising in the back of her mind. Was this why Josie had refused to let her see him? Did she already know what his reaction would be?

"Listen, sweetheart, I appreciate the effort you're putting into this. I really do. But you're not fooling anybody. I don't know how you convinced a paladin to help you, if he truly is one, but your trick won't work on me. I know a scam when I see one." He smirked like he'd just played a winning hand in a game of cards.

Jill's temper snapped. She marched forward, drawing the knife from her belt and pressing it up against his throat. "I'm done playing games. Believe me or don't, but *I'm* responsible for thousands of refugees. They need supplies to last through the winter, and people tell me you can get those supplies. So, will you help me, or will you allow children to go hungry?" The words flew from her mouth like a torrent of hail, each one landing with extreme force. She would knock this man down a peg if it was the last thing she did.

Peter glared at her, his breath warm against her skin. "You really are the princess, aren't you?"

"Yes." She stepped back, still clutching the knife.

"Sorry, I just pictured someone a little more . . . impressive." He took another swig of his drink which he hadn't dropped despite the blade at his throat a second ago. "Though your temper certainly screams spoiled princess."

"Sorry. Didn't have much chance to change into a ball gown before fleeing for my life from my power-hungry brother."

Peter's glare softened just slightly. "Power-hungry brother indeed."

Jill pulled away her blade, but didn't sheath it. "Will you help me, yes or no?"

"No."

"What? Why not?" She'd thought he'd do as she asked once she revealed her identity. Another stupid mistake.

When will I learn?

Peter picked up his glass, turning away from her to stare into the fire. He shrugged. "I don't really help royals, least of all the sister of the man who's taken everything from me."

"He's taken a lot from everyone." Jill swallowed. She wished she could tell people the truth, that the man on the throne may have Jack's face but it wasn't him at all. It was that monster, Malum. The irony was that Jack was the most important thing Malum had taken from her.

Peter shook his head. "You don't understand. His

monsters, what they've done . . ." His voice dropped low, taking on a tone that chilled Jill to her core.

"I know."

"No, you don't!" Peter spun, face pinched and red.

Grimzy stepped closer, a deep rumble emanating from him.

"Those creatures are beyond vile, and they have only one desire—to destroy and consume."

Quiet settled over them. "Who did you lose?" Jill asked. She would never forget the day in the Deadwood when she'd rescued those people from the vulgan's webs. A shiver ran through her body.

"Many. So many. But the worst are the ones that came back."

Jill's head tilted, a new uneasiness weighing on her. "Came back? What do you mean?"

"You don't know then?" He raised a brow.

Reluctantly, she shook her head. She hated how little she knew.

Peter stared into the depths of his drink, as if it might have answers for him. He sighed then chugged the rest of it in a single gulp. And though he didn't sound pleased, he said, "Come, I'll show you."

THEY FOLLOWED Peter away from the tavern and into the haunted darkness. Frost crunched underfoot and a pale moon lit the path faintly before them. Grimzy walked behind them, leading Jill's horse by the reins.

Peter's steps were nearly silent. His back hunched as they walked farther from the tavern, as if an invisible weight rested on his shoulders, growing heavier with each step forward.

Jill's palms were clammy despite the cold, and she gripped her butterfly swords for comfort. Or rather her sword. She'd lost one the day she'd fled. It felt like a part of her was missing as well.

She wasn't entirely sure what Peter meant when he spoke of the ones who'd come back, but she suspected she understood far better than he knew. Jack had come back, and yet part of him had died at the well that day.

Ahead sat a small wooden shed, boarded up and looking like it hadn't been used in ages. The door had several locks, including an iron bar latching it shut.

Jill's heart slammed against her ribcage as they approached in near silence. This was no ordinary shed. Jill stopped but Peter continued forward, unlatching something before he lifted a square piece of wood. It was a window, but thin iron bars placed close together lined the opening.

Peter motioned for Jill to come closer. Everything in Jill wanted to run, to flee this terrible dread settling in the pit of her stomach. Her mouth was parched as she stepped up to the window, peering through the bars.

A figure huddled in a corner, wearing nothing more than shredded rags. The woman—at least it looked like a woman— rocked back and forth, muttering under her breath.

"Who is this?" Jill hissed. "Why do you have this woman locked up?"

Then the woman launched herself toward them with blinding speed, screeching like a wraith. Jill screamed. A fist grabbed the back of her hood as a taloned hand shot through the bars, reaching for and clawing at her.

The woman raved and screeched on the other side of the bars, gripping them with pale hands and long, razor-sharp nails. Her gaunt face was accentuated by the clumps missing hair. Scratches covered her arms and face.

"Liza, shh. It's okay. It's all right." Peter's voice had turned soft, and Jill was reminded of the way Will had calmed spooked horses. "Liza, it's okay."

The woman stopped screeching but stared at them, bloodied fingers gripping the bars. Her chest heaved.

Peter took a step forward, holding a tentative hand out. He hummed a song with a sweet melody. The woman's breathing slowed just a fraction. Peter took another step forward, his fingers barely brushing against the woman's face. The woman leaned into the touch just a bit. Then she growled and snapped her teeth at Peter's fingers like a feral dog.

Peter jumped away in time but watched as the woman yanked on the bars. He wiped his face as a tear slipped out. She pretended not to see it even as the sight of it punched her in the gut.

"Who is this?" she asked again, breathless.

He turned to her, a grim smile on his face. "Well, princess, this is my wife."

8

DAVID

David still felt like he was staring at a ghost. Surely, the man in front of him couldn't be alive, could he? But it was Luca. Luca who sat cross-legged in front of the flickering fire, holding a tin cup of tea, wearing his somber but thoughtful look. He would know his friend anywhere.

Guilt lashed at his chest. Luca was right. David and Grimzy had been assigned to hunt down the vulgan and simply assumed the man had died. To find out that he'd been looking for them all this time only made David feel worse.

He and Luca had faced many things together over the years, having been new recruits at the same time. He could still recall their first day of training when they'd been paired together for combat lessons. Luca had moved so quickly David was on the ground before he'd blinked.

"I wish I came with better news, David." Luca set his cup on the ground, glancing at the others in the hut. Kylian and Bo were talking in the corner and, after exchanging introductions, Zyla had set herself to practicing her stitches, determined to be the best healer she could be.

"So do I."

"Where is Grimzy?"

David sighed but explained the last several months to his friend. He told Luca about his curse, about how he and Grimzy had set out to hunt down the vulgan, how he'd run into the princess of Erinya and recruited her help, how they'd wound up at the well only for Jack to seize control of the vulgan and lose his humanity in the process.

When he was done speaking, he felt like he'd been emptied out. He was tired. Tired of this hard, laborious life where every day brought new horrors and no reprieve. It didn't seem fair.

Since when has life ever been fair?

The thought irritated him. He knew life wasn't fair, but that didn't mean you gave up on the idea though, right?

"So Grimzy is with his people in the Whitesaw Mountains?"

"I assume so, yes." David stared into the fire.

"And the princess?" Luca arched a brow, a smirk playing at the corner of his lips.

David's stomach flipped despite himself. He tried his best not to think of Jill these days. It only made him angry. And if he were honest, a chord of longing struck deep inside him. It was like hearing a beautiful song from far off, calling to him, making him ache. He missed her.

David swallowed, shoving the treacherous thoughts away. She'd made her choice, and he'd made his. Whatever had grown between them in the short time they'd known each other meant nothing now.

"She's at the palace I assume, dutifully serving her brother and king." That thought burned him up inside. His respect and admiration for her was tainted by the knowledge that she remained complacent as the kingdom was laid to waste. For that, he didn't think he could forgive her even as he longed for her.

"You know this?" Luca asked, skeptical.

"Where else would she be?"

Luca shrugged. "I suppose you could be right. But you said she fought harder than anyone to save Jack, do you think she'd stand by while this happened?"

The way Luca said the words, like she could be somewhere else, gave him a flicker of hope he did not want to entertain. It was easier to let her go if he hated her.

"You said you had news?" David wanted desperately to change the subject before the hate and longing within him got any more tangled.

The feline man's gaze dipped and his pointed ears flicked.

Bad news then.

"The Ohans have taken control of the army at the border of Carthesia, where we were stationed. No longer are they following the king's commands, though they're doing their best to keep that knowledge from going public. I barely managed to flee in time."

David's mouth went dry.

"There's more," Luca continued. "They have weapons unlike anything I've seen before. Where they got them, I can only guess at. They must have dealings outside of Erinya."

"You mean, with the impendium?"

Luca shook his head. "Impendium is strong and powerful, but it doesn't hold a candle to the weapons they have now. They don't fight with swords or bows—they fight with something else. Powerful projectiles similar to arrows but with more power and force then a person could muster. One shot can kill a man in the blink of an eye."

David's insides turned to ice.

"What are they planning?"

"I'm not sure exactly, but they want control of Erinya. And they're no friends of the king."

"This is why we must find the rest of the Saints' Heirs," Kylian interjected, unashamed that he'd obviously been eavesdropping.

David's chest pinched in irritation. "What exactly are the Saints' Heirs going to do against weapons like these?" he asked through gritted teeth.

"You seek the Saints' Heirs?" Luca's ears perked.

"*He* does," David spat, "I'm just trying to stay alive." An incredible feat considering his blasted curse.

Luca gave him a look that asked why he was here with these people if he didn't want to be. David looked back into the fire, content to let his friend wonder.

"I do," Kylian said, answering Luca's question. "The Black King has returned, but the heirs of the Saints' have returned as well. Their powers are returning, and we can only assume that a great battle lies ahead." Kylian spoke with such fierce conviction that David himself was nearly convinced.

Luca's head tilted. "This explains a great deal."

"What?" David's head snapped back to his friend.

He nodded. "Our people have long believed the Saints would return someday. We have always honored the feline Saint, Nadia the Peacemaker."

Kylian scooted closer toward them, staring at Luca with fascination. "What do you know of the Saint? I can't find anything on her."

David disliked how Kylian edged closer to them.

"According to the traditions of my people, they say that Nadia was a beautiful young woman with the voice of an angel. Many men sought her affection, but her father forced her to marry their town's head merchant, hoping to give her a good life. But the merchant was a wicked, vile man. On their wedding night, he hit Nadia. Many, many times." Luca's chest fell as if he knew this girl personally and she weren't a mythical figure from centuries ago.

David had always admired his friend's empathy for those affected by injustice.

"The young woman, not knowing what else to do, did the only thing she could. She sang. The melody was so haunting and beautiful that it put the man into a sleep from which he never awoke. When the townspeople learned what she had done, she was exiled from the town despite the bruises covering her body."

Quiet settled over everyone. Zyla stilled, Kylian didn't speak, even Bo turned to listen to Luca's story.

"What happened after that?" Bo asked, cracking the silence.

"The kingdom of Erinya was facing dark times. The king had siphoned all the magic from the land, threatening the balance of life. But she met others like her, others with strange power they did not understand. A gift, it would seem, but from whom they did not know. And they became the Saints we know today, banishing the Black King to a realm beyond our world." Luca glanced around the room. "But he has returned, perhaps more powerful than before."

Bo's head dipped and she sat back against the wall.

"He has," Kylian asserted. "Which is why we must find the Saints' Heirs and free the Order from the Ohans. It's our only chance to vanquish him once and for all."

"And you do not wish to help them, David?" Luca stared meaningfully at his friend.

David bit his tongue, swallowing back his initial response. "I'm here because I have nowhere else to go."

"Could you not go to Grimzy's people in the mountains?"

Another flutter of irritation rippled through David's chest.

He could have gone to Grimzy's people. Something told him he would be accepted without question. So why did he feel so resistant to the idea, even as he complained about the company he traveled with?

"Luca, will you help us in our search? Will you join us?" Kylian asked.

Luca pursed his lips and glanced between David and Kylian. "I would like to, but . . . I've spent this time searching for David and our friend Grimzy. I believe that is where I'm needed at this moment."

Kylian sighed. "Of course. I would have loved for you to join us on our quest. Your knowledge and skills could be useful to us."

David snorted. The way Kylian spoke of "their quest" reminded him of how a young boy might romanticize his purpose in the world.

"Just because you're a pessimist, David, doesn't mean I have to be."

David frowned. "I'm not a pessimist. I've just lived enough life to know that things are rarely as simple and easy as we'd like them to be."

"Fear is not becoming of you," Kylian said, shaking his head.

The words were a knife to David's gut. He wasn't afraid. He was cautious. He'd been reckless before and it had rewarded him with an unbreakable curse. He was mutilated, broken, and destined for a horrific death. How could he possibly be optimistic? How could he still have hope when the only person who'd given him hope had betrayed him to help her ruthless brother?

"I think you're right, Luca." David's words were hard as steel. "We should find Grimzy." He looked at Kylian. "I think it's best if we part ways."

"If you're certain," Kylian said. Luca eyed David with suspicion, which only served to irritate him more.

"I am."

Kylian shrugged. "I think you're making a grave mistake, David. And I think you know it."

"Do I? Because it seems to me, Kylian, that you're in this for the glory. For the tales they will tell and the songs they will sing of the man who found the Saints' Heirs and brought them together to take down the Black King."

Kylian stood, brushed invisible dirt off his sleeves, and peered down his nose at David. "Perhaps, you're right. It *is* time for us to go our separate ways. We're heading north. There's an Order safehouse near the Whitesaw Mountains. We can travel together to that point and then part, if you'd like. I suspect it's still safest to travel together as long as possible." Kylian paused and considered David, but instead of looking into his eyes, Kylian seemed to be looking at his scars. Then his lips twitched. "I hope you find what you're looking for, David."

9

MILLIE

Millie saddled her horse, something she'd grown more accustomed to thanks to Master Ravala's help. The feathery light of dawn encroached on the citadel, the white marble structures and teal-colored domes glowing faintly in the sunrise. One of the vulgan would accompany them on her hunt for the princess.

Ice shot down her spine. She could sense it even as it stood sentient outside the stables. Its presence touched some dark part of her soul, leaving her perpetually uneasy. The horses sensed it too. They snorted and whinnied and stomped their hooves, eager to be far from the vulgan. She sighed. This was going to be a long journey.

The stable door opened, letting in a draft that rippled Millie's cloak. She knew who stood behind her before she turned.

"Malum." She finished tightening a buckle before she turned and dipped into a bow.

Her breath caught. The king stood before her, wearing all black and gold, his ebony crown blending into his dark locks.

Behind him stood a familiar form Millie had hardly seen since she'd begun her training.

"Doon!" She ran forward, forgetting her fear as she wrapped her older brother in a hug. Hesitant arms wrapped around her as well.

"Hey, sis." Doon's voice was soft, a feature that contrasted with his tall, bulky frame. She pulled away, looking at Malum.

"What is he doing here?" Millie's eyes narrowed. She didn't trust Malum in the slightest, but some part of her was grateful he'd brought her brother here to say goodbye. Doon began to wander the stables, greeting the horses he hadn't seen since his imprisonment.

Malum glanced around, refusing to meet her eyes. He sniffed at the air, his disgust evident. "Doon will be joining you on your journey. Who better to keep you safe than your older brother?"

His dark eyes slid to Millie, and she swallowed. She could see it for the threat it was.

Indignation flared in Millie's chest. "Older brothers should protect their younger sisters, *Jack*." She said the words slowly, twisting them back at Malum, letting him see the jab for what it was. Once, she would never have dared defy the king so openly, but she was beginning to see the power within her, however small it might be. Ever since Malum had ordered her to hunt down Jill for her execution, Millie could not stave off the anger that burned within her. This was not the Jack she'd known, the Jack she'd cared about.

Malum grabbed her forearm, his fingers bruising her skin. Millie gritted her teeth. She would not let him see her fear. She would be like Jill. She would be strong.

"He will serve as a reminder of what will happen should you fail. Again."

Millie's stomach clenched, and she glanced at her brother,

who now wore a patch over one eye. Or rather, he wore a patch over the empty socket where his eye had been before Malum removed it. He released her arm, which throbbed as the blood flow returned.

"I've heard rumors of army compounds and supplies from villages going missing near the Whitesaw Mountains. I'm certain Jill is close. Find her. Bring her to me." He turned and sauntered away without another word.

THE SUN WAS NEARLY up as Millie, Doon, Master Ravala, several attendants, and a vulgan neared the edge of the Citadel. The lower towns looked even worse than the last time Millie had traveled through. Silence reigned over the district. The only sound was the wind whistling through the gaps in the rickety houses. No smoke rose from chimneys despite the chill. She saw few townspeople, as if they dared not leave their homes.

Occasionally she caught movement from the corner of her eye, only to see a ragged curtain fall back into place in the window of a house.

Soldiers patrolled the streets, far more than she'd ever seen in the lower towns. They made no sound save for the rattle and clink of their armor, each of them bearing that strange, distant gaze.

A sideways glance at Master Ravala told her she wasn't the only suspicious one. His jaw clenched and unclenched while white knuckles gripped his reins.

"What's happened here?" Millie asked, her voice not daring to rise above a whisper. Even as she spoke, she saw the soldiers' eyes flick toward her. They *were* listening.

Master Ravala heaved a ragged breath. "The king has

lowered the conscription age to fourteen for those who cannot pay the increased taxes."

Millie drew her horse to a halt. This was news to her. No wonder these people were terrified.

A scream wrenched the air, followed by shouts and clanking armor. The chill in Millie's veins sparked into flame as she urged her horse into a canter toward the ruckus. Doon and Ravala followed close behind.

Her horse rounded a bend in the road, and Millie leapt from the saddle as she took in the scene before her. A young woman lay crumpled on the ground, clutching a bundle of cloth in her arms as one soldier yanked on her hair while another soldier held a blade to her neck.

Millie stormed forward, emboldened by the fire flowing through her chest.

"What is happening?" The authority in her voice surprised even her as the woman and soldiers turned toward her.

Millie's spine straightened as she pictured the princess in her mind. The woman had tear streaks running down her dirty face, and Millie could see a bruise forming under her eye.

One of the soldiers, a spindly inkwell man missing several teeth, stepped forward. "This woman could not pay the taxes."

Millie glanced back at the woman, realizing then what she clung to so desperately. A wail sounded from the bundle as the mother shushed the crying infant.

"Release her." Millie's voice boomed and once again a ripple of shock passed through her.

The man scowled, revealing his remaining yellow teeth. "But the taxes—"

"Will be paid by me," Millie finished for him.

"But—"

"But what?" Millie leveled him with a glare. Over her dead

body would she let these men take this woman's child. A fourteen-year-old was bad enough, but an infant?

"The king has ordered—"

"I will deal with King Jack. I am Paladin Millie, and you will obey me." Vaguely, she was aware of her brother's and Ravala's horses clopping up behind her.

The soldier's scowl deepened, but he nodded to the man who still held a blade to the woman's back. The other soldier let go but did not acknowledge Millie beyond that, instead staring off into the distance.

Something is very wrong with these soldiers.

"Payment, *paladin?*" The man sneered at her. Unlike some of the other soldiers, this man seemed entirely in control of himself. The thought was nauseating. She was certain this man demanded far more than even the king's taxes to fill his own money bags.

Millie yanked the bag at her waist, fishing coins from it and tossing them at his feet. He dove for them like an orphan after a scrap of bread.

"Do not return to this woman. If I catch you here again, I will throw you in Murderer's Row myself."

The man blanched, rising. He spit at her feet, turning away before she could react.

Millie tried to get her breathing under control as the soldiers walked away. She watched their backs until they disappeared down another alleyway.

At last, she turned to look at the young woman, still sitting on the ground, rocking her fussing child. Millie released a sigh and knelt in front of her. She had two black eyes, one still forming and one Millie could tell was several days old. Her scalp was red from where the soldier had yanked on her hair.

"I'm so sorry," Millie whispered.

The woman wouldn't meet her eyes but remained

hunched over the child, as if she were still too terrified to move.

"What's your name?"

The woman inched away from her and Millie stiffened. The girl wasn't just afraid of the soldiers, she was afraid of Millie.

"I'm not going to hurt you." Tears leaked from the corners of her eyes. Jill would never be caught dead crying in front of anyone, but here Millie couldn't hold it together for more than a few minutes before her emotions got the better of her.

Finally, the woman looked up at Millie. Her face was thin, the skin yellow from malnourishment. She was feline, her slanted cat eyes a shocking blue. She would be beautiful if not for the state of her health.

"Keyanna," she croaked.

"Keyanna," Millie repeated. "Where is your home, Keyanna?"

The girl looked at the ground again, cheeks turning red before she pointed at a building down the road. It was one of the nicer establishments, but Millie recognized the red flags hanging above the doorway.

A brothel.

No wonder those soldiers thought they could harass her.

She was the lowest of the lows by Erinyan standards. A slave and a prostitute, likely forced into the trade just to survive.

"Stand up," Millie commanded as gently as she could. The young woman rose on shaking legs. Millie could see now that the girl was around her own age. Millie could have been in her shoes had she not been born to one of the wealthier servants.

The child had quieted, now asleep in his mother's arms. A tear slid down the woman's cheek and she bowed her head. Millie knew that feeling all too well. The feeling of being looked down on, of being subject to other peoples' wills. She wouldn't allow Keyanna to raise her child like this.

Doon slipped off his horse, as if reading her mind. Keyanna shrank back as he approached, and Millie shuddered to think of what she'd been through.

"It's all right. We won't hurt you. You'll be staying somewhere else tonight." Millie nodded at one of the attendants, ushering them over. "Please escort Keyanna back to the palace. She will stay in my quarters and remain under my protection."

"Millie," Doon's voice was a whisper. "Are you sure this is a good idea? She belongs to someone."

"She is a person. She belongs to no one." Millie gave the girl a meaningful look. "Not anymore."

Keyanna's eyes widened.

"But the king—" Doon's voice rose in pitch, his single eye burning into her.

"I'll deal with him. And I will deal with the girl's master as well." Saying the words aloud made her feel slimy. That one person could be master over another's life felt entirely wrong. "Go. You are free."

The attendant, a young inkwell girl, bowed before Keyanna then motioned for her to follow. Reluctantly, the feline woman followed, turning to glance back at Millie.

"Paladin Millie?"

"Yes?"

"Thank you. I am eternally in your debt." Keyanna bowed her head and continued following the attendant, her steps timid at first then growing stronger with every step she took.

"Who are you?" Doon asked. Millie spun back to her brother, his single eye boring into her, his brows taught.

She swallowed. "What do you mean?"

"The Millie I knew would have been far too afraid to step into a situation like that, let alone defy the king's orders."

Her heart skipped, and she fought back the tremor that threatened to make her body cave in on itself. He was right. Never in her life had she been so bold. Even a few months ago she would never have dared place herself in such a situation, no matter how moved with pity she might be.

Was that such a bad thing? How often had she stood on the outskirts, watching helplessly as the lowly were oppressed and taken advantage of? No. She would not let that happen anymore. Especially not now.

Let Malum be angry with her. Let him torture her. Let him do whatever he liked to her. She would not yield. Not anymore. She was done running and hiding.

"I'm not a scared little girl anymore." She looked up at the Citadel behind them. "I am a Paladin. And I will fight for those who can't fight for themselves. No matter what."

10

BO

Their traveling party left at dawn, the gray light casting everything in somber tones. Bo leaned heavily on her crutch as she walked, a light rain pattering against her shoulders. She hadn't spoken to anyone since the night before when they'd decided the group would be splitting up.

David and his friend Luca walked at the front while Kylian and Zyla followed behind. Bo hung back, in part because of her leg but mostly because she wanted to be alone. Or rather, she didn't know how to be anything but alone. Even before she was bound to the vulgan, it had always been just her and her mother. In the last few months, she'd been constantly surrounded by people, and she wasn't sure how she felt about it.

Rain continued to drizzle as they left the feline village, headed northeast. The land out this way was barren, leaving them far more exposed than they would have liked. Trees were sparse and only strange rock formations broke up the dreary brown and gray landscape. Each formation was the same, with three pillars of rock clustered together in descending height and faint carvings on the sides that had been worn away by wind and rain.

"Burial sites," Luca explained. "My people honor the dead with three important aspects of their lives. The tallest is usually their spouse, the middle their children, and the shortest is often their cause."

"Their cause?" Zyla asked.

The feline man nodded. "Yes. Their cause is what they dedicate their lives to. For some, it is their chosen path of study or occupation. But for others their cause goes deeper. It is often predicted by the glyphs from their Naming Ceremony. Some make it their life's cause to feed the hungry, or to study medicine and heal the sick."

"So, like destiny?" Bo asked.

"Yes and no. No one's destiny is written in stone, not until they're gone." Luca motioned to the burial site. "A feline's cause is different. They have a choice in what they pursue as their cause, but they are not ruled by it. A destiny can be decided."

Bo slowed her steps, absorbing the man's words. She wasn't feline but if she had a cause, what would it be? Once she'd believed her cause to be keeping the vulgan away far from civilization, and then she'd failed at that. She glanced around at the group, each person lost in thought, as if considering the same question for themselves.

They walked for several hours in silence after that, the landscape changing slowly from grass and rocks to a more wooded landscape. A village lay ahead in the distance as they followed a main road. None of them liked being on a road, but so far, they'd yet to cross paths with any other people. Occasionally, they heard animals scuffling through the undergrowth nearby, but none bothered them.

As they drew closer to the village, they passed decimated and abandoned fields and crops. A sinking feeling hit Bo's stomach. One crop of corn had been burned, leaving the stalks black and brittle and the ground covered in ash. Another crop had been abandoned, rotting squashes and gourds decaying into the earth.

The closer they got to the village, the worse it got. Corpses lay on the side of the road, with birds and insects picking away at the bodies. The smell was nauseating, and Bo did her best to look away from it all.

"What happened here?" Zyla's soft voice shook.

"The vulgan happened," David growled.

Bo shrunk back. *She* had let this happen. These monsters should have stayed deep in the mountains, away from anyone they could hurt. Bo's attention snagged on a smaller corpse, the bare feet black and blue with cold and decay. A child. Just a child.

Bile rose in her throat, and she couldn't keep it down, collapsing to the ground to vomit. Everyone stopped and Bo could feel their stares, but she couldn't meet their eyes.

Kylian knelt beside her, motioning for the others to keep moving. Reluctantly, they did so, and Bo was grateful, even as a flush burned her cheeks.

"This isn't your fault, Bo." Kylian's voice was so steady she almost believed him.

Fierce anger burned through her, and she looked up at him. "Stop lying to me! The vulgan should have been a hundred miles away from here! They should never have left without my permission, and if they had, I should've been able to call them back!" Her voice rose higher as tears spilled from her eyes. "These people died because of them! Because of *me!*" Panic clawed up her throat. Kylian reached for her hand, but she yanked it away.

"Bo, what happened to your foot?"

Bo blinked, confused. That was not at all what she'd been expecting. "I was born with a clubfoot. What does that have to do with anything?"

"You were born with it." Kylian looked thoughtful for a moment, his jaw flexing and relaxing.

"What? Why are you curious about my foot *now?*"

"You were born with it."

"Yes," she hissed through gritted teeth, glaring at him.

"You had no choice. No control over it." He motioned around them. "You've had so many choices taken from you," he paused. "And I don't mean your foot. I mean everything. The vulgan should never have been your problem to deal with. You were a child. And being taken from your family—" He shook his head, his cheeks growing red. "That wasn't your choice either."

Bo looked up at Kylian. "Why are you saying all of this?" She gripped her crutch, her knuckles turning white.

"Because you need to hear it. What happened here is awful. But these creatures, the Black King—these are things that were set into motion generations ago. You cannot blame yourself for the actions of others."

Bo nodded, but she still felt heavy. She may not have had control over most of the things that had happened to her, but she had managed to screw up the few things that were inside her control, and she hated that.

When they entered the town, they found the others searching for supplies, but it appeared they weren't the first who'd had that idea. Luca found a rusty kitchen knife while Zyla found a bag of onions.

"There's not much else here," David said.

"We keep moving then," Kylian said.

David eyed Bo and Kylian, a disapproving frown pulling at

his scarred face. "We should camp here tonight. The next compound is still a day's walk away, we won't make it there before dark."

"Fine. But we leave at first light tomorrow." Kylian looked at Bo. "I don't want to be here any longer than we have to be."

"Finally, something we can agree on," muttered David.

Kylian rolled his eyes but sauntered off, checking out each of the village houses to find one suitable for their needs.

"Bo, can I speak with you?" David's frown had deepened.

She shifted, a bit uncomfortable. "Uh, sure."

He nodded at the front porch of someone's home. Reluctantly, she followed him as he sat down on the edge. The wood was worn from years of neglect. She sat beside him but put several feet between them. She didn't think she'd ever had a one-on-one conversation with David before.

"I wanted to discuss something with you."

Bo sighed. Why did everyone want to talk to her? Why couldn't people just leave her alone to sulk in peace? "What is it?"

"It's Kylian. Something about him feels . . . off to me. His attention to you, his fixation," he sighed. "I don't like it. He's much too old for you." David crossed his arms as Bo looked over at him.

"What?"

"It's clear he cares for you, Bo. But why, I can't say. I'm worried about you and about you staying with him. I think—" He released a heavy sigh, "I think you should come with Luca and me to the Whitesaw Mountains."

Shock and uncertainty swirled in the pit of her stomach followed by discomfort. Was he really worried about her being with Kylian? And yet, she was supposed to follow two men to an unknown location, leaving behind the only people who'd ever given her a chance?

I wouldn't have to see the Order again.

That was strangely appealing. As guilty as she felt for betraying them to the Ohans, part of her longed to never see the Order again, especially now that she'd caused such devastation.

"I don't know." She shook her head. "But I think you're wrong about Kylian." He may have shown more kindness to her than he had to anyone else but nothing about it seemed romantic. No. There was something else about Kylian, a strange connection, yes, but it wasn't what David thought.

"Just—think about it. I know you don't know me well, but I don't want to see you get hurt."

"I can take care of myself just fine," Bo snapped.

David chuckled. "I'm sure you can. You remind me an awful lot of someone else I know." His face drooped.

"Is it that princess?"

David flushed, rubbing the back of his neck. "Maybe a little."

Bo pursed her lips. "If you like her, why'd you leave her?" She didn't care how blunt the question was. It was nice to see someone else squirm for once.

"It's not that simple." He stared ahead at nothing, his expression turning stony.

"Right."

He rose to his feet suddenly, fidgeting with his bow. "Anyway, just think about it. It's like Luca said. Your destiny isn't written in stone. You can choose to join them or come with us." He turned and walked away before Bo could respond.

For the first time in weeks, Bo was alone. Her thoughts whirled inside her head, leaving her with an ache behind her eyes. What was she supposed to do? She couldn't undo the past, like Kylian had said. But her magic hadn't manifested, and she didn't know how she could be any help to people without it. Then there was Kylian himself. David clearly thought the man was giving her too much attention, but she was a Saints' Heir, so it made sense. Right?

Bo sighed. She had one day before they reached the army compound. One day before she'd have to make a choice one way or the other. She could follow Kylian and Zyla, or she could go with David and Luca.

A scream cut through the silence.

Zyla.

Bo was on her feet in an instant, moving as fast she could on her crutch and good leg. The clash of steel rang out, followed by grunts and growls that sounded like no animal Bo had ever heard before.

She rushed around a corner. Zyla had fallen to the ground, her eyes wide with fear as Luca and David fought off another person.

It took several seconds before she understood what she was looking at. It was indeed another person, thin and clothed in rags. The person had stringy hair and walked on all fours like an animal, lunging at Luca while releasing a blood-freezing shriek. Sharp nails dug into the side of Luca's face.

Thwip.

The person froze, an arrow protruding between its eyes before it fell back into the dirt.

No one moved. At last David stepped forward, yanking the arrow from the person's head. Everyone moved closer and sucked in a collective gasp.

No blood flowed from the wound in his head. The body looked like someone who had been dead for some time, not someone who had just died. His nails were sharp and long and coated in dried blood.

"What is this?" Kylian asked.

David kicked the man with his boot, rolling him over onto his stomach. On the man's shoulder were two large puncture holes crusted in blood, something like black ink seeping through the man's veins.

"I've seen this before." David glanced around at them. Bo's heart was a quick, dull ache in her chest. "I don't think the vulgan are just eating people anymore. I think they're turning people into monsters."

11

JACK

Jack was a prisoner within his own mind, helpless as he watched Malum issue orders and commands Jack couldn't stomach.

Higher taxes.

Lower conscription age.

More soldiers.

More fear.

Hunting Jill.

Jack hated the looks he received from his people, even knowing it wasn't him who wreaked havoc on the kingdom. Every servant, every guard, every attendant refused to meet his gaze, trembling when they saw him. And for good reason. Even the general and Paladin Salazar had come to fear him.

It's not you they fear, not really. Malum smirked.

You wear my face, my body. They know no different. Jack wanted to scream, wanted to wrench himself from this body, but he was powerless. Was this what Malum felt like when their roles were reversed?

It was.

Jack didn't respond, but he was certain Malum felt his anger. Even Jack could feel it as it rolled through the body they shared.

Perhaps the most infuriating part of being trapped within his mind was the way Millie now looked at him. Not as Jack, but as Malum. Her fear and loathing were evident, palpable, and each time he saw her he felt his heart fracture more.

This is the cost of saving her.

And I'd do it again.

Jack found the assertion true. Millie may look at him with fear, but at least she was alive. At least she'd been reunited with her brother.

Her brother.

Disgust roiled through him as he recalled that day. She'd helped Jill escape and while Jack was thankful, Malum had been furious. It was his own hands that dragged her brother into the throne room. His own hands had held the whip that struck him. He could still feel the blood that had splattered his face. He could still feel himself carving Doon's eye from his head. Worst of all, he could still feel Malum's glee overpowering Jack's hatred and disgust.

Doon had deserved none of this. It was Jack's fault he'd been imprisoned in the first place. Now it was Jack's fault he'd been tortured as well.

My elixir saved him.

You just needed a bargaining chip, Jack hissed.

After Doon lay in a puddle of blood on the throne room floor, Jack had begged Malum to do something. To heal him. The sound of Millie's sobs and protests wrenched something loose inside him. Somehow, Jack managed to force Malum to save her brother. He doubted he'd ever be lucky enough to have such influence over Malum in the future.

Of course, then Malum had another way to hurt Millie.

Malum inhaled, walking Jack's body over to a large window overlooking the sea. It was perhaps his one mercy toward Jack. He was forced to watch himself do so many terrible things but to be able to glance at the sea, even for a second, gave him a reprieve like no other.

Do not presume to know my intentions, prince. I know more of heartbreak than you could ever hope to understand.

You have to actually have a heart to suffer heartbreak, Jack sneered.

I did, once. Malum's voice was filled with a sorrow Jack had never heard or felt from him before.

A scene unfolded before Jack's eyes. A man stood in the Erinyan throne room. His skin was dark, and he stood taller than any human man Jack had known. A golden crown rested on his brow, and he held a goblet in the air, a warm smile on his face. The throne room was filled with people. All the animal clans, the mountain men, the boreads, the inkwells, even the dryads were in attendance. Jack also spied several people bearing the colors of Welynn, Carthesia, Jahdala, and Sunaria. All five kingdoms were present— something that hadn't taken place in well over a hundred years.

The day of my daughter's birth.

Jack suddenly saw a young woman, sitting on a throne beside the king's, holding an infant in her arms. If Jack could, he would have gasped. He had never seen such a beautiful woman. Her skin was golden bronze with a splash of dark freckles across her nose. Vivid green eyes peered through thick lashes, and her black hair hung in curls and braids. A silver circlet rested on her forehead.

My wife, Anoora.

Again, sadness laced Malum's words with a warmth and longing Jack never expected to find in him.

She's beautiful. Jack couldn't help but picture Millie who, although different in looks, captivated him in the same way this woman had captivated Malum.

She was the love of my life.

Jack could feel that it was true. Malum's fierce joy and devotion was tangible, and Jack felt every ounce of it.

And my daughter was the most precious thing I'd ever laid eyes on. We named her Corina, for she was our heart.

The memory sped up in front of Jack's eyes. It was a dazzling night, full of joy. There was music and dancing and drinks. And then abruptly, everything stilled.

Malum held his daughter with a faint smile on his face, ignoring the world as he watched her sleep in his arms. His wife sat beside him, her hand resting on his arm. The light in the throne room had shifted, the murky gray pre-dawn light filtering through the windows. Only a few guests remained, most having retired for the evening.

A figure in the corner caught Jack's attention. Unlike the rest of the partygoers dressed in vibrant colors, this person wore a dark hooded cloak, concealing his face. The memory seemed to slow.

The figure walked closer to the dais, the sound of thunking boots booming in the now quiet room. The figure's face was still shadowed by his hood as he knelt before the king.

In a single burst, the memory returned to normal speed. The queen leapt from her throne, throwing herself in front of her husband and child.

A knife struck her in the throat.

Jack's blood froze. It was too similar to Millie's wound.

The queen collapsed and Malum roared, calling for guards as he handed the now-screaming infant off to a nearby maid. He fell to his knees, lifting his wife's body into his arms. She was already losing so much blood.

The party descended into chaos. Frightened attendees screamed and fled, running in every direction. Guards shouted orders but little could be heard over the panic. And all the while, Jack watched the cloaked figure slip out of the throne room and out of sight.

The noise around Jack quieted until it was nothing but a distant roar, like ocean waves pounding against the shore, heard from a long way off.

Anoora died that day.

Jack felt numb, like he'd been hollowed out. Millie had nearly met the same fate. No. She had met the same fate, only Malum had brought her back.

My daughter passed the next week. She would not nurse for anyone but her mother. Malum spoke the words with a cold resignation.

I'm sorry. The words felt strange and out of place. No apology could make things right or undo a wrong that had been done. They say time heals all wounds, but Jack knew better. Death was not a thing to be healed from. It was a divide that could not be crossed.

But Millie did.

Everything faded until Jack and Malum stood back in his quarters, overlooking the sea. The somber memory seemed to paint the world in shades of gray. Thick silence filled the room, and Jack could not sense any of Malum's emotions.

What did you do? Jack feared the answer. He didn't want to know, yet his burning curiosity wouldn't let him ignore this.

I consulted the great apothecaries and learned

of a source of magic strong enough to bring my wife and child back. They considered it evil. I considered it justice.

Jack recalled the story he'd learned as a kid, of the Black King who had stolen the magic from the land of Erinya itself, destroying everything and everyone on his quest for vengeance. Until the Saints rose to stop him. Where their magic came from though, no one knew.

Ahh yes, the Saints. They did indeed stop me, banishing me to that realm between life and death. A punishment for disobeying the laws of nature, they said. Vehemence filled his tone.

"And now they will try to rise again," he said aloud. "But this time, I am ready. I will destroy every last one of them."

JILL

To say Jill was disturbed by what had happened to Peter's wife would be an understatement. The woman's gaunt face and sharp teeth were made of nightmares, nightmares she'd rather forget. But the rescue mission to the Deadwood where so many souls were lost to Malum's monsters lingered in her memory. Clearly, the vulgan did far more than wreak havoc and devour people.

They were transforming people. That must have been what nearly happened to Grimzy when the vulgan bit him. That black, inky substance seeping through his veins would have turned him into one of those . . . things. What did you even call them? They weren't monsters themselves, but they were no longer people either.

Jill's head whirled with so many questions and so few answers as they rode silently along the hidden trail. Reluctantly, Peter had agreed to accompany them to the mountain men's domain. When she'd promised him revenge against her brother, he had at least agreed to hear them out. His main protest had to do with leaving his wife. He feared what others might do to her in his absence. Thankfully, Josie the barmaid, who was his wife's sister, had agreed to look after her.

A wildwind whipped through the barren trees, carrying the scent of snow and smoke. Her stomach churned. Back home, it would be nearly time for the Yuletide festivities that took place each winter—her favorite time of year. Roaring fires blazed in every hearth. The Citadel would be decorated with lanterns and strings of ribbons and bows. Servants brought in large trees and placed them all over the palace, trimmed with red berries and gold-painted apples.

The red berries represented the blood of the people, for despite their many peoples, the blood of all was red, a reminder of the connection they shared despite their physical differences. The golden apples represented the peace and wealth of Erinya, that all people who came to this land would be welcomed and given a chance to lead their own lives and destinies.

Now the black blood of the vulgan fractured every belief she'd held of her beloved kingdom.

How ignorant she'd been. Once, Jill had believed in all of this. But after seeing her kingdom as it truly was, she felt cheated and betrayed. Would her people ever know peace? Would they ever be free of the fear that ruled over them all?

"What exactly is your plan?" Peter asked.

With another gust of wind, the first snowflakes began to fall.

Jill ground her teeth. She rode one of the few horses the mountain men cared for. Living in the mountains and being far too large to ride the average sized horse, they had very few. Peter had his own, of course. Grimzy, with his long stride, never faltered in keeping pace with them.

"We need enough supplies to care for the refugees through the winter."

"That's not exactly a plan." Peter's tone was dry as he brushed snow from his shoulders.

"I'm aware of that," Jill huffed, her breath clouding the air before her. Another shiver rolled through her. As much as she loved Yuletide, she disliked the bitter cold.

"Where are you going to get these supplies?"

"Well, we were sort of hoping you could help with that."

Peter's mouth turned up in a half smirk. "I'm flattered, princess, that you think I have such power and resources. But alas, even my impressive reach extends only so far."

Jill pursed her lips. "Don't call me princess." She gripped her reins tighter. "And I don't think you have unlimited resources or power. This was merely a suggestion from the people who sent me."

"The people who sent you?" Peter raised a brow. "I'd like to meet these people who feel they can command a princess."

A spark flared in Jill's chest. She hated feeling like she had to submit to the council, but here she was. And why? Would this prove anything to them? Or was it just their way of using her for their own ends?

"Yes," she said, irritated, "They thought you might know of somewhere we could get supplies or have the connections to get us the supplies we need."

Peter was silent. Jill glanced over at him. The man's brows were furrowed, and he bit his bottom lip. He was not what she'd expected of a smuggler. He seemed far too smart. Gentlemanly even. He looked like a man born of nobility, not a man who'd climbed the ranks through deception and thievery. But perhaps that was the point. Maybe that was exactly why he'd become so successful.

"I do have one idea." He spoke with slow, measured words. "But it's risky at best."

"Everything's risky these days. Have you seen the state of this place?" Jill made no effort to hide her animosity.

"Unfortunately, I have." Peter stared at her, his lips pinched and jaw tight.

"So, what is it?"

"It would involve making enemies."

"I already have a few of those."

"Not enemies like these."

"My brother controls a horde of monsters, chased me from my home and my kingdom, and is likely hunting me right now. I can handle enemies."

Peter chuckled but it was devoid of any true amusement. "Fair enough." He slowed his horse, taking a steadying breath. "What do you know about the Ohans?"

"Absolutely not." Elisha's voice was as condescending as Jill had ever heard it, and she had to fight the urge to snap at the woman and remind her of her place.

Jill and Grimzy stood around the table in the council's meeting tent while Peter lounged in a chair in the corner, his feet propped on a box as he snacked on roasted chestnuts. Peter's idea was to raid the Ohans' fortress for their wealth of supplies. No one seemed happy about this plan—except Peter. He watched them, a smile tugging at his lips in a way that Jill found beyond irritating. Had he come all this way just to laugh at them?

Now the council was angry with Jill for Peter's suggestion when they'd sent Jill to find Peter in the first place. It all struck her as very unfair.

Life, like battle, is never fair. The sooner you realize this, the stronger an opponent you will be.

Master Ravala's words came to her, both a comfort and a source of grief. She'd nearly forgotten him in all the chaos of fleeing the citadel. Where was he now?

"The last thing we need is to make enemies of the Ohans." Javyn wrung her hands.

"And what would you have us do instead?" Grimzy asked, folding his arms across his chest. He seemed as annoyed with the turn of events as Jill.

"Anything would be better than risking upsetting the Ohans," Elisha said, calm and unbothered by Grimzy's simmering temper.

"The Ohans are already our enemies. They've never had Erinya's best interests at heart." Jill leaned forward, resting her hands on the edge of the table. She'd never trusted Ohan-Jin, and after he'd tried to establish himself as a regent instead of Jack, it had only confirmed her suspicions.

"You really are better off leaving them be," Peter piped up from the corner.

Every head swiveled in his direction as he popped another nut into his mouth, grinning.

"Then why even suggest it?" Jill ground out. He was making her look like a fool in front of the council. Not that she needed his help.

Peter shrugged, nonchalant. Jill would never have guessed the man had watched his own wife be turned into some sort of mutant creature given the way he acted now. "You want supplies? The Ohans have supplies to spare. They are their own stronghold. They have a reach even greater than mine. Pair that with the slaves and weapons they have under their control, and they're probably a force more powerful than the king even realizes."

Jill's heart stuttered, the breath leaving her chest. "I'm sorry. What did you just say?"

Peter popped a few more nuts into his mouth before brushing his hands off. "Which part are you referring to? That they're probably a force more powerful than the king knows?"

"No. What you said about the slaves. And the weapons. What do you mean?" Jill's heart was a frantic drum in her chest. Slaves? Slavery didn't exist in Erinya. She'd heard of distant countries employing such barbaric methods, but not in Erinya. It was outlawed. Right? She was suddenly horrified by her own ignorance.

"Yes. Slaves. Essentially, at least." Peter stood from his chair and swaggered over to the table.

A glance at the other council members told Jill she wasn't the only one disturbed by this revelation. And what were these weapons? Were they different from the weapons the king had access to?

"The Ohans control the Impendium mines. But of course, they need people to do the mining for them. So, the people in their territory are forced to work the mines, relying solely on the Ohans as their 'generous benefactors.' In their minds, since the Ohans are supplying the people with everything they need to live, then the people must repay them by serving in the mines, among other things. They're not free to leave, free to find another profession, or even free to have children without the Ohans' permission. Essentially, slaves."

Silence overwhelmed the group. Distantly, Jill was aware of the sounds of the camp beyond the tent but even that was muted. Her eyes found Grimzy, who sat cross-legged on the other side of the table, his gaze burning with a fury she'd never seen before, not even when she'd been denied to see Peter.

"So," Jill cleared her throat, "The Ohans have kept these people enslaved and no one knew?"

Peter's lips flattened to a crisp line. "King Cole knew."

Jill's face burned as all eyes turned to her, as if this information somehow meant she'd known too. But her father had rarely shared anything of importance with her. As far as he was concerned, her sole purpose was to secure an alliance with Welynn through her arranged marriage. To him, she was good for little else.

If only he could see me now. Though given her lack of political prowess, perhaps her current situation wasn't something to be proud of.

She realized everyone was waiting for her to speak, to offer some explanation. She shook her head. "I didn't know. If I had . . ." Her breath caught as overwhelming emotions rushed through her. Sadness. Anger. Disgust. And the most haunting question—if she'd known, *would* she have done anything about it?

She knew her answer to the question now, but a month ago? A year ago? The knowledge of her own cowardice and selfishness left her unsettled, like a bird that could find no safe place to land. She was barely staying aloft as it was. Now this?

"Anyway, that's probably the least of your problems." Peter continued speaking as if the rest of them weren't still grappling with this new knowledge. "The biggest problem is the new weapons they have."

"You mean, from the Impendium?" Elisha narrowed her eyes at Peter.

Peter laughed. "Yeah, no. The Impendium is the least of our problems. The weapons they have now make Impendium-crafted weapons look like children's toys."

"What kind of weapons?" Grimzy asked.

Peter picked a metal instrument up off the table, fiddling with it for a second before answering. "The weapon itself is called a gun. Imagine a bow and arrow, but far deadlier.

Instead of arrows, they have bullets. You load an explosive powder and the bullet into the gun. When you pull the trigger, the bullet launches faster than any arrow ever could and rips through everything in its path. Now imagine you can fire off bullet after bullet in mere seconds. And imagine every man in an army has one. They need only stand back and fire at their enemies, and those enemies, who only have close-combat weapons, can't even get in close enough to use them." Peter paused. "Just ten men with guns could take out an entire regiment in a matter of minutes and live to tell the tale."

A shudder rolled up Jill's back. How had the Ohans kept so much of this secret from the rest of the kingdom? Why continue mining Impendium if they had access to better weapons? Surely, those could be used in the war against Carthesia.

Unless it was all an illusion. Mine the Impendium for the king, keep the better weapons for themselves. But they'd only need better weapons than the king if they were planning something. Something big.

Jill wanted to rip her hair out. Fire raced through her veins, washing away all reason and logic. The Ohans needed to be stopped. They had undermined Jack's reign, had gone behind her father's back, enslaved people, and hoarded dangerous weapons. They didn't care about Erinya. They wanted to conquer it.

"We must stop them." Jill's voice was low but certain. She left no room for argument. She was tired of being undermined herself. "The Ohans are a threat to this kingdom."

"And what, exactly, do you suggest?" Elisha raised a brow, but her tone lacked its usual condescension.

Jill rolled her shoulders back, meeting each member of the council's gazes one by one. "We launch an assault on the

Ohans. We take their supplies and their weapons. And then we free our people."

"It would be a suicide mission," Javyn said.

"She's right." Elisha nodded.

Jill slammed her hand on the table, the bang echoing around them. "And what else should we do? Stand by as our people suffer? The Ohans have what we need, and we can save our people at the same time." She glanced at Peter, who was glancing at the tent entrance, possibly wondering if he'd made a mistake in revealing this information.

To her surprise, it was Grimzy who spoke up. "The king himself did not cross the Ohans. They were a force to be reckoned with even before they had these weapons. To launch a full-scale assault would require numbers and resources we don't have. And even if we could free the people, how do we get them out? Many will be weak and unable to make a journey here." He didn't add what everyone else was thinking. That they didn't have any more room in the caverns for more refugees. And traveling across Erinya with the vulgan on the loose was asking to be attacked.

Jill huffed, a gnawing sensation building in her stomach. She couldn't accept that. There had to be some way they could get what they needed and free the people. *Her people.*

She looked down at the table, scanning the various maps of Erinya. Something tickled the back of her mind, and she glanced back over at Peter, folding her arms across her chest.

"How do you know so much about the Ohans?"

Peter's eyes widened for just a fraction of a second before he flashed them all a crooked smile. "Because I have dealings with them, of course." Jill glared but he remained unaffected.

"We'll deal with that later," she said through gritted teeth. Her attention returned to the maps, studying them once more.

Her eyes landed on a fortress to the north, Fenric's Keep. The wolfmen's domain.

A wisp of an idea clutched at her thoughts. "What about the wolfmen? Do you have any dealings with them?" Her gaze flicked back to Peter, whose smile had dropped.

"No one has dealings with the wolfmen."

Jill stared at the map. Fenric's Keep bordered the icy coast of the northern Ataran sea. While the wolfmen kept to themselves, she knew they had a large fleet, opting to trade with other countries and kingdoms rather than Erinya.

The Ohan's territory also bordered the coast. Maybe, just maybe . . .

"What are you thinking, Your Highness?" Grimzy asked, studying her.

Jill looked at the council again, her heart thundering with the suggestion she was about to make. "What if we asked for the wolfmen's help? Their fleet could easily carry the rescued people to safety, and with their numbers, we might actually have a chance against the Ohans."

Peter laughed again, but it was devoid of any humor. "I just told you. No one has dealings with the wolfmen. Not even me. And I have dealings with almost everyone. They would never agree."

"Why not?"

"Because. They keep to their own kind. They're practically independent from Erinya. The only reason they're still here is because of the treaty they signed after the assassination of Queen Anoora."

Jill frowned. How did Peter know so much about Erinyan history? And why didn't she know?

Perhaps more disturbing to her were the fractures within her kingdom. The Ohans were plotting nefarious deeds. The wolfmen refused to engage with the rest of Erinya. Even the

Whitesaw tribe had kept mostly to themselves until the refugees arrived.

And you think you can make a better ruler? She asked herself the question, once again disturbed by her answer. To become queen would mean more than just taking the throne from her brother, it would mean uniting her people. But she wasn't sure they *wanted* to be united.

"I don't see any other way. If there's even a slight chance they might aid us, we have to try. For the people."

For Erinya.

Elisha's head tilted as she stared at Jill. For once, she looked curious rather than haughty. "And you are willing to do what it takes?"

"I am." Jill's voice was strong. "I will fight for the people of Erinya. No matter what." She looked at each of them in turn. "I will die for them if it comes to that."

13

DAVID

ind lashed against the window of the wooden building, clawing its way in through the cracks. David breathed heat onto his hands before rubbing them together. The group had been hunkered down in the abandoned army barracks for the last several days despite their plans to part ways, opting not to light a fire in case more of the blackbloods were present.

The blackbloods. That's what they'd nicknamed the people the vulgan had transformed. They'd encountered two more since the initial attack, though these had ambled through the street. Their skin was pale to the point of looking blue and that inky black substance coursed through their veins. They were crusted in dried blood and ice and filth.

David recalled Grimzy's encounter with the monster that had bitten him, its poison seeping into his veins. When they'd slayed that vulgan though, the poison had vanished and Grimzy had returned to normal. Would the same happen if they killed all the vulgan?

"How many do you think there are?" Luca's voice was a whisper.

"Impossible to say. But I'd wager there will be many more before this is over," David said.

Luca gazed sideways at him. "This?"

David ground his teeth together. His friend had a point. What was this? What were they doing? What was *he* doing?

Your destiny is as changing as the wildwinds. Mother Goose's words echoed in the back of his mind. But he remembered all too well the visions he'd seen in the Enchanted Wood. His dreams were haunted by the sense of falling, of shattering into a million pieces, all at the hands of Jack. Jill's brother. The brother she'd defended and returned to. The brother who had unleashed these monsters on the citizens of Erinya.

"You seem lost, David." Luca said, then he rose from where they'd been sitting and shuffled across the room to get himself more tea.

A shudder rolled through him, and he fiddled with the new arrows he'd been working on. He'd been stuck in this building with Kylian, Zyla, and Bo for too long, venturing out only to relieve himself. Kylian seemed intent on finalizing some master plan before continuing their journey, insisting David stay close even though he'd planned to leave. Reluctantly, he'd agreed.

Now he felt too hot, despite the freezing barracks. He couldn't seem to catch his breath, no matter how hard he tried to slow his breathing. With shaking hands, he grabbed his bow and headed for the door. He needed out. He needed out right now.

Without a backward glance at his companions, he stepped outside. A frosty wind stung his cheeks but the ache of it soothed him. He could handle the cold. He'd been hunting in the cold all his life. Shouts came from behind him, but he slammed the door shut.

He just needed to take a walk and clear his head. Too much information and too many questions vied for his attention.

With his bow slung over his back, and the promise of snow in the air, the tension slowly seeped from his body. Nothing like mind-numbing cold to keep your thoughts from running wild.

He'd been plagued by bouts of panic since he was a child. His heart would race, the room would spin around him. The air in his lungs felt thick and syrupy, like he was choking on it, trying desperately to breathe. His mother could always calm him and was the one who suggested he take walks outside. Over time, he'd learned what triggered such attacks and did his best to avoid such things.

It was why he'd started hunting. The focus required, the outdoors, and the peace and quiet of a forest in the early morning set him at ease.

David continued down the desolate street, his breath returning with each step forward. They needed to keep moving. If they waited much longer, the snows would come, and they would be stuck here until the spring thaw. Their supplies were dwindling even though Zyla did her best to ration their food, using the same tea leaves over and over until it was slightly colored hot water.

He needed to go to Grimzy's people. They would help him. Maybe they'd even have answers about the vulgan and the blackbloods. The Whitesaw people often had knowledge the rest of the world had long forgotten.

The clopping of horse hooves broke through the silence. David's senses went on high alert as he whirled toward the source. Voices followed, but they were muddled by the distance and the wind.

He examined his surroundings, trying to recall which barrack his friends had been in. How far had he walked? Normally he paid attention to that sort of thing, but he'd been so restless he'd ignored his surroundings. An amateur mistake.

He did know one thing though; few people besides soldiers had horses.

Spying a large broken crate that had been tossed aside, he ducked behind it just as the entourage rounded the corner. David stilled, peeking through a crack in the boards. Three people sat on horses, while several other people escorted pack horses.

The first was a gruff looking inkwell man armed with several weapons, including a sword and daggers. Beside him rode a young man with dark skin, a patch over one eye. But it was the third person who gave David pause.

Millie Muffet. King Jack's paladin.

He recognized her from the battle at the well. He remembered her power to transform into spiders. A Saints' Heir, Kylian explained later. Kylian had been displeased to learn she'd chosen the king's side.

"It doesn't look like anyone's here," Millie said, glancing at the barracks.

"We should check each building to be certain," the inkwell man said, swinging himself off his horse. "If the princess was hiding out here, they'd want it to look abandoned."

David's heart gave a sudden lurch.

If the princess was hiding out here . . .

What did that mean? Did that mean Jill wasn't at the palace? And if so, why were they looking for her?

Unless she'd left. And if the king's paladin was looking for her it couldn't mean anything good.

Panic edged into his veins. He had to play this carefully. He needed to know what was going on, he needed to—

A knife pressed into his back. "Who are you?"

David angled his head back, catching the squirming tattoos on the man's wrist. His gaze flicked back to Millie and her entourage, but the inkwell man had vanished from their group.

"Why are you slinking in the shadows?" The man's voice was cool and calm, but David sensed the danger underneath.

The knife dug deeper into David's back giving a subtle click as it touched his glass skin. For once, he was grateful for his curse as he didn't feel any pain unless the skin cracked or broke.

The man prodded David forward, toward the paladin who'd dismounted. At the sight of him her eyes widened.

"You."

"Me," David said, keeping his voice as steady as possible.

The girl marched up to him. Saints, she was short. At least two heads shorter than him, but something in her gaze was different from the last time he'd seen her. A fierceness and strength he felt sure hadn't been there before.

"What are you doing here?" she asked, her voice cold.

"Just seeking shelter. Something wrong with that?"

David glimpsed clearly her entourage now. It was a small party, probably meant to keep a low profile. The man at his back seemed to be the greatest threat at the moment. The young man with the eye patch eyed him warily but remained on his horse.

"Where's the princess?"

"Last I heard, she was at the palace," David said.

The knife dug deeper into his back. Any more pressure and he'd crack.

Millie pursed her lips. "The princess fled nearly two months ago after refusing to swear fealty to King Jack."

A burden that David hadn't realized he'd been carrying lifted from his shoulders.

She fled. She refused to swear fealty and left the only home she'd ever known. Guilt pounded into his stomach like he'd been punched in a tavern brawl. He should have known she'd never sit idly by. He should have been there for her. Instead, he'd run from her. Like a coward.

"I haven't seen her since we parted ways at the well."

"I don't believe you." Millie's voice was flat, her eyes searching.

He recalled how the girl had spent her life as a maid in the palace. Jill likely underestimated the maid. But David knew better. The servants and maids saw more than they ever let on. They were always watching. This girl wasn't any different, and that made her dangerous.

"It's the truth." And he was glad for it. Something told him if he had any clue where she was, Millie would sense it.

A thought struck him at that moment. A thought he wished he could have wiped from his mind because Millie did indeed sense it. He may not know where she was, but he had a feeling he knew where she'd gone.

The girl stepped forward, her gaze burning with a fire that reminded him of Jill. She drew a knife, pointing it at his chest. "But you know where she went."

Briefly, David wondered if the girl stabbed him through the heart if it would actually kill him or just wound him. He didn't intend to find out.

"When Jill spoke of you, she described a meek, timid girl. Do you really have what it takes to plunge that knife into my heart?"

Millie's face hardened, and though she was much shorter

than him, a flicker of fear rolled through his chest. He'd recognize that look of determination anywhere. She sheathed her blade, nodding to the man behind him.

"Tie him up."

David let himself be dragged along by the stout, burly man, his mind reeling with the knowledge this girl had just given him.

Jill had refused to swear fealty to her brother. She'd fled her home. She was being hunted down by the very girl who had bested her in the Paladin Tournament.

He needed to warn Jill.

A kick to the back of his knees sent David to the ground, a sickening crack and a blast of pain shooting through his kneecaps and down his shins. He hissed.

Millie wandered over to the other young man while the inkwell man bound his wrists behind him. If he noticed the scars that spiderwebbed around David's hands and forearms, he said nothing.

Flurries of snow settled around them. Movement down the center of the compound caught his eye. Bo peered out from behind a crate and dread kicked him in the stomach.

Don't do it, Bo.

While he'd only known the girl a few months now, he'd learned quickly that she tended to act first and ask questions later. He tried to shake his head at her, to let her know he had this under control, even if he wasn't certain he truly did. Pretty much anything was better than Bo's misguided help.

To his displeasure, the girl kept inching forward, her gaze burning as she eyed Millie. This was not going to end well.

Ravala must have seen her too, because he shouted at Millie, right before Bo launched herself forward, tackling Millie to the ground. The young man jumped from his horse and grabbed for Bo's waist, pulling her off the paladin. But Bo was determined, still clawing at Millie even as she was dragged away.

Millie's form dissolved, a thousand spiders taking her place.

Bo bucked and kicked against her captor before biting his hand and elbowing him in the groin. The man dropped. Millie's spiders lunged forward, crawling up Bo's legs and up her body.

David swore under his breath. He knew he could escape his bonds easily, but it wasn't going to be pretty. He bit his tongue as he wrenched his arms apart, shattering his wrists. The ropes slid off but now both of his hands were lying in the dirt. He cursed again. He should have broken only one hand. Still, he stood and spun on his captor, kicking his inner thigh.

An arrow zipped through the air, catching the inkwell in the shoulder. The large man cried out, dropping to the ground. David spun to see Luca in the distance, another arrow nocked and aimed for the young man holding Bo.

Before Luca could release the arrow though, a scream wrenched the air. Black mist spewed from Bo's mouth as she threw off the man holding her. The spiders flew off her as well, screeching and cowering before that black shadow.

The mist grabbed at Millie's spiders and the young man, tendrils like tiny fingers pulling them all away from Bo until she stood protected in an invisible forcefield. Bo's shadows sent the young man up against the wall while the other half of the shadows grabbed at every one of Millie's spiders, smashing them together in a ball until Millie reformed in front of them.

Bo screamed again, the force knocking everyone to the ground.

David's back cracked and his ears rang as the scream continued. He looked up to see Zyla rushing forward, the only one who dared approach the girl. The others must have heard the commotion and followed Luca. Behind Zyla, Kylian lay on the ground, staring in awe at the young girl.

Zyla shuffled forward, pushing against whatever force Bo was using to pin everyone down. The girl reached for Bo's hand, clasping it tight.

At last, Bo's screaming stopped, and she collapsed into the girl's arms, unconscious.

While the others remained dazed, Luca hurried over to David, catching sight of his hands on the ground. David had no time to explain.

"Could you give me a hand or two?" he asked. He would have laughed at his own dark sense of humor had their attackers not started coming to.

Without a moment's hesitation, Luca grabbed his hands. Zyla and Kylian ran toward them, the latter carrying Bo in his arms.

"It's time to go," Kylian said, only sparing half a glance at the broken hands Luca held.

David nodded, limping forward as his back slowly healed itself. They all turned and fled to the Northeast, headed toward the Whitesaw Mountains. He was certain of it now. Jill would have gone to Grimzy and his people. And if she was being hunted, then he had to warn her, even if it cost him his life.

14

MILLIE

Millie woke to the sound of whispering voices and a crackling fire. Night had descended and she was keenly aware of the heavy blanket over her and the roots jabbing into her back. Opening her eyes, she saw her entourage sitting in a small clearing, trees sheltering them from the light snowfall.

She sat up and wrapped the blanket around her shoulders, trudging over to the fire where Ravala sat while a palace healer tended his shoulder. Doon sat nearby, seemingly entranced by the roaring flames. He glanced up at her as she approached, coming to settle in beside him.

"What happened?" Millie whispered to her brother.

His jaw tightened but his gaze remained on the fire. "That girl used some sort of dark magic."

Images tore through Millie's mind, sending waves of pain rolling through her as she recalled the fight. That girl had done something to her, to her spiders. The girl had forced her to reform. The pain was unlike anything Millie had ever experienced. Burning pressure had pounded in her mind, like her skull was stuck in a fiery vise. Every nerve in every one of her spiders was ripped apart, overwhelming her until the blackness had consumed her.

"Are you all right?" Doon asked, turning to look at her. She was still getting used to his eye patch, but she could read the concern in his other eye.

"I'm okay."

He nodded. "We decided it was probably safer to set up camp here than risk staying in the army barracks. Who knows what other characters we'd find there."

Millie swallowed. She would never have thought of that. Jill would have though. Despite her magic and her improvement in fighting, she would never be as skilled as the princess.

What would have happened if she'd simply let Jill win the Paladin Tournament all those months ago?

She wouldn't be here now, that was for certain. She wouldn't have watched her brother be tortured in front of her, she wouldn't have fallen for the charming prince with a demon in his head.

Her head was spinning, and her lungs constricted. She had to get up. She needed to be alone.

She rose to her feet, letting the blanket fall to the ground, the chilly air nipping at her like a playful pup. The cold was a relief.

"I'll be back in a bit. I need—I need to think. Figure out our next move."

"Be careful." Doon's voice trailed after her, but she was already disappearing into the shadows.

Moonlight hung through the trees like a gauzy curtain, casting everything in its pale light. Pine needles crunched beneath her boots, and as the sounds of the camp faded, her heartbeat slowly returned to its normal pace.

No part of her wanted to hunt Jill, but she recalled Malum's threat with crystal clarity. If she didn't bring him the princess, if she failed in any way, Doon's life would be forfeit. She couldn't risk that, not again. Doon deserved none of this and she'd protect him, no matter the cost.

"You should be careful wandering off by yourself." The sultry voice cut through the silence.

Millie whirled, heart in her throat as she grabbed for her knife. "Who—"

A figure stood before her, leaning up against the tree with nonchalance that, for some reason, sent her blood roaring through her veins. She sheathed her blade.

"What are you doing here, Malum? How are you even here?"

Jack's body stepped forward, wearing the same crooked smile he'd worn the day they'd met. The smile of a prince who knew he was handsome. The smile Millie knew better than to fall for.

Malum stopped a foot away from her, his dark gaze pinning her where she stood. "I came to see how you're doing, to make sure you're all right. Is there something wrong with that?" His tone was a touch too mischievous, and she pictured a cat playing with a mouse.

"But *how* are you here? Shouldn't you be in the palace?" They were fifty miles from the Citadel by now. He couldn't have followed them all this way.

Malum raised a hand, darkness swirling between his fingers. The shadows danced through his fingertips like it lived and breathed. Like it answered only to him. It reminded her of the girl's gift, but Malum's magic carried a note of something darker.

"My magic is returning, albeit slowly. With it I can travel

wherever shadows exist." He smiled at her. "Though it is harder the farther away you are."

Millie shivered. It unnerved her to think how Malum might use such a power, and that he thought it worthwhile to visit her. To keep an eye on her.

Something in Malum's face—Jack's face—softened, taking in every detail of her. Millie looked away, wrapping her arms around herself.

"Well, I'm fine." She pursed her lips.

"I sensed you were in trouble earlier. I came as soon as I could."

Her eyes flicked to his. "How could you know that?" Unnerving indeed.

His eyes shifted color for an instant, flashing from black to green. "Millie—"

"Jack?"

His eyes shifted back to black. "I'm sorry." Malum's voice was soft, as if he truly meant it.

Millie knew better. Fire lit her tongue. "Why do you do this to him? Why do you let him out only to push him back? It's cruel. It's sadistic." The words were harsh in the quiet night and to her surprise, Malum flinched at her accusations.

"You think I'm cruel?" A lethal quiet laced his tone, and Millie wanted to reel her words back in, if only to protect Jack and her brother. Who knew what Malum might do in retribution.

They stood mere inches apart now, their breaths clouding in front of them. She wanted more than anything to step back, to put distance between them, but she held her ground. She may have been speaking to Malum, but she was staring at Jack's face.

"I think you know the answer to that." Her heart raced like a galloping horse.

"If I were different, if I were better, could you love me the way you loved Jack?" His eyes held a hint of pleading.

Millie jerked away and cold seeped between them. *Love.* Is that what she'd felt for Jack? She wasn't sure. "Why would you ask such a thing?"

Malum took a step toward her and Millie's blood pounded faster. Jack was truly handsome, even with Malum's darkness in him. Sometimes it was hard to forget it wasn't really him.

But he's still in there.

Malum grabbed her wrist, his fingers surprisingly tender. She wondered if he could feel her racing pulse. "Millie." His voice was solemn as a vow, as quiet as a whispered promise, as deadly as poison. "I see why Jack was charmed by you. Your quiet strength, your humility, your fierce heart."

She pulled her wrist from his grip, grateful when he let it slip away. His hand curled into a fist before flexing at his side.

"Jack was a good man, *is* a good man. But you are not him, *Malum*, even if you wear his face."

Before she could lose her nerve, she began to walk away.

"Perhaps someday, Millie, you will see the world as I do."

She glanced back at him. The expression on his face was impossible to read, soft and yet carved from stone. "Or perhaps, you will come to see the world as I do, as a place to be protected rather than conquered."

She slipped between the trees as Malum vanished into shadow.

15

BO

Bo woke feeling more exhausted than ever. A dark shadow loomed in her mind, melting away any attempts at coherent thought. Her skin prickled with warmth, and she realized strong arms carried her. It was the kind of warmth Bo had long forgotten, the warmth of being cared for, tended to. It made her vastly uncomfortable.

A snarl tore from her throat as she shoved out of the person's hold, eyes snapping open as she hit the ground with a less-than-graceful thump.

Kylian frowned down at her. "Was that really necessary?"

"Who do you think you are?" She snapped. "What's going on? Why are you carrying me like I'm some damsel in distress?"

She stood and glanced around, catching sight of Zyla, David, and Luca. They all stared at her, tension evident in their shoulders, in the way they gripped their weapons. Why did they look so wary?

Kylian pursed his lips. "Do you remember anything?"

David pierced her with a hunter's gaze—as if she was the prey.

"Remember what?"

"Bo," Zyla stepped forward, quiet and calm. "You attacked those people back there with—with your magic."

She froze, dumbfounded. Magic? She really did have magic then.

"You used a lot of magic far too quickly. You drove yourself to exhaustion," Kylian explained. "We've been taking turns carrying you for the last several hours."

Her knees buckled, whether from the exhaustion, like Kylian had explained, or the knowledge that slammed into her gut. She'd hoped she would be done with her "gift" after the vulgan fled her grasp. She squeezed her eyes shut. She didn't want to think about this, didn't want this magic, didn't want any of this.

"We should keep moving. We need to find shelter before nightfall." The urgency lacing David's calm tone cut through the tension. His meaning was clear. They didn't have time for this.

Gritting her teeth, Bo stood, snatched her crutch from Zyla, and started moving. She would not be carried. She'd made do so far in life.

She was grateful when David turned, continuing as if nothing had happened. He was one of the few people she'd encountered who didn't seem to think her weak or that she needed help and protection.

The party trudged on though Kylian continued looking at her, concern lingering in his gaze. She ignored him.

Zyla walked beside her, her presence as calming and steady as a bubbling brook. She didn't need to say anything, didn't need to do anything other than walk beside Bo to put her at ease. Bo had no idea what Zyla's sister was like, but she felt certain Zyla would be an excellent healer someday, if only for her calming presence.

"Can I ask you something?" Bo's voice was scratchy and raw.

Zyla nodded. "Of course."

"How long have you known Kylian?"

Zyla's head tilted, considering. "He's been working with the Order for several years now, feeding us information from the king."

They walked a bit farther as Bo considered this. "But why? Why work for the king? Where did he come from? And how does a man so young become the king's adviser anyway?"

Zyla gave her a sidelong glance. "There's a lot about Kylian we don't know. He's the one who found us, asking questions about the Saints' Heirs and how many we'd found. As far as I'm aware, he's the first person to ever discover the Order's secret cause. We didn't trust him at first, being the king's adviser and all, but he said working for the king was a necessary evil. I don't think anyone ever figured out what he meant by that."

Bo stared at Kylian's back, ramrod straight and proper even though they were hiking through a forest. His clothes also seemed like he'd put them on just this morning, freshly washed and pressed. He reeked of nobility, and yet . . .

"David thinks I should go with him and Luca to the Whitesaw Mountains."

Zyla's gaze snapped to hers. "And?"

Bo shrugged. "I don't know. David said he thought there was something off about Kylian, said he didn't trust him." She didn't mention that David was concerned for her safety. It was still too weird to even consider.

"Do you always push people away, Bo?"

The question was like a slap to the face, unexpected and painful. She frowned. "What is that supposed to mean?"

"When you first came to the Ohans, I had to practically beg you to let me clean and treat your wounds. When I offered you the Order's help, you agreed, only to turn around and betray us. Then, the second you had another offer, you ran off with complete strangers to abandon the Ohans. Now, you want to leave us too. Will you ever let somebody in?"

Ice shot through her veins, and she fought back a shiver. "I did what was necessary to survive." Her words escaped in a low warning tone.

Zyla stopped walking, forcing her to stop as well. "I know you did. You've been surviving so long on your own that you don't know how to live. So, tell me Bo, when are you going to try? When are you going to decide you have a life worth living?"

Bo had no answer. So, she kept moving, ignoring Zyla for the rest of the day.

Night fell and they rested against the trees, not daring to light a fire despite the bitter cold. In the morning, they continued east toward the mountains. Zyla's question from the day before lingered in Bo's head, sending a wave of anger through her each time she recalled it.

What did Zyla know? She hadn't been forced to live in hiding all her life. She hadn't been trapped by a bond with literal monsters. She didn't know anything.

"I've been thinking about that man, the first blackblood we came across," David said to the group, breaking the silence. "I don't think it's safe for our group to split up."

Kylian halted. "Really now? And I suppose you think we should follow you all the way to the Whitesaw Mountains?"

"Actually, yes, I do." David's scarred face surveyed them all. Bo remembered he'd been a captain or something in the army. She could see why. His confident leadership could be jarring at times, especially for someone who was normally so quiet.

But Kylian had become the king's adviser for a reason, despite his youth. The two men stared at each other. One, the picture of grace and nobility. The other a war-hardened man who knew what it meant to survive.

"I don't think you understand the power being held captive within the Convent. Without the Saints' Heirs, we have no hope of winning this war."

War. Is that what this was? Is that what they faced?

David stepped forward. "Listen, I understand you want to get your friends out of there, believe me, I do. But what can five people do against the Ohans? I've never been inside their territory before, but you should know better than anyone what a fortress that place is."

The trees overhead bent and sighed against the gusting wind. Bo looked between the two men then glanced at Zyla, who stood still with pursed lips and downcast eyes. Zyla had served in the Ohan's mansion. If anyone knew what they were capable of, it would be her.

"He's right, Kylian," Bo heard herself saying.

Kylian's head whipped toward her, his brow pulling together for an instant before his face relaxed, ever the diplomat. "I suppose I should expect that coming from you."

"What?"

Kylian's cheeks colored. "You betrayed us. I should have known you wouldn't want to help." The words were smooth as glass. Cold and calculated. Rehearsed. He'd just challenged her, and he knew it. He glared at her. Some question lurked in those hidden depths, something beyond his carefully cultivated exterior. He wanted Bo to push back, to say something.

Instead, she looked away.

Will you ever let somebody in?

Bo wanted to feel angry, to feel the heat of injustice roll through her. She wanted to lunge at the man and claw his eyes out with nothing but her dirty fingernails. But all she felt was cold, like a snuffed out a candle.

She glanced at David again. Luca stood behind him, taking in the scene with those watchful cat eyes.

"I'm coming with you," she said. She refused to stay with Kylian any longer than she had to. Zyla gave her a sad smile, but her look held no surprise. It seemed she'd known what Bo would choose.

"If you come with us, we can plan to get your people out. You don't stand a chance on your own." David said the words as if he wished they weren't true, and Bo believed him. But would Kylian?

Kylian's expression faltered, a look of anguish passing over it. "I can't just leave them. The Ohans—" The king's adviser shook his head, as if he didn't want to picture just what the Ohans would do. "I *must* free them."

David nodded gravely. "And we will. I promise. But we must be smart about this. If you come to the Whitesaw Mountains, I will speak with Grimzy, and we will see what we can do to rescue your people. Together."

Kylian glanced northward, to the direction of the Ohans' territory and fortress. For all his quirks and pretentious behavior, he clearly cared for those he'd left behind.

Zyla touched a hand to Kylian's elbow. "They're right. We do them no good if we're captured. I know the Ohans better than most. We have no chance against them right now. We need help."

Kylian's fist clenched, his knuckles whitening. "Fine." He marched toward David, jabbing a finger into his sternum. "But I will hold you to that promise. We get them out, no matter what."

"We will."

16

JILL

ill rubbed her eyes, struggling to hold them open as she read through the scrolls of parchment in front of her. She sat at a desk carved into the smooth rock of her quarters. A crystal light glowed above her, hung from the alcove above the desk. She'd spent the last several nights here, poring over old documents and maps, treaties, and recorded taxes and loans from various officials throughout the land.

Most of it was rather boring, though a few of the writings interested her. She'd even found a firsthand account of the Battle of Shadows, a legend regarding one of the first recorded encounters with a wraith, and an archaic poem about some nameless Deity. One article appeared to be the philosophical musings of someone named T. Whitesaw. An ancestor of Grimzy's perhaps? In it the writer spoke on forgiveness and redemption, about refusing to believe anyone was too broken to be loved and something about the broken putting the broken back together. It was all very nice but highly irrelevant to her.

She needed to learn as much as possible about the wolfmen before she left. And so far, she'd found very little.

Of all the animal clans, they were the most reclusive. It seemed they'd always kept to themselves, venturing out of their keep only for the occasional diplomatic journey. Even then, plenty of compelling and bribery took place to get them to leave.

None of the information she'd found was particularly reassuring.

In one account dated back to a historian from a couple hundred years earlier, she'd learned that a wolfman had assassinated the first queen, Queen Anoora, as Peter had rightly explained in their meeting. However, despite catching and executing the assassin, they never learned his motive for killing her, and the wolfmen offered no reason. She could find no other information.

A knock at Jill's door startled her. She turned a bit. "Come in."

Peter walked in, closing the door behind him. Jill's heart stuttered at the sight of him. His trimmed beard had turned scruffy in the few days he'd been in the mountains, and it reminded her of David.

"Thought you might be awake still." He crossed his arms, leaning back against the doorframe.

Jill glanced over at the bunks carved into the stone wall. Lyra and Asif were fast asleep and would likely stay that way. This had become their strange new routine. The kids would fall asleep. Then Jill would spend the late hours reading until she fell asleep at her desk, waking only when her neck began to ache. Then she climbed into bed for an hour or so until the gemstones glowed brightly, signaling dawn.

"Well, you thought correctly. Did you need something?"

Jill turned back to the desk. The words and numbers blurred before her eyes. Saints, she was tired.

He walked across the room to lean against her desk, staring at her. "I need you to get some rest. We head out tomorrow, and the last thing I need is to be eaten alive because you couldn't keep your eyes open." He smirked, but his jaw was set.

Jill sighed, rubbing her temples. "I know. I just feel like there has to be more here. There has to be something the wolfmen want."

"The wolfmen want to be left alone. That's all you need to know."

"I'm serious, Peter. I want to know why. Why the secrecy? Why are there hardly any records about them? What have they been up to all these centuries, tucked away in their keep?"

Peter stared at her. "I'm serious too. You need to sleep. And—" he stopped himself, debating something. "And you need to be prepared." He turned back to the door.

"Prepared for what?"

He glanced over his shoulder at her. "For them to say no."

Hours later, Jill met Grimzy and Peter at the edge of the mountain men's city. The main entrance was a large tunnel carved by the first mountain men long ago. It stood twice as high as the mountain men, dwarfing average people. Its wide mouth stretched open, revealing more stalactites with glowing gems hanging from the ceiling to light the path.

Jill knew the mountain men had created more ways in and out of the city, especially since they could manipulate the earth with their voices, but she had yet to see any others. On either side, some of the few guards in the entire city stood watch. Apparently, they were far more concerned about threats coming into the city than any within.

"Did you get some rest?" Peter asked as Jill double-checked her pack and belongings.

"Yes," she lied. She had laid in bed for hours, trying her best to sleep, but Peter's warning had only paranoid her. Without the aid of the wolfmen, they couldn't attack the Ohans and hope to live. It was indeed a suicide mission.

Peter's green eyes pierced her. Jill brushed off his concern, however, wanting nothing more than to get going. While she'd enjoyed the hospitality of the Whitesaw Tribe, she was anxious to see open skies and trees and feel the wind on her face.

"A word, Your Highness?"

Jill turned to see Javyn standing several feet away. So, she'd come as the sendoff for them then. Behind her the rumbling city was slowly waking. Asif and Lyra would wake soon, staying behind with the chief. Distantly, the sound of wheels clattered over the stone streets, the smell of hama bread and spices wafted toward them, as if trying to coax them to stay. Jill wanted to, even as something called her to leave.

The inkwell woman's eyes darted all around as Jill stepped toward her with a tightness forming in the pit of her stomach. She sensed something off in the air between them.

"Yes?"

Javyn's voice dropped to a breathy whisper. "I know you are a capable woman, but far darker works are at play than even you could imagine."

Jill felt Peter's and Grimzy's eyes on the back of her neck, the hairs raising ever so slightly. "It's a dark world we live in right now, Javyn."

The woman's eyes darted to Peter, her gaze resting on him until Jill heard the scuff of his boots walking away from them. When he seemed far enough away, the woman pulled up her sleeve to reveal a tattoo of a bird in flight. One that, unlike her other tattoos, did not move, meaning she hadn't been born with it.

"Do you know what this is?"

The princess pursed her lips, giving a slight shake of her head.

"This is the symbol of the Order of the Saints."

Jill shifted, fiddling with her belt strap. "And?"

"There is something you must know. The Saints live. Even now as darkness closes in, they rise, just as they swore they would whenever trouble came to Erinya. You must find them. They may be our only shot at—" Javyn stopped herself, but her meaning was clear.

They may be our only shot at winning this war.

The reality hit Jill then. She was no longer a princess vying for the position of paladin. She was a fugitive and traitor to the crown, hoping to win the throne and overthrow her brother.

This was war.

She swallowed hard, her mouth dry as dust.

"Why are you telling me this now?" And what did she mean the Saints were rising again? She'd heard that somewhere else before, but where?

Jill blinked, thinking back to several months earlier when she sat around the dying embers of small fire across from Grimzy. *The rise of the new Saints,* he'd said. She hadn't understood then. Still didn't, but—

"Some think the Saints are dangerous and do not wish for them to return. They wield magic that could turn the tide. You must find them."

"Who thinks they're dangerous?"

Javyn glanced around again, fear etching itself deep into her catlike features. "I wish I could tell you more, but we have no time. You must go to the wolfmen but do what you can to find the Saints' heirs. They're our only hope."

Jill nodded. She didn't know what else to say, and she didn't have time for this. For any of this. But she sensed the woman would be displeased if Jill said that aloud. Javyn gazed at her with eyes full of hope, then turned and wound down the main road back to the refugee camp.

"What did she want?" Peter's voice was low, tight. She glanced at him, noting his stiff posture.

Jill just shook her head. "To be honest, I'm not entirely sure. But I suppose we'll find out sooner or later."

Peter's lips pursed, a shadow crossing his face, but he said nothing. He returned to his horse, double-checking the straps she knew he'd already tested. Jill watched him, her mind writhing with this new information. The Saints' Heirs. What did it all mean? And why had Peter suddenly become so tense?

"Are you ready? We should be going soon," Grimzy rumbled, ambling up to her.

She looked up at the giant of a man. "Yes."

The trio led their horses into the tunnel. They'd brought a packhorse to carry their things. They wound through the tunnel in silence, the air growing colder the closer they got to the surface. Jill did the math in her head. They only had a month or two before winter arrived in full force. Then it would be too cold and dangerous to travel until the spring thaw.

When they reached the dead end of the winding tunnel, Grimzy laid his hand on the wall. A deep rumble echoed through the earth beneath their feet. The stone in front of them slid sideways, grinding and scraping open. Piercing light shot through, nearly blinding Jill after months of living underground. When she'd left to find Peter only days ago, she'd left at night, the transition much easier on her eyes.

Jill blinked away tears, inhaling the scent of crisp winter air and pine trees. The snows may come even sooner than anticipated, given the smell in the air. She fought back a shiver and mounted her horse.

"Grimzy, you've heard of Saints' Heirs, correct?" Jill asked, her voice trembling.

Sitting on her horse, he was only a few heads taller than her, rather than twice her height. Peter rode alongside her, his eyes shifting to the mountain man, but he said nothing.

"I have."

"You once told me the world was changing, that the new Saints would rise. What did you mean?"

Grimzy nodded, grimacing slightly. "Indeed, Your Highness. The Saints' Heirs are rising. You've already met one. But there are more."

Jill's heart thundered. *Millie.* Somehow, she knew. She knew the girl she'd treated so poorly, the girl who had risked her own life to help Jill escape, was one of them.

"Tell me everything."

17

JACK

*D*espite being imprisoned within his own mind, Jack still dreamed. And as Malum rested—for he'd learned the Black King did still need rest like any other person—Jack dreamt of the first girl he ever loved. The girl who had stolen his heart before Malum had stolen his mind. The girl with ivory skin splashed with dark freckles. The girl with tattoos that lived and breathed. The girl who had told him she could never love a spoiled, rotten prince. To his face.

Anna.

Such a simple name for such a complicated girl.

In his dream, he recalled the day they had first met, when the girl had become his sister's new maid. When he'd entered Jill's quarters, he'd expected a blushing, swooning servant who couldn't keep her eyes off him. That was the nature of Jill's previous maids. His sister never could keep one for long.

Instead, he'd walked in to speak with Jill and found himself transfixed. But Anna either hadn't noticed or couldn't be bothered, continuing with her work tidying Jill's room as if the presence of the second and third most powerful people in Erinya was nothing out of the ordinary.

He'd watched her, barely absorbing Jill's words as the girl dusted the furniture, swept the floor, and cleaned out the fireplace.

Her dark straight hair was pulled back into the typical servant's braid, yet it suited her perfectly. She swiped at her brow, brushing soot across her face.

"Jack, are you listening?" Jill's stern voice intruded his thoughts.

He'd tossed her the grin he knew drove her crazy and usually ended with him being smacked upside the head. "Actually, I wasn't."

Behind Jill, Anna snorted.

The twins turned to face her.

A normal, sane person in her position would have looked terrified that she had possibly offended the prince and princess. Not Anna. She merely pursed her lips and returned to her work.

Jill frowned at the girl. "Is there something you want to say?"

"Nothing I'm allowed to say," Anna quipped without looking at them.

Jack had sensed his sister's rising anger, her indignation at being treated that way by a servant. Before Jill could say something that got the girl in trouble, Jack spoke. "And what would you say if you were allowed?" he asked, folding his arms lazily. "I'm curious."

The maid slowed her scrubbing of the fireplace, considering. He later learned she'd debated voicing what she truly thought or making up something else.

She stopped scrubbing altogether and turned her gaze on the prince, those jaded eyes staring at him with distrust, and it was the first time he noticed the tattoo of a line that stretched from beneath her right eye, all the way to her chin. They said the inkwell's tattoos prophesied significant moments in a person's life. What did that one mean? He couldn't help but wonder as he stared at her.

"If I were allowed to say such things, I would tell the princess she shouldn't be surprised the prince isn't listening to her. That listening may be one of the many skills he could improve upon."

Jack's jaw dropped as Jill, to his surprise, burst out laughing.

He closed his mouth, glaring at his sister. "What do you mean, one of many?"

Jill just patted his shoulder, chuckling. "You don't have to answer that," she called to Anna. "I know exactly what you mean."

The prince glared at the maid, who shrugged, looking unapologetic. Although the words had stung, he admired the girl's bravery and knew somehow it wouldn't be the last time she humbled him.

That first day faded, the dream giving way to another day with Anna. A day he recalled almost as vividly as the day he'd met her.

Erinya had been plagued by a relentless summer heat, suffocating even for the middle of the season. The North Plains had become kindling for the fires that swept through, the smoke and heat combining to miserable effects. Troops had been dispatched to the plains to help quell the fires and keep them from getting too close to the Citadel. The king had sent Jack and Jill along to oversee the troops. Jack later realized his father had also wanted to keep the two of them out of his meetings with Ohan-Jin.

Anna had come with the princess, handling everything

from planning the transport of the Jill's things to personally caring for her horse. Jack had learned how hard working the girl could be, even if she'd made her distaste of the prince well known. So well known, in fact, that even some of the legionnaires Jack trained with learned of it, heckling him endlessly during their duels.

They had just reached the outskirts of the plains when they decided to set up camp and hold a barrier against the fires. In a foul mood from the smoke that clogged his lungs and stung his eyes, Jack began unloading the wagon that contained the officers' meeting tent and immediately set to work pounding stakes into the ground, tying the canvas even as the wind whipped it about.

"Didn't know you were capable of doing grunt work." Anna carried a basket of Jill's personal belongings, that judgmental gaze leveled at him. It was an ironic statement considering his sister wasn't bothering to help unload any of her own personal things.

Jack wasn't sure if it was the smoke, the heat, or the taunts the men had given him, but it was the first time the girl's words had truly gotten under his skin.

He whirled around and stepped toward the girl, towering over her. "Did I do something to offend you? Is there a reason you seem to hate my very essence?"

Anna's eyes widened, the first hint of fear he'd ever seen from her. It lasted only a second before her cheeks flushed, making her freckles stand out even more.

"You don't have any idea who I am, do you?" Her voice was like ice that cut away at his core. Dumbfounded, he stared at her, scouring his memory. Anna let out a humorless laugh, shaking her head. "Of course you don't remember. Why would you?" She turned to go, anger rolling off her in tangible waves.

"Wait." He grabbed her forearm, and she stiffened but halted.

The glower in her eyes was frightening enough that he quickly let go.

"Please, just tell me what I've done and how I can make it right."

"You can't."

"Please!"

"Why do you even care what I think?" Anna's entire face had turned red now, her chest heaving. And so did his.

Save for his sister, no one had ever gotten him so riled up before. Why *did* he care what some serving girl thought of him? She was no one. Nothing.

And yet . . .

"I care because I hate that you look at me with such fury, that you think so little of me. I know I'm not perfect, but if I've done something wrong, please, let me make it right." He hated how he begged. What a sight it must have been, a prince begging a maid, and yet he felt no pride. Something pulled him toward her. In the months they'd known each other, and despite her hostility, every interaction had left him wanting more. Wanting to know her better, wanting to peel back that hardened shell of hers and learn why bitterness had overtaken her.

Anna's jaw clenched and unclenched until she finally spoke in a violent whisper, like the calm before a storm. "You know I've lived in the palace my entire life."

"Okay," he said, frowning.

She turned her head, meeting his eyes. "I've watched you grow up. I've cleaned up your messes time and time again. All the serving girls have at one point or another. And so many of them think of it as an honor. An honor to clean up after the prince. An honor to be the next girl in line to have her heart broken by you." She fell silent.

Jack swallowed, suddenly not sure if he wanted to hear anymore. "And I'm guessing you thought those girls were foolish?"

"I was one of those girls."

Never had Jack heard such anger voiced so quietly before, save for his father's.

"And?" He sensed too late that he'd said the wrong thing.

Anna wheeled around to face him, dropping the basket. "And? *And?*" She heaved a frustrated sigh. "Do you remember the girl you asked to meet you under the apple tree in the courtyard, but you never showed up? The girl you gave a bouquet of wildflowers? The girl you even promised was different from all the other girls?"

Jack stared, memories flashing. Many girls. Too many girls. Even when he was a boy, he'd asked countless girls to meet him under the apple tree. He forgot about them more times than he cared to admit. Especially to Anna.

"We were both kids, I know." She swallowed, a tear tracing its way down the tattoo on her face. "But I thought you'd at least remember me. At least acknowledge that day you didn't show. But no. When I started working for your sister, you acted like I was a stranger, like you never even knew me."

Still Jack flipped through his memories, not daring to say he didn't believe her. Not daring to mention that after all her prompting, he still couldn't remember her face, her name.

"I'm sorry." He knew the words weren't enough. Never would be. Still, he couldn't stand the pained silence between them.

"Don't be. I'm just glad I learned my lesson long before the other girls did." She swiped the basket off the ground, shoulders tight.

"Anna, stop."

This time she kept walking.

"Anna, please."

"I need to get back to work."

"What can I do?" He didn't know why his feet moved to follow, as if some invisible tether bound him to her. He knew he shouldn't chase after her, that he should let her be. But he couldn't stop himself.

"Nothing, Jack. You can do nothing." She picked up her pace, refusing to look at him as she made her way to Jill's tent, already assembled though his sister was nowhere to be found.

The words caught him off guard. The girl continued to surprise him. This strange girl who called him by his first name without any fear of the consequences. Only his sister and father had called him Jack with such boldness, such familiarity.

"Am I not worthy of forgiveness? Can't a person change?"

Anna swept through the entrance of the tent and still Jack followed. She slammed the basket on the table and spun to face him.

"Why won't you leave me alone? You want to prove that you've changed? Leave and forget that you ever knew me. You've done it once before, and I have no doubt you can do it again." Each word was laced with venom as they fileted Jack to his core.

Even in her fury, her appearance was striking. But that wasn't why he stood rooted to the spot. It wasn't simply because her words struck him like physical blows but that every word she uttered was hopelessly, painfully true.

His mouth had gone dry. "I forgot you once. But I could never forget you again."

She sighed, shaking her head. "What do you want me to

say? Do you want me to forgive you to ease your conscience? Soothe your spoiled soul?"

"I want to know why you're so angry. So angry that after all these years you can't let go of this."

"You think I should just forget what you did? Forget how you treated me?"

"I think you wouldn't be angry if you didn't still care about me." As Jack said the words, he suddenly noticed how close they stood, their chests inches apart, her eyes, her lips, so close to his.

He should have met her under that apple tree. He wished he *had* met her under the apple tree.

Anna noticed too and stepped back, folding in on herself, wrapping her arms around her middle.

"I could never love a spoiled prince like you, Jack."

"I wish you could, because I think I'm falling in love with you."

"Don't say that." Her voice wobbled. "You don't know anything about me."

"I know you love daffodils." The words were out before he considered them, before he considered how crazy he was acting. She was a maid, and he was a prince.

"What?" Genuine confusion pulled at her features.

He forged on despite the bleakness that threatened to swallow him. "I know you take a walk through the gardens every morning and stop when you reach the daffodils. I know you hate fish and love apple tarts and have a sister named Helene who died when you were little. I know you spend every free moment you get with your nose in a book and that your favorite book is *The Knight's Bride,* but you'd never admit that to anyone. I know your middle name is June, and I know you're one of the most beautiful girls I've ever seen."

Anna stood frozen, her mouth parted in a slight *o*. He

watched as another tear fell, perfectly tracing the line of her tattoo.

"How?" she breathed.

He swallowed the lump that had formed in his own throat. "I *know* you, Anna. You can hate me for the rest of your life, and that's fine, but I do care. And you're right, I was an arrogant, spoiled brat. But I was a kid. And I'm sorry, but I can't stand the way you look at me with such hatred. At least let me apologize."

Another tear slid down her cheek and she brushed a quick finger over it. "Fine. You can apologize."

"I'm sorry, Anna."

She pursed her lips, as if still debating whether she'd forgive him. Her eyes were red, but no more tears fell. "I forgive you."

A weight unlike any he'd ever felt lifted off his chest. How long had he carried it around? How long had he known the way he felt about this girl?

"Can I meet you under that apple tree in the courtyard when we get back?"

She stepped forward then, her lips pressed to his for too short a moment and then she pulled away with a genuine smile playing on her face.

Heat climbed up Jack's face. "Is that a yes?" he asked, rubbing the back of his neck.

"We'll see," she answered. And then she sauntered out of the tent.

They continued stealing kisses when they could. Finding spaces and times to be alone. Jack was fascinated by her. She had such strong opinions about everything from the Ohans' trading practices to the ingredients purchased by the palace chef. When he could, he would find a night for them to steal away together and walk along moonlit paths, take her dancing in the pubs where no one knew him, and whisk her away on picnics in the countryside.

He was indeed falling in love with her. He couldn't picture a future without her. Some part of him even realized he was willing to defy his father to be with her. Whether that was on the throne with her at his side or somewhere else. Anywhere else really. He couldn't care less, so long as they were together.

Then one day, she left.

No goodbyes. No explanation. Only a note slipped under the door of his room. He'd read it so many times he'd memorized it, though that was easy given its brevity.

Jack,

I'm so sorry, but I must leave. Please don't come looking for me. And please know I always loved you. I don't think I ever stopped loving you. But it's better this way. You were born to be a king, but I was not born to be your queen. I wish you all the best.

With love, Anna

Malum had invaded his mind by then, and her letter had left him reeling. Instead of spending his days with her, he'd hidden away in his room, battling the nightmare within his head. Alone. Was that why she'd left? Because she thought he was pulling away? Did she think he'd forgotten her then?

He'd never learned but, true to her wishes, he'd never looked for her, though every part of him wanted to. He wanted to explain. He *wanted* an explanation. He wanted one last goodbye at least.

It was the first time he'd truly hated his throne, his position. For the first time, he wished to be a nobody. He longed for the freedom and anonymity to be with her. But he let her go.

That picture in his head, that future he'd come to imagine with her, slowly faded. And soon he could go one day without thinking of her. Then two days. Then a week. He refused to forget her, but over time the details of her face became blurry. The memory of her lips on his drifted away like mist in the wind. Somehow, letting go of her felt like losing her all over again.

Then Malum sank his teeth deeper into Jack's mind until he filled the place where Anna had been. But what she had filled with light and warmth, Malum filled with darkness and ice. Where happiness once lived, sorrow and pain intruded. Where she had lifted his spirits, Malum reminded him he was a failure. Shadows swarmed his heart, lies attacked his mind, and Malum slowly cut his soul to pieces.

He was nothing but a prince of ruin.

And so, he did the only thing he knew how to do, the only thing he could think of to fight back the demon plaguing him.

He gave in.

18

DAVID

avid stood at the top of a tower with Jill beside him and Jack in front of him.

This scene had haunted his dreams night after bleeding night. It was always the same. Jack would yell and charge at him. He would kick David in the chest, sending him off the tower. Jill would scream, a sound perhaps more haunting than anything else.

And then he would shatter.

David woke, a sharp pain digging into his back. He'd deliberately positioned himself against the base of a large oak tree so a knot in the bark would poke into his back and keep him awake. He was sick of the nightmares. Clearly, it hadn't done any good.

He rose to his feet, early dawn light leaking down from above. They needed to keep moving. No one would be happy about it, but they needed to outrun their pursuers. Over the last day and a half, they'd all made impeccable time, stopping only twice when no one could keep going. Through it all Bo hadn't complained once, keeping pace with them despite leaning heavily on her crutch. The girl was tough, though something told him it had little to do with her foot and more to do with her spirit.

They were close to the Whitesaw Mountains now, perhaps only a few more hours of travel if they continued to move quickly.

"Kylian."

The young man had propped himself against a tree, with his arms crossed and eyes closed, but David couldn't tell whether the man was sleeping.

"Yes?" He answered without opening his eyes.

"Time to get moving."

He sighed. "I know."

The king's former adviser stood, brushing off the dirt and pine needles that clung to his clothes. The girls were curled up next to each other against a log and covered in dirt and leaves.

A soft thud sounded behind them and David turned to see Luca crouched before them, having kept watch up in the trees. His feline eyes helped him see better in the dark, making him an ideal person to keep watch overnight.

"We should hurry," Luca said, a slight frown pulling at his cheeks.

"I know," David said, grabbing his pack and bow.

"No. We should really hurry. I've seen no sign of our pursuers, but another strange scent lingers in the air. Something I don't recognize."

David and Kylian exchanged glances and nodded. They may not see eye to eye on everything, but David could respect the man's intelligence and drive.

"Bo, Zyla."

The girls groaned in unison but were on their feet a moment later, and then they were off again, hurrying through the trees. David followed, doing his best to cover their trail. If they had more time, he would have insisted they zigzag and backtrack to cover their tracks better, but they couldn't afford to waste any more time. Not when Jill's life was at stake.

Jill.

Anger and longing twisted inside him. He wanted to see her again and yet part of him never wanted theirs paths to cross again. Images from his dreams clouded his mind, weaving into his every thought and fear.

Mother Goose had told him the Enchanted Wood would show him visions of things that *might* be. Was it possible the future in his dream wouldn't come to pass?

"Are you thinking about her?" Luca's voice was barely above a whisper.

David pursed his lips. It would do him no good to lie. David had kept his descriptions vague as he told Luca about the princess, yet he'd easily guessed David's feelings for Jill.

Reluctantly, David nodded.

"You're afraid of seeing her again."

"Yes." David gripped his bow tighter, always finding comfort in its weight, in the smooth texture of the time-worn wood. "And no."

Luca nodded as if this made perfect sense to him. "Do you think she will want to see you again?"

David looked ahead, scanning the path before them. The temperature was dropping gradually, and he could smell the snowfall that would be here in a few hours.

"I don't know. After everything happened, I was so, so angry. And up until a day and a half ago, I thought she was still at the palace, letting Malum terrorize this kingdom. But—" He stopped, shaking his head. "I just don't know anymore."

"Does she deserve your anger?" Luca arched a brow, piercing David with an intensity only a true friend could manage.

David grimaced. Once he might have said yes. When he'd first met the princess, he found her arrogant and selfish. But something had changed in the time he'd known her. She didn't deserve any of his anger, and yet it burned through him. While the betrayal he'd experienced at the well made him want to never see her again, another part of him longed to simply stand at her side. To fight her battles with her. To let her know she wasn't alone.

The wind shifted, carrying with it the scent of earth and loam and something else. Incense? Luca stilled beside him. "The Whitesaw's domain is close."

"Up ahead!" Kylian called back in response.

A rock outcropping appeared before them, butted up against the base of the mountains. Snow began to fall, coating their party within minutes.

Behind the outcropping stood a Whitesaw man, shorter than Grimzy but still several heads taller than David. The man wore cropped pants with a leather belt and a linen vest that revealed his large, tan chest. The belt held weapons among other things—tinctures, fire starters, a coil of rope, and a large horn made of bone.

"Who goes there?" The Whitesaw man asked, his large arms crossed. He made no move to draw any weapons but that only unnerved David more.

Unsurprisingly, it was Kylian who spoke first. "We come seeking refuge. We also bring news that pertains to the princess."

David swallowed, his throat dry. This was the test, the moment they learned if Jill was truly here. But would the man lie to them?

Tension wrapped around them as they all prepared for the worst.

The Whitesaw man looked at each of them in turn, the

silence pierced only by the wind rustling the trees. Several minutes passed before he deigned to respond.

"And from where does a group of misfits like you hail?"

David and Kylian exchanged a glance, but it was Zyla who spoke up first.

"We have traveled as allies together in hopes of safety. Our differences mean nothing. We seek only refuge in times of great trouble."

"And how are you acquainted with Her Highness?"

David's heart soared, but he immediately squashed the feeling back down. *She's here.*

"I served under Paladin Grimzy in the army. The princess and I became traveling companions a while back. You may verify this information with the paladin and the princess." David's blood pulsed faster. What would they do if the man didn't believe them? Would they still be granted refuge?

The mountain man's jaw clenched, his knuckles tightening around the knife at his belt. "We will give you shelter for the time being, but you must go before the council if you wish to stay."

A collective sigh released from the group, but David noticed Luca's body remained taught, eyes narrowed at the man guarding the entrance.

The mountain man continued, "However, I'm afraid your information will be rather useless as the princess and Paladin Grimzy have both left on a secret mission and will not be returning anytime soon."

David's chest seemed to collapse in on itself. Of course she'd be gone. He fought back the urge to punch the rocks nearby. Maybe shattering his hand would feel better than what he felt now.

"You can give this information to the council, and they will decide what to do with it."

David glanced at his new companions. It seemed everyone else was just as uneasy with the solution as he was.

"What is this council you speak of?" Kylian asked, taking a step forward. With his shoulders rolled back and head held high, he quickly established himself as their leader. David fought the urge to roll his eyes.

"The council of the Lost Tribe. They will determine your fate," the man rumbled.

David stiffened. So, the Lost Tribe had made it? But what was this council, and how much power did they have?

"So, are you going to let us in or not?" Bo ground out, her voice like a knife scraping against stone. David wished she'd just keep quiet.

The mountain man turned to the girl. Bo, to her credit, didn't look the least bit intimidated by him even though he was more than twice her height. Perhaps that was what happened when you had power like hers.

"We will grant you shelter for now." The man's voice dropped lower. "But know that we will not tolerate liars, traitors, or those who seek to disrupt our peace."

Without further explanation the man turned, pressing his large hand on the stone behind him. Closing his eyes, the man began to hum. It was deep and vast and reminded David of the sound of thunder, of roaring waves crashing against a shore, of wind winding through a valley.

The man stopped and pulled his hand back. The earth beneath their feet began to rumble and groan, and the group watched in awe as the mountain in front of them parted like a curtain to reveal a long tunnel diving into the rock. From the ceiling hung stalactites with large stones, filling the space with warm light.

"Enter under the protection of the Whitesaw Tribe. Bring with you only peace."

Luca nodded. "Thank you, friend. Peace be with you and your people."

The group murmured additional thank-yous then entered the long corridor that sloped into the mountain's darkness. Behind them, the rocks groaned shut, reminding David of the day he and Jill had entered the Enchanted Wood. He prayed this endeavor would turn out much differently.

The further they trudged into the tunnel, the wider it became. All the while David fought the urge to turn around and head back the way they'd come. He didn't want to waste a single second searching for Jill. Every moment he waited was another moment Millie came closer to finding her.

But would the young paladin actually hurt the princess?

David wasn't entirely sure. She was clearly loyal to the king, despite knowing what lived inside him. Perhaps she believed hunting down Jill would help Jack in some way. Maybe. Either way, David's skin crawled with worry, but he did his best to school his features, clutching his bow for comfort.

Ahead, the tunnel brightened, and they stepped into the underground city of the mountain people. For a split second, all thoughts of Jill vanished as he beheld the behemoth city.

A large main road wound through the city toward a massive red clay palace at the top. Buildings were carved into the rock on either side, and a sparkling river flowed down the center of the main road before disappearing back underground at the head of the cave.

Smaller roads jutted out in winding paths throughout the city, forming a sort of circular pattern that could only be viewed from above the city where they stood. High above them were those massive gems, bleeding light down onto their domain, filling what should have been a cold, dark cavern with warmth and light.

Luca drew up beside him on silent feet, a twinkle in his feline eyes. "It's incredible," he breathed.

David nodded mutely, his gaze following the path ahead of them that sloped down to a plateau jutting out before the city. A cluster of large tents sprawled outside the city, no doubt where the inhabitants of the Lost Tribe dwelled. The smoke of small fires twisted up from the camp.

"Who goes there?"

David's gaze ripped away from the city, now focused on the two Whitesaw men guarding the entrance. They each wore similar outfits to the guard outside, but these men had two vertical stripes of red paint on either side of their face under their eyes. David recalled Grimzy mentioning the red-paint markings indicated the mountain men's rank within the tribe.

Kylian stepped forward, his silver tongue dripping with niceties as he explained their situation and the news they'd brought for the princess.

The tribesmen only nodded and the man on the left turned, heading down the main road.

"Follow me," he rumbled.

David glanced at the others. Bo appeared to be in a foul mood, as usual. The others remained cautious but followed the man without question.

The road before them sloped gently down, the red rock smooth from centuries of use. It reminded him of the feline village where Asif had lived, though much more populated.

They walked in silence, though the noise of the camp ahead grew louder. Children sprinted between tents, much nicer than the ones that had burned to the ground. People shouted at one another as more tents were constructed. The river gurgled past, its spray catching the light overhead.

"David?"

He stilled, spinning toward the familiar voice. "Asif?"

Before he knew what happened, David was nearly tackled to the ground as Asif crashed into him, wrapping his arms around David so tightly he thought the boy might crack his skin. Another body did send him to the ground as Lyra slammed into them as well.

David laughed, the sound foreign to his own ears. He couldn't recall the last time he'd laughed, but as the kids released their grip and he rose to his feet, he found himself smiling for the first time in forever.

He gripped the kids by the shoulders, kneeling in front of them.

"Asif, what happened to you? You've grown!" It was true. The feline boy stood nearly a head taller than when David had last seen him, looking less like that scrawny kid he'd found hiding in a hay pile and more like the legendary feline warriors of old. No doubt eating regularly had helped him shoot up. "Soon you might even be a match for me."

Asif just smirked. "I already am."

David gave him a playful punch on the arm. He turned to look at Lyra, her cat eyes stunning in the warm amber light. Her brown skin looked healthy and full, not gray and ashen like it had when he'd cut her from the vulgans' webs.

Luca approached from behind and David stood. "Asif, Lyra, this is my friend Luca. I taught him everything he knows about archery," he said with a wink.

Luca rolled his eyes. "Quite the opposite, actually. He was a mediocre shot at best when I met him."

The feline children looked up at the man in awe and David smiled. He was certain the children would practically worship Luca. His stomach twisted as his smile faltered.

"We need to speak with the council, Asif. It's about Jill."

Asif's eyes snapped back to David, his expression souring. "Jill's gone," he said sharply.

"She didn't say goodbye," Lyra explained, crestfallen.

David frowned. "Do you know where she was going?"

The boy looked between him and Luca. Asif really had grown in the past few months. But it was more than that. The way he held himself was different. Gone was the paranoid, fearful kid ready to pick a fight even though he knew he'd lose. Instead, the boy stood tall and proud, a confidence present that hadn't been there before. And, David noticed, Asif's arms were toned and more muscular than before. He'd wager the kid had continued practicing swordplay.

"I'm not sure. She left with Grimzy and Peter yesterday morning. Their mission was kept secret." Asif's voice held an edge that told David he wasn't too pleased about this.

David's attention snagged on something else. "Peter? Who's Peter?"

Luca eyed him from the side.

"The smuggler. Not sure why they need his help, but he seemed to know a lot about the Ohans."

David's brows raised. Smugglers? The Ohans? And Millie was hunting her. He swallowed. He had to figure out where she'd gone. He had to . . . what, exactly? Would he track her down in hopes of warning her? Once he'd told her, then what? Would he come back here, his task completed? He wasn't sure, but he needed to know where she'd gone first.

Ahead, Kylian, Bo, and Zyla followed the mountain man, on their way to speak to the Lost Tribe council. The glass soldier steeled himself and followed. It was time to get some answers.

19

MILLIE

Millie rode alongside Doon in silence. The clopping of horse hooves penetrated the terse atmosphere as their entourage followed at a distance behind them.

How had she come to this place? Hunting down the princess on the orders of a man she might have loved once, a man now imprisoned within his own mind.

She gave her brother a sidelong glance, only to find him already staring at her, his eye patch a constant reminder of what she'd done. Of what Malum would do if she failed.

"What happened when you disappeared last night?" Doon asked.

Millie's throat swelled, her heart a skittish, frightened animal in her chest. How had she come here indeed.

"I needed to be alone." She gripped her reins, her leather gloves crinkling in the cold.

"And were you?" The tone of Doon's voice made her eyes snap to his.

It had been three days since their run-in with Jill's former companion. Each night Malum had come to visit her in the shadows, looking and sounding like the Jack she'd known. He was kind and sincere despite the way she treated him. She could almost believe he was Jack.

Except for his black eyes, filled with a darkness that belonged solely to Malum.

"He's dangerous, Millie," Doon said, her silence answer enough for him.

Despite everything, her chest flamed with indignation. "You don't know him, Doon. Who he was before." She paused, looking ahead at the mountains that loomed before them, snow dusting the tops like a sugary confection the royal chef made. "He's still in there."

Doon's face twitched, his lips forming a tight line.

Millie yanked on the reins, her horse stopping instantly. These royal horses had been trained well.

"What is it?" she ground out.

Doon kept riding, forcing Millie to follow. His brown mare had been his favorite when he'd worked the stables, and he'd always longed for a chance to ride her out in the wilds like this. She wished the circumstances were different.

"Doon," she sighed.

"Don't, Millie. Just don't." He looked ahead, refusing to meet her gaze. That Saints-forsaken eye patch would haunt her for the rest of her life.

"You must believe me when I say that he *was* different."

Doon choked on a dark laugh. "Was that before or after he carved my eye out of my skull?"

Millie's magic rolled through her, sharp and sudden as lightning, and she had to resist the urge to dissolve in a swarm of spiders.

"That wasn't him. That wasn't Jack." Her voice was barely

a breath, tears of anger already pricking the corners of her eyes.

Doon wheeled his horse around, blocking her path. Fire gleamed in his eyes, fury twisting his features. Millie had often wondered why he didn't have magic like she did if they were both Saints' Heirs. In that moment though, she was grateful he didn't.

"And what about when he killed my friend and framed me for his murder? Was it Jack then?"

Millie hardly dared breathe. She couldn't answer that question. Didn't want to.

"I don't care who he was. I care who he is now. The prince you thought you knew is gone. That man is a monster," he growled.

"Quiet," she hissed, glancing at the party behind them. "Jack isn't a monster."

"But Malum is. Yet that doesn't stop you from spending your evenings talking to him instead of me."

Millie's face flushed with heat. Whether from anger or embarrassment, she herself wasn't sure. "Is that what this is, you're jealous I'm not talking to you?"

"Not even close, Millie," he said. "I'm frightened for you. You can't trust him."

"It's not that simple." She refused to meet his gaze.

"Millie, look me in the eye and tell me he isn't a monster?"

The eye.

She stared at her brother, her closest friend and protector. The brother she'd risked her life to save in the Paladin's Tournament. The brother who was tortured because of her.

His eye bored into her like a dark, burning sun. She swallowed and turned away.

"That's what I thought." He huffed and urged his horse into a trot, kicking up dirty snow in his wake.

Millie stared at his back, and though they weren't visible now, all she could see were the scars he bore from Malum's brutal lashes.

~

Millie volunteered for first watch that night, knowing full well Doon wouldn't argue. He'd always loved his sleep and his time in the royal dungeons hadn't changed that.

The tree bark bit into her back as she sat in the silence of the quiet forest. She closed her eyes, her body instantly dissolving into spiders. She inhaled, opening her eyes and taking in the sight of every spider.

It should have overwhelmed her, the amount of information she took in when controlling so many sets of eyes and ears. It had once, but now she could easily sift through it all, following the sight of each spider with precision.

As one, her spiders crept through the forest, their scurrying only audible to her ears. In addition to having several extra sets of eyes, Millie could also see better in the dark in her spider form.

She crept along the forest floor, the trees that were tall in her human form now dwarfing her exponentially. It made her a little dizzy.

When she had ventured far enough from the camp, she re-formed. It was getting easier to do so and took less energy than when she'd first discovered her powers. She inhaled the chill night air, the sensation biting at her lungs.

"I wasn't sure you'd come." His voice was soft. A whisper. A dark promise.

Millie turned as Malum stalked out of the shadows. His edges were blurred, whispers of black smoke curling off him.

"I wasn't either." Guilt twisted Millie's stomach as she thought of Doon, practically begging her to let Jack go.

But she couldn't. As long as Jack was still trapped and fighting to free himself from Malum's grip, she wouldn't let go. Jack had fought for her. Now she would fight for him.

Malum stepped closer. "Your brother does not approve of me."

Millie wasn't surprised he knew, though perhaps she should have been. Few things these days surprised her. Things had been strange ever since she'd woken up to discover her powers.

She shook her head, crossing her arms against the cold. The first snow had fallen, just a light dusting, but more would come, and she wanted to be back in the Citadel by the time it did. With the storms that rose in the North and whipped through the Whitesaw Mountain range, being here without shelter was a death wish.

"And you do not know if you should trust him or not." Malum's gaze caught hers before sliding down to her lips.

She glanced away, infuriated by the heat that roiled through her.

He isn't Jack.

She bit her lip. "I trust my brother. It's you I can't trust."

Malum stepped closer. Millie willed herself to take a step back but found she couldn't. Looking at him was like looking down at a valley while standing at the edge of a precipice. Dangerous. Deadly. Yet, for all the world she could not step away.

"Do you want me to be trustworthy?"

Millie released a breathy laugh, the heat clouding in front of her. "What is that supposed to mean? Of course I want to trust you."

"Do you want to trust me or Jack?" His steely black eyes

latched onto her, and she felt like prey caught in the line of a hunter. Frozen and terrified.

"I know Jack is still in there, and I will free him." Her voice wobbled and her cheeks heated with embarrassment. Bold words and yet she couldn't even say them confidently.

"I'm sure you will try." Malum smiled and it was so unlike Jack's real smile that for a moment Millie could see the difference between the two men who inhabited the same body.

He stepped forward and Millie stepped back, coming up against a tree. She bit back a curse.

"I don't wish to harm you, Millie. I respect Jack enough for that."

"And what about Doon? What about Jack's sister? Do you respect him enough to care for them as well?" The words snapped out of her like the whip that had lashed against Doon's back. "You think you can be soft and kind to me while pretending that your hideous actions haven't stained your hands forever? That they haven't stained Jack's hands forever?" Anger lit her tongue, her throat, her entire body.

But not anger with Malum. Anger with herself.

Jill had tried to warn her. That day at the well. The princess had told her that if Jack drank the water he would be lost. He would be gone and Malum would take control of him.

She had not listened.

Hot tears rolled down her cheeks, but she barely felt them as she stared at the man in front of her with a loathing she'd never felt before. She loathed him and herself and Jill and Doon. Everyone. It wasn't fair. She hadn't asked for any of this. She'd never wanted to become a paladin beyond wanting to free her brother. Never wanted this cursed power. Never wanted to be caught up in royal politics and dangerous feuding siblings.

And then for a second, Malum's black eyes shifted to green. The color of the trees. Of the ocean waves cresting along the shoreline. Of the grass on a warm summer day.

"Millie." It was Jack's voice.

A sob released from her chest as she surged forward, wrapping him in a hug. She knew he would be gone within seconds. Malum never let him stay for long.

Jack's arms wrapped around her, pressing her head against his chest. She could hear his bounding heart, feel his breath as it brushed against her ears and neck. She inhaled, breathing in his scent. That same pine and smoky smell. It was him.

His body went rigid in her arms, but Millie didn't pull away, letting her tears soak his shirt. She knew he was gone, that Malum held her now. Still, she clung to him, her heart breaking with every passing second.

"I'm sorry, Millie."

She pulled away, looking up at him. She swiped away her tears, knowing how weak it made her look. But she didn't fear weakness. More than anything, she feared the brutal cold that strength could become.

"Why do you do this to me? To him?" She looked to the ground, refusing to meet his eyes, to acknowledge the cold that wrapped around her as she let go of him. Refusing to admit that she wished his arms were still around her, even if it was Malum.

"I cannot let him regain control—you know that. But I know what he means to you and what you mean to him."

His form rippled and then vanished, leaving her alone in the dark of the woods. She stood there in the silence, the pale moon and stars giving off a watery light. She wanted to vanish like him, to leave this place and never return. She wanted—

A yell tore through the air.

Millie was racing before she'd realized she'd moved. More screams and shouts. And up ahead, flames.

Oh Saints! She was supposed to be the one keeping watch. She was supposed to alert everyone should any threat approach.

Instead, she'd left.

More screams. Blood curdling. More flames, growing bigger and brighter. And hotter.

Panic propelled her forward even as a wind whipped the flames into a fury. Ahead she spotted servants fleeing into the darkness while Doon and Master Ravala fought against their attackers.

Smoke curled through the trees as she burst into the clearing they'd set up camp in, quickly taking stock of the fight. To the left, several servants were trying to free the frantic horses as flames danced near them, eating away at the underbrush. To the right, Master Ravala wielded his sword against three reptile men, swinging and dodging blows with an effortless grace for such a stout man. And Doon—

She whipped around, searching for him in the chaos. Trees cracked as the fire soared upward, smoke billowed, filling her lungs and burning her eyes. This had happened too quickly to be a natural fire.

"Doon!"

A figure launched himself at her and she narrowly dodged the blow, drawing and fumbling her sword. It was another reptile man, gleaming red scales lining his cheekbones. He slashed at her with his kukri knife, the angled blade sharp and treacherous. She managed to bring her sword up in time, but she was no match for his strength.

In an instant she dissipated, hurling her spiders forward at the man. She chose larger spiders, the size of a man's hand, and sent them crawling up his legs, biting into his scaly skin. The man screamed, spinning around to try to shake her off. Around them the fire continued to burn.

"Stop," a lethal voice commanded.

The man spun and Millie froze, her spiders' many hearts rallying together in a frantic rhythm.

Ohan-Jin stood at the edge of the clearing with a knife pressed against Doon's throat. Blood trickled down his neck as the reptile man pushed the blade into his skin.

As if for the first time, Millie noticed the suffocating heat around her. She shuddered and found herself returned to human form, kneeling on the ground. Sweat dripped down her neck, her brow, yet her chest was cold as ice.

Off to the side Ravala had ceased fighting as well, his weapon still drawn but more men surrounded him.

Ohan-Jin smiled, revealing sharpened teeth. "Good."

"What do you want?" Millie growled, resisting the urge to transform again. But she'd never make it before the man slit her brother's throat. No, she could not fight her way out of this. Saints, what she'd do to have Jill here.

"Your cooperation." He did not elaborate but motioned to the men surrounding Master Ravala. A strange weapon smashed against his temple and the inkwell man crumpled.

Millie screamed, half rising to her feet. Hands grabbed her from behind, binding her wrists. "Why are you doing this?"

Ohan-Jin's smile receded, his oily gaze looking her up and down. More men stepped from the shadows, each armed with knives and swords as well as weapons she'd never seen before. Gone were the servants who'd accompanied them, and Millie could only hope they'd gotten away.

"I know what you're attempting, young paladin, but I have no plans to divulge my secrets to you here and now, not when you'll know soon enough. Suffice it to say, I need your help."

"I'll never help you," she hissed, surprised at her own

bravery. Once upon a time, she would have quaked with fear, her words lost to trembling and terror. But she was not that girl anymore. She had faced her greatest fears and survived. She would do so again.

Ohan-Jin's eyes twinkled in the dying firelight, as if he knew something she did not. "You will help whether you want to or not." The man shoved her brother at one of his henchmen, the strange weapon pointed at Doon's back as he was bound and gagged.

Ohan-Jin sauntered forward until he stood inches away from her. He ran a taloned finger down her cheek, a gentle caress that sent shivers down her spine.

"King Jack will hear of this. He will come for me," Millie said, glaring up at him.

That oily smile again. "Oh, I'm counting on it."

Pain exploded through her head and then everything went completely, resolutely dark.

20

BO

The Whitesaw Mountains were something to behold. Bo had never quite seen anything like them before. Dazed, she followed the group until she was walking through a refugee camp, the noise overwhelming after the silence of the long tunnels.

She stumbled after Kylian, the man watching everyone and everything through keen eyes. Bo observed him for a moment. Kylian's knuckles tightened and released several times, as if he had to remind himself this was not a fight. In the last few days of travel, the bags under his eyes had grown heavier, his cheekbones more pronounced. It seemed the man was not nearly as unbothered as he made himself out to be.

Behind her David stalled, his name ringing out throughout the camp, and she watched as two kids crashed into him. She frowned at the kids, a fuzzy feeling nudging the corner of her mind.

"Bo?"

She turned back and found Kylian staring at her with a raised brow. "Everything all right?"

She rolled her eyes and kept moving.

Kylian easily caught up with her. "When we meet with this council, let me do the talking," he said.

"Of course. Because what else would we expect from you?" Bo leveled a stare at him. She knew it was petty, but being petty was what she did best. Or rather, being petty was what she did best when she didn't know what else to do.

The dark magic she'd used several days back had left her exhausted, like a void had opened up inside her and nothing, save the nothingness of sleep, could fill it. No words could describe that moment when she'd released, well, whatever it was. The shadows had slinked back inside her, waiting for the moment she released them again. Waiting for orders.

She'd often wondered what her life would have looked like had she not been raised in the heart of a dark forest with a woman who'd stolen her away as a child. Wondered again what life would have been like without being tied to the monsters. Now it seemed she had her answer. She was always destined for darkness.

David and Luca caught up to her, the two kids at his heels.

"So, you made some friends." The young feline boy said to David, examining her.

He must have been roughly twelve or so, just a few years younger than she was, but he stood a head taller than her. She tossed him her most seething glare. The boy frowned at her.

"What's wrong with your face?" he asked.

David smacked the kid on the back of the head.

"Nothing. What's wrong with yours?" she quipped.

David looked up at the cavern ceiling high above them as if to say, *Saints help me.* "Asif, this is Bo. Bo, this is Asif."

Asif looked her up and down, staring at her twisted foot before meeting her eyes again. She raised a brow at him, daring him to say something about it.

He remained unfazed. "What happened to your foot?"

"Asif!" David snapped. "Knock it off."

"What? I'm just curious!" He tossed a smug smile at her.

"Just, get along you two. We have to speak with the council." David shook his head, then jogged to catch up to the others.

"Wow. Someone's jealous." Bo smirked. She kept her gaze forward, a surge of glee passing through her as Asif's smile turned to a grimace.

"What's that supposed to mean?"

"Oh please. It's clear you practically worship him."

Asif grabbed her arm, spinning her toward him.

"What the heck? Get your hands off me!" She shoved him away, surprised when he only took half a step back.

The boy glared at her. She growled at him. She often found growling was enough to make people keep their distance.

But Asif only responded in challenge, stepping forward. Their eyes locked. This kid had no clue who he was dealing with. She never backed down.

That strange fuzzy feeling washed over her again, distracting her. The feline girl who'd been with Asif approached them as Bo glanced around, suddenly dizzy and overwhelmed by the chaos of the camp. An inkwell woman was scrubbing a pair of pants in a bucket. A feline man sharpened a pathetic looking knife. Children screamed as a horde of them trampled through the walkways of the camp.

She gritted her teeth until her jaw ached. "I have to go." Before she saw his reaction she shuffled off after David and the others.

They entered a large tent up ahead, the fabric swishing closed behind them. Bo found herself strangely riled as she took in the people sitting before her. There was a gazelle woman, a boarman, an inkwell woman, and a feline man, all of whom looked vaguely irritated as they surveyed the traveling party.

Bo glanced at their own group, struck by their ragged appearance. Covered in dirt and smelling like an outhouse, even Kylian looked worse for wear. And that was saying something. The prima donna took every chance he could to bathe and improve his appearance.

So, she was unsurprised when he stepped forward to speak first.

He bowed deeply to the council, and Bo rolled her eyes before feigning a yawn when Zyla caught her gaze.

"Greetings, council." Kylian's voice was like dripping honey. "We thank you for your generosity in allowing us here, and we are honored to be with you."

The gazelle woman looked unimpressed. Bo liked her instantly.

"We know who you are, Kylian Doyle." Her voice was sharp as glass. "Skip the pleasantries and tell us why you're here."

Bo smirked. Oh yes. She liked this woman a lot.

Unruffled, however, Kylian continued. "Of course. We come on behalf of Princess Jill, who we believe is among you. We think she is in danger and came to warn her." His words were smooth, calculated, as always. No mention of wanting the Lost Tribe's or the Whitesaw people's help. Not yet.

"And why do you think someone wishes harm to the princess?" The gazelle woman leaned back in her chair and crossed her arms, looking very much like she couldn't care less about the princess's safety.

"Because we were attacked by someone looking for her," David said, stepping forward. She didn't miss the tightness in his shoulders, the way his jaw locked. He continued, "All I ask is that you tell me where she's going so I can warn her."

The gazelle woman pursed her lips. "I remember you David, how you helped rescue our people from those monsters. But I'm curious," she paused, eyeing him. "If you're so concerned for her safety, why did the two of you part ways?"

Bo recalled that day at the well. David had fought Jack so he could drink the water himself, to break his own curse. He'd never told them exactly what his curse was, but she suspected it had something to do with the unnatural scars covering his body.

"We did not see eye to eye. So, we parted ways. But that doesn't mean I wish her harm." David's voice was strained.

The gazelle woman looked at each of them in turn, her gaze resting on Kylian again. "That explains why you're here, David, but not the rest of you."

Bo's hands were sweat-slicked within seconds as the gazelle woman's deadly stare fell on them one by one. What would the woman do if she learned the truth, that they needed the council's help to find the Saints' Heirs? Would they help, or would they turn their backs? Would any of this even matter? With the vulgan under Malum's control, who knew what it would take to stop them. To stop him.

Kylian met the woman's eyes. "We seek sanctuary. You must know that nowhere in Erinya is safe right now, not with the vulgan on the loose. We have—" he swallowed, as if bracing himself for something painful. "We have nowhere else to go."

The defeat in Kylian's voice struck some broken chord within Bo's chest. Could it be that the self-assured, pompous, charming Kylian felt just as terrified as the rest of them? She'd always thought of him as being so much older and wiser, but he was only twenty-five, only a decade older than her, still very young.

But as she looked at him, she noticed the slight droop in his shoulders, the dark circles under his eyes, the scruff that had grown along his chin. Was it all a mask? A clever façade? A forced confidence so the world would never know how truly scared he was?

She hated how much the thought reminded her of herself.

The gazelle woman tipped her head forward. "Many have come seeking sanctuary. We will grant it to the best of our ability. But I sense there is more you wish to ask of us, otherwise you would not have come offering your warnings so freely."

Beside her, David stiffened. Kylian didn't look surprised by the comment though, as if he'd hoped the topic would venture into this territory.

The woman continued. "Yes. I know you, Kylian Doyle. Your history is impressive, becoming the king's adviser at just twenty years of age, a feat accomplished by no one else before you. I've heard some call you a genius for your strategic intelligence. So, forgive me if I can't help but feel this is a ploy to receive our help."

Kylian's charming smile faded into a stern slash across his face, changing his features from a cunning fox to a brutal negotiator.

"Yes, we seek sanctuary. Yes, we come to warn the princess of threats against her." His voice hardened to a wicked edge. "And we come to request your aid in rescuing the Order of the Saints from the Ohans before they are killed. Or worse."

The council before them stilled at this, each set of eyes turning to the gazelle woman.

They know something. Bo was certain.

"What do you mean, worse?" The woman's eyes narrowed

as she clenched the arms of her chair. "What could be worse than death?"

A war waged itself on Kylian's face and Bo knew he was struggling with how much information to share. Say too much and it might put everyone at risk. Say too little and it might not be enough to win their trust and aid.

"They could turn Saints' Heirs into weapons. Weapons to be used against us."

"How so?"

Zyla reached forward, resting her hand on Kylian's arm, nodding gently.

"The Saints are rising again. Their power may be the only thing that can stop Jack and his vulgan. But if the Ohans kill them, or use them against us, Erinya will fall."

Nobody spoke. No one dared utter a word into the silence that bathed the tent.

"You speak of the Saints' Heirs, do you not?" It was the feline man on the council who shattered the claustrophobic quiet. Beside him, the inkwell woman looked more curious than afraid.

"I do."

More silence, all eyes coming to rest on the woman who sat at the head of the table. A woman whose face had paled three shades.

"I have heard whispers of these returning Saints. Rumors. Each one more far-fetched than the last. And even if they're true, why should we believe you?"

Bo's stomach somersaulted even before Kylian turned to her and smiled.

"Because. We have one right here."

KYLIAN

$\mathcal{B}$o practically snarled at him. Kylian was certain he would pay for it later but so be it. The girl was sharp edges and jagged pieces, but he didn't fear her. Whipped dogs always growled the loudest. But deep down, they wanted what everyone wanted, to be loved.

"Show them what you can do, Bo." He kept his voice calm, soothing. So much about the girl was like a frightened animal.

The gazelle woman—Elisha—arched a brow, her narrow eyes taking in every sliver of movement. Beside him, Zyla pierced him with a look that suggested she thought this was a very bad idea.

Bo glanced between him and the council, her face twisted in a scowl. Kylian could practically read her thoughts, and he suspected many of them included swear words so foul even she didn't dare utter them in front of everyone.

"What he says is true, but I can't control it."

Kylian stiffened as Elisha pursed her lips. It was the wrong thing to say. To imply that Bo had no control would just get them tossed back outside.

"Somebody better explain. Now," Elisha snapped.

Kylian sighed inwardly but forced a smile to his face. Years of court politics had trained him well. He had the laugh that was both humble and easygoing, a demeanor both approachable and trustworthy while still establishing his authority. He knew how to spread rumors and how to shut them down. He commanded nobles and commoners alike, assessing every person he met like they were a riddle to be solved, and solve it he would. He knew which nobles truly feared the king and which ones paid him lip service. In a single breath, he could dispatch an assassin to take care of an unruly noble and order a feast for another who was easily flattered and manipulated.

He was a puppet master, pulling on strings no one else could see. He had risen to the position of king's adviser at so young an age for a reason.

Make them see a man who never doubts, who always has a plan. And a contingency plan. And a contingency plan for the contingency plan.

Most of all though, never let them see the fear that always lurked just below the surface.

"Councilwoman, I will not insult your intelligence by pretending I have all the answers." A compliment, to cast himself in a humble light. "What I can tell you is this, the darkness plaguing our land now is only the beginning." He fought back a shudder. "King Jack has deadly monsters, the vulgan, at his disposal, as you know. Carthesia pushes farther into Erinya. The Ohans gather their own forces and weapons."

At this the council's faces darkened, eyes flicking to Elisha, whose face was a stone mask.

"The Saints' Heirs may be our only hope. Help us and in turn—" he paused, sweeping his gaze across the room. He was an actor, and they were his audience, held in rapt attention. "They will save us all."

He could feel Bo's anger, radiating toward him, but he didn't care. He knew that feeling all too well. In fact, hers wasn't the only emotion he could sense. Wariness from Zyla. Disapproval from David. Skepticism from Elisha and the rest of the council members. Except for one.

The inkwell woman, Javyn.

Javyn, it seemed, had hope.

Her eyes shone with a brightness undimmed by the gravity of their situation. Her fingers clutched each other, her chest swelling. She was a loose thread in the tapestry of stone the council had woven. And he would pull on it.

He dipped his head toward her. A sign of trust. A bond forming between them with unspoken words.

"You know." Two words. And all he needed to plant a seed.

Javyn swallowed as the council members turned to her. Elisha's skepticism twisted into suspicion, then curiosity.

"I do," she said.

"Help us." He looked again around the room, forcing just the right amount of pleading into his voice. It must sound sincere, but not desperate. He could not let them know they held all the cards. Instead, let them believe they were making an impact, a difference. Inspire them to greatness. "Help us save the world."

Javyn turned to Elisha, lips pursed. Kylian knew it was enough. Enough to cast doubt in the minds of the council, get them talking, get them wondering.

And wondering was a powerful tool. He didn't need to sow discord or strife, not here, not now. He would play to their desires. Deep down, they all desired to see the world changed and made into a beacon of light rather than a realm of darkness. And now they would wonder if the Saints' Heirs would do just that.

"We will discuss the matter further," Elisha said. "Until we've come to a decision, you may make yourselves comfortable. Asif will show you around."

"I can't stay here."

They had made it only twenty feet from the council's tent before David had grabbed his arm and pulled him aside.

Kylian resisted the urge to roll his eyes at the lovestruck soldier. The man was clearly infatuated with the princess, even if he tried to deny it. But he kept his face neutral, knowing he could not afford to make enemies with the man before him.

"You can't?" he questioned, though he knew precisely what David's next words would be. Zyla and Bo had followed the feline boy, Asif, who'd begun showing them through the labyrinth of canvas tents. Luca kept his distance from Kylian and David but made no secret of staying with his comrade.

"I have to warn Jill before Millie finds her."

Kylian allowed himself a small smile. In truth, he didn't care what this man did. His primary concern was the hold he seemed to have over Bo. He didn't like it. Not one bit. But outright hostility would get him nowhere. No, it seemed much better for the man to go on his fool's errand to find the princess. From the sound of it, he wouldn't be far behind her.

"I would expect nothing less."

It was strange to him though. He'd known the princess for years, though Jill rarely paid him any mind. At one time, he himself had been under her spell, though only briefly. She had a determination that he admired, but despite her good looks, nothing about her was soft or sweet. She was a formidable character, but so was he. They would have torn each other to shreds.

But David, the loyal soldier with a soft heart, was head over heels for her, though Kylian doubted even he realized it.

What had changed in the princess since the last time they'd seen each other? Was she truly worthy of David's feelings, or was he being played?

A curious thing indeed.

His gaze slid over to Bo where she stood with Zyla and Asif, waiting in a line for food being passed out.

"You don't answer to me, David." He looked back at the man of scars. So many scars. Part of some curse he'd been put under. "It's finally time we part ways. Ironically, I believe this is my place for now. And yours is with the princess."

David dipped his head. The closest the man had come to showing him respect. However, Kylian had to admire him. David's respect did not seem a thing easily won. His cautious nature had made him a good soldier. No. He wanted David as an ally, not an enemy. Respect, however begrudging it may be, was the first step to forming an unbreakable bond with this man.

"I'll return after I've warned her."

At that Kylian frowned. "You don't intend to go with her?"

David's jaw clenched. "I'll warn her. But I can't join her."

Interesting. Very interesting. He tucked that piece of knowledge away to examine later. For now, he had bigger problems. Different priorities.

His eyes slid back to Bo, who had moved ahead only a few feet in the ever-growing line.

"Doyle?"

"Hmm?" He continued to watch the girl as she limped, leaning heavily on her crutch. Her foot must be giving her more trouble today after their mad dash to reach the mountains. He'd noticed some days were better than others for her.

"What's your interest in Bo? I know she's one of the Saints' Heirs, but it seems you have a particular . . ." David seemed to search for the word. "Fascination with the girl. You're ten years her senior."

Kylian chuckled, turning to look at David. His respect for the man grew, realizing he would be so concerned about Bo. Kylian supposed he'd be suspicious too if the tables were turned.

"Ah. I see. I assure you, it's nothing like that at all." A spike of pain shot through his chest. After all this time, it was still hard to think about that day. "She reminds me of my own sister, I suppose. The girl died when she was very young. She'd be about the same age as Bo now." For once, he could not hide the sorrow in his voice. Nor did he care to. That moment was forever frozen in his mind. He doubted the fear and sadness would ever truly go away.

David dipped his head a fraction. "I'm sorry. But I had to make sure."

"Of course." He inhaled, clearing away the negative thoughts. "When will you be leaving?"

"Tomorrow at the latest."

"Best of luck then." He nodded toward David and then Luca, who came to stand beside his friend. "I hope you find the princess."

"Me too."

KYLIAN SAT SILENTLY beside Bo and Zyla, dipping his pitiful excuse for bread into a strange lentil soup with sharp herbs and bitter spices. He might've enjoyed it if it had any salt. After months away from the Citadel, he'd almost grown accustomed to the lack of luxury, but he would always love salt. And there never seemed to be any when he desired it most.

Bo seemed just as enthused as he was about the meal, but Zyla remained upbeat, never wavering in her optimism. Her sister was no different. It was one of the many things he liked about her.

"Zyla, have you heard from Ymira?" He kept his voice casual and his eyes on his food, as if he were asking about any member of the Order. He still couldn't stop the skip in his heart at the mention of Ymira though.

Zyla glanced at him sideways, her eyes seeing far more than she ever let on. Another trait she shared with Ymira.

When Kylian had first come to the Order offering help, everyone had been suspicious, and rightly so. Why would the king's most trusted adviser offer to help a secret Order? They knew he must have some ulterior motive, and they were correct about that. They still didn't know why he'd chosen to help them. His plan was years in the making.

Ymira had been the first to trust him, the first to offer him kindness. She was also the first person to see him for who he was, much to his initial discomfort. Despite his best attempts, the girl always seemed to know what he was thinking and feeling. More than once, he'd wondered if her healing abilities extended far beyond seeing into the physical body and into the mind as well.

"You know as much as I do. Ymira and Aaira planned to go with Hasani to his people." Zyla studied him carefully, perhaps sensing the heat that rose up the back of his neck as he forced himself to take another bite of stale bread. "She's in good hands though. Hasani will take care of her."

"I have no doubt he will." The words came out snippier

than he intended, an unfortunate slipup. Zyla and Bo glanced at each other, something unspoken passing between them.

Hasani.

For as kind and trusting as Ymira had been, Hasani had been equally as hostile and suspicious. He also wasn't overly fond of Ymira spending any time with Kylian either.

He pursed his lips, resisting the urge to throw the ceramic bowl on the ground. No. He was calm, collected, easygoing. He inhaled, forcing his body to adopt a relaxed position. He was air. He was water. He was in control of his body, not the other way around.

"Is everything all right?" Zyla asked.

"Of course." Kylian smiled, the picture of ease. "Just taking stock of who escaped that night. And who didn't." He didn't need to force the somber tone that invaded his voice.

In his mind, he ticked off the Saints' Heirs they knew and the ones they still needed to find.

Ymira, heir of Uri the Bright.

Orion, heir of Briar the Cunning.

Hasani, heir of Inerys the Terrifying.

Millie, heir of Zillah the Vengeful.

And Bo, heir of Keiran the Unbreakable.

Five in total. Only five. One of whom had sided with Malum. Still seven left to find, and so little time.

He counted the remaining Saints off in his head. Torryn the Gentle, Jin the Resilient, Cairn the Strong, Nadia the Peacemaker, Felix the Trickster, Moroz the Unyielding, and Amari the Eternal.

He knew most of the original Saints were of different races, so their descendants would be as well. One of them was Whitesaw so perhaps they would find one here. The original Saints' number included another human and gazelle, a feline, a boarman, and a wolfman.

And one from the Reptile Clan.

That heir made him the most nervous. If the Ohans knew an heir was among them, and sought to use the heir's power against them, it could be disastrous. They would have little hope of winning that heir over to their side.

"Kylian?" Bo's voice yanked him from his thoughts, and he turned to look at her. They sat on the outskirts of the camp, their legs dangling over the edge of the walkway above the river. The water rippled below them, dark swirling eddies carrying clean water to everyone. There was something beautiful about that thought.

"Yes?"

Bo frowned, like she hated what she was about to say. "Thank you."

For all the masks Kylian was used to wearing, genuine surprise tossed the current one away. He smirked at her, "I'm sorry, did I hear you correctly? Did you just thank me?"

Bo scowled. "Don't push it."

Kylian chuckled. "What for exactly?"

Her scowl evaporated and she looked out across the river. "I've never had friends before. For so long, it was just me and my—my mother. And then the vulgan came to me and I felt like my life was over, like I was doomed to live the rest of my life hiding just to keep people safe. I never thought anybody could ever care for me. Especially after, well, you know."

Bo's honesty touched something cold in his chest. Something he'd shoved down so deep he'd nearly forgotten.

"You know, I don't think we're too different." He swallowed. It was hard to allow himself to be so honest. "I've spent my life studying people but never joining them. It seems safer that way. To stay away. To love anything is to give it the power to hurt you. And we've both been hurt." An ache clawed at his chest. For one fleeting second, he would allow himself to feel it. To feel that deep, nagging sorrow that burrowed inside him.

Bo nodded, still staring out across the river.

"But isn't pain what makes love so much stronger? I don't think anyone was meant to live this life alone. And sometimes risking pain is worth it."

Bo looked back at him, opening her mouth to speak when a shout tore their attention away. Asif was running toward them, his face lit with panic.

The trio stood, Bo easing up with the help of her crutch. Kylian became aware of shouts and screams that had been overpowered by the sound of the river.

"What's wrong?" he asked the boy.

He stared at them, wide-eyed and gasping for breath. "There's a riot, and I can't find my sister."

2 2

JILL

rincess. Traitor. Usurper. Queen.

The words echoed through Jill's mind like the clanging of an ancient bell, tolling in the distance. The snow had started falling, only a light dusting for now, but her breath clouded in front of her and frost coated her skin.

Their plan was to wind through the mountain range as far north as they could before cutting to the east toward Fenric's Keep, home of the wolfmen. They led their horses on thin mountain trails used mostly by wild animals. The rocky terrain would be treacherous should their mounts slip.

Fortunately, Grimzy guided them, walking ahead and clearing a path. She was surprised how nimble and agile he was. He moved like water, like the wind, yet he was as solid as the earth.

For two days they traveled in near silence, finding caves to camp in at night, lighting only the smallest of fires to keep from freezing to death.

In the last several hours, they had descended the thin mountain trails, and now the path before them widened so their steeds could walk side by side, so they mounted them once more. The jagged rock faces gave way to barren trees coated in pristine snow.

Jill inhaled deeply, relishing the cold in her lungs. Here, she could almost forget about the troubles her kingdom faced. Here, she could almost pretend that she was another girl, living another life, far away from the responsibility that weighed on her shoulders. At the end of the day though, she couldn't forget entirely.

A howl penetrated the air, a mournful pained cry. On it went, growing quieter and quieter until it tapered off completely. The sound brought tears to her eyes.

"It's been separated from its mate," Grimzy rumbled.

Jill glanced at Peter, whose face was drawn tight. His gaze clashed with hers, the sorrow replaced by something else.

"I don't need your pity." Though the words were harsh, they held no bite.

Jill looked ahead, instead locking on the tattoos that adorned Grimzy's back like a work of art.

"I know," she said. "We've all lost people." Her mind turned first to Will, then to David. The ache in her chest threatened to burst, and she wondered what would happen when it did. She didn't think she could bear the weight of such despair, not on top of everything else.

It shouldn't have mattered. She knew that. Not with so many other more important things happening. So many were dying. So many more would die. And yet, she grieved a man who had promised to follow her. A man who'd left her.

"Josie's taking care of Liza," Peter said in a gruff voice. "She's in good hands." He sounded like he was trying to reassure himself.

"Good."

Another howl cut through the trees, farther away. Even

without Grimzy Jill would have known the pain of that cry, the utter hopelessness. The wolf hadn't simply been separated from its mate; its mate had died.

"How exactly do you plan to negotiate with the wolfmen?" Peter asked, his voice dispelling the gloomy thoughts settling over them.

Jill gripped her reins tighter, shoving away thoughts of David, of Will. The time for grieving was over.

"I'm still not sure. Their solitude shows they don't need anything from the rest of Erinya. They've hardly had any dealings with Erinya in the last century." She shrugged. "I doubt that will change now."

Ahead, Grimzy slowed, falling into step beside them, his footfalls soft on the cottony snow.

"Jill, you mentioned that Alpha Volkov attended the Paladin's Ball," Grimzy mused. "That would be the first time an emissary from the wolfmen has visited in well over a decade."

"Why is that?" asked Peter.

"I'm not sure. The last time one of the wolfmen visited, they wanted to break the Anooran treaty," Grimzy explained.

Jill tilted her head. "This treaty, what is it exactly? What is their agreement with us?" The seed of an idea formed in the back of her mind. This wasn't the first time someone had mentioned the treaty, and yet she knew nothing about it.

"I don't know all the details, only that the wolfmen signed the treaty nearly four hundred years ago. After the assassination of Queen Anoora, the king wanted to eradicate the wolfmen entirely."

Jill stilled, her blood freezing in a way that had nothing to do with the temperature outside. "And?" Her question was barely more than a breath.

"They came to an agreement. The wolfmen would live, so

long as they never committed any crimes against Erinya. Any crime, no matter how small, would result in execution," Grimzy explained.

Jill realized they'd come to a halt. The only sound came from their horses huffing out plumes of hot air.

"Any crime?"

"Yes," Grimzy nodded. "From pickpocketing to murder. Any infraction was an automatic execution."

"No wonder they've kept to themselves all this time." Peter chuckled darkly.

A crack echoed through the trees, and they all spun toward the sound.

Jill's blood pounded as she scanned the trees, searching for the source of the sound. Likely an animal, she told herself.

Another crack split the silence, coming from the opposite direction. The horses began stamping their hooves, flicking their tails.

"Grimzy—" Jill barely got the name out before a body launched itself at Peter, taking him to the ground.

Jill drew her sword just as another figure launched itself at Grimzy. Her horse spooked, rearing back and dropping her in the snow. Snarls and shrieks filled the air.

It was two people, a man and woman, their skin as pale as the snow around them except for the black veins covering their body. The woman, nearly bald and wearing shredded rags, slashed her talon-like claws across Peter's forearm as he wrestled her in the snow.

Jill rushed forward, tackling the woman and pinning her to the ground. Up close she could see how hideous the woman was. Her fingers were black and blue from frostbite, and her bones poked through her skin. She was covered in scratches and scabs, some of which oozed black pus.

The woman reached for Jill's face, trying to buck her off.

She only succeeded in knocking the blade from her hand, hissing and growling like a feral beast.

Distantly, she was aware of the man attacking Grimzy, slashing at the mountain man with claws. Peter had joined in the fight, swinging his blade at the man but narrowly missing each time.

The woman bucked again, spewing black saliva in Jill's face. The spray felt like acid on her skin. Without thinking, she released her grip on the woman, clawing at her face.

Saints it burned!

A scream tore from Jill's throat as the woman pounced, pinning Jill to the ground with a strength she should not have. Jill twisted, heaving breaths clouding the air between their faces.

The woman stilled, looking down at her, then smiled. Black blood coated her teeth and Jill tensed. She knew this woman; she'd been part of the first Lost Tribe. Fear unlike anything she'd ever known pierced her chest like a poison blade, like the black bile splattered across her face.

"Hello *princess,*" she hissed. More saliva dripped from her lips, landing on Jill's cheek.

A whimper loosed from her chest.

"We've been looking for you. *He's* been looking for you."

Jill couldn't move. The woman's hands encircled her wrists like iron, claws digging into the supple skin and drawing blood. Tears slid down her cheeks, dropping into the snow beside her head.

She was frozen. The woman above her would end her now, would gut her with those razor-sharp nails. Her blood would run and melt the snow around her.

She would never see the Citadel again, would never witness another morning looking out over her kingdom, the domes glinting in the sunlight, the distant sound of waves crashing on a sun-beaten shore.

She would never see Jack again.

Her brother. Her twin. Her other half.

The woman raised her bloody claws, preparing to swipe them across Jill's throat. A faint *thwick* sounded above her and the body slumped to the ground, an arrow protruding from her temple.

Jill wriggled out from beneath the woman, rising to her feet. Her heart clenched. An arrow.

She spun, time stilling as her eyes landed on the figure in the distance. He rode atop a black steed, bow clutched in his fingers. The scars on his face were present as ever, but Jill didn't care. A sob wrenched from her chest as she shot toward David, who was already dismounting.

They crashed together, his arms wrapping around her, clinging to her like she was a raft in the middle of the Ataran Sea. Jill buried her face in his chest and felt his fingers running through her hair, felt the solid, steady weight of him against her.

He peeled himself away from her, holding her at arm's length. The warmth in her chest vanished as he penetrated her with that searing gaze.

"Are you hurt?" His thumb brushed over the tender burn on her cheek.

She licked her chapped lips, shaking her head. She didn't think she could speak. Her throat felt too tight with unshed tears, unspoken hopes and dreams and wants and needs. *Saints* why couldn't she speak? Why couldn't she tell him everything she'd thought for the last several months? Everything she wished she'd said the day he'd left.

David gave a curt nod, his body stiff. "Good."

Before she could utter another word, he stepped away

toward Grimzy and Peter, who had slain the man whose body now bled out in the snow beside the woman's.

Jill's stomach threatened to empty itself, a fresh wave of terror washing over her. She looked at the bodies before them, still and silent as the snow ran black.

Every sound was wrapped in gauze, the world slowing to a single heartbeat. Grimzy and David embraced. Peter shook his hand.

Still, she stared at the couple in the snow. She remembered them clearly now. The bright young woman, a gentle kindness in her features, forever erased by the poison that pounded through her veins. The man, strong and broad, now sallow and sickly as he stared with a hollow gaze up at the snow-gray sky.

Aeyla and Baedor. The couple she and David had met in the Lost Tribe.

Dead.

Their son was nowhere to be found.

23

PETER

*J*ill's face went pale as the snow as she stared down at the dead bodies before her. A man and woman lay there, dark blood turning the snow crimson. The scarred young man shouldered his bow as a feline man dropped from a branch high above and landed noiselessly, walking over to the princess.

Sometimes Peter still had trouble believing he'd become tangled up with the princess. Liza would never believe it.

His ribs tightened, the air caught in his chest. Thinking about Liza was still so hard. Would she understand why he'd left? Did she remember him at all? Or was her mind lost forever?

He suppressed a shudder. How easily it could have been her who lay at their feet bleeding into the snow. Thank the Saints—or whoever—that he'd found her when he did, before she'd completely turned. Her urging convinced him to lock her in the shed in the woods. The memory of locking her away, of slamming the door shut on her as she screeched and howled, as she clawed at her arms and face until blood streaked down her skin in thick rivulets, would haunt him as long as he lived.

"Luca?" Grimzy's eyes widened as he looked at the feline man who slinked toward them, a smirk tweaking his mouth.

"Didn't expect to see me alive, did you?"

The mountain man chuckled, rumbling the earth beneath their feet. "I should have known it would take more than an explosion to kill you."

Jill turned, her face frozen in mute horror as she glanced between the newcomers, a tear sliding down her cheek.

Peter stepped toward her. Something was wrong. "Jill?"

The scarred young man also froze.

"You remember them, don't you." The words were a whisper in the wind, but they were not a question.

She knew them.

The man knelt in the snow, brushing his fingers over their eyes. Then he stood, turning away from the couple. Peter's stomach churned, thoughts whizzing through his mind too fast to grab hold of.

Don't picture Liza. Don't picture Liza.

Too late. Power surged through him and the scene shifted before his eyes, an image of Liza's slain body replaced the woman's, blood leaking from her. Her beautiful face forever marred by self-inflicted scars. He closed his eyes, trying to shove the images away, but they burned into his mind, twisting his reality.

These visions were the worst. The ones that were too real. Too easy to believe.

Liza will be fine.

He prayed no one else had seen what he'd done. What he'd become. His whole life he'd breathed and uttered lies. Now, thanks to his illusions, he lived trapped in one perpetually.

"We need to keep moving." The mountain man spoke with

a quiet authority, daring anyone to challenge him. "More of them—" he nodded to the man and woman on the ground, "could be lurking anywhere."

Peter turned away, returning to his horse. Swinging a leg over, he adjusted himself in the saddle as he sealed the cracks in his mind. He couldn't let the princess know, not yet at least. Not until he'd sorted through everything himself.

For the love of Saints.

He was one of them. One of the Saints' Heirs.

Somehow, he'd known, if not the entire truth, then partially. He could create illusions with a flick of his fingers, conjure images with a thought, drive a person insane with a mere word.

Peter, heir of Saint Felix the Trickster. Perhaps the least beloved of all the Saints. Even with the dark powers the other Saints wielded, Felix had a mischievous nature few trusted. Most people didn't really worship the Saints, but they were revered. Or they had been once. Now all that lingered these days were stories. And Felix the Trickster had many, though few of them were flattering.

How fitting, he thought bitterly.

Of course, the power had come in quite handy over the years. It had given him the ability to pull off cons and deals even the best smugglers couldn't handle.

He glanced over at Jill, whose face seemed more sullen than usual. Stiff-backed, she mounted her horse and glanced over at the newcomers.

Fatigue pulled at Peter. He'd told Jill to rest but hadn't been up for resting himself much lately either, thanks to the nightmares. The scarred man looked him over, his gaze dragging down Peter's form. He didn't miss the tightness in the man's jaw.

"The name's Peter," he offered, a smirk tugging on his lips as he pushed the fatigue away.

The man pursed his lips. "David." He nodded to his companion. "And this is Luca."

Because he sensed David's tension and because he simply couldn't help himself, Peter flashed David a dazzling smile. "So how do you know the lovely princess?"

David bristled, then frowned. "We traveled together a while back." The response was curt, his tone clipped.

Peter's smile widened. So, it was like that then. *A trickster indeed.*

"I see. She does make a fair traveling companion."

The feline man's eyes darted between the pair, perhaps sensing what Peter was doing. Peter didn't care though. He'd had little entertainment the last few days and needed something to take the edge off. He climbed onto his horse and urged it forward.

"She has her strengths." David wouldn't meet his eyes, the coldness practically radiating from him as he mounted his horse and followed him.

Jill and Grimzy had already gone ahead, the silent pair locked in grief. David kept his distance, and Luca seemed keen to follow him.

"She most certainly does." Peter laced his words with a suggestive tone and nearly burst into laughter as David's cheeks reddened, his gaze burning so hot it could have melted glass. "Tell me about yourself David. I'd love to hear more about your travels with Jill."

The man said nothing, refusing to even look at Peter.

"The silent type then, I take it? I can respect that." Peter's horse ambled beside them, and he studied David's scars from the corner of his eye.

They seemed unnatural, the lines too crisp and straight,

like cracked pottery. Everything about it screamed of magic. Or a curse.

Peter wracked his brain for the curses he knew. In his line of work, it was critical to know what goods he transported and whether an apothecary had taken the initiative to curse his wares.

He'd run into several over the years. Once he'd stolen a cache of jewels from a violent Lord. After Peter had liberated the jewels, he'd discovered they had a sticky fingers curse placed on them, each one of the jewels fusing to his fingers until his hands were entirely covered and weighed more than the king's crown.

Then there was the outbreak of sores after he'd liberated medicinal tinctures from yet another noble who was intent on hoarding them despite his township's population suffering from deadly Necora.

It must be some sort of curse then. But how did he get it? And why hadn't he asked some apothecary to break it? That's what Peter had always done. Granted, he'd had to travel to the elves' domain in Welynn where most of the apothecaries lived now, but they had magic enough to break even more sophisticated curses. Allegedly, Erinya once flowed with magic that everyone could access. Now only the apothecaries with special magical objects and plants had magic.

"How'd you get that curse?" Peter could be cordial and charming and cunning when he wanted to be. And when he didn't want to be, he was blunt. He had little patience for beating around the bush when it didn't serve a purpose. He was a businessman after all, not a politician.

David's whole body went rigid, if that were even possible given how tense he already was.

Bullseye.

Peter smirked.

David slowly turned his head to look at him. Peter expected anger, rage for prying into the life of such an obviously secretive man. He did not expect to see pure terror on his pale, marred face.

"How." It wasn't a question but a demand. A cold, whispered demand. But once again Peter caught the subtle shift of David's eyes as they flicked toward the princess.

"She doesn't know?"

The man gripped his bow, his knuckles turning white, revealing spiderwebbed scars across his wrist. "Not everything."

"What did you do?" Peter kept his voice as neutral as possible—he didn't want to spook the poor man—but he was dying to know.

"I hunted down the Silver Stags of Torryn the Gentle."

Luca stopped his horse and inhaled sharply. Even Peter halted his own mount.

Saint Torryn the Gentle's Silver Stags were mythical, legendary. Only the best hunters had ever caught sight of them, let alone slay one. Normally, he'd never have believed such an outrageous claim. It was absurd. Only David said it without a hint of arrogance, instead trembling with fear. Clearly, he'd underestimated the man.

And apparently David had underestimated the cost of the kill.

Peter recalled now something about a blessing placed on them, and a curse on anyone who killed one. A curse worse than death.

"Does Grimzy know?" Luca spoke with a reverence laced with anger, his chest heaving.

Peter's gaze fell to Luca then drew back to the mountain man in front of them. Understanding opened in his mind. Saint Torryn the Gentle hailed from the Whitesaw Tribe. No doubt the Silver Stags were precious to the mountain people. If the man ever learned—

"He does."

Peter's head whipped back to David. The man seemed to shrink inside himself, his back hunched and eyes drooping.

"And he forgave you?" Luca asked sharply.

David remained silent. Then at last said, "I don't think he would have if I hadn't left two alive, male and female. They should continue."

"You got all but two of them?" Peter failed to hide his awe, and both men glared at him. He shrugged. "Say what you want, it's still impressive."

The tether on David's temper snapped. "It's atrocious. What I did was unforgivable. Those stags are said to bring healing and light, and I killed them all to prove some hideous point that I was better than the father who abandoned me. They were blessed by a Saint, a Saint who spoke with them, who considered them friends. And I killed them. I deserve this curse, and it will be my undoing." His voice faltered on the last line as his rage dissipated, leaving fatigue and shame in its wake.

Luca stared at his friend, pity in his eyes. Interesting that he was learning this alongside Peter.

"It's intriguing though, don't you think?" Peter mused aloud. Yes, it was very interesting. And though he'd never consider himself a pious man, he didn't believe in accidents. Not on this scale.

"What is?" David spat, incredulous.

"Curses can always be broken. That's the nature of them. Nothing is made that can't be unmade. What I find interesting is that you've wound up in the company of a mountain man searching for Saints."

"And?"

"And they might very well be the people who can break your curse." Peter wasn't sure why he was offering a broken man hope. He knew better than anyone the danger of it. But maybe Peter needed to hear it too.

Nothing is made that can't be unmade.

Perhaps there was hope for Liza after all. If they could find a way—

An axe split the air an inch from Peter's nose, driving itself deep into the black bark of the tree to his left.

Tall, willowy figures materialized, wielding bows and axes. Luca's ears flattened as he and David both drew their bows, but it didn't matter. Within seconds, they were completely surrounded.

Peter examined the figures, taking note of the spiraling horns that protruded from the tops of their heads. They wore fluttering robes and furs, beads dangling from the braids woven in their dark hair.

Except for two girls, one with bronze skin and cat ears, and one who was paler than the others, and bore a fluttering tattooed flame on her forehead. By her side stood a young gazelle man who held himself taller than the others, and Peter caught the glances as the group looked to him.

The leader. It was important to know that information quickly.

"Who goes there?" He spoke with the cool authority that comes from never being questioned.

Jill raised her hands, back stiff as she surveyed the group. "We're just traveling through." She replied in a similar icy tone.

The leader smiled tightly. "That does not tell us who you are."

"Our mission favors secrecy," Jill explained.

"Not if you're traveling through gazelle territory." The

man shrugged. "You don't take another step until you tell us who you are."

Peter stared at the back of Jill's head, almost sensing the war waging in that mind of hers.

"Wait," David was off his horse in a second. "You—" he pointed to the inkwell girl. "Are you Ymira Halissa?"

The girl's face morphed, her eyes widening. She held no weapon, only her hands remained outstretched, bracelets of light glowing at her wrists. She glanced at the leader whose face darkened while the feline girl glared at them.

"Explain. Now. Or we shoot."

"David—" Jill hissed, glaring at him with such ferocity it could've frightened a stone giant.

"I know your sister, Zyla."

All was still for a heavy second and then Ymira was rushing forward, collapsing in front of David. Peter glanced again at the entourage as hesitation flickered in their faces.

The young man's eyes narrowed, unconvinced. "How?"

"She and I traveled together, with Kylian Doyle."

Jill's head flicked to David, confused. "Doyle? What—"

Ymira looked back at the man. "They're alive." Tears were suddenly streaming down her face as she wrapped David in a hug. "Is she safe? Where is she? Did they find Bo?" The questions spewed from her and a strange pang struck Peter in the gut.

A girl who would do anything for her sister. It was touching, really. He just wished he weren't so damn cold.

David politely pulled himself out of the girl's embrace, holding her at arm's length. "She's safe. They found Bo. They're with the Whitesaw Tribe in the mountains."

A sob wracked Ymira's body as the young gazelle man strode forward, dark braids hanging to his shoulders. He motioned to the others, a smooth wave of the hand and they put their weapons away. His narrowed gaze remained though.

"I am Hasani Zibiah, son of Tabitha Zibiah, chieftess of the Gazelle Clan." His eyes slid over the princess and the mountain man at her side then landed on Peter, recognition making the man's expression grow colder. Peter gave him a wink and a smirk. For some reason unbeknownst to him, it made Hasani's frown deepen.

"You make for an odd traveling company. Come with us. I'm dying to know why a princess, a paladin, and a smuggler are traveling together."

MILLIE

Millie woke to the scent of mildew and blood. Darkness blinded her until her vision adjusted. Rocks and roots dug into her back and oozing mud squelched between her fingers. Pain radiated down the back of her head, and she sucked in a sharp breath.

She was in an underground cell.

Watery light spilled from a small hole above her, the only source of light to be seen. She tried to rise, but her spinning vision sent her to her knees.

"Millie, are you awake?" Doon's voice flooded her heart with warmth.

He was safe. He was here.

"I am." Her throat was raw, her voice croaking in protest. She could just make out Doon's features in the dim quarters. He sat across from her, knees pulled to his chest.

"Doon, where are we?"

"We're at an army base near the border of Carthesia."

Millie started. She must have been out for days if they'd

traveled that far. But that wasn't all that disturbed her. An army base should have been under the authority of the king. If it wasn't . . .

"The Ohans have allied with Carthesia and taken control of the camp. To my knowledge, anyone who swore fealty to the Ohans lived and those who didn't . . ." He didn't finish.

"Where's Ravala?"

"I'm not certain. Probably another cell like this. I think they want information from him."

Millie tried to think, but the pounding in her head commanded her attention. She rattled through what Ravala had taught her should she ever be captured. Take in the state of her body and then the state of her surroundings.

She wasn't bound but she was injured.

Only one way out, the exit being the small hole nearly ten feet above her head. She saw no way to scale the wall as it arched above them. Her weapons, of course, had been confiscated, including the long hairpin that doubled as a lock pick.

But they couldn't take her power from her.

She closed her eyes, searching for that thread of power. It was effortless now. Where once she'd struggled to find it, grasping at it like a blind beggar, now it came to her like a trained pup when its master calls.

Her form dissolved. The muddy cell they were in brightened thanks to her heightened vision. It was all mud with two posts that held up the barred entrance above. Millie sent her spiders climbing up the wall, thankful for their ability to go places normal people could not.

Her first goal—escape.

"Millie, wait!" Doon's voice was a harsh whisper. "They'll kill you!"

She couldn't respond in this form, but it didn't matter. She would get her spiders through the bars and then—

Something fell through the bars and landed on the ground. A second later a blinding flash lit the entire space. And then darkness.

Millie's spiders fell, trapped in that darkness. She reformed in the air then landed hard on her leg.

Something snapped and she screamed. Her leg!

It was twisted at an odd angle, searing pain shooting up the left side of her body. A piece of broken bone jutted out through the skin. Doon was at her side, saying something and trying to grab her, but she couldn't hear him. Not through the sound of her own screams.

Blinding pain rolled through her. Blood. Misery. Gasping breaths. She couldn't think straight.

Doon was yelling now, but she still couldn't make out the words. She heard the creaking of iron, watched through blurred vision as a rope ladder swung down to graze the earth, and felt strong arms grab her and haul her up.

And just as she reached that elusive gray daylight, her vision clouded once more, and she slipped into a sea of nothing.

Agony ripped her from the dark's clutches. Fire spread through her veins, burning up and down her leg. Her throat ached from screaming, though she didn't remember uttering a sound.

She lay on a metal table, the cold cutting through her clothing. Someone was mending her leg, applying salve, sewing, and wrapping. She thrashed against the pain, as if it were an enemy she could simply shake off, but thick ropes bound her wrists and ankles, keeping her strapped down. Tears streamed down her cheeks and blood filled her mouth. She'd bitten her tongue and it had swelled, only adding to her torment.

An undignified whimper escaped her.

"I'm sorry," a soft voice said. The healer fixing her leg. "Unfortunately, the pain will get worse before it gets better. You're lucky the injury isn't infected." She managed to crack her eyelids open. A gazelle man bent over her, tending to her leg. Short horns protruded from his head, and his skin was several shades darker than her own.

She heaved a rattling breath as he finished wrapping the bandage around her foot. Several more tears slipped down her face, dripping onto the table with an audible plop.

Plop. Plop. Plop.

She couldn't stop them, yet exhaustion tugged at her core, imploring her to shut her eyes and never wake again.

And so, she listened.

To LIVE WAS to know pain. And Millie felt intimately acquainted with it. The healer had come and gone many times, his frown deepening with every visit and inspection of her leg.

Fever plagued her. Nightmares plagued her. She'd lost all concept of time, of day and night, of reality and dreams. Was she being tortured on purpose? Was the healer actually trying to help her? If so, why? Did they need her for something?

They must, otherwise they would have killed her by now.

She almost wished they would.

Until she thought of Jack. Of Doon. Even Jill, somewhere out there. What would she do in this situation?

She wouldn't have been stupid enough to break her leg while trying to escape.

New anger flooded through her, but not at Jill. Not even at Jack. But at herself. She shouldn't have agreed to this quest. Perhaps then she wouldn't be here now, sitting at death's doorstep.

Or did it go further back than that?

Did it start with helping Jill escape months ago? Or at the well when Jack drank the water, succumbing to the evil residing within him? Or perhaps it started with the tournament, where she'd gotten it in her head that she could be something more than she was destined to be.

She was a child pretending to be a king's paladin. She knew that now. Jill had been right. More than right. In her strange, backward way, maybe Jill knew not letting Millie become paladin was a mercy.

How different things would be if she hadn't.

The door creaked and there was a scuffing of boots. Only now did she notice how large the room she was in was, how fine the things inside were, even as she heard rain clinking on the rooftop. Chair legs scraped against the floor, and then a familiar figure sat by her head, staring down at her.

Scales gleamed and slitted eyes slithered up and down her form.

"Welcome, Paladin Millie. I trust you've been well taken care of," Ohan-Jin said.

She swallowed back the acid that burned the back of her throat, but she couldn't speak without shaking, stuttering words that would betray just how frightened she was.

A sharp fingernail traced a line down the side of her face, and she recoiled, trying to pull away from him.

The reptile man only chuckled, a dark throaty laugh that

sent her skin crawling like the spiders she summoned. "You've seen better days, little Miss Muffet."

What would Jill do? What would Jill do?

The words were an anthem in her mind, a steady drum beat to march by. She could do this. She could be strong. She was *not* weak.

"What do you want with me?" she croaked out. Her throat was still raw, her tongue still swollen. Had it been a day or two since she'd broken her leg? Or had she screamed more when she did not remember?

Ohan-Jin stood, walking down to examine her leg. It was then that she noticed another figure lurking in the corner.

The healer watched mutely as Ohan-Jin unwrapped her bandage. Sweat slipped down the gazelle man's forehead, his hands clenched into white-knuckled fists at his side. The healer looked between her and Ohan-Jin, his chest falling and rising with gathering speed.

She winced as the last of the bandage came undone, the air hitting the wound like a kiss of death. Her breathing sped up as his fingers traced their way over the stitches. She didn't know how the healer had staunched her bleeding long enough to put the bone back into her body but somehow, he'd done it. And he'd sewn her skin, kept her from losing the leg entirely. She supposed she should be grateful.

"This will be a very simple process, *paladin*." He rested two hands on either side of the stitches, the sensation sending fire shooting up her spine. "I am going to ask a question. You will answer it." His reptilian eyes met hers. "And if you do not, I will break you."

Millie's gaze latched onto the healer's, his olive skin paling as their eyes met.

What would Jill do?

"Why?" She felt like an insect caught in a web—cornered, small, insignificant. How ironic.

"No one is closer to the king than you."

Despite the pain, the looming torture, the fear that coiled around her like a snake, she laughed. It was the mirthless laugh of a broken person. "I am not nearly as close to the king as you think." Her words held a bitter edge. No, she wasn't close to the king. Yet every part of her wanted to be. Even now.

"We shall see." Ohan-Jin snapped his fingers. "Esmeray." The healer, Esmeray, stepped forward, refusing to meet Millie's eyes as he handed a long thin needle to Ohan-Jin.

Before she had time to wonder, Ohan-Jin stabbed the needle into the puckered skin around her wound. Her back arched off the table as an explosion of pain ripped through her, twisting up her leg and releasing itself as a scream through clenched teeth. He pulled the needle out

"Wonderful. I just needed to be sure you weren't too far gone." Ohan-Jin spoke with the calculated nature of someone conducting experiments, not torturing another person.

Millie sucked in several breaths, fighting back the tears that blurred her vision.

She would be strong. She would withstand. She would not succumb.

"King Jack. He is inhabited by the Black King Malum, correct?"

Sweat beaded along Millie's forehead, her jaw tight to keep from ripping against her bonds. Dried blood encircled her wrists, the ropes gnawing away at her flesh like maggots at a corpse. It was a pain she could focus on, rather than her leg, to keep her from divulging too much. She didn't know what the man wanted with the knowledge of Jack, but some instinct told her to keep it secret as long as possible.

She shook her head. "I don't know what you're talking about."

Ohan-Jin's lips thinned. "So, this is the game we're going to play then." He stabbed the needle into her leg again, letting it remain there.

Her entire body shook.

She would be strong.

He pulled the needle out. She was dimly aware of the warm blood dripping down her leg and felt her body growing cold with every drop. The pain was enough to torture her but would do very little damage.

"Let's try a different question then. The princess, Jill. You were her maid." He paused, as if waiting for an answer.

She swallowed. Was this a trick? Everyone knew she'd been the princess's maid. She nodded, not trusting herself to speak, afraid of how horrific her voice would sound.

"You helped her escape?" He dragged the tip of the needle along her thigh, down toward the wound, taunting her.

She would withstand.

She shook her head.

The needle stabbed her wound again, driving deeper than the first two times. It struck bone, digging and searing its way further down.

She screamed again, a rasping hollow thing. The sound made her hate herself more. What did he want? Why did he want *this information* from her? She was nothing, no one.

Ohan-Jin heaved a sigh of great disappointment. The sound of a father whose child has broken something irreplaceable. "If you refuse to tell the truth Millie, this will be much harder for you. Tell me again, did you help the princess escape?"

Millie glanced over at Esmeray, who stared at the floor.

Rage curled through her like smoke, soft at first, but now billowing greater and larger. *Coward.*

She didn't know him but that's what he was. A coward. And with it came the frightening realization that she was *not* a coward. No.

She would not succumb.

She shook her head again.

The needle slammed straight through her leg and into the table beneath her. And there it stayed.

2 5

BO

*B*o didn't care for Asif—though she didn't much care for most people—and she hardly knew his sister, but as her eyes scanned the growing riot, fear shot through her like a lightning strike. The girl was young and small and lost in that angry mob.

Her feet moved without a thought, instinct taking over as she headed toward the people who swarmed like a hive of angry hornets. Kylian and Zyla followed closely, their toes biting at her heels. Any other time it would have irritated her. But something stronger than anger consumed her for once.

As she dove into the fray, a strange thought struck her as quickly as the fear had clutched her. She couldn't remember the last time she *wasn't* angry. But she couldn't think about that now, not with so many other angry people. At what, she wasn't sure, but fighting had broken out and spread until people were stampeding and crashing into each other. People screamed and shoved, fighting their way through the chaos and panic. She wondered how many had simply been caught in the wrong place at the wrong time and how many truly sought destruction.

Bodies pressed against her, an elbow struck her in the ribs, a large man shoved her from behind, and then someone grabbed at her arms, yanking her back. Breathing became difficult as she fought her way through. The scent of smoke struck her nostrils, only adding to the mass hysteria and confusion.

Saints. If this didn't calm down soon, people were going to die.

"Lyra!" She shouted into the din, but she may as well have been whispering for as loud as the world around her was.

Breathing grew more difficult, the air too thick to inhale. Someone slammed into her, sending her to the ground. The light around her disappeared. A heavy foot stepped on her leg, and she screamed, fighting to rise against the crush.

Panic raced through her veins.

Where was Kylian? Or Zyla? They'd been right behind her seconds ago and now they'd disappeared, lost in the cacophony.

Saints, if Lyra was stuck in this . . .

More feet kicked her as she tried to get on hands and knees. Someone tripped over her, landing on the ground beside her, a young boarman, blood flowing from his temple. A large boot landed on his chest, the sickening crunch deafening despite the sounds of screams.

Bo froze in horror as the man lay there, unmoving even as the crowd pushed against him and more booted feet stepped on his limbs and chest and face. She had to get up—had to keep moving.

Then a high-pitched note rose above noise, haunting and melodic. For a second, Bo wondered if she was already dead, listening to the Saints singing her into the afterlife, if they did that sort of thing. She wasn't actually sure. Beside her, a person stilled, also entranced by that single note swelling and tumbling like a flowing river.

More feet stilled, enough that she found purchase and pulled herself to standing. Her foot ached, her mouth tasted of dirt, and bruises already discolored her skin. Despite the pain, an overwhelming sense of calm flowed through her. Her shoulders relaxed, her heartbeat slowed, and her eyelids grew heavy.

A warning rang out in the back of her mind, yet she couldn't fathom why.

She felt more at peace than she had since, well, ever. The anger that consumed her dissipated.

A memory surfaced. She was walking through a field full of wildflowers, her chubby hand gripping a tiny crutch. Tall grass reeds stood only a head shorter than her; the hiss of bugs sounded in the air as she pushed through, following the tall woman ahead of her.

Sunlight beat down on her and she swiped a hand across her wet forehead, damp hair clinging to her skin. She didn't care. Her mother had a surprise for her.

She followed mother, whose flowing red dress tangled around her legs as she led Bo deeper into the woods. Still the sunlight kissed their skin, warm and bright. A moment later they arrived in a small glen, hemmed in by ash trees.

Her mother pressed a finger to her lips, her bright eyes glowing with mischief. She waved a hand to Bo who scooched closer, plopping herself down into her mother's lap. Her mother pulled the grass reeds aside to reveal a doe the color of silver with two fawns curled up beside her. Their fur shone bright in the sun, glinting like the sparkle of gemstones.

Bo watched in awe as her mother clutched her tight. She glanced down at her mother's hands, their fingers intertwined.

Bo's light skin contrasted sharply against her mother's dark skin, but she didn't care. She didn't know any different. All she knew was warmth and love.

Tears suddenly streaked Bo's cheeks, and she found herself back in her body, that heart wrenching song still rending the air. No words, just notes that twisted into a melody unlike any she'd ever heard.

Everyone around her had stilled, rendered immobile by that haunting tune. Many had tears in their eyes as well, some with a trace of a smile on their face. Others wore expressions of pain, of sorrow so deep one might never find the bottom.

The song continued. It fluttered high, the tune like a butterfly twirling in a summer breeze, then dropped low, like a roll of deep thunder.

Bo glanced around, looking for the source of the song. Something tickled the back of her mind, a sensation she couldn't shake. It wasn't the first time she'd felt this.

Someone was using magic.

The Saints' magic.

Bo stepped through the crowd which, while still packed, was easier to navigate now that everyone stood still. So still. In fact, Bo was the only one moving.

She pushed forward, following the song that grew and swelled. More tears dripped down her cheeks, though she wasn't sure why. The song made her immensely happy and deeply sad at the same time. It reminded her of sunny days and thunderstorms. It made her want to dance and weep. It made her want to lie down and rest and yet march off to war.

People parted before her as she wriggled her way through the crowd, the song growing louder and the magic growing nearly impossible to resist. She slid between a boarman and a feline man, finally arriving at the source of the song.

A girl stood at the center of the crowd. A small girl with cat ears and almond shaped eyes.

Bo inhaled sharply.

"Lyra," she breathed.

Speaking her name seemed to break some sort of spell as Asif's sister stopped her song, her eyes taking a moment to focus. For a handful of seconds, all was quiet.

Then murmurs raced through the crowd like the swishing of golden wheat on a windy day. Bo didn't need to hear them to know what they said.

Magic.

Saints.

Dangerous.

Kylian was at Bo's side a second later, eyes just as wide as everyone else's. Asif arrived and skidded to a stop beside them, a frown pulling at his lips. He shot Bo a glare, as if Lyra's power was somehow her doing. Bo returned the look with equal intensity.

Kylian knelt beside the feline girl, who looked so small and timid. She clutched her arms around her midsection, staring at the ground.

"Where did you learn to do that?" Kylian asked her.

The girl shrugged, her eyes darting all around.

"How long have you been able to do that?" Bo asked.

Again, the girl shrugged.

Around them, the quiet stillness had begun to wear off. Hushed whispers had evolved into shouted accusations.

"How'd she do that?" Someone yelled in a trembling voice.

"Did she use magic?" Someone else hollered.

"Bloody *witjka!*"

Bo's blood froze, her heart rate spiking at the accusation. She recalled what she knew of the apothecary war. If they thought Lyra was a witch, or any of the Saints' Heirs were witches for that matter, they were all in trouble.

Bodies began pressing in again, this time moving toward Lyra. Kylian whisked her up in half a second, Asif at his side.

"No one is to harm the girl." Kylian's voice was hard as ice and twice as cold. Fire burned in his eyes as he glared at everyone around them. Even Bo found herself intimidated by the look. Rarely was Kylian so blatantly aggressive. "Let us through," he growled, plowing into the crowd, Zyla at his side.

People parted quickly, eager to be out of the way. Asif and Bo followed behind, keeping their heads low as eyes followed them. Bo's shoulder brushed against Asif's, and she resisted the urge to snap at him and tell him to back off.

Finally, the crowd began to dissipate, whatever initial fight that had broken out long forgotten. Apparently, they had more important things to tend to than fighting. It didn't stop the side glances and sneers tossed at them as they headed for the edge of the camp.

Minutes later they entered their tent. Lyra had fallen asleep in Kylian's arms, and he placed her on a small patch of blankets in the corner.

Bo could relate. Not simply because she shared an understanding of the physical toll magic took on the body, but because of everything. It was traveling through infested lands, the fear that clawed at her heart from one moment to the next, the anger that burned and burned and burned inside her.

She was so *tired*.

Tired of hiding. Tired of running. Tired of never belonging. Tired of being angry.

She glanced around the tent, her eyes passing over Kylian and Asif and Zyla. Shadows cupped their eyes and dirt smeared their faces. She'd wager she wasn't the only one who felt that way.

Instead of commenting on it though, Bo collapsed to the ground and recalled her vision, the memory of the day her mother had shown her the silver fawns. Confusion twisted inside her like oil and water. She'd loved her mother. She still wanted to. But how could she? Her mother had taken everything from her. Yet her mother *had* loved her. But what about her real mother? Had her real mother loved her like that?

For the first time ever, she allowed herself to imagine her family. Her flesh and blood family. It was a thought she had ignored up until that point.

What if they're still out there?

She hated the hope that flickered in her chest, a dim candle in the darkness. She pressed her eyes shut, willing the thought away. It didn't matter. She would never know one way or the other. Her mother, her only family, was gone.

"Did you know?" Kylian asked, staring at Asif.

The feline boy looked over at his sister who snored softly in the corner. He swallowed and shook his head.

"So, she's . . ." Bo trailed off. She knew some of the Saints but not all of them.

"Heir of Nadia the Peacemaker," Kylian finished.

Peacemaker.

The girl's power had lulled an entire angry, riotous mob. In mere minutes the song that permeated the air with such ethereal sweetness had indeed brought peace. Until the song had faded. Then the people's anger had turned on Lyra instead.

Bo's skin crawled, a shiver running down her spine. What would happen when everyone learned of the Saints' Heirs? Would they see them as heroes like Kylian did? Or would they only see the dangerous enemies the Heirs could become?

Bo sighed. Not belonging was something she'd grown

accustomed to, and yet, she hadn't even realized how close she'd come to hoping things could be different.

"I don't understand." Asif's soft voice split the silence. "Lyra and I, we're full-blooded siblings." The boy looked to Kylian, raising a brow. "Which means we're both heirs, right? So why does she have power, and I don't?"

Kylian's entire body stiffened, then he swallowed. "Well, the legend goes that the power will be inherited by the one most worthy of the gift." Kylian's tone was measured, careful. Beside him, Zyla stared at the ground, her shoulders shrinking ever so slightly. Her sibling was an heir as well. How must it feel to know your sibling possessed a power that you did not?

An interesting thought came to her.

"What if an heir dies? Does the power go to a sibling?" Bo asked. She wasn't sure why her heart was suddenly thundering in her chest, why her hands quivered.

"We don't know," Kylian confessed. His eyes flicked to hers and then away a split second later.

Asif crossed his arms, frowning. "What if some of the lines ended? I mean the Saints lived hundreds of years ago. How do we even know all twelve of them still have descendants?"

Bo glanced as Asif, somewhat surprised. It was a fair question. She was rather annoyed she hadn't thought of it sooner.

"They must," Kylian said.

"But what if they don't?" Bo asked, her voice turning hard. The back of her neck prickled, irritation welling up inside of her. What if they'd been led on some wild goose chase? What if their mission was doomed before it even began? What if none of this mattered?

"They do," he insisted, pinning her with fierce glare.

"How do you know that Kylian? How do you know any of

us stand a chance against Malum and the Ohans and these monsters?"

"I just do, okay?" Kylian's voice had lost its diplomatic tone, the words coming out harsh. He rose to his feet, his cheeks unnaturally flushed.

Bo followed suit, rising to her feet. "But how?"

"Because I do!"

"Kylian—"

"That's enough, Addie!" Kylian's voice boomed, his breathing ragged.

Bo drew back, her anger giving way to confusion. "Addie? Who's Addie?"

Kylian froze, eyes wide. Zyla and Asif stared at him as well, looking just as lost as she was.

A second later, the young man had regained his composure. His face returned to its neutral, calculated expression as he straightened out his coat before brushing the dust off his sleeves.

"She's no one. A slip of the tongue is all." He shook his head as if the last few seconds had all been some terrible misunderstanding and nothing more. He turned to exit the tent then paused, "You ask me how I know the Saints' Heirs are out there? How I know they exist?" He looked at each of them in turn, leveling them with a gaze so intense they each looked away. "Because great evil is coming. And when evil rises, good rises to challenge it. It must, otherwise it wouldn't be good. The light will always rise to push back the darkness. I know they're out there because we've dwelled in darkness for too long. It is time for the sun to rise."

26

MALUM

The princess was headed north. Malum could feel it. One of his many spies had spotted her and her companions, right before their sight had vanished completely.

Someone had killed them. No matter though. He had many, many more. The vulgan had ensured that. Each of his pets had done their work well, turning as many people as they could into weapons at his disposal.

You're cruel, said Jack.

"Perhaps," Malum said aloud, his gaze taking in the ocean as he stared out the window yet again. Too many times now he'd caught himself staring out at it, lost in the prince's thoughts rather than his own.

His face twisted, Jack's reflection staring back at him in the glass. Malum turned away, striding across his quarters and to the door. Smug satisfaction slid through him as he felt the prince's disappointment. That would teach the boy to have him staring at the ocean.

Out front his guards stood sentry, their stares unwavering as they faced the opposite wall. His body loosened as he examined them, the only movements from them their slow, even breaths.

Good.

His powers increased exponentially each day as more and more soldiers came under his influence. And with the vulgan roaming the country, it wouldn't be long now before he turned more to his side. An entire army subject to his every whim and desire—it would be glorious.

In this section of the palace, all was quiet save for the whisper of his boots against the emerald rugs that lined the marble corridors. The guards trailed silently behind him. He didn't need them of course. It was all for show. But a king without his guard would have been suspicious, asking for trouble.

He could not afford trouble.

Since he'd lowered the conscription age, unrest had grown within the Citadel. Someone had started a fire in the upper city, and he'd been forced to institute a strict curfew. For a time, it had sufficed, since the punishment for being out after curfew was being strapped to the whipping post. Another new thing he'd added. He was rather shocked old King Cole didn't already have one, the old king's methods were certainly barbaric enough.

Even my father had some decency.

Your father preferred to let people rot in prisons so far underground they forgot what the sun looked like. Tell me, which is worse?

The prince fell silent, but Malum could feel him seething. He ignored it. Malum had grown accustomed to the feel of Jack's loathing, his hatred. It wrapped around him, a constant ache, like a sore that never heals.

It made no difference to him whether the prince approved of his actions. He was in control.

He strode into the throne room, the whispers of a crowd silencing as he cut a path through the center of the room, straight for his throne. Four vulgan stood on either side of the white marble dais, silent and ominous, shadows twisting around their forms. He inhaled, smelling the fear in the room. In front of the steps leading up to the throne, several figures sat hunched over on their knees, bags over their heads and hands tied behind their backs.

Malum stepped lightly on the stairs, turning back to face the crowd. Guards loomed at each of the arched doorways, stoic. Among those gathered in the room, in addition to the traitors tied up before him, were some of the lesser nobles who'd yet to swear fealty. He hoped this. . . demonstration would change their minds.

Five figures were tied up. He sauntered up to the first, ripping the bag off to reveal curved horns and matted hair.

Madame Sorelle.

He'd arrested her the day after Jill fled, hoping to learn where she might go. The woman had not deigned to tell him anything useful. Not only that, but she'd also informed him she wouldn't betray Jill's location even if she knew. He'd merely rolled his eyes. Jill did not deserve a woman of her caliber's loyalty.

He'd hoped several months in the dungeons would loosen her lips, or at the very least, bring about some humility in the old woman. Judging from the defiant look in her bloodshot eyes, that had only kindled her wrath.

No matter. He didn't need her any longer anyway. Not now that he knew precisely where the princess was thanks to the hive mind of his spies.

"Madam Sorelle, how was your stay?" His voice dripped dark sarcasm, and he flashed a smile at some of the other nobles standing behind. None met his eyes.

"As good as can be expected, *Your Majesty,*" the woman spat out.

He slapped her face. The sound echoed in the marble hall, but the woman didn't even have the audacity to look surprised. Instead, she smirked, even as her cheek bloomed red.

"Do you take pleasure in being an insufferable old woman?" Malum growled.

The woman's smirk remained. "Talk to me after you've been locked up for weeks on end. We'll see how amiable you're feeling."

He tilted his head, examining the other figures before him. Among them were Paladin Salazar and his son, Paladin Willa, and a rebel who'd been caught breaking into the army's food stores. Paladin Salazar had been caught freeing a young girl who should have been conscripted into the army, and that was all the leverage he'd needed to have the man and his son thrown in the dungeons.

Malum nodded at the nearby guards. They ripped the coverings off the prisoners' heads. One by one Malum examined each of them.

Paladin Salazar and Paladin Willa, while disheveled, pinned him with fierce glares. The boy, Salazar's son, trembled as he stared at the floor. The scales on his cheekbones shone like dull copper and his chest sagged as if pulled to the floor by an invisible string.

The last in the lineup was the rebel, a young man, one neither he nor Jack had ever seen before, yet there was something oddly familiar about him. He couldn't have been older than sixteen. He had dirty blond hair and a nose that looked like it had been broken before, maybe more than once.

"What is your name?" he asked the rebel.

The young man remained silent, refusing to meet his eyes.

Malum planted a kick into his gut. The boy collapsed to

the floor, wheezing and curling in on himself. Malum sighed. He hadn't even kicked the boy that hard.

"Name. Now. I won't ask again."

"My name is Braddock," he hissed through clenched teeth, tears clumping at the corners of his eyes as he lay on the ground.

"Braddock." Malum rubbed his chin. It didn't sound familiar, yet the boy's face reminded him of someone. He sifted through his memories.

A dark night in a shadowy stable came back to him.

"Ah. You must be Will's brother."

The boy stilled, staring up at him with wide eyes. Malum smiled, then knelt before him.

"How?" Braddock asked in a breathy voice.

He pulled the boy up before him, leaning in close so no one else could hear. He whispered in the boy's ear. "Because I killed your brother."

Braddock was on his feet a second later, face red and twisted in fury as he tried to headbutt Malum. He screamed as he charged at him, but Malum only stepped back.

The screams stopped. Braddock looked down at the shadows protruding from his chest, blood already seeping from the wound to his heart. The boy's knees hit the ground, then he slumped to the side, his body smacking the floor with a wet thunk. He lay there unmoving, his eyes unseeing.

Malum glanced around the room. Everyone had paled, staring at the boy's prone form and the growing puddle of blood around him.

A sob cut through the silence. Paladin Salazar's son. His shoulders quivered as his tears hit the floor.

"What did that boy ever do to you?" It was Paladin Willa who spoke. Yet another nuisance. "What have any of us done to deserve this?"

Malum heaved a great sigh. It was all for show of course. He'd planned to make an example out of someone. He'd hoped it would've been Paladin Salazar, but there was still time for that.

"He was a traitor. Caught stealing food, from our soldiers no less."

"Only because no one else has enough food to eat thanks to *your* taxes," Paladin Salazar said.

Behind them, the vulgan stepped forward, their smoky claws clacking on the ground. Paladin Salazar quieted but made no effort to hide his rage.

"How else would you have me protect you? If you'll not forget, paladin, I suggested that families could turn over a child of fourteen instead of paying the taxes. An order which I believe you *deliberately* ignored."

The two men stared at each other. But Malum was not the one in chains now. He smiled.

"Do you deny it?"

"No."

"Then it's settled." He turned to the guards, motioning for one to come forward even though he didn't need to. One thought and they would obey him.

The guard yanked back the boy's head, pressing a blade to his neck.

"No! Please!" Paladin Salazar yelled, rising to his feet, even as more guards yanked him back down. "Kill me! But leave my son alone!"

Malum turned, arching a brow at the paladin. Things were turning out even better than he'd hoped.

"And why should I? I Imm?"

The man shook with anger, the guards struggling to hold him back. "Is this how you plan to rule, Jack? Through fear and violence?"

Malum's smile fell. "You're not answering my question."

Paladin's Salazar's jaw flexed. "Kill me instead. Kill me so I can show you what a father who would die for his child looks like."

The words hit like ice water splashed in his face. Malum schooled his features, though. Before he was cognizant of the order, a guard stepped forward and sliced his knife along the paladin's throat. The man slumped forward, and the pool of blood on the throne room floor grew.

Salazar's son sobbed again, a sound so loud it almost twisted Malum's own dark heart.

What have you done? Jack's horror was tangible, his fear so potent that even Malum had trouble differentiating between his own feelings and the prince's. *You've murdered a paladin!*

"Take them back to the dungeons." He said to no one in particular. Within seconds, guards hurried forward, dragging the prisoners through the blood, leaving a trail of gore in their wake. He turned to face the nobles. Few were of noteworthy importance, but he could not have any turning on him.

"Swear fealty now or join them in the afterlife."

HALF AN HOUR LATER, Malum returned to his chambers. Each of the twenty gathered nobles had sworn fealty. It was too easy. He'd hoped one of them might try something. But no.

He shouldn't have killed the paladin. He needed them on his side. Instead, he feared he'd made a martyr of the man.

Kill me so I can show you what a father who would die for his child looks like.

The words sent anger burning through his veins, hot and wicked. It was the words that were the problem. A man dying as a traitor to the throne was justice. A man dying in the place of his child was powerful.

And he could not afford to cede power to anyone, not even a dead man. Especially not a dead man. People really didn't give them enough credit for the sway they could hold over the masses.

As he rounded a corner, electricity pulsed through him like a bolt of lightning. He paused. Power snaked through his bones, his nerves sparking in pain. Something was wrong.

The vulgan had seen something.

What is it? Jack asked.

I'm not sure.

The minute Malum let those words slip he knew he'd made a mistake. He could feel the prince pressing against his mind, gaining a foothold in the face of his uncertainty.

Malum's mind slammed shut, locking the prince away. He would not allow Jack to slip through even the smallest crack in his head. To do so could prove devastating.

Instead, Malum shut his eyes, feeling his essence blur into darkness. Vanishing into shadow, sliding through space and appearing somewhere else, was easy. When he opened his eyes, he stood where the vulgan following Millie was.

He'd ordered a vulgan to follow her, to keep watch from a distance. He knew the creatures unnerved her, so while he'd insisted she take one, he kept it far from her. He didn't want to see the fear of him in her eyes.

Since when do you care what Millie thinks of you? Jack asked, his tone like the dangerous low growl of a threatened dog.

Malum blinked. When *had* he started caring what the girl thought of him? He ignored the prince as he stared at the landscape in front of him, a barren gray prairie that mushed into the southern marshes. Light rain drizzled on a brown encampment where thousands of soldiers flitted about.

Soldiers wearing the Carthesian crest.

And working alongside them was the Reptile Clan bearing the Ohan crest.

Fire burned up Malum's throat, stinging his eyes and face. Rage hurtled through his blood. Yet something else disturbed him.

Millie should have been close by. She shouldn't be anywhere near the Carthesian border. Unless . . .

He drew the shadows to himself, twisting around him like a dark cloak before his form vanished once more. He reappeared a second later, tucked in the dark corner of a large tent. Soldiers trudged through mud, a thick coating slathered across their boots and wrapped around their calves.

Malum's heart pressed up against his ribcage, every pounding like the roar of tempest. He scanned the area, observing and listening.

Where is Millie? Jack's panic mingled with his own.

In the distance, he caught sight of two soldiers standing guard outside a cement compound with a flag bearing the Ohan's insignia.

A heartbeat later, Malum was inside, wrapped in shadow as he surveyed the scene before him in horror. A table sat in the center of the room bearing Millie's still form, dried blood caked on her.

What have they done? Jack's rage was tangible, spilling over into Malum like a tidal wave. What unnerved him was the anger he knew belonged to him and him alone.

Malum was by her side instantly, fire spreading through his body like a coursing river, fast and swift and deadly. He pushed the hair out of her face, which was far too pale and gaunt for his liking. His hands shook as he felt for a pulse. It was faint but there. Barely.

They will pay for this. Jack's tone was livid, but Malum felt the boy's fear, or was that his own? He couldn't be sure. They were all tangled together now, he and Jack.

The door creaked open, rusted hinges squealing in the silence. Ohan-Jin stood in the doorway, gray light silhouetting him.

Yes, they will.

27

DAVID

He'd lost a piece of himself somewhere. A small piece, but the skin around the black hole on his forearm ached. Soon the cracks would spread, and he wondered when the cracks would become so wide he couldn't put the pieces back together right. Perhaps he would just simply fall apart at that point.

David glanced at Peter, who walked alongside his steed with a confidence that bordered on arrogance, even though they were now in the presence of people who wanted nothing to do with them.

It was sheer luck David had figured out Ymira was Zyla's sister. The girls bore a strong resemblance to each other, but David distinctly remembered Zyla describing her sister's power and the flame tattoo that burned on her forehead.

Light snow had begun to fall again from gray clouds overhead. Birds chirped from their nests and squirrels scampered through the undergrowth. The scent of the forest eased the tension in his shoulders just a bit. Under any other circumstance he would have loved being outside. But when he caught sight of Jill, his entire body tensed.

He could still feel her embrace as she'd wrapped her arms around him, that look of pure relief when she'd seen him. The relief he'd felt as well, seeing her alive. It was quickly replaced by an agitation he couldn't place his finger on.

She was fine. She didn't need him here. He knew how this ended—with him shattered into a million pieces. And yet he'd still come to her, still found himself at her side, following her into whatever treacherous unknowns lay before them.

"You seem troubled," Luca said, his footsteps so light even David hadn't heard his friend sidle up beside him.

"Maybe because I am." He clenched his jaw. Normally, he'd tell Luca what was going on. But he didn't feel like talking.

"What do you know about the Gazelle clan?" Luca's eyes shifted to the figures escorting them.

David pursed his lips. "Very little, I'm afraid."

Luca frowned. "Me too. And I dislike that very much."

"Why's that?"

"The Feline Clan has long since separated themselves from the other animal clans. I thought perhaps our pride kept us from interacting with the other clans and tribes. But it seems we're all divided from one another. The wolfmen hide in their keep, the Ohans have their own territory, and even the Gazelle Clan seems unwelcoming to strangers." Luca's frown deepened as his gaze scanned the group. "Has Erinya ever been united?"

David couldn't help looking at Jill, nearly ten feet ahead of them. Her hair had grown a bit longer since he'd seen her last. He liked it. But something about her seemed off.

"I don't know," he answered honestly, still staring at her.

"But I suspect Her Highness might be the key to doing just that." His stomach churned as he looked at her.

He'd learned to trust his instincts in the years he'd spent as a hunter and in the army. They'd helped him find the silver stags, helped him become a captain, helped him stay alive. Right now, they were screaming at him to run as far away from here as he could. But duty would forever war against those instincts, and it compelled him to stay. To stay with her.

Ahead of them, wisps of smoke curled through the trees, beckoning them forward like crooked fingers. Hasani halted, Jill and Grimzy following suit. He turned to face them, his eyes catching David's, his face a dark unreadable mask.

"You will leave your weapons here."

Jill shook her head, her red hair collecting snowflakes like they were flowers. "You can't ask us to walk unarmed into a camp without knowing why." Her voice was hard as the rock of the Whitesaw Mountains, but he didn't miss the slight warble to her tone.

David walked forward before he knew what he was doing, snow crunching beneath his boots. Grimzy pierced him with a knowing gaze.

"You will leave your weapons here or you will be denied passage through our lands." Hasani's tone was colder than the air around them.

"Your lands?" Jill scoffed. "How dare—"

David caught her forearm, swinging her around to face him. Blotches appeared on her cheeks, her eyes wide and brow furrowed.

"Jill," his voice was soft. Everyone watched them now.

She yanked her arm out of his grasp, her lips curling in disgust. It was like taking a blow to the chest. One that shattered skin and bone and every part of him. He'd never once wondered whether his internal organs could crack like his skin did. But now, as his heart ached, he was beginning to consider it.

"This doesn't concern you," she said through gritted teeth, turning back to face Hasani.

A storm rumbled inside him, thunder and lightning arcing through his veins. How long and far had he traveled to reach her? To make sure she was safe? To warn her about Millie? He'd killed that monstrous woman before she could kill Jill and suddenly, she was upset with *him*?

Heat flared along the back of his neck, but he stepped back. "Forgive me, *princess*."

Hurt flashed in her eyes before they hardened like polished onyx, cold and hard and unfeeling. Good. It was better this way.

"If you two are finished, I'd like to invite you to join us. But I must still request that you lay down your weapons," Hasani said.

Jill stared at the young man for nearly twenty silent seconds before she loosened the belt at her waist, her blade falling to the snow. Beside her, Grimzy removed the knives he kept strapped to his belt. Peter and Luca followed suit.

David gripped his bow, pulling it off his shoulders as slowly as he could. He hated this as much as Jill did. Hated relinquishing this part of himself, relinquishing the security. He handed it to the feline girl who took it with a silent nod, eyeing him with suspicion.

"Don't mess with it."

She smirked but remained silent.

As one, the group moved forward through the trees, a smoky curtain appearing before them, concealing whatever lay on the other side. Hasani walked through it first, the smoke twisting near the ground like silvery serpents. One by one each person in their party followed them through until David and the girl who held his bow remained.

The girl motioned with her head to go first. David swallowed, stepping through the smoke.

He'd pictured stepping through it like one might step through a waterfall. But as he passed through the gauzy veil, darkness drew near him. Silence swallowed his senses and for one terrifying moment he thought he might be dead.

An instant later, sunlight came rolling at him, burning away the haze that had settled over his vision.

They stood in a large clearing devoid of snow or even a cold winter breeze. Instead of pine and spruce trees, twisting purple and orange daru trees clumped together to form houses in the bases. The roots twined around each other like snakes, flowers he'd never seen before sprouting up in between the cracks.

He was suddenly sweating. He'd been bundled up to protect against the freezing weather, but now balmy air coated him.

A glance to his side told him that his companions were as awestruck as he was. Jill's eyes couldn't seem to focus on any one thing and even Grimzy relaxed.

"How?" Jill breathed.

Hasani smiled, the first one David had seen from him. "We have our ways. Now come. My mother will want to speak with you."

He turned, everyone else following behind. All except for Ymira. She fell into step beside him, her lip quivering.

They wandered through throngs of bulging coiled roots, a path winding through the village that grew larger by the second. Green glowing lanterns hung from the trees above them, dappling the spongy forest floor. People were hard at work. A group of men sharpened blades on a spinning grinder.

Others fashioned arrows from the bark of the daru trees. Children ran around, nubbed horns sprouting from their heads as hammers pounded against metal, ringing through the trees. High above their heads large birds flew from tree to tree, tiny scrolls tied with ribbons around their feet. Foreign spices hung in the air, mixing with the scent of a burning forge.

David inhaled sharply. Though so much around him was different, a familiarity crept up his spine, sharpening his senses.

"They're preparing for war." He hadn't meant to say words aloud but suddenly they were hanging in the air.

Ymira didn't bother to deny it. "They've been preparing since the day Hasani, Aaira, and I arrived. I'm still not certain it will be enough."

David said nothing. Did Jill sense it too? Did she catch the sidelong glances cast in their direction, the tightness in people's bodies and the lips thinned to grim, sharp lines? People bustled about and made noise, but no laughter—save for the children's, no casual conversations, and no gossip about the latest sweethearts or neighborly squabbles sounded.

The sun passed behind clouds overhead, shadows darkening everything around them.

Ymira stopped walking, grabbing his wrist. "Tell me again that my sister is okay." Tears pushed at the corners of her red-rimmed eyes. The feline girl, whom he presumed was Aaira, waited quietly behind them. Like she didn't want to leave Ymira's side.

David placed a hand on the girl's. "She's safe. I promise." He didn't mention that Bo might have been the most dangerous person he'd come across lately but fortunately she was on their side. Probably.

Ymira nodded, brushing away a silver tear. "Thank you." She licked her lips. "I just needed to be certain. After the

Order fell, we all escaped, but then we parted ways, and I'd heard nothing from them since."

The group ahead of them kept moving, but no one seemed to notice that they had fallen behind. David glanced around, taking in the weapons and the preparations. Kylian had told him all about the Order and their mission. About how they'd fallen to the Ohans and barely escaped. Is that who the Gazelle Clan was planning to fight against now?

Ymira shook her head, forcing a smile. "Come. The chieftess will be upset if we keep her waiting." She strode forward, her pace picking up as if she could outrun the knowledge David had just given her. He caught sight of the glowing bracelets at her wrists, warmth emanating toward him. Her traditional gazelle-style robes swished around her legs.

How had an inkwell girl come to befriend the Gazelle Clan? What about the feline girl, Aaira? Was it their friendship with Hasani that had brought them here? It seemed the wary glances from the gazelle people were aimed at them as often as they were aimed at him. Did the girls notice how people stared at them with sour faces and arched brows? Did they care?

Ymira seemed oblivious, her gaze instead locked on Hasani —who, to David's surprise, glanced back at her with a soft smile on his face. She returned the smile, the slightest blush rising up her neck. Aaira rolled her eyes, but David couldn't help but notice that they flickered to Luca and stayed there.

He didn't have time to ponder the looks as they arrived in a new area of the gazelles' domain. Two large daru trees stood like the legs of giants in front of them, their trunks as wide as a mountain man was tall. Roots curled up and out of the earth forming an archway high above, several feet taller than Grimzy, who walked under without having to duck at all.

David heaved a breath and followed.

Beyond the arch they entered an area that resembled the inside of a bird's nest, if instead of sticks and twigs birds used vines and roots and veins of gold and silver. More green lanterns and colored beads and baubles hung from above, the trinkets catching the light and throwing it around like scattered jewels.

At the head of the room, a group of people sat on tree stumps around a small table with wooden cups of steaming tea and a small platter of nuts and berries and bread. At their entrance, a woman stood, her horns larger than any he'd ever seen. This must be the chieftess.

A circlet of gold hung above her brows. Her dark ebony skin looked oiled and polished, gleaming in the light. Her gray and black hair wrapped around her horns in a series of intricate braids.

Hasani dipped into a deep bow before walking over and pressing a kiss against the woman's cheek. She smiled then turned her gaze on the rest of the group. The smile faded as she assessed them.

Somewhere along the way, the party that had found them in the woods had slipped away, leaving only their group, Hasani, Aaira, and Ymira.

"You are a long way from home, Your Highness." The chieftess's voice was rich and deep. She turned to Grimzy, tilting her head. "Paladin. Welcome to the Oasis. We've heard of your feats of both strength and justice." Her eyes glided over Peter and Luca then landed on David, but she said nothing.

Jill stepped forward, her hand reaching for a sword that wasn't there before curling into a fist. "Please chieftess, we mean no harm. We only seek to travel to Fenric's Keep and must cross your lands to do so."

The woman barked out a throaty laugh, surprising everyone.

Hasani's mouth settled into a tight line across his face. Beside him, Ymira stood with her hands folded in front of her. Aaira lingered close by as well, a faint scowl on her face.

"Why in Inerys' and Amari's name would you want to go to the wolfmen?" the chieftess asked.

Inerys and Amari. David recognized the names as the two Saints hailing from the Gazelle clan. They were twins if he recalled correctly, each inheriting their own power. That was all he knew of those Saints' though.

"The princess seeks their aid to rescue those held captive by the Ohans." Grimzy spoke with such authority everything went still. Even the chattering birds fell silent. As if every living thing in that room listened to the mountain man.

Ymira stepped forward with Hasani close behind. At this, Aaira finally looked interested.

"Truly?" Ymira asked, breathless.

But Hasani shook his head. "You have no idea what you're up against."

"Which is why we need the wolfmen's help," said Jill.

"They won't help you." The chieftess strode forward, coming to stand only a few feet from the princess. "Many times, I've sought to build a relationship with the wolfmen. Every time they have denied even my messengers, with whom they bear no ill will. I'm afraid you stand little chance, princess."

Jill's shoulders sank. "I must free my people from the Ohans."

"Is it justice that motivates you? Or is it your own pride that seeks to free them?"

Jill looked like she'd been slapped.

Anger surged through David, and he was about to step forward when he stopped himself. Had he been any different when he'd first met the princess? Had he not treated her with similar animosity? He'd thought her shallow and spoiled. But then he'd learned about Will, the boy she'd loved who had been murdered. About her arranged marriage. About her cruel father and dead mother. About her twin brother who was possessed by an evil king hell-bent on destroying the world. Is this what everyone thought of her? Did everyone judge a princess by her title rather than her character? Here she was, fighting for her people, and it still wasn't enough for them.

These people didn't even know her. But did *he* know her?

"The princess has more honor than anyone I've ever fought beside." Grimzy's voice was soft, but that did not hinder the truth and power of his words. "You would do well to remember that." He glanced back at David, something unreadable in that gaze. Did he mean to imply that she had even more honor than David? Did Grimzy judge him for abandoning Jill?

A small bird alighted from a nearby tree, coming to land on Grimzy's shoulder. David tipped his head at the sight of the tiny bird on the massive mountain man. Strange.

"We will allow safe passage through our lands. But it's a fool's errand." The chieftess turned her eyes again on David, following his scars. Few people stared so openly at him, most choosing to pretend they weren't staring while they so obviously did. He preferred the open examination, honestly.

"We could help them," Ymira said, turning to the chieftess. "They're our people too. The Order lived near the Ohans for so long and did nothing. But your clan could help, even if the wolfmen do not." Her voice rose in volume and sped up, carrying a lilting hope through the room. Everyone stood a little taller, bolstered by the girl's words. Even Aaira's suspicious frown had disappeared.

The chieftess sighed and flashed the girl a condescending smile. "And where are *your* people Ymira? If I recall, the inkwells defected to the crown long ago. They don't even have their own refuge like the other tribes and clans. They just mixed themselves in."

The flame on Ymira's forehead flickered.

David shot Jill a glance only to find her looking at him already. He could practically read her thoughts from her downturned lips.

Your people.

Mountain men. The Gazelle Clan. The inkwells. The Feline Clan. The wolfmen. It was just as Luca had suggested. All of them were so separated. It seemed none were willing to work together for the common good.

Chills skittered down his spine. What did this mean for Jill? For Erinya?

"We thank you for your generosity, Chieftess Zibiah," Grimzy rumbled. "We seek only to pass through your lands in peace."

The woman nodded. "So be it. But you should know," she paused looking at each of them in turn. "Peace is an illusion. All we can do now is hope we survive the storm of war that approaches."

2 8

KYLIAN

ylian paced in his tent, trying to quell the anger slowly taking over. He'd never lost control like that before. He'd always prided himself in keeping his emotions checked, his feelings reined in. But he'd lost his temper, lashing out at Bo like she was nothing more than a nuisance. And he'd called her Addie.

Addie.

Saints alive he was stupid. So stupid to let such a thing slip off his tongue.

Addie. His adorable, smart, fierce little sister. The sister with a clubfoot, stolen from him as a child. But the sister he'd loved and adored, she was gone. She'd been subjected to a life of exile, of torture, of monsters and darkness and fear.

He'd suspected it from the moment he'd first met her. After a few days, he became certain.

Bo was his sister.

Their features were too similar. The same nose, the same hair color. Her skin was lighter than his, but it always had been. Of course, her clubfoot had been a tell, but it was more than that. The fierceness he had seen from her even as a small child, she'd never lost it. It was probably why she was still alive after all these years despite the atrocities she'd endured.

How many times had he wanted to tell her? How many times had he tried, only for the words to die on his tongue? He rarely found himself at a loss for words with anyone else. But with Bo things were different.

It wasn't as if Bo had simply been living with someone else all this time. No, she'd endured so much. Not to mention, she barely tolerated Kylian. Would she even believe him if he told her the truth? Would she despise him?

Worse yet, what if she accused him of never seeking her out, not knowing that's all he'd been doing since the day she'd been taken?

Eventually, he would tell her. When the time was right. That was always the key to diplomacy. Revealing the right thing at the right time. Too much too soon and it could overwhelm a person. Too little too late and who knew what dark consequences might be wrought.

No. It was better to keep the knowledge to himself. Just for a little longer.

The pacing marks on the ground in his tent caught his eye. He scuffed them up with his boot just before Zyla walked in with crossed arms and a gaze that always saw too much. She was one of the few people who could see through even his most flawless façades. She found chinks in his armor and stabbed him with her words of harrowing truth.

It was as frustrating as it was refreshing to be seen for who he really was when he'd spent his entire life curating a mask for everyone to see.

"Lyra and Asif are sleeping," she said, plopping onto the ground, ignoring the way the dust coated her dress. Dirt was streaked across her tired face and Kylian suddenly felt guilty.

Zyla had followed him from the moment they'd fled the Ohans. Not once had she complained and yet she'd done so much for him and for their group. He still hadn't thanked her.

"Thank you," he said. "For everything you've done."

She just nodded. "Of course."

It was such a Zyla answer. As if risking her life time and again, peacekeeping, and helping everyone they met was something anybody would do.

"The council wishes to meet with you again." She swallowed. "Everyone is concerned about Lyra's new power."

Kylian huffed. "You mean her power that prevented an all-out riot that would've ended with countless deaths? A riot caused by the infighting of their people? And they're disturbed by *her*?"

Zyla pursed her lips. "They worry about a young girl with the ability to control such a large crowd."

Kylian's teeth ground together. It should have delighted him that they'd found another heir. After all, they'd searched for months with no luck and now they'd simply stumbled across one right before chaos should have unfolded.

But an uneasiness had settled over his skin like spiderwebs, its sticky feeling clinging to him. He'd hoped they'd be safe here. He'd hoped the council would see reason. He'd hoped for so many things. Too many it seemed.

Hope was a fickle thing. Did it make one naïve or brave? Or both? He could never be certain.

"We've been here all of a day and things have gone poorer than I could have imagined."

"What did you expect, Kylian? That these people would welcome us with open arms? Embrace the Saints' Heirs and place all their hopes in them? These people are afraid. They've spent their entire lives under the thumb of those more powerful than them. The Saints don't sound like saviors, they sound like conquerors."

"But they're not!"

"They don't know that." Zyla stood, her face pleading with Kylian. "They have been without hope for so long they cannot imagine a future where things could be different."

Kylian stared at the girl before him. He had known Zyla for years, since she was a kid. But she wasn't a kid anymore. She was eighteen, a young woman, taller than she was even a few months ago. She might even be taller than her older sister at this point. Their features were similar—the blond locks tied back in braids, their knowing eyes. But Zyla didn't have the power her sister did, and for some reason it made her stronger. He was suddenly aware how close she stood, only inches from him. The tent was sweltering, his heartbeat erratic.

He stepped back, the air around him cooling as he put space between them. *You are seven years her senior,* he told himself. Not a large gap by any means, but He was in love with Ymira, who was in love with Hasani. Wasn't he? Why did he suddenly feel so confused? He shoved the thoughts away.

"How do we convince them?" He turned away from her, unable to meet her gaze. He could feel her stare lingering on him, newfound uncertainty tainting the atmosphere.

"It's simple really."

"Yes?"

"We must show them a better future is possible."

A WEEK PASSED. News of the near riot had spread through the entire Whitesaw domain, and the knowledge that a Saints' Heir was among them only put people more on edge. The Whitesaw people increased patrols in the camp, and where they'd been relaxed on the first day Kylian's group had arrived, they now walked stiff-backed with hands on their weapons.

The camp began separating itself as well. The Feline Clan resided in one corner, gazelles in another, and the few boarmen seemed ostracized to the outskirts of the camp. Whether by choice or because they weren't welcome anywhere else, Kylian wasn't sure.

Now he walked side by side with Zyla and Bo as they wound through the spiraling marketplace toward the chief's home. For the last several months, the children had stayed with the chief in what was perhaps their first true home since their parents had died. Clearly, the man had a soft spot for them. And since the riot, the two hadn't left, so they'd all agreed it was safest for Lyra if they met there.

Meetings. So many meetings.

As the king's adviser he was used to them. Yet still they wore on him. Each day it was something else as he spoke with the council and the Whitesaw chief, debating what to do and how to do it.

They'd learned that Jill planned to seek the aid of the wolfmen in freeing those held captive by the Ohans. But everyone knew her chances were slim. It gave him a little comfort to know she had plans to infiltrate the Ohans. Perhaps she had changed since he'd last seen her.

Then there was the matter of the vulgan. And the blackbloods.

It was enough that even Kylian's control on his emotions had begun to slip. Still, nobody would listen when he insisted the Saints' Heirs could help. In some cases, he'd even been met with outright hostility. Mostly from the council of the Lost Tribe. The Whitesaw chief though, a looming presence he might be, kept silent on the issue.

As they walked, Kylian's hand brushed against Zyla's, and

he recoiled just a touch too fast. Another area of uncertainty. One he couldn't bring himself to dwell on yet. He'd had feelings for Ymira for years. It seemed wrong that he should be feeling strange things for Zyla now.

Zyla cleared her throat, either oblivious or feigning ignorance, he wasn't sure.

"Bo, have you made any progress with your powers?" he asked suddenly. The chief's home was less than a quarter of a mile away but somehow felt so far. He wanted to forget the confusion that occupied his mind.

The girl scowled. "Very little."

"I see. And has Lyra had any success?"

Bo's scowl deepened, if that were possible. "She's had some. But no one likes it. Even the chief is uneasy."

"Why is that?" Kylian asked.

Bo leaned on her crutch. Sometimes he forgot about it, she moved so deftly. He supposed when she'd spent her whole life learning to maneuver through a forest, flat ground was probably nothing at all.

The young girl, his sister, pursed her lips, eyes shifting around them. The marketplace was quieter than usual. Stares followed them like hunting hounds. Whispers trailed at their backs. Rumors had multiplied like rabbits and taken on a life of their own, each rendition of the story darker than the one before. Last he'd heard, Lyra's song had been the cause of the riot. That rumor could get them all killed.

"I don't know what's true and what isn't, but something's brewing. People don't trust Lyra. They want her gone. They want all of us gone." Bo said the words under her breath with her gaze set ahead of them.

Kylian swallowed the lump in his throat, choosing to focus on the sound of his boots scuffing against the stone path. The scent of searing fish and fragrant teas wafted toward him. He inhaled deeply, forcing a smile to his face as he continued forward.

Never let them see you're scared.

This rule was more important the more scared he was.

Eyes followed them, leering and watching, knowing full well where they were headed. The path up to the chief's house was lined with more of those glowing gemstones, alternating between red and amber.

Inside, the chief's home was simple but large. The mountain men had no use for the sort of façades put on by so many other people. Orange and white marbled hallways led to various rooms while bats hung from the ceiling. They were tiny, harmless creatures—the Whitesaw equivalent of pet cats. But Kylian had been unnerved by the thought of walking beneath one that might be relieving itself.

A mountain woman with a servant's gauge in her ear greeted them and they followed her through a series of corridors, each one twisting and turning like cave tunnels. As far as Kylian had gleaned during his visits to the Chief's home, the layout had no rhyme or reason whatsoever. He'd also come to suspect the occupants rearranged the home regularly as each time they visited the layout seemed slightly different.

They descended a set of large stairs, Bo maneuvering down them easily before they came to a dead end. The gemstones hanging above dimmed until they stood in suffocating darkness. The mountain woman began to hum, and a deep rumbling shook the space around them. Kylian inhaled deeply, pressing his eyes closed so he wouldn't panic.

Despite knowing the routine, he wasn't thrilled about being so far underground and feeling the earth shake. Only the logic that the mountain men knew precisely what they were doing brought him any sort of comfort.

The sound of grinding rock echoed and then light spilled

from an arched opening, blinding after the pitch darkness. They stepped into the chief's personal meeting room.

A large fire blazed in the center of the room, the smoke escaping through a hole in the ceiling. Kylian had no interest in knowing how far up it went. Better to imagine he was relatively close to the surface.

A human-sized table sat off to the side with platters of Whitesaw delicacies spread across it. The platters held roasted nuts, braised fish, herbed sauces, carafes of hot tea, a ridiculous number of sweet treats, and many other things Kylian had only come to recognize after several visits. The food, however, remained largely untouched by the other occupants who sat on cushions on the ground around the fire. The entire Lost Tribe council was already present, along with the chief, Lyra and Asif, and the chief's right hand, a lean mountain man who resembled a very large rat.

The chief dipped his head to them, and they all returned the greeting. The mountain men did not have royalty, and every man, woman, and child was greeted in the same fashion. To bow to anyone was considered an insult. Kylian appreciated the mountain men's pursuit of equality, even if he wasn't particularly convinced it would work outside of these caverns. Sadly, the rest of the world was bent on elevating themselves. Hence why this meeting was even necessary in the first place.

They found seats on the unoccupied cushions, Zyla sitting only a few inches from Kylian. Heat radiated from her, and it took all his effort to pretend she wasn't there. Only Bo didn't join them immediately, instead heading to the table full of food. Kylian cringed inwardly. Didn't she understand why they were here? It wasn't for the food.

"Thank you for coming," the chief spoke. "We were about to discuss the matter of the peoples' complaints about Lyra."

Kylian held back an exasperated sigh. It had been the same thing in each meeting. The council brought forth new complaints, even though Lyra hadn't used her power again—except within the chief's home—and Kylian did his best to assuage them. Each time, the council left dissatisfied. All except Javyn who seemed to be the only council member on their side.

Kylian glanced at Lyra. "What are the complaints this time?"

"There is growing concern not just about Lyra, but about all of you," Elisha explained, a sour look on her face. "While the Saints are worshiped as heroes, the Saints' Heirs are not. The longer Lyra stays here, the more dissatisfied people become."

"And what exactly should we do with her? Throw her out and let her fend for herself?" Kylian growled.

Lyra's eyes went wide, and she looked to Asif, who shot Kylian a glare.

"Don't worry Lyra, I'm not suggesting we do that," he said, trying to reassure her. "Quite the opposite, actually." He gestured to Asif and Lyra. "These two have already been ostracized as orphans, it is our responsibility to make sure they're protected and cared for now."

Elisha's gaze bored into him. "I am not suggesting we toss her out. But I am suggesting that she leave."

The sound was sucked from the room. The fire flickered wanly, as if it too were surprised by the words from the gazelle woman.

"And why would you suggest such a thing?" Kylian said, his voice dangerously low.

Elisha looked at everyone in turn, her horns reflecting the red glow from the fire. Kylian was distinctly reminded of the stories he'd heard of horned devils who whispered lies in people's ears, seeking to cause mischief and chaos. He was fairly certain he'd forever picture her as one of those mischievous devils from now on.

"You think me cruel, but I say this for the girl's safety. Rumors of an assassination attempt run rampant. She cannot stay here without risking her life."

Kylian's mouth went dry. He should have known. For all his diplomatic prowess, he'd underestimated the unreasonable fear that drove people to irrationality. A stupid mistake. The one thing you could guarantee was that people's fear would drive them to stupidity.

"And where, exactly, is she supposed to go?" Kylian asked, his hands bunched into white fists. Zyla rested her fingers on his arm, and he stiffened.

"We think it would be best if you all sought out the princess and her entourage in Fenric's Keep," the chief said, flashing them all a sad smile.

This time Kylian could not hide the look of surprise on his face. "So, we're no longer welcome here?"

Javyn spoke, "It's for your safety."

"Really now?" Bo quipped. "Our safety? Or theirs?"

"Both." The deep voice of the Whitesaw chief echoed through the room. All turned to him.

He sat cross-legged like the rest, but his face drooped, and his body sagged. For the first time, Kylian truly examined the chief. His bronze skin was dull and waxen, his eyes were milky, and his breath seemed to escape him. A shocking realization struck Kylian.

The chief was dying. Was that why he'd been so quiet on all these matters?

Kylian pursed his lips as the chief turned to look at both children, giving them sad smiles. "Asif and Lyra, I want you to know that you will always have a home here. The world has not been kind to you, first by taking your parents, and then by casting you out. You have known cruelty many of us have not. But fear is often the source of cruelty, however misguided it may be. Now is no different." He paused and Kylian was painfully aware of the rapid thumping in his chest. "We stand on the edge of a great war, a time of change. I sense you both will have a part to play before this is all done. And when it is," he paused again, his eyes glistening, "You two will come home."

Lyra leapt forward, wrapping her arms around the man's large neck and the room tensed. The small girl looked even smaller as she hugged the mountain man and Kylian half stood, preparing to pull the girl from the chief. A scathing glare from the large man made him promptly sit back down.

Fat tears dripped down Lyra's cheeks as the chief grabbed her shoulders to look her in the eyes. A large finger tucked a stray piece of hair behind her feline ear. He hadn't realized Lyra had grown so close to the chief.

"Lyra, you are an orphan no longer. By the earth below me and the stars above me, I adopt you as my own. Though our differences are stark, our hearts beat with the same love. My daughter, it is time for you to be brave. Find the princess and unite our people. I make this vow to you and to your brother. You are loved and wanted. You are coheirs with my son Grimzy, and you shall return home." The earth rumbled with the chief's declaration, as if fate itself was being written in stone, as if the stars had moved in the heavens to obey his words. As if these were the final words of a dying man.

Kylian had never witnessed a moment of such gravity, and of such beauty.

Shouts interrupted the sacred moment, the earth around them rumbling again. The room they were in shook violently. Furniture fell over. Glasses broke. Was this part of the chief's vow? He looked around and the panicked looks told him this was something else entirely.

"They've come." The chief's voice, though quiet, could be heard over the sudden chaos. "You all must leave."

Behind them, a doorway opened in the rock revealing a cloaked figure wielding a crossbow. Before anyone could react, an arrow launched through the air, aimed straight for Lyra.

A scream rent the air, followed by a flurry of movement.

And then stillness.

The doorway that had been opened was sealed, the assassin gone. Where the chief had once been sitting, now he stood in front of a shell-shocked Lyra, an arrow piercing his torso.

"It is time for you all to leave," he said again, glaring at the wall where the figure had been moments before.

The earth rumbled again as another cleft in the rock opened to the side of the antechamber.

"Go now, all of you. Find the princess. Find my son. We will deal with the assassin." He spoke the words to Kylian, who was still sitting and trying to understand everything that happened in the last few seconds.

Then Kylian rose and grabbed Lyra, whose tears began falling fresh. Zyla and Bo were close behind, dragging Asif toward the opening.

"Wait!" Asif called, a tear sliding down his own face. "Please, chief!"

They hurried into the dark tunnel, even as Asif continued to struggle.

"Asif, my son, we will meet again," the chief said and then the tunnel closed behind them, sealing them all into the darkness.

29

MILLIE

illie stood at the base of a hill with skeletal trees surrounding her, their spindly limbs the picture of decay. At the top of the hill stood Jack, raising a wooden cup to his lips. Jill raced toward him.

The moment was both infinite and seconds long.

She should have listened to Jill that day, should have listened when the princess told her Jack was something else. Now she relived this moment over and over and over. Watching as he drank from the well. His body seized and convulsed, and he tumbled down the hill. Millie ran to him, but the distance between them only grew, stretching out eternally before her.

She would never reach him. She would never again see those playful green eyes, that mischievous smirk, the charming smile and laugh.

The memory started over.

She was back at the base of the hill. Jack pressed the cup to his lips again. Jill raced toward him again. Jack seized and tumbled again.

Again and again and again.

Each time the distance between them grew wider. She watched from farther and farther away, shouting into the void as if she could somehow change the past.

The scene before her twisted, smoke rising from the ground, swirling in ghostly figures around her. Something watched her, red eyes staring back at her through the darkness.

Well, this was new.

Figures stepped out of the smoke, surrounding her. The red eyes grew bigger until a strange creature she had never seen before stood in front of her with a figure riding on its back. It looked like a large cat, sleek black fur pulled taut over coiled muscle. Its red eyes softened to a pale orange, warmer than the harsh red they had first appeared.

The figure slid a leg over the creature's back, hopping down. A dark, slender hand brushed down the cat's head and side. The cat leaned into the touch and purred so loud it rumbled through the space around them.

At last, the figure stepped forward, lowering the hood to reveal a young woman with skin the deepest brown Millie had ever seen. The woman's hair was pulled back in hundreds of braids, and moonlight hit her cheeks, casting her skin in a glow that made her look like an ethereal goddess.

"Millie Muffet," the woman said, her voice quiet but brimming with authority.

Millie froze. The other figures had drawn closer, and she could see them more clearly as the fog rippled behind them.

Twelve people.

Humans. A wolfman. An inkwell. A boarman. A mountain man.

"Do you know who I am?" The woman asked. Her voice was higher than Millie would have thought, and she stood only a few inches taller than Millie herself, which wasn't saying much, but there was something about the way she held herself that exuded regality.

Millie inhaled. "Saint Zillah the Vengeful." Was this a dream? Or was she losing her mind after days of torture? Surely, this couldn't be real.

The young woman nodded. For someone with the title of vengeful, she was not at all what Millie had imagined. She had pictured someone fierce and strong and hardened. Someone who was capable and ruthless. From the moment Millie had learned she was Zillah's heir, she'd wondered how she could live up to such an ideal.

As if the young woman knew what Millie was thinking she said, "People have assigned many names to us over the years. Once I was called Zillah the Avenger. But the stories have changed over time, as all stories do."

Around the circle, the other figures nodded as if they also knew this to be true. As Millie glanced around, she could see what Zillah meant.

When Millie pictured the Saints, she'd always imagined the fiercest of warriors. The tallest, the strongest, the bravest. But as she glanced around, she thought they seemed a rather ordinary lot, like people you might meet on the street every day. Nothing about them stood out.

It was a testament to how stories could change history, for better or worse.

"Where am I?" Millie asked. Mist swirled all around them, reaching for them, twisting and eddying but never dissipating.

Zillah glanced back at her large black cat, who had settled on its haunches, tail flicking the mist back and forth.

"We are caught in that realm between life and death, the Shadowlands some call it. The place where the Black King was trapped for so long. You meet us here because you too are trapped between life and death. You have been since Malum brought you back. And we come to prepare you in the battle against the darkness."

Millie wasn't sure that it answered her question but sensed it was as much of an explanation as she would receive.

Her attention caught on five words though. *The battle against the darkness.*

"War is coming." Millie's lungs squeezed in her chest, making her feel dizzy. Somehow, she had known no other way would work. When Jack drank from the well and Malum took control, some deep, distant part of her had known war was inevitable. And when Jill had fled . . .

Zillah nodded again. "You have an important role to play Millie, you and the princess both. You are two sides of the same coin. Only together can you vanquish evil once and for all. Only you two can restore the magic to Erinya and free us all."

Millie felt nauseous, a heavy stone resting upon her shoulders. She was just a girl, a maid. She may have this gift but that didn't mean she could fight an evil king determined to destroy everyone and everything. She barely knew how to use it.

"It is a burden too heavy to carry on your own, I know." Zillah gave her a sad smile, her deep golden eyes piercing her to the core. "But the princess is your ally, not your enemy. You must find her. Only together do you stand a chance."

Millie swallowed the lump in her throat. "And what of Jack? Can he be saved? Is he even still in there?" Her voice was a whisper. The words felt painful to say aloud. She wasn't sure she even wanted the answer, but she couldn't leave without knowing. Her heart thundered within her. Could she leave him? Could she abandon him after his sister had done the same?

Zillah pursed her lips. "I don't know. But if he is, I do not think he has the strength to fight against Malum."

The air whooshed out of her and tears formed behind her eyes. She wasn't sure what answer she'd expected.

"You must not give up hope," Zillah said, once again reading her mind. "There is always hope."

Millie shook her head, teardrops falling to the ground. Hope seemed so flimsy, so uncertain. Like crossing your fingers and making a wish. There was no guarantee.

"Do not despair, or Malum has already won," Zillah said.

"I don't know if I can do this," she croaked. Her legs wobbled. They were asking so much of her. She would fail them. She would fail Erinya.

She would fail Jack.

Zillah stepped closer to her, lifting her chin in a motherly way. Millie was suddenly struck by an odd thought. This woman was her ancestor, her many greats-grandmother. Warmth flooded her chest, seeping down her limbs and into the tips of her fingers and toes.

"You are stronger than you know, Millie. *You* became a paladin. *You* helped the princess escape. *You* are the only one who might still reach Jack. You must fight. You must not give in."

Millie could only nod, silent tears still dripping down her face. She didn't want to do this. She didn't want to keep fighting, keep pressing forward. She didn't want to keep hoping when all it did was break her heart.

"Our time grows short." Zillah backed away, the other Saints following suit. "Find Jill. Find our heirs. Stop Malum. Fight back the darkness." Zillah smiled at her, climbing back onto her large black cat. "You are not alone Millie. You never have been."

Millie still had so many questions but the scene around her

was fading, the mist swallowing the Saints as they vanished into thin air.

A sob escaped her as she opened her eyes. She was still a prisoner in the Ohans' camp.

Distantly, she was aware of some commotion outside the room where she'd been held captive. Her legs ached. Her head pounded. Her wrists were bloody and torn from the ropes that bound her.

But then fingers were untying her bonds. Hands lifted her from the table, pulling her to a solid chest. She inhaled the scent of woodsmoke. She had come to know this scent as well as she knew her own shadow.

Jack.

She clutched him, his arms strong and steady as he held her. She struggled to open her eyes, to look into his face twisted with rage. Darkness emanated from him as he marched forward.

Ohan-Jin stood in the entryway, with a grin that chilled her to the bone. She'd seen that look of glee before, right before he'd stabbed a needle straight through her leg.

"I was hoping you'd come, Your Majesty," he said in a silvery voice.

"You've made a grave mistake." Malum's voice was a low growl, the warning of a predator before it attacked. "You will pay for this treachery."

"Will I now?" Ohan-Jin smirked, not looking the least bit frightened. "Burn this camp to the ground if you like, but it won't stop me."

Once Millie's heart might have raced at the thought, her blood pounding, sweat pumping. But all she felt in that moment was exhaustion and pain.

"I know the prince is gone, Malum."

Malum stilled, then inhaled slowly, a dark chuckle rising

in his throat. Anyone else might think he was surprised, that he'd believed his secret was out. But Millie knew better.

Malum smirked. "You finally figured it out then, did you? I suppose you must feel rather pleased with yourself."

Ohan-Jin shrugged. "I knew something had changed. You were not the pathetic, simpering prince who'd left on his quest."

Millie glanced between the two most powerful men in the kingdom standing off against each other.

"We need not be enemies, Malum. On the contrary, I'd hoped we could unite."

Malum looked the reptile man up and down. "Is this how you make allies? By torturing the people they love?"

Millie's heart clenched at that word. *Love.* Did Malum love her? Or was that Jack talking?

"I needed to be certain it was you. And I needed you to see what I've built, what we could build together." Ohan-Jin gestured around him.

Millie's eyes grew heavy once more, exhaustion tugging at her like a river longing to drag her below its surface.

"I think we have little to gain by allying ourselves." Malum marched forward, his arms never wavering in their strength as he headed for the door that Ohan-Jin blocked.

"And what about your sister?"

Malum froze. Or perhaps it was Jack that made him do so. Millie could no longer be certain which one was in control.

"Yes. My spies say your sister rides north, to the wolfmen."

Malum's brow furrowed, his confusion evident. Millie tried to understand why Jill would do such a thing, but her thoughts grew murkier by the moment.

"I have my own spies, Ohan. Now get out of my way, before I kill you where you stand."

Ohan-Jin smiled. "No."

A blade shot through the air, slicing Millie's arm, but before she could even cry out, she was drenched in darkness.

A few seconds later, they stood in the shadowed corner of the camp, soldiers bustling about, campfires crackling, a sulfur-scented mist hanging in the air.

Blood dripped down her arm. The cut wasn't deep, but Millie could tell the blade must have been poisoned. It burned like acid, searing through her bloodstream.

"Are you all right?" Malum set her gently on the ground.

She looked up at him. At those eyes. Mottled black and green. She didn't understand. How? Why? Her throat was too dry to answer, so she shook her head. Pain threatened to tug her under again, clawing at her like a rabid animal.

"Doon," she said, her throat scratching.

Malum nodded. "I'll be right back. Stay hidden."

He vanished into shadow. Millie crawled over to a few large crates that sat tucked away and slipped in between them, her strength fading. Her muscles ached. Her bones ached. Her heart ached.

Is this how you make allies? By torturing the people they love?

What did it mean? Millie's head spun too fast to make sense of it all. Was it Jack who said that? Or Malum?

Did it even matter? Jack was gone.

How could she be hiding at a time like this? Jill would never cower in a corner. Jill was brave and strong. And Millie was . . .

Tired. So tired.

Her eyes drooped shut despite the chaos in the camp. Explosions of darkness shook the air. Smoke billowed through the tents, thick and sulfurous. The clang of armor and metal rang out.

Malum was a one-man army.

Shadows swirled nearby and Malum appeared, covered in soot and blood, his face a dark mask of rage.

"Millie!" He called.

"Here," she replied weakly.

An instant later, she was in his arms. She could feel his heart pounding furiously inside his chest as it heaved. The world turned dark around her, shadows pulling her into their depths like the tide pulls one under. The blackness was sudden yet comforting. That frightened her more than anything else, that she could be so comfortable in Malum's darkness.

Just when she thought it might never end, the darkness lifted, revealing a deepening blue sky, the first stars just beginning to shimmer overhead.

They must have been several miles from the camp, yet she could still smell the smoke, still hear the sounds of battle. What would the Ohans do to Malum? What had he done to them?

The Ohans had allied themselves with Carthesia and had paid the price. Would Malum's destruction be enough, or would it insight further bloodshed? Would he ever ally himself with Ohan-Jin after what he'd done to her?

She shook those thoughts away. She would worry about it all later.

She looked up at Malum again, those black and green eyes swirling together like a tidal pool. His steps were steady as he carried her in his arms, the warmth of his body flowing into her.

"You came for me." A tear slid down her cheek.

"Of course I came for you," he said in a gruff voice. "I became the villain for you, and I would do it again. I would burn the world for you."

Millie's stomach somersaulted. Suddenly, she couldn't breathe. Her heart was beating too fast, her mind reeling.

He'd saved her life twice now. Another tear escaped, dripping down her face as she pressed it to his chest. She squeezed her eyes shut, leaning into him.

Her heart was fracturing piece by piece. She cared for Jack —she did. But Malum scared her. She'd stayed for Jack, hoping, wishing, praying somehow that he was still in there, that he could be saved, and maybe he still could be.

But she did not want someone to burn the world for her.

And so, as he carried her toward freedom, Millie wept, silently saying goodbye.

30

JILL

Jill splashed her face with warm water, relishing the heat. She hadn't realized how cold she'd been until she'd stepped inside the gazelle's domain. After the meeting with the chieftess, attendants led their group to another courtyard nearby and their weapons had been returned to them. Off the courtyard were several rooms within the large daru trees, and she'd quickly claimed one with the most privacy. The room itself was small, with only a mat on the floor and a basin of water on the stand, a dim candle flickering beside it.

She examined her face in the polished metal above the basin that served as a mirror. She hadn't seen her face in ages, and it seemed unfamiliar somehow. Her features were sharper, her skin paler, the bags under her eyes darker. It was a face haunted by these past few months.

Jill gripped the side of the basin and stared at her feet. An insurmountable wall blocked her path to freeing her people. Her brother. The vulgan. The Ohans. The blackbloods. The

Carthesians. The wolfmen. The Saints' Heirs. The discord between her people.

It was too much.

Her breathing came quicker, and she squeezed her eyes shut. Her heart pounded too fast; her knees buckled. The next thing she knew she was on the floor, her throat closing.

Had she been poisoned? Why couldn't she see straight? Why couldn't she breathe or stand or think? The candle was too bright. Every sound was too loud.

She dug her nails into the soft dirt floor as hair fell into her face. So much hung in the balance. Everyone was counting on her, whether they wanted to or not. And it seemed many did *not*. They wanted a real leader.

How was she supposed to save a kingdom that didn't want saving? How was she supposed to unite a people that loathed each other? She'd never wanted this burden to begin with, but now that she'd shouldered so much, she could not just disregard it all.

It was all too much.

"Your Highness?" David's voice cut through the noise in her head, the questions that had no end and no answers.

She looked up at him, standing in the doorway of her room. Heat rose up her cheeks as she imagined what he must be thinking. She had been so relieved to see him, and she thought he'd felt the same way until he'd given her a look so cold it rivaled the oncoming winter.

Even now his gaze remained wary, as he stood with one hand on the doorway, another on his hip. She glanced away, and despite every protest within her, a single tear slid down her cheek and landed on the earth.

She wanted him to leave.

She wanted him to stay.

She wished he would speak.

And she wished he would stay silent.

Footsteps padded forward and then he knelt in front of her. Everything was still and silent, save for the sounds of their own breathing.

Gentle, calloused fingers found their way under her chin, lifting it up to look him in the eyes. His thumb caressed her cheek, the touch so light she might have imagined it.

"A queen should hold her head high."

He turned and left without another word.

MORNING CAME SWIFTER than Jill would have liked. The sunlight pushed its way through the window carved in the base of the daru tree. Fitful though her sleep had been, she longed to roll over and continue sleeping. In sleep the world melted away, becoming a distant memory. She dragged her fingers across her cheek, the warmth of David's touch still lingering in her mind. It was everything she'd hoped for from him, yet not enough. She closed her eyes, relishing this last moment of peace before she would rise and—

A low horn blew in the distance.

Another sounded, a pitch higher.

A third joined, creating an ominous howling that had her on her feet in seconds, scrambling as she strapped her sword to her waist and stumbled into the courtyard.

Grimzy, David, and Luca were already there, and Peter dashed out on Jill's heels. His red hair was disheveled, his eyes bleary. Jill doubted she looked much better.

Hasani, Ymira, and Aaira swept in soon after, panic evident on their faces.

"We're under attack. Those creatures must have followed

you here," Hasani accused, anger punctuating every word. "You need to leave now."

"Wait, we can help," said Jill, stepping forward.

"This isn't your fight, Your Highness," Hasani said. "Our warriors will handle it."

"But we can help," she repeated. She would not leave these people to fend for themselves. Not after they'd taken them in at great risk. She spun toward the courtyard entrance.

"He's right Jill," Peter said. Jill turned back to face them all. They all stared at her. Peter, David, Luca. Even Grimzy remained silent, a small bird perched on his shoulder.

"We can't just leave them here." Her voice was harder than the steel of her blade. "I won't abandon them."

"You aren't abandoning them," said Grimzy. "You are the future queen of Erinya. You must live to fight another day."

Jill squeezed the pommel of her sword. "These are my people. I have vowed to fight for them, to protect them." Anger and desperation swirled up inside her. How could they ask her to leave?

Shouts and screams sounded in the distance. The clang of metal rang out. Several figures stumbled into the courtyard, their emaciated forms covered in blood.

They all froze, staring as more of the blackbloods ambled in. Rotting flesh drooped from their limbs, pus oozed from their sores, and that inky substance flowed through their veins. Still more came, blocking their exit.

Jill glanced at her companions, recognizing the grim determination on each of their faces. She still had so much to learn about becoming queen. She didn't know what the next day held, but she knew more trials would come. Even now a thousand fears threatened to suffocate her.

But she knew how to fight.

She drew her sword, still light without its twin. An arrow

whizzed through the air, piercing a creature through the throat.

And then the blackbloods charged.

Jill's blade sliced through rotting flesh like butter. David and Luca's arrows kept flying, taking down one creature after another.

Grimzy fought with his hands, black blood covering his knuckles. Peter used his knives to get in close, slashing and stabbing at the creatures.

Chaos ensued but they all fell into a rhythm, even as more creatures arrived, piling into the courtyard. They trampled each other, led by some blind instinct.

Flashes of light burst around her, and Jill traced the flashes with her eyes, only to see Ymira's wrists glowing. Light rose from her bracelets, firing off in bead-sized orbs that struck the blackbloods, knocking them to the ground.

The blood drained from her face. She glanced at Hasani and Aaira, who both seemed unfazed by Ymira's power. Then she noticed that Hasani was getting in close, grabbing onto the blackbloods. Jill struck down a creature as it lunged at her, then she paused to watch.

Hasani gripped one of the blackbloods's forearms. The flesh turned purple and blue, color traveling up its arm as it shrieked. As the colors reached the creature's face, sores began bursting with blood. Then the blackblood collapsed.

Ymira and Hasani had magic.

Another blackblood crashed into her, knocking her sword out of her hand and pinning her to the ground. What had once been a woman now nipped at her like a feral dog, stringy hair clinging to her yellowed skin. Jill tried to buck her off, but though the blackblood was small, she was ferocious. Her nails sank into Jill's skin, drawing blood.

Panic began to set in as she shoved at the creature, flailing and squirming. She reached out for her sword, but her fingertips just brushed the hilt as the woman sank her teeth into Jill's neck.

Pain like she'd never known burned through her veins. She screamed as her vision turned red, then black at the edges. This couldn't be the end. She would *not* die here.

A wet schlick sounded and the woman slumped forward on top of her, dead. Jill shoved her off and scrambled out from beneath her, looking up to see David staring at her with wide eyes. Saving her for the second time in two days.

"Thanks." Her voice shook as she stood.

He nodded and fired another arrow.

The fighting had died down a little, but more of the blackbloods crowded the courtyard, the scent of rot and decay gag-inducing.

"We can't hold them off forever," Grimzy said as he bashed one over the head. "They're after you, princess. We must lead them away from here."

She nodded, and the ground beneath her spun. Her neck and shoulder burned, and her entire body ached. Fear struck her like one of David's arrows.

Will I turn into one of them?

Her breathing shallowed and she staggered forward, her legs buckling before she fell into someone's arms. They held onto her, holding her upright as the world continued to spin.

"We have to leave!" someone shouted. Was it Hasani or Peter?

"They're blocking the only exit," David said.

"No, they aren't." That was Hasani, she was certain. She looked around for him, but the motion made her nauseous. "There's a secret path out through one of the rooms."

"How do we escape so they won't follow?" Luca asked, sending an arrow into another blackblood.

Peter swore loudly, cutting down another creature. "Leave it to me."

Jill's vision cleared a bit, and she looked up into David's face as he guided her toward one of the rooms off the courtyard. She tried to pull away but was too weak.

The blackblood's poison was setting in fast. Her heart pounded faster. She *was* turning into one of them.

"Your Highness, we must go." David started toward one of the trees.

She hated that he wouldn't say her name, but she had no strength left to argue as she watched the group continue fighting.

Then the scene in front of her shifted. Jill blinked. One second, Ymira, Hasani, Grimzy, Luca and Aaira were all fighting. The next, they vanished. Or seemed to. She didn't understand what she was seeing, or rather, what she wasn't seeing.

The blackbloods stopped fighting and looked around, confusion evident on their rotting faces. A second later, the rest of their group reappeared, but the blackbloods acted as if they could not see them.

Everyone in the courtyard was frozen as they turned to Peter, with a hand outstretched and eyes closed in concentration. Hasani and Ymira exchanged a glance, but Grimzy stared at the man with a furrowed brow.

"You guys better go now," Peter said through gritted teeth. "I can only hold the illusion for so long."

Hasani and Ymira were the first to move, Aaira and Luca close behind. David started moving forward and Jill let herself be led along, not trusting her own feet to carry her.

Sweat beaded along Peter's forehead and his face turned red. His entire body trembled. "Bleeding Saints' Grimzy, get out of here!"

Grimzy inhaled as he closed his eyes. Then he let out a low whistle that seemed to shake the earth and echo through the wind. Jill stopped moving to stare at the paladin.

"What are you doing?" Peter asked, glaring at Grimzy.

But somehow Jill knew. Somehow, she sensed what was coming even though she didn't understand how she knew.

Rumbling sounded through the trees, hooves and paws and wings beat against the air. The sounds grew louder and then animals burst through the trees. Birds and deer and rabbits and bears and insects and squalls and several other creatures Jill had heard of only in name. They stampeded into the courtyard just as Peter's magic failed. They crashed into the horde of the blackbloods, trampling and clawing and pecking and tripping them, driving them back.

"Go!"

Jill didn't need to be told again and followed Hasani and the others, helped along by David. Behind her, Peter and Grimzy rushed into the side room. Hasani shoved aside a mat on the floor to reveal a trap door.

Within seconds they were all down in the tunnel beneath the room. Grimzy pulled the trap door shut, leaving them in darkness.

Ymira's glowing bracelets sent light into the tunnel, illuminating everyone's harrowed faces.

Jill looked up and found them all staring at her, waiting for her to say something. She glanced at a crouching Grimzy, whose head still brushed the top of the tunnel. Their eyes locked, and a sudden sadness overwhelmed her. He'd never told her.

"You all have a lot of explaining to do," she said. Then Ymira's light faded, and she sank into darkness.

31

BO

They traveled through the tunnels for half a day before the cave spat them out on the snow-caked surface. Bo's leg had started to throb. Normally, it didn't bother her too much, but the colder weather changed that. Her twisted ankle ached, and every movement sent pain up her leg.

They'd been woefully unprepared for any sort of journey. They had no food, no water, and the clothing they wore in the mountains would not hold up against the snow coating the ground and their shoulders.

Bo shivered. One winter when she was a child, she and her mother had nearly frozen to death. They'd been snowed in for weeks as their firewood slowly dwindled and their food stores stretched to the limit. She and her mother snuggled together by the fire for those weeks, her mother telling stories of her homeland, which was drenched in sunlight and turquoise seas. She had never seen snow before coming to Erinya. Bo had always imagined those stories of sun were the very thing that had kept them warm during those cold weeks. As she trudged through the snow, body going numb, she couldn't help but think of that very cold winter.

Ahead of them, Kylian collapsed onto a stump, burying his face in his hands. A swirl of emotions twisted in her stomach as she watched him. Uncertainty. Fear. Anger. Pity.

Zyla stood close by tending to Lyra while Asif lingered behind Bo. His presence unnerved her, the hairs on the back of her neck rising as she turned to stare at the feline boy. Even though he was younger, they were the same height and that ticked her off.

"What are we supposed to do now?" Asif asked, shivering.

She looked back at Kylian.

"What's our plan, Kylian?" she asked, fully aware he had none. But he always had a backup plan. Surely, he had something.

Kylian rubbed a hand down his face. Shadows hung under his eyes and his golden hair had fallen from its tie, hanging at his shoulders. During their entire journey, he'd kept himself impeccable. But now he looked defeated.

"We head north. To the princess," Zyla answered.

"And what about food?" Asif asked, an edge to his voice. "What about clothing? Or a map? Or weapons?"

Kylian looked up at them, swallowing.

Asif marched forward, pointing a finger at him. "This is your fault," he accused. "Lyra and I were fine before you guys came here. Then you show up and suddenly everyone's after us! They want Lyra dead. They want me gone. And none of this would have happened if you'd just stayed away."

"Asif—" Bo started.

Asif whirled to face her. "No. You don't get to speak. You have no idea what it's like! We have been outcasts our entire lives, and just when we'd finally found a home, a family, it's ruined! And it's because of you." He jabbed a finger at her.

Her breath fled her lungs. "Me? Are you serious right now? How is it my fault that your sister is one of the Saints' Heirs?"

"She was totally normal before you guys showed up, then suddenly she has this magic?"

Bo's skin grew warm despite the freezing air. "I think you're just jealous she has magic, and you don't."

Asif's face twisted and he shoved her. She tried to step back, but her club foot wouldn't budge, and she tumbled back into the snow. For a second, she sat there stunned. Then red-hot anger surged through her veins.

"You little—"

"Enough." Kylian rose from the stump, looking between the two of them. "We don't have time for this. The princess heads north. She's our only hope of freeing the Order now." Kylian's mouth was a dark slash on his pale face. Even a few days underground had not been kind to his tan complexion. "And let us pray our hope is not misplaced."

They trudged through the bitter cold for a day and a half before they came across an abandoned village. Sleet-sloshed streets splattered mud on their boots and clothes. Circular homes with latticed wood on the interior with thick furs and pelts wrapped around the outside filled the village. She didn't know who'd lived here, but they'd been prepared for winter. They raided the homes, scrounging clothing and supplies, including a large sled they loaded and took turns pulling. The grueling part of winter was still a few weeks off. But any setbacks in their journey would be deadly. Bo just hoped the Wolfmen would let them stay. If not . . .

Well, she tried not to think about that.

IT WAS Kylian's turn to pull the sled. Lyra sat bundled in furs, her gaze settled on the footprints in the snow behind them. Kylian's mood had soured more every day, until he was barely speaking more than a few words at a time. Bo worried about him, a strange new feeling for her. She'd never worried about anyone other than herself before—and her mother, when she'd been alive. Certainly not about a prick like Kylian.

She wondered if there was more to Kylian than she'd initially thought. Unease snaked through her every time she found herself staring at him. He really was so young to carry the weight of an entire kingdom on his shoulders.

Groaning, she picked up her pace to walk alongside him, leaning heavily on her crutch. She cleared her throat, hoping to grab his attention without actually speaking to him.

His eyes slid to her then back to the path in front of them. The Whitesaw Mountains lay to their right, dense forest to their left.

She sighed. "You're awfully quiet."

He grunted in response, tugging the sled with a jerk. According to their map, they were still a few days out from Fenric's Keep. Thanks to the tunnels, they took a slightly different route than the princess.

"You wanna talk about it?" Bo couldn't believe her own ears. Was she really asking him to talk to her? Did she even actually care about him or was his silence just too weird to handle?

"There's nothing to talk about," he said flatly.

"Right." She swallowed. She didn't want to talk either. All she really wanted was . . . well, she wasn't sure what she wanted anymore. Several months ago, she would have said she wanted to go back to her corner of the woods to live out the rest of her days alone.

But somewhere along the way that had changed. She'd

spent her entire life alone. Once because of her mother, and then because of her monsters. The monsters were no longer her burden though. So where did that leave her now?

They shuffled through the snow in silence for several more minutes. Bo's nose was so cold she was sure it would turn blue and fall off eventually. Her breath puffed up in front of her face, and snowflakes clung to her hair and lashes.

"It's not your fault, you know," she said. She glanced up at the trees overhead, remembering he'd once told her the same thing. It felt strange to be on the other side of that comment.

"Yes, well. That doesn't keep me from blaming myself." He gave the sled another tug, his pace slowing. He'd been pulling it for hours, dragging it up hills, over logs, through ice-coated brambles. He hadn't complained once, accepting the burden as if it were his alone to bear.

Perhaps they weren't so different, she and Kylian. The thought sent her pulse skittering. She didn't care for his haughty air, his prim manners, or flawless image. But was that who he really was? Or was it a mask to keep people out? To keep them from getting too close?

"Someone once told me that I place a lot of responsibility on myself that was never mine to bear." Beside her, Kylian stopped walking but still refused to meet her gaze. "I think the same could be said of you," she whispered.

He finally looked at her. Their gazes locked and his jaw clenched and unclenched, looking like he wanted to say something.

"What?" she asked. "What is it?"

He stared a few moments longer then shook his head. "Nothing. I just thought . . ." He pursed his lips.

"You thought what?" Her curiosity was piqued. He was hiding something. He knew something she didn't. And it mattered.

He rubbed a mittened hand down his face. "Nothing. Forget I said anything." He started walking again, picking up his pace.

"You were going to say something. What is it?"

Kylian's face pinched in agitation, turning red. "Another time." He wouldn't look at her.

"Is it about Addie?" She wasn't sure where the question had come from. Who was this, Addie? Why had he called her that name? Did he know something she didn't? Did he know about her—

No. She would not allow that hope to blossom inside her. The hope of a family out there somewhere. How would he even know where she'd come from? She shook her head.

"Addie's dead."

This time it was Bo who stopped walking, frozen in place.

"I—I'm so sorry." She swallowed. She didn't know who Addie was to him but judging from the heaviness in his face, they'd been close. "What happened?" She knew she shouldn't ask, shouldn't pry. But curiosity prompted her tongue to move despite logic telling her to keep her mouth shut.

Kylian sighed, a sound of defeat like she'd never heard from him. "It was all my fault, and I lost her."

32

DAVID

David trembled as he watched Grimzy carry Jill, who remained unconscious. His friend, his paladin. The Heir of Saint Torryn the Gentle. The very Saint who had blessed the silver stags David had hunted and killed.

He'd told Grimzy the story of his curse ages ago, even knowing Torryn the Gentle was the mountain people's patron Saint. He'd feared then what Grimzy might say, how he might condemn David for his atrocious act.

That was nothing compared to the fear he felt now.

Panic filled his lungs; his head throbbed behind his eyes. Once, he'd hoped to break his curse. Now he believed he deserved it. He deserved every broken piece, every crack, every fracture. Every single scar.

He lingered at the back of the group as they hurried through the tunnels, guided by Ymira's light. Another Saints' Heir. Hasani and Peter were heirs as well.

It seemed too perfect, too coincidental. Four Saints' Heirs just happen to find their way to each other? It felt too good to be true. Rarely did things work out so perfectly. Unless fate or some great Deity had brought them together. But he'd never believed in such things. Faith seemed more fitting for better men, not a man tainted by the sins of his past.

David glanced at Jill, safely cradled in Grimzy's arms. Black liquid spread through her veins where she'd been bitten. His fear of Grimzy transformed into fear for Jill.

Would she turn into one of those awful creatures? When Grimzy had been bitten, the venom disappeared after the vulgan that bit him was killed. But Jill had been bitten by one of the blackbloods, not by the vulgan.

Their pace slowed until they reached a dead end, a rickety wooden ladder leading upward. They all turned to face Grimzy, who still held Jill. She rasped several wheezing breaths, as if she couldn't get enough air.

"Let me see the bite wound," Ymira said.

Grimzy knelt, holding Jill as carefully as one might hold a newborn baby. A wave of envy struck him. He wanted to be the one holding Jill. He wanted to be the one to care for her.

Instead, he balled his fists and stood off to the side, a wordless observer as Ymira tore at the collar of Jill's tunic to reveal her wound. The wound was far more gruesome than he'd been prepared for. A crescent of puncture wounds sank deep into the spot between her neck and shoulder, black blood leaking everywhere while muscle and tissue threatened to burst.

"This isn't good," Ymira said, almost to herself. "It's spreading fast."

David's heart dropped to his toes, and bile collected in the back of his throat. As a soldier he'd seen death many times. He'd seen war and loss and bloodshed. But nothing could have prepared him for watching the girl he cared for fighting for her life.

Jill's entire body shuddered, and her eyes rolled back into

her head. David struggled to remember life before her. He'd been so alone, so angry. He hadn't even realized it until this very moment, but she'd broken through the darkness that had hung over him since his mother had died. The darkness that lied to him, telling him he would be forever cursed and alone.

"Grimzy, hold her down." Ymira's voice was calm and soothing, like a peaceful brook whispering through a sunny glen. The tightness in his chest eased just a bit.

Ymira's bracelets glowed as she pressed her fingers to the edge of the bite wound. Blood oozed as she pinched the skin together. Jill bucked beneath Grimzy's grip, her tortured scream seeping into David's bones. He stood frozen, fear tightening his throat.

Tendrils of light rose from the bracelets, twisting in pirouettes and flips like a graceful dancer before settling on the bite wound. The black venom flowed backward, leaching out onto the ground. The putrid scent made him want to gag. Ruined skin began easing back together, new flesh growing and connecting over the tissue.

Jill's body relaxed as Grimzy's grip on her loosened.

The last bit of light from Ymira's bracelets flowed into the wound, knitting the skin together until all that remained were a few crescent shaped scars, so light he wouldn't have noticed them if he hadn't watched them heal. Jill took another deep breath then her body fell limp.

Ymira slumped against Hasani, bruise-like circles appearing under her eyes. Hasani's arm wrapped around her shoulders, holding her in a way that sparked a flame of jealousy in his chest. How he longed for Jill to lean into him like that, to trust him, to want him.

But he'd left her in the Enchanted Wood. He'd treated her as though she would be the death of him.

The images of his vision in the wood flashed back to him,

the living nightmares unfolding before his eyes. He was afraid of falling for her, because he knew she would break him.

But the truth was, he'd fallen for her long ago. And he was prepared to shatter for her.

HASANI SET A BRUTAL PACE, but David didn't mind. It kept him from thinking too hard about Jill's sleeping form in Grimzy's arms. The mountain man carried her without complaint across freezing streams, into dipping valleys, and up steep hillsides. Hasani, Ymira, and Aaira had not intended to join them, but after the attack on the Oasis, it made sense for them to accompany the princess to the keep. From there, they would decide whether they would stay or return.

The snow fell harder the farther north they traveled but no one complained. It was a far cry from the enchanted warmth of the Oasis. Fog clouded in front of David's face like a phantom. The cold grew almost unbearable, and he wondered if his condition would allow him to be affected with frostbite.

Beside him, Luca remained silent, his eyes flicking to Aaira every few seconds. Despite the dire situation, he couldn't help the grin that slid up his face as he eyed his friend. Their eyes locked and Luca gave him a sheepish look, confirming his suspicions.

"We're nearly there," Hasani called, his horns glinting obsidian against the bright white snow.

David's stomach tumbled. Even as he knew why they were here, what they were walking into, he feared what the wolfmen might do. At best, the wolfmen would turn them away. At worst, well, he tried not to think about that. He only hoped Jill's presence would at least keep them civil.

Light filtered ahead of them, signaling the end of the

forest. David heaved in a cold breath as they approached a large open space. A pristine carpet of snow and ice stretched out before them, touched only by a handful of skeletal trees here and there as if warning them to stay away.

In the distance, Fenric's Keep stood like a soldier at attention. Turrets of black stone soared upward along the outer wall of the keep, which must have been a mile long. Backed against the mountainside, the keep loomed like an ominous warning. Even the temperature seemed to drop as they stared at it, dark clouds of snow swirling above it, obscuring its full height.

David shivered in a way that had nothing to do with the freezing temperatures. He turned to Grimzy. "You need to put her down."

"She shouldn't be walking yet," Ymira said, "She needs to rest."

David's jaw clenched. "Unfortunately, we don't have time for that. She must walk this final stretch if we're to have any hope of the wolfmen helping us."

Ymira pursed her lips but said nothing as Grimzy set Jill down with her back against a tree. Grimzy nodded at him, then backed away. Her eyelashes fluttered as David knelt before her. He wanted to reach out and touch her, to tuck the loose strand of hair behind her ear. He wanted to see if her lips were as soft as they looked, if—

He stopped that thought before it could fully form. Instead, he grabbed her shoulder, gently shaking her until her eyes fluttered open. He pulled his hand away like he'd been burned. He couldn't allow himself too close, not after what he'd done to her.

Jill sat up straighter, blinking at the wintery landscape. Exhaustion tugged at her and, not for the first time, he wondered what she'd been through these last months. Initially, he'd assumed she was still in the Citadel with her tyrant brother. But she'd been on the run and in hiding. David wondered if she'd rested at all since then.

Guilt and shame washed over him, and he couldn't meet her eyes.

"We're nearly to the keep," he said gruffly. "You'll need to walk this last bit. You can't show any signs of weakness."

Jill nodded. Her body seemed to protest as she rose to her feet. Her legs wobbled and he began to reach for her but pulled away at the last second. She was steady. She was fine. She didn't need him.

More than that, he didn't deserve her.

"Good," he said, swallowing the sudden lump in his throat before turning away. If he looked at her any longer, he would be tempted to reach out to her, and he couldn't do that.

"They will see us coming," Hasani warned.

"Correct," David said. "We will have nowhere to hide." He looked at all of them as if asking if anyone wished to turn back. No one did.

Jill straightened her back, rolling her shoulders as she stared at the keep. "I can go alone if I must." Her words carried a heavy yet tentative hope, as if she were prepared to forge ahead on her own but secretly did not want to.

"I will follow you," said Grimzy.

David swallowed hard as each person agreed to follow her until Jill's eyes landed on him. He looked away, feeling her disappointment like a battle wound. He'd promised to follow her once and had broken that promise. He would not make the same mistake twice. He nodded at her but remained quiet, not trusting himself to speak.

They moved as one, exiting the safety of the tree line and pushing through the deepening snows. They remained on high alert, watching the bulwarks ahead for any signs of attack.

David had no idea what the wolfmen would do to them, for surely, they must have seen them by now.

The wind gathered speed, pelting them with stinging flakes of ice. Jill stood tall at the front, her hand never leaving the handle of her blade. She did not look back. Nor did she show any fear.

They drew closer but still saw no signs they'd been spotted. What if the wolfmen simply ignored them, leaving them to freeze to death only feet away from safety and warmth?

At last, they reached the monolithic entrance that looked more like the doorway of a giant tomb than anything else. They all stilled, waiting for something to happen. But the only sound was the howling of the wind. Or was that the wolfmen? Did wolfmen howl like wolves? David wasn't sure.

After nearly ten minutes, the grinding of rock and stone drew their attention to a smaller door off to the side. Out stepped two wolfmen, dressed in dark blue and gray uniforms, only knives at their belts.

"Who goes there?" One of them asked, a jagged scar across his wolfish nose.

"Princess Jillianna of Erinya." Jill's voice was strong and proud, unwavering despite the cruel gleam in the guards' eyes.

"Interesting," the scarred one said. "And what are you doing here?"

"I've come to speak with Alpha Volkov."

The wolfmen grinned to reveal razor sharp canines. "Is that so?"

"Yes," Jill said, her voice hard as the stone keep looming over them. "You will let us enter or be in danger of committing treason against the crown."

The older wolfman stepped forward. "I believe, *Your Highness,* harboring a royal fugitive is already considered treason. Do not think you can fool us. We want nothing to do with you. I suggest you leave now before I no longer find this amusing."

Jill's shoulders tensed and David could see the wheels in her head turning, searching for some foothold.

"I've come to make an offer to Alpha Volkov he cannot refuse, one I believe will benefit all the wolfmen. It is in all our best interests for you to let us in."

The scarred wolfman considered her, his smile slowly fading. Seconds passed. Then minutes. David's heart started beating painfully in his chest. This was a mistake. They should turn back. But Jill wasn't backing down, she wasn't taking no for an answer.

He fell in love with her just a little bit more.

Finally, the wolfman smiled again, raising a bushy brow. "So be it, princess. But don't say I didn't warn you. Few who enter Fenric's Keep ever leave. I do not expect it will be any different for you."

JILL

The keep seemed colder inside than it had outside. The wolfmen guards led their group down a long narrow corridor with blue fire torches reflecting against the black stone. Jill held herself tall even as they passed other wolfmen who eyed them suspiciously.

From what Jill gleaned during her research, the wolfmen housed their military forces in the keep, and the regular wolfmen citizens lived up against the mountain behind the keep. Thousands lived in the keep and thousands more dwelled in the valley, sheltered from attacks on every side.

They walked in silence through the endless halls, passing barrack after barrack filled with soldiers. They rounded a corner then made their way up a spiraling staircase, the stone steps worn from hundreds of years of boots stomping up and down.

At last, they reached the top, only to be led through more hallways and up more stairs. Jill was used to walking since the palace was large, but she'd mostly traveled from her quarters to the training grounds and occasionally to the throne room for various ceremonies.

Just when her legs began to burn from all the stairs, they arrived at a larger hall with thick beams crisscrossing above them. The stone here was lighter, a pale gray rather than black. Regular torches lined the walls, giving this section a far warmer feel than the rest of the keep. Ahead stood large double doors, the thick wood covered in centuries of dents and dings.

"Your friends may wait in the mead hall," the older guard said, motioning to the doors. "If you'll follow me, I can take you to Alpha Volkov." He gave her a grin that seemed to suggest he could not wait to see what would become of her.

Jill swallowed hard and nodded at the others to go into the hall.

"I'm not sure this is such a good idea, Your Highness," David said, though he refused to make eye contact with her.

It stung, him not looking at her. She wanted to grab his scarred face and force his eyes to meet hers. She wanted to shake him until he finally glanced at her. She wanted him to break the way she did every time he called Your Highness instead of Jill.

She did none of those things. "It will be fine. Alpha Volkov wouldn't dare hurt a princess in his own home. To do so would risk outright war." She tossed a glance at the guards, but they were unaffected by the threat. Either they didn't care about war, or they were serious when they'd called her a fugitive. She wasn't sure which worried her more.

Grimzy didn't look pleased but dipped his head and ushered the others toward the hall. She turned and followed the guards.

With the others gone, the guards walked much faster, quickly outpacing her as they herded her through more hallways and steps. She tried to keep track as she went, a left here and then a right, another right, up a staircase. At times she felt as if they led her in circles intentionally. They passed several other large rooms and hallways, and Jill swore she even saw several humans congregating in a meeting chamber before the wolfmen guards called back at her to keep moving.

Finally, they approached a door that, while not dissimilar to other doors in the keep, had a giant wolf-head knocker hanging in the center of the door. Two guards stood outside, silent and unmoving. Only their eyes followed as Jill stepped through the doorway.

Alpha Volkov stood on the other side of a desk and set down several papers as she entered. He held his head high, his wolfish features keen and observant. With a nod, he dismissed his guards. The door slammed behind her. She was suddenly, painfully alone.

Had she been a fool coming here? What if the wolfmen denied her request? What would she do? Would they be allowed to leave?

She grimaced. Even if they were allowed to leave, she wasn't sure where they'd go. Winter was on its way and a journey back to the Whitesaw Mountains without supplies would be deadly.

It all came down to this moment. It all came down to her.

The study was sparsely furnished with a large desk, old wooden chairs, and a fireplace where a small, fire smoldered. It did little to push out the cold that enveloped the room, but she was learning quickly the wolfmen liked the cold.

Alpha Volkov stood nearly two heads taller than Jill, his face passive as he stared down at her, no doubt watching her every move. His navy-blue robes were neatly pressed, and a black sash tied around his waist signified his rank as their leader.

"Welcome to Fenric's Keep, Your Highness. I trust my men have been accommodating?" His voice was gravelly but even, diplomatic.

"Accommodating enough."

He didn't hesitate to jump straight into matters. "With all due respect, Your Highness, I'm a very busy man. But I'm also curious. What brings the princess so far from home and all the way to my doorstep?" His sapphire eyes pierced her to her core. He didn't move, standing tall and proud like a statue, assessing her. He was far more intimidating than Jill cared to admit.

She swallowed hard. Jill had practiced in her head what she would say to the wolfmen, how she would win them to her cause, over and over. But now that she stood before him, the words fled from her mind. Alpha Volkov did not seem the type so easily persuaded by fancy speeches.

"I've come to seek your help."

"Is that so?" The man raised a brow but looked thoroughly unimpressed. Still, he stood as rigid as if he were made of ice, as if he were carved from the same stone as the keep.

"Yes." She gripped the pommel of her sword. They had not taken it from her, either because they were foolish or because they didn't fear her. She suspected the latter. "As I'm sure you've heard, my brother rules with monsters—the vulgan—by his side. Carthesia presses into our borders, and the Ohans have their own sinister plans." She didn't let her voice waver as she listed out the threats mounting against them. The path to becoming queen filled with new obstacles each day.

"I've indeed heard all of this. What I don't understand is what it has to do with me?" He sounded bored, annoyed even.

Jill decided, in that moment, that she was not above begging. Not if her people's lives were on the line.

"My people take refuge in the Whitesaw Mountains, but

winter is coming, and they need supplies to last through the months. The Ohans have those supplies, along with terrible weapons." She swallowed. "They also have slaves I intend to free."

Despite her best efforts, her heart slammed against her ribcage. All her cards were laid on the table before him. She had given her power away to the man in front of her. He alone could determine the fates of so many people.

Outside the wind howled, as if it too understood her plight.

"How bold of you." At this, Volkov crossed his arms, his first movement aside from his blinking eyes. "Tell me, how exactly do you intend to free so many from captivity and traverse safely across the kingdom?"

"We need your fleet," Jill said before she could lose her courage. "With your boats we can launch an attack from the shores, commandeer supplies, and bring the people to safety here."

Silence. And then a smile.

"Interesting proposition. You want to use my men, my boats, and my keep for *your* people."

"They're your people too."

Volkov barked out a throaty laugh and Jill tensed.

"Of all the things you've told me in the past several minutes, Your Highness, that's perhaps the most ridiculous." He shook his head, as if genuinely amused. "The answer is no. You and your friends may see yourselves out." He looked down at his desk, picking up a piece of parchment, the dismissal clear.

"Wait, no." She didn't bother to hide the desperation in her voice. "We can't do this without you."

"And what do I get out of it, *princess?*" he sneered. "You're asking me to risk much for people who hate my own."

And there it was.

She played her last card. "I would see the Anooran treaty overturned."

"And?" He pressed his hands into the desk, a smile toying on his lips.

Her stomach flipped. *And?* And what? Was it not enough? What more could she offer?

As if reading her mind he said, "Nearly four hundred years of hatred of my people and you think you can undo all of that in a heartbeat simply by annulling some treaty?"

As a matter of fact, that's exactly what she'd thought, but she didn't dare admit that. It seemed she still had so much to learn about politics.

"Tell me, princess, do you know the history of your people?"

She remained silent, unsure what he meant in asking the question.

"Humans do not hail from Erinya, did you know that?"

She nodded slowly. She sensed she was treading dangerous waters and any moment something would drag her under.

"I'm sure the history you've been taught is different from ours." His eyes glazed over, as if watching something off in the distance, as if Jill were not present at all. "But humans came as conquerors, seeking to rule this land for themselves. And those who lived here first—the wolfmen, the felines, the inkwells, even the mountain men—were subjected to their reign. How exactly humans have remained on top for all these centuries, I have no idea."

Jill felt nauseous. It wasn't that she doubted the wolfman's words, on the contrary, she felt the truth in them press down on her heart like an anchor. The father of the Black King had come to Erinya, subjecting it to his rule. Then for a reason no one knew, Malum killed him.

Volkov continued. "And with them, the humans brought tales of wolves, none of them kind. Big bad wolves." He enunciated each word. "In their eyes, we were villains, monsters, savages in need of a king who would put them in their place." His gaze seared her soul. "Six feet underground."

She inhaled sharply.

"So, you see, even before the Anooran treaty came to be, the wolfmen were vilified. The assassination attempt on Queen Anoora only secured that belief in the minds of Erinya. Even the other animal clans began to ostracize us. We were outcasts. Demonized. Hated." Volkov's voice revealed a deep sorrow, as if he truly wished things were different.

Jill's words failed her. "I'm sorry." It was all she could think to say, despite knowing how little those two words could do. Tears pricked her eyes, but she forced them down.

"I am too." The hard edge returned to the Alpha's voice. "We will not be helping you. I will not risk the lives of my people for a petty sibling squabble."

The words were a spark in her belly and fire began to flow through her veins.

"You're right. What has happened to you and your people at the hands of mine is awful, and for that I am truly sorry. No words could ever atone for the wrongs done to you." She paused, rallying her courage to keep speaking. "But you and I have no quarrel. I have not harmed you, nor you me. Together we could change everything. Help us and let the world see the wolfmen as heroes, who aided Erinya in her time of need. More than four hundred years of animosity is far too long."

Alpha Volkov heaved a tired sigh. "Pretty words from a pretty princess."

The words were a slap to the face, but she did her best to stay calm, even as the statement boiled her blood.

"I'm almost inclined to like you, Your Highness. Your naivety is admirable. But I'm afraid nothing you can say or do would change my mind. Our people are divided, and we will stay that way."

"You don't think I know that?" She let her frustration drive her, the words spilling forth like a split sack of grain. "Every clan keeps to themselves, quarrels and disputes driving a wedge between the people of Erinya. The Ohans are corrupt, the clans and tribes too proud to interact with each other, and my brother has been taken hostage within his own body by Malum, the Black King himself. We cannot afford to fight among ourselves, otherwise the war is already lost. I cannot make right centuries of wrongs, but when does it end? With us? With you and me right here and now? Or must we wait another four hundred years before there is peace between us?"

Volkov's expression darkened, his eyes narrowing. "You ask me to simply choose to forgive you and your people?"

"So, you admit forgiveness is a choice?" Her words were a blade. They were not nearly as sharp as Jack's had been. Jack had a rare gift for diplomacy, charming everyone he met. But she'd be damned if she didn't try her hardest to win the Alpha to her side. Even if she had to beg, to plead, to lay everything down on the line. She would do whatever it took to make him see.

"You're right. And perhaps that is the truest thing you've said so far. Forgiveness is indeed a choice. And I choose not to." He bared his teeth, revealing sharp canines, the leash on his anger as far as it would extend. "Now, you and your people will leave my keep and not return on pain of death. I do not care if you will be queen someday. If you remain any longer, I cannot promise no harm will come to you. You may see yourself out."

"Please—"

"Out now!"

The door to the study opened behind her, the Alpha's guards marching in and grabbing her with frightening strength. They hauled her into the corridor and the door slammed shut.

JILL FELT HOLLOW as she trudged down the long stone halls of the keep all alone. No guards led her back, so she was left to wander by herself, wallowing in despair. The others all waited for her somewhere. Waited for her to give them good news of the treaty she'd secured. Instead, she would come bearing ill news.

She'd been naive to think she could rally the wolfmen to her cause.

Peter would agree. Possibly even Grimzy and David. Still, they'd followed her, and not because of what she could give them. She could give them nothing. She had nothing to offer. She could make promises about what she would do when she was queen, but if she never saw that day, if Malum destroyed her, they were left with nothing.

Nothing. Nothing. Nothing.

That's all it amounted to. That's all *she* amounted to.

Lost in thought she wandered the halls, in no hurry to find the others and tell them of her failed negotiations. Blue fire torches lined the corridors, their flickering flames casting eerie shadows on the stone walls.

"Princess Jillianna?"

She jumped, looking up in time to stop before running

headfirst into the man in front of her. A human man. Or—she noticed his pointed ears—an elf?

She'd never seen an elf before. To her knowledge, none resided in Erinya, only in Welynn. What was he even doing here in Fenric's Keep?

The broad-shouldered elf stood before her with a blade strapped to his back. Fine blond hair hung to his shoulders and facial hair clung to his chiseled jaw. He was handsome in a rugged sort of way.

"I'm sorry, do I know you?" She wasn't sure why she'd asked the question. She knew no elves. They were just another group that wanted nothing to do with her kind. The thought made her want to scowl, but she managed to keep her face neutral.

The man gave a tense smile. "Well, not exactly."

Her mind was blank. "What do you mean?"

He swallowed. "Well, Your Highness, my name is Prince Tiernan, and I'm your betrothed."

34

MILLIE

illie woke to the sounds of a crackling fire and the smell of cinnamon and nutmeg wafting from a cup on her bedside table. She inhaled, sinking into the velvety bedding beneath her. She tried to sit but a sharp pain snaked through her leg, eliciting a hiss.

Movement to her left caught her eye. Malum sat slumped in a chair by her bedside, his head resting on a fist, eyes closed but brows pulled tight. For a moment, she could almost pretend it was Jack sitting next to her. For a moment, she could almost forget the horrors of the past several weeks.

She swallowed the nausea that suddenly plagued her. He wasn't Jack. Jack was gone, just like her brother had said.

Doon.

This time she sat up, wincing against the pain. Malum woke, shaking off the sleep and kneeling by her side an instant later.

"Are you all right?" Jack's kind voice spoke, but his eyes were black.

Not Jack. Keeping that in mind was a struggle.

"Doon. Ravala, where—"

"They're safe." He brushed a sweat-soaked strand of hair out of her face, tucking it behind her ear. Her skin crawled at his touch, and she pulled away, finally looking around the room. She lay on a large four-poster bed with dark green bed sheets covering her. The chamber was massive, housing a bathing salon, office, and sitting area. A fire blazed in the large hearth beneath a painting of Erinya's former ruler, King Cole. Her heart stopped.

She was not in her chambers. She was in the king's room. Malum's room.

The nausea rose again, and this time she couldn't stop it. As if reading her thoughts, Malum conjured a bucket just before she emptied her stomach into it. Her heart hammered like a battle drum; her stomach ached. Everything ached. And despite it all, she wondered what people would think of her staying in the king's rooms. Perhaps they'd already made their assumptions, but she still hated the idea.

"What happened?" she rasped. Malum handed her the spiced tea, and she sucked it down, ignoring how it burned her already sore throat.

"After we escaped, I brought you here." He leaned back in his chair, fingers pressing into the black velvet arms. "The Ohans have betrayed Erinya, and yet Ohan-Jin still seeks to become my ally. I don't know what he's playing at."

The teacup finally cooled in Millie's hands, and the tip of her ring finger brushed against a chip in the porcelain. The room had begun to spin but she forced herself to look at Malum, whose dark eyes stared intently at her.

She still recalled Ohan-Jin's silver tongue during the meeting after King Cole had fallen ill. The silky smile that didn't reach his eyes. How he'd goaded Jack into attacking him. She was certain Ohan-Jin had never been a friend to Erinya.

"Perhaps he wishes to trick you?" Millie offered.

"I'm sure he does, but why?" Malum continued to stare, his brows furrowed. Millie allowed herself a few moments to truly look at him.

Was Jack really still in there? The way Malum acted made her think he was, but perhaps it was a test to see if she'd let down her guard. Malum couldn't actually care for her, could he?

She pushed the thought away. Even if Malum cared for her, his idea of love was tainted by his obsession with power. He could never truly love anything.

But what of Jack? Her heart whispered those words.

Malum eyed the large clock by the bed. "I must go. I have matters to attend to. I will be back soon to check on you." He rose from the chair, crossing the room.

"Malum," she said, and he paused. Her heart skipped in her chest, as terror climbed up her throat. She had to know. "Did you save me or did Jack?"

His gaze landed on her, softening in a way she'd never seen before, even when he was just Jack. "We both did."

Millie woke to a soft rapping at her door. Candlelight tossed shadows against the wall, their flickering fingers clawing at nothing. She shivered.

"Come in," she rasped. Her throat still felt raw despite all the tea and honey she'd been drinking.

A young woman bustled in, carrying a tray loaded with soup, a hunk of sprouted rye bread, and an assortment of chocolate covered fruits. Her stomach grumbled. The woman continued forward, a cloth-wrapped bundle at her back, and Millie started as recognition hit.

"Keyanna! You're safe!" Millie had almost forgotten the feline woman she'd sent to the palace the day she'd left the Citadel.

Keyanna smiled, dipping her head in respect. Her face was flushed with healthy color, and she looked much fuller than when Millie had last seen her. The swaddled baby slept peacefully curled up against his mother's back.

Keyanna set the tray on Millie's bedside table.

"How are you?" Millie asked.

"I am well, thank you. You have done me a great service by allowing me to become your maid in waiting."

Millie's stomach curled. She hadn't intended for the girl to become her servant. She'd simply hoped to provide her safety. "You don't have to be my maid, Keyanna. I wished for you to be able to take care of yourself and your child. Nothing more."

The girl fixed her with a sad smile, folding her hands in front of her. "I cannot live off your charity, Paladin. Besides, I've never had a real job, and I enjoy the work."

Millie swallowed. They were similar in age, yet their lives had turned out so different. While she'd been born a maid, living and working in the palace meant she'd never gone hungry. She'd never spent a night on the streets. She'd never had to worry about her safety or resort to selling her body just to survive the week.

"Well, have a seat. I wouldn't mind the company."

The girl pursed her lips but obeyed. She pulled the child off her back and held him as she perched stiffly on the edge of the seat. She gave Millie a faint smile and looked around the room.

In those awkward seconds, Millie realized she knew nothing about this girl beyond her name and where she'd come from. With shaking hands, Millie grabbed the hunk of bread, tearing a piece off and popping it in her mouth.

"I'm sorry I never asked. What's your son's name?"

Keyanna's face softened. "His name is Asher."

Millie chewed the bread in her mouth slowly, looking at the little feline baby. His ears had their traditional point, soft orange fur coating the tips. Thick dark locks covered his head like his mother's.

"I've never heard the name Asher. Is it a feline name?"

Keyanna shook her head. "No." She looked down at her feet. There was clearly a story there, but Millie wouldn't push it. When she was ready, if ever, she would share.

"He's adorable."

"Thank you."

Asher released a small cry and Keyanna rocked and shushed him until he settled once more. The girl looked at home as a mother, yet it made Millie sad she had no one to share that with. But perhaps the father wasn't one Keyanna would want to share a future with. Still, it must be lonely.

Keyanna looked up at her, opening her mouth then closing it, her eyes shifting around the room.

Millie straightened. "What? What is it?"

Keyanna swallowed. "Would you like your soup?" She lifted the bowl, handing it to her before she could respond.

"Uh—" Millie accepted the bowl, confused, then felt the crinkling of parchment underneath. The girls locked eyes.

"I was instructed to make sure you ate your soup." Keyanna's gaze pierced her.

Millie nodded, though she could not fathom why the girl was acting so strange. Unless—

Unless they were being watched. It made sense. Malum could linger anywhere with his shadowy magic.

Asher released another cry and threw his tiny fists in the air, squirming in his mother's grasp. Keyanna stood.

"I'm sorry. I must go and feed him. Is there anything else I can do for you, miss?"

Millie shook her head as she clutched the parchment between her fingers. "Please, do what you need to do."

The girl began walking back to the door.

"And Keyanna?"

She paused, turning back to Millie, her brow furrowed.

Millie smiled at her. "Thank you."

"Of course."

The girl exited without another word and Millie quickly set the bowl on the table and tucked the note into the bedsheets to read it discreetly.

We need to talk. I will find you in a fortnight at the stroke of twelve. Be ready.

    —MG

Millie read and reread the note, trying to understand it. Who was MG? And why did they want to speak with her? Why go through the trouble of roping Keyanna into this?

Uncertainty settled in her stomach as she glanced out her window, lost to her thoughts. Snowflakes dusted the edge of the window like frosted treats. In the distance, the wildwinds howled through the Citadel like a warning.

Something came over her then, a vision appearing in her head. Millie pictured the winds twining through the streets, pounding on doors, telling people to flee this dreadful kingdom. She imagined them sneaking into the tiniest cracks of doors and windows and rousing people from their sleep, urging them to their feet. Parents would gather supplies while sleepy children clutched their teddies. They would slip from their houses under the cover of dark, keeping to the shadowed corners of the city and avoiding patrols. Each house they passed, more would join them, and though it defied all logic, they would be silent as death, never meeting any soldiers who would bar their path. Even nursing babies would not cry, somehow knowing silence meant life. And then they would leave the city, escaping to freedom.

The wildwinds howled again at her window, an array of colors fluttering in the snow like dancers in the moonlight. She swore it smiled at her.

Millie could not smile back.

35

PETER

*P*eter did his best to look at ease in the mead hall, though it was a challenge with so many wolfish eyes fixed on him. He pretended to ignore them, all the while scanning every inch of the place, filing away any information he could glean.

Most of the wolfmen wielded spears with feathers tied on the shaft below the head of the spear. The feathers presented an array of colors, perhaps some signal of rank?

Someone set a mug of mead in front of him, the bubbly drink sloshing over the sides. Peter glanced up at David, whose mouth was set in a grim line.

"For you," David said without looking at Peter. The man slipped into the seat beside him, clutching his own mug, though looking as if he had no intent to drink it. Instead, David merely stared at a bronze brazier hanging from the stone walls.

Grimzy remained by the door, refusing to sit while Hasani, Ymira, Luca, and Aaira warmed themselves by the fire, speaking in hushed tones.

"So," Peter started, "Grimzy is one of the Saints' Heirs.

Did you know?" He didn't particularly want to have this conversation, not now. Actually, not ever. But David's moping since the princess had gone to meet Alpha Volkov had Peter longing for a change in topic.

David shook his head, then gave Peter a sideways glance. "And how long have you known you're an heir?" He raised a brow as he took a sip from his mug.

Peter's pulse spiked but he forced a lazy grin to his face, shrugging as nonchalantly as he could manage. "I've had this magic for a while. Didn't know it was because I was an heir though. Just thought I was special."

"Of course you did," David said bitterly.

Despite the erratic thumping of Peter's heart, he leaned back and crossed his arms, smirking at the broken man. For as hard as his skin was, it sure was easy to get under.

"It seems Grimzy and I aren't the only ones." He nodded at Hasani and Ymira, the pair standing much closer together than really seemed necessary. "How convenient."

"That's a word for it." David took another swig of his drink, though he grimaced like it was the worst drink he'd ever had.

"So, we might want to consider our exit strategy," Peter said, eyes flitting about the room again. He counted ten wolfmen total, each armed with spears and knives at their belt. The keep was a fortified labyrinth, easy to lose people but also easy to get lost. He hated going in anywhere blind but seeing as they hadn't had much choice in this endeavor, they would have to make do.

"Our exit strategy?" David raised a brow.

Peter pursed his lips, trying his best not to appear condescending. "For when Jill comes back empty-handed. Unfortunately, that is more likely than not."

David chuckled. Another swig. "Perhaps. But I wouldn't bet against Her Highness."

"Neither would I, but the first rule of any con is always have an exit strategy."

"This isn't a con," David said flatly.

"Isn't it though?" He leaned forward and finally took a long drink from his mug. The mead was quite good. He didn't understand David's reaction to it. "Find a way in, convince people to help, use their supplies and their people for something of a fool's errand. Then take the glory for yourself. A perfect con to convince them they'll be heroes."

"Keep your voice down," David hissed, eyeing the guards near them.

"They've heard every word we've been saying. You should be far more concerned that they pay us no mind. Means they're not the least bit worried about us and what we can do."

David shifted uncomfortably. "Well, it seems we can do quite a lot actually." He gave Peter a meaningful look. It was Peter's turn to be uncomfortable.

Four of the Saints' Heirs were together in this very hall. It did change things. But not by much. The wolfmen still didn't appear threatened by them.

At that moment, the large double doors they'd entered through burst open again. Jill stood in the doorway, her face paler than usual. And beside her . . .

Well, I'll be damned. It was an elf.

How long had it been since he'd done business with the elves? Three years? Four? He racked his brain as the pair walked forward.

Beside him, David rose then stopped, clearly uncertain about the role he now played in the princess's life.

Peter eyed the newcomer, noting his weaponry, finer than any other weapons he'd seen in the keep so far. He noted the blonde hair and stubbled jaw. Then the crest he bore on his left shoulder and the emerald ring on his right hand.

A prince then. And judging by the crest of a winged horse with a horn atop its head, this was High Prince Gaelor Tiernan Acanthus of the Princedom of Chivalry, or Tiernan as he preferred to be called. What was he doing here? Last he'd heard the man had been seeking a marriage alliance—with the Erinyan princess.

Peter stilled. No wonder Jill looked so pale. He eyed David from the side. The man's expression grew darker as he assessed the newcomer.

"I think it's time for us to leave," Peter whispered under his breath. He was striding over a second later, not bothering to see if David followed. Luca and the others watched warily from a distance.

"How'd the meeting go?" Peter asked, his eyes flicking between the princess, Grimzy, and Prince Tiernan, who stepped away to give them space. Though Peter knew for certain the man could hear every word they said, at least he was polite.

Jill pursed her lips. "They won't help us."

Peter's stomach clenched. He hadn't expected them to help. In fact, he'd spent most of the trip thinking of alternative plans. And yet, some part of him had hoped. Hoped the wolfmen would see reason.

Foolish. They were invested in their own kind, just like everyone else they'd come across, save for the mountain men. He couldn't blame them though. He wouldn't be here now if he didn't somehow believe Jill held the key to curing Liza.

Peter stiffened at the thought, glancing over at Ymira. *No, not Jill. Ymira.* Ymira had healed Jill when she'd been bitten, drawing out the poison before it could turn her into one of those creatures.

"I feared as much," Grimzy rumbled. He knelt on one knee beside Jill, placing a hand on her shoulder. For a split second, she seemed on the verge of tears, and then the expression vanished. Her face became as still as tempered glass and sharper than its jagged edges.

"It doesn't matter now. We can't waste time. Grimzy, how long will the food stores of your people last?" Jill crossed her arms, looking to the ground.

"We may have enough to last us through the winter, if we ration and no more refugees show up."

Jill grimaced. The others finally joined them. "Hasani, what do you think it would take to convince your people to help us?"

The gazelle man winced. "I fear my mother refuses to see reason. Though perhaps after the attack, she would be more inclined. But I have no idea how my people fare." He forced a small smile as Ymira grabbed his hand, clenching it tight. Right. They'd left the Oasis to be destroyed by the blackbloods.

They all stood in silence, and Peter was painfully aware of all the wolfmen's watching eyes. One looked far more interested than the others, his eyes slightly widened, his gaze never tearing away from them even when Peter shot a glare in his direction.

Saints' blood. He hated how vulnerable they were. They shouldn't be discussing any of these things here and yet they had nowhere else to go. They were completely at the mercy of the wolfmen.

"Excuse me," a lyrical voice cut in, and they all turned to the elf man. "I couldn't help but overhear. It seems like you need help."

"You could say that," Peter muttered. "Think you'll give it to us? Not sure how the wolfmen would feel about their trade agreements with Welynn being put at risk." Peter flashed the man a smirk as the others looked between the two of them. Peter shrugged, crossing his arms.

Prince Tiernan cocked an eyebrow. "Have we met?" His eyes were shockingly blue, like a piece of sky had been frozen in them.

"Not officially. But I make it my business to keep tabs on those in power. Even the princes of Welynn."

Jill stiffened, and her gaze lowered to the floor. Clearly, she didn't want to do this right now.

"Prince of Welynn?" David asked, his voice lower than usual. Even Grimzy looked intrigued. Peter doubted any of them had ever met an elf, save the mountain man. He knew a few traded in the markets of the Whitesaw Mountains. "Why are you here?" David did a horrific job of keeping the suspicion from his tone. It took a surprising amount of Peter's strength to resist rolling his eyes.

"Trade agreements, as this fellow so kindly pointed out," Tiernan said, gesturing to Peter. "And your name is?"

"Peter," he said flatly. He had zero intention of cooperating with the prince. Peter had tried to secure trade with the wolfmen before, but they preferred to do business with Welynn rather than Erinya.

He may have also attempted to steal the crown jewels from Prince Tiernan at one point in time, but that was beside the point.

Instead of being offended, Tiernan looked amused. "Peter, huh? I once knew a smuggler with that name. A lousy one."

Peter kept his face neutral and shrugged. "Never heard of him."

"Right." Tiernan said with a smirk. The elf turned back to the princess, looking her over with interest. "You need help, correct?"

"We can manage on our own, thank you." Jill's voice reminded Peter of a bow string pulled too tight. Soon enough it would snap. He just hoped she wasn't aiming at him when it did so.

"What are you trying to do?" the elf prince pressed.

"It's really none of your concern." Jill wouldn't meet his eyes. "We're leaving. I doubt there's anything you could do." The princess looked at each of them, signaling that she was done with this conversation, and then she turned away.

"You plan to free the Ohans' slaves, do you not?"

Jill froze, spinning back to the man. "How could you know that?"

The prince simply pointed to his ears. "I have very good hearing, princess. How do you think I found you?"

Jill glared at the elf prince, who looked quite pleased with himself. Peter didn't miss the quick glance Jill stole at David, whose body remained taut as he watched the exchange like a spooked animal.

At this, the man finally turned to the rest of the group, laying a hand on the pommel of his sword and bowing low. "How rude. I haven't officially introduced myself. My name is Prince Gaelor Tiernan Acanthus of the Princedom of Chivalry of Welynn. Two months ago, I was supposed to wed an Erinyan princess of legendary beauty. But imagine my surprise when I discovered she'd fled her kingdom and was lost, only to find her in the last place anyone would have ever expected. Here."

Ymira let out a gasp. Grimzy's brows raised. David's expression turned darker than even Peter could have dreamed. Meanwhile, Jill looked like she was about to pass out.

"I know the Princedom of Chivalry is one of the lesser princedoms, but your stunned silence is less than reassuring." The broad man straightened, his smile slipping just slightly.

"What are you doing here?" David practically spat the words.

"I believe I already answered that question—trade agreements. Right, Peter?"

Peter only stared, annoyed by how unaffected the man remained in the awkward silence. Even the wolfmen shifted uncomfortably, like simply watching the exchange was difficult.

Despite this, the prince forged ahead. "I heard what you discussed with the Alpha. With all due respect, Your Highness, freeing your people is a worthy goal. It's noble. I admit I did not expect such behavior from the princess."

"I'm not a princess anymore," Jill snapped, her words like a dagger slicing through the air.

"If there's any way I can help—"

"You can't." Jill spun back to the door, walking away from her betrothed before she paused again, as if remembering something else. "And in case you were wondering, we are no longer engaged. You made that deal with my father. Not with me."

"Your Highness—" Grimzy started to say but a loud bell clanged, ringing through the mead hall. Alarm bells.

"What the—" David said, spinning around.

The double doors swung open again, and one of the guards rushed in. "Zima, Ivan! Check the gates. The rest of you, maintain your posts."

Two of the wolfmen closest to the entrance ran from the room, their metal armor clanking.

"What's happening?" Grimzy asked the man who'd shouted orders.

"Alarm was raised," he said gruffly.

Jill was the first to flee the room, following the soldiers, everyone else followed close behind. They ran through the long corridors, more soldiers joining as they wound up the stairs until they reached the battlement. All the while the bells continued to ring.

Soldiers lined up against the wall, awaiting orders. Peter approached. His hands suddenly felt slick with sweat despite the bitter wind whipping across his face.

Not half a mile away were eleven monstrous creatures, twisting shadows of ash and smoke swirling around their forms.

The vulgan had arrived.

And in front of them, hundreds of the blackbloods.

3 6

―――――

KYLIAN

*E*veryone spoke very little as they trudged through the snow toward Fenric's Keep, chasing after the princess like lost puppies who couldn't fend for themselves. He hated it. But they needed her. And staying in the mountains hadn't been an option.

He heaved the sled behind him as his breath clouded in front of him. His muscles burned. During his time as the king's adviser, he'd made it a point not to exert himself unless absolutely necessary. Doing so would muddle his appearance, and appearances were everything.

Unless you were going to die in a blizzard. Even he had to admit appearances suddenly became much less important.

He was thankful for Zyla, as usual. She had been keeping everyone together, keeping everything in order. It was Zyla who'd thought of using the sled and blankets to keep Lyra warm. Zyla who'd found a map and planned their route, stopping at every potential rest spot until they reached the keep. And Zyla who'd talked with Bo and the others when Kylian couldn't think straight, let alone speak.

It had been days since he'd gotten a proper nights' sleep. Truthfully, it had been longer than that. Ever since he'd fled the Convent months ago now. He couldn't rest until he knew they were safe, until he rescued them.

He'd failed once to rescue someone he cared about. He refused to let it happen again. They were counting on him.

Did anyone actually say that? His traitorous mind whispered.

A small part of him wondered if he might be putting more pressure on himself than anyone else ever had. Well, even if that were true, this was a matter of life and death. He couldn't afford to cut himself any slack. People were depending on him, and he would do everything in his power to save them.

And if it still isn't enough?

He gripped the rope tighter, the rough little hairs digging into the palms of his freezing hands despite the gloves he wore. Until he failed, he would not let himself imagine defeat. It was the oldest trick in the book.

Imagine defeat and you've already lost. Imagine success and nothing can stop you.

"Kylian," Zyla's soft voice somehow cut through the sound of his ragged breathing and the sled crunching over the icy terrain.

He ignored her, pretending he hadn't heard. He didn't want to talk to her and listen to her soothing words. He didn't want to be placated. What he wanted, more than anything, was to be angry. He wanted to feel his rage burning through his veins, inflaming him from the inside. He wanted it to consume him.

"Kylian," she said again, louder this time.

Still, he pressed forward, refusing to acknowledge her. It was a tactic he'd used before. Convince someone you couldn't be bothered to hear them, and they would do one of two things. They would either be forced to reveal their true motivations in seeking you out, or they would give up. Of course, you had to be careful when you implemented such a tactic. If you weren't careful—

"Kylian!" Zyla's voice turned angry, and he spun toward her, ready to unleash his fury on her.

"What?" he snarled. "What is so important that you have to keep speaking to me? Can't you see I don't want to talk to you?" His words seemed to echo in the space around them, despite the dampening effect of the freshly fallen snow. His heaving breaths clouded in front of his face, and he glared at the shocked faces staring back at him.

Zyla stilled, her face taking on a pained expression. "The children need a break," she said, breathless.

He stared at her. Then without another word he dropped the ropes and walked toward a large log jutting out of the snow, ignoring the way his heart twisted at the look of disappointment on Zyla's face. He sat, crossing his arms and staring into the distance.

Fine. He'd take a break. Let the world fall apart while he sat on a log, doing nothing productive. What good was he if he couldn't *do* anything?

Bo stomped over to him. "What the hell is wrong with you?" Her face burned red, and he could practically see the steam rising off her.

Good. He wanted someone to feel the way he did. He wanted to fight. He was ready.

"What?" he snapped at her.

Bo blinked at him like he was an idiot. "Ignoring everyone? Yelling at Zyla? Scaring Lyra?"

He shoved to his feet. "Oh, I'm sorry, did I hurt your feelings while I was trying to save everyone's lives? Did that make you feel bad?" The words were cruel, but he didn't care.

Something had broken inside him, and he wanted nothing more than for someone else to feel his pain. Even if it was his little sister. She didn't care about him anyways.

Bo seethed. Before he could utter another word, a shadow rose from her skin and swirling darkness took the form of a fist that smashed straight into his face.

He flew through the air and landed in the snow nearly ten feet away, struggling for breath. His lungs couldn't take it in. Blood dripped into his eyes and leaked from his nose. Pain blurred his vision—his ears rang.

He heard yelling distantly but couldn't make out any of the words.

His anger dissipated as a wave of guilt and shame crashed into him, far more painful than the wound Bo had inflicted.

A hand yanked him from the ground, hoisting him into the air. Bo stood before him, holding him in the air with her shadowy fist. She was no longer angry but didn't look as satisfied as he would have guessed. Instead, she looked resigned.

His blood dripped into the snow. He deserved the blow, deserved her wrath.

Stupid. Stupid. Stupid.

Since when had he allowed his emotions to control him like this?

"I have half a mind to leave you here to die in the snow," Bo said. Her blank expression told him she wouldn't hesitate to do exactly that, and a new fear spliced through him, colder than the freezing wind that bit his skin. "But I think that would be traumatic for them." She nodded at the others. "Especially Zyla."

His feet hovered several inches off the ground. His throat tightened. What had he done? His little sister had just threatened to kill him. He'd spent over a decade searching for her, seeking to make things right. And now that he was so close, so close to getting her back, his outburst had undone everything. He could never tell her the truth now. She would hate him more than she already did.

"Snap at me, take your anger out on me—fine. Whatever. I don't care. I've done nothing but provoke you since we met. I'm the one who betrayed your friends. I'm the one who can barely control her magic. But—" she paused, taking a step toward him. "You don't. Yell. At. Zyla." Her shadow hand dropped him into the snow.

He looked over at the others watching the scene unfold. Asif looked as angry as Bo, clutching the pommel of his sword. Lyra's terror-stricken face buried into Zyla's side.

But it was Zyla's expression that killed him. Not one of anger. Not even sadness.

No, she looked disappointed in him. These were the people counting on him, and he'd let them down.

"Zyla—I—I'm so sorry." He stood, wiping the blood from his face, ignoring the way it pounded and ached in the cold.

Zyla pursed her lips and shook her head before turning away from him. She picked up Lyra and put her into the sled then grabbed the ropes and started walking.

No words. No complaints. Just quiet indifference. It was like taking another blow. In fact, he would have preferred physical pain over whatever he felt now.

Bo and Asif followed her, not deigning to give him another glance.

He trailed along after them, cursing himself as he wiped more blood from his face. For all his political prowess, he could see no way to make this right.

37

JILL

*J*ill's entire body shook with fear. It curled through her chest, splitting her veins, choking her lungs, and tightening around her muscles like a vice. A hundred wolfmen soldiers stood on the battlements of the keep, some grim-faced, others slack-jawed.

Fear prompted her to run and hide, but it would do no good to ask for an army, only to crumple at the first sight of danger.

This isn't simply danger though. This is a massacre. Malum had sent them not just to end her life but as a warning.

All those people, instead of losing their lives to the vulgan had instead been corrupted. How many of them had gone on to attack their own friends and families? How many had committed horrific acts they would never remember? How many more people would he turn to his side with the aid of the vulgan?

She had been so close to meeting that same fate. Even now her memories of that moment felt murky at best. She shuddered to think what she might have done had the transformation completed. Was there any returning after that happened? She couldn't be sure, but it presented several moral dilemmas within her mind.

If there was even the slimmest of chances these people could be saved, what would slaying them say about her? Was there a way to minimize casualties? Or would it be cruel to restore their minds if their bodies were mutilated beyond recognition?

And then there were the children. Her stomach turned at the sight of a small child with blackened hands shuffling through the snow far below. He still clutched a stuffed toy to his chest, though it was covered in mud and ice.

"What do we do?" David was at her side, his bow in hand. She looked at him, an agreed upon truce in the look they shared. This was no time for—well, whatever they were doing.

"Yes, princess," another voice said. "I'm eager to know how you'd fight such a unique battle." Alpha Volkov had arrived silently and now stood behind her.

She glanced up at the Alpha, who studied her openly. A plan. She needed a plan, and quickly. She quickly took stock of their defenses and their opponents.

Eleven vulgan stood at the rear of the blackbloods, ushering them closer to the walls of the keep. A quick glance along the length of the wall told her there were four ballistae.

"We need fire," she said. "Have your men gather as much oil as can be spared. We need to launch those bolts at the vulgan in the rear. If we can slay one, that should release its hold on the people under its control." Or so she hoped. Grimzy had nearly been turned once but she'd killed the vulgan before the transformation was complete. She had no idea if that would be the case for the people whose transformations were complete.

She turned to see Luca standing behind David and

realized more people were looking to her than she'd initially realized. Hasani, Ymira, and Aaira stood there, along with Grimzy and Peter. Even Prince Tiernan had come to stand beside the Alpha. Good. She would need all of them.

"Luca and David, head up the archers. As soon as the vulgan draw close enough, have them launch flaming volleys. Grimzy and Aaira, I want you in charge of the ballistae. Set up guards around them. Do *not* let them fall. The vulgan can materialize across large spaces at will, and we must be prepared for anything. Hasani, Ymira, and Peter, I need you to do something dangerous. Are you up for it?"

They nodded, grim but determined. She inhaled slowly, calming her racing heart. She couldn't let them see the fear her own plan gave her. She must display confidence, even if she could very well be sending them to their deaths.

"I want you three on the ground. Peter, create an illusion that will hide you. I want you to round up as many children as you can. We can't save everyone, but we must try."

Peter's expression soured. "And how are we supposed to get hold of one, let alone bring several back here?"

Jill's heart faltered, her mind blanking. It was a fair question.

"Think of something," David ordered, embodying the voice of a captain.

She was grateful he'd spared her from giving an explanation, but she refused to look at him. It would only convey weakness if she doubted herself now.

"Ymira, see what your healing abilities can do. Hasani, you have your gift. Figure something out." Her voice was hardened steel. "Now, go."

Instantly, the group scattered, each person finding their assigned place and gathering the necessary weapons. She cast a glance at the approaching army of blackbloods. They were still a quarter mile off, slow as they slogged through the snow. But they would be here before they knew it.

"And what will you do, Princess?" Alpha Volkov asked. She'd nearly forgotten he was there. Beside him, Prince Tiernan watched her with interest, the playfulness in his gaze completely at odds with their current circumstances.

She turned to the Alpha. His gaze was cunning and scrutinizing, dissecting her as if she were nothing more than an intriguing test subject rather than the future queen of Erinya.

She leveled him with her best glare. She refused to be cowed by this man, intimidating as he might be. "I will fight."

He said nothing as he continued to stare at her. Of all the animal clans, the wolfmen were the most animal-like. Fur lined his face in the form of thick sideburns. His nose and mouth protruded like the snout of a wolf. His eyes, the color of blazing sapphires, were sharp with animal instinct.

"How convenient that you arrive at my keep with a chance to prove yourself following so close behind you."

The accusation was clear. He thought her cruel enough to intentionally bring harm to his people if it meant winning them to her cause. And if she were honest, she might have if she'd thought of it. If she hadn't been so terrified of this army of monsters set before them all.

"I'm tired of mincing words Alpha," she said, a new surge of confidence blossoming inside her chest. "I did no such thing. But Malum will not rest until I am dead, and the kingdom is fully his. This is the world that awaits us if we do not join forces."

The wolfman's gaze softened—just slightly. "How old are you, princess?"

The question caught her off guard and she had to think about the answer. Her and Jack's birthday was only a few weeks before Yuletide.

She'd missed her birthday. Their birthday. She'd never spent one apart from her twin before. A strange sadness to feel with everything happening around her.

"Um—eighteen," she said at last, ignoring the pit in her stomach.

Snow began falling lazily from the sky, dusting their shoulders, adding to the centuries of ice and snow packed into every crevice of the keep.

"You are young and unpracticed," he said, finally looking away from her. "Nevertheless, I hope you lead us to victory, Your Highness." He dipped his head and strode off before taking a position further down the battlement, his perfect stance honed from years of fighting.

She returned her attention to the battlefield before them. How many lives were within and behind these walls? How many more would seek refuge here? She needed to win this battle not only to prove herself but for them. For her people with nowhere else to go. No matter who they were or where they came from, she would fight for them.

David appeared at her side. "Ballistae are ready and await your signal."

She nodded and drew her sword from its sheath, raising it into the air. Cold metal clinked as a hundred soldiers shifted on the wall. They turned to face her, waiting for orders. Waiting for *her*.

Her mouth went dry, and her body froze, not from the upcoming battle, but instead from the weight that rested on her shoulders. Should she give a speech? Say something poetic and encouraging?

You are not your brother.

She had few words, but what she did have was love. Love for these people—these beautiful, messy, broken people.

"To arms," she yelled, her voice echoing in the mountain

peaks around them. "To fight is to hold hands with Death. Death before disgrace!"

"Death before disgrace!" Grimzy echoed, his voice deep and bellowing.

Jill eyed the vulgan, who'd edged closer now. "Ready the ballistae! On my count!"

Feet shuffled and wood creaked. The scent of oil and smoke lit the air.

"Three, two, one—fire!"

38

BO

*N*ight descended on the forest and the perpetual wind died down, momentarily giving them a reprieve. Bo and Zyla lit a fire while Kylian gathered more firewood. Asif sat with his back against a tree, Lyra tucked beneath his arms.

It would be a long night. They were only another day's journey from the Keep, but they'd had to stop to set up shelter for the night.

With her own back pressed against the woody bark of a tree, Bo stared into the blooming firelight. The flames rippled and shuddered, smoke curling up into the black sky through the trees. Soft bird calls sounded but other than that, the snow muffled everything.

"Thank you," Zyla said, interrupting the silence.

Bo looked up at her across the fire. She crinkled her nose. "What for?"

"For talking sense into Kylian."

"She didn't really talk sense into him," Asif said. "More

like beat it into him." He gave her a sideways grin. She turned away and shrugged.

"Someone needed to do it." Her stomach twisted as she recalled the encounter though. She was still learning what her powers could do, how they worked. In truth, she hadn't meant to hit him so hard. It had done the trick though.

Still, she didn't like it. Kylian was the one who was supposed to hold it together. The one who always had a plan. The one who exuded confidence even in the face of terrible odds. But he was losing it. Mean words were one thing, but something, some subtle shift, was corroding his self-assured nature. She feared where it might lead. As much as she hated to admit it, they needed him. He knew more about the Saints' Heirs than anyone else.

"He cares about you," Zyla said.

Bo eyed her. "Pretty sure he cares about you too."

To her surprise, Zyla's cheeks flushed in the firelight, but she didn't respond. Perhaps . . .

Well, it didn't matter. It was none of her business one way or the other.

She truly didn't understand it though. Her mother had told her love stories, but they'd never much interested Bo. It was fine for others, sure, but she just couldn't see herself ever falling in love. She'd rather do so many other things instead. Though she imagined not being alone would be nice.

Something crashed in the bushes nearby, and Bo was on her feet in an instant. Kylian stumbled through the undergrowth, eyes wide with fear. He carried no firewood but shook visibly.

"What's the matter?"

"We have to go, now!"

Without explaining further, he ran over and started throwing snow on the fire and gathering their things.

"What happened? What's wrong?" Bo asked as she helped toss their few belongings into the sled.

Asif had already secured Lyra in the sled and had drawn his sword.

"They're here—the blackbloods. We have to leave now!" He threw another handful of snow on the fire. It sizzled and melted before going out completely.

More crashing sounded through the undergrowth and then they all fled into the night, screeches and howls chasing after them.

Snow coated Bo up to her knees, soaking her pants and freezing her toes as she tried to run. The snow deepened, and every step pulled her further into its clutches. During the day they'd constructed special frames they tied to their shoes to help distribute their weight and keep them from sinking into the snow. But they'd had no time to put them on.

Bo looked behind her, catching sight of the grotesque figures lumbering toward them. But the deep snow hindered the blackbloods just as much as it did them. The rotting frozen corpses tripped and clawed their way over the icy terrain.

An ear-splitting wail shattered the silence of the night around them. A monster made of shadow materialized in front of them. A vulgan stood there, its jaw snapping open and closed as it slinked forward on its smoky, spindly legs, unbothered by the snow.

Asif shot forward, stepping lightly on the snow without sinking and swung his sword at the creature's legs. It vanished before the blade made contact, spinning around behind Asif and whipping a leg toward him instead and sending him flailing through the air.

Lyra screamed.

Bo's heart thundered, sweat dripping down her despite the bitter cold. She needed to think, needed to—

Another scream and she turned to see a blackblood pull Zyla to the ground. Kylian raced over and fought off the creature, which snarled and hissed.

Lyra screamed again as a vulgan grabbed her and lifted her from the sled by her leg. She dangled upside down and wailed, thrashing against the monster's strength, but it was no use.

And Bo stood still. Her friends needed her, and she couldn't move. *Her friends.*

She'd never had any of those before. It was a strange thought to have in such chaos, but it was true. Zyla, Asif, and Lyra, even Kylian—jerk that he was—were her friends.

Something shifted in her chest, like the snap of something locking into place. She cared about these people. For the first time ever, she cared.

She would not let them die here.

Magic flooded through her entire body. Colors burned brighter, sounds sharpened, and her breath deepened. Shadows lifted her into the air, swirling around her like a whirlwind. In the past, she hardly remembered using her powers, let alone controlling them.

Now it was different.

Time seemed to stall as she examined the landscape below her now, her power lifting her face to face with a vulgan. Kylian and Zyla still fought off several of the blackbloods. Asif was trudging back through the snow, his face a mask of red-hot anger as he caught sight of the vulgan still holding Lyra by her ankle. Briefly, Bo wondered if Lyra's power of song would work on these creatures. But it didn't matter. The girl was too panicked to sing.

A whip of shadow shot out from Bo, splitting into several arms that grabbed the blackbloods, pulling them off Zyla and Kylian before ripping the creatures' bodies apart. More poured onto the path, but she split her shadows into more arms, dismembering the creatures two and three at a time, tossing their black-blooded bodies into the snow.

Bo turned to the vulgan, unconsciously keeping the blackbloods at bay with her other shadows. She sent a shadow forward, aimed straight for the monster's face. It struck the vulgan directly in its face and shot out the back of its skull.

The monster screamed, dropping Lyra and reaching for its face with its claws. Asif raced to Lyra's side and grabbed her, moving her away from the ongoing battle.

Bo shot forth another shadow, piercing the other side of its face. The vulgan thrashed against her, the motion moving through the shadows and whipping Bo through the air. She gritted her teeth as she flung about, the cold air stinging her eyes and skin.

She sent another shadow toward the vulgan's throat, but the monster batted her shadow away before it could strike. The momentum pulled her through the air and her magic faltered as she crashed into the snow. A shock vibrated through her bones, knocking her teeth together and making her vision spin.

She shivered, sweat beading at her brow. Distantly she knew sweating in the snow was dangerous, but it didn't outweigh the threat looming over her. Bo rose, her club foot buckling slightly.

She tried to reach for her magic again, but the vulgan disappeared then reappeared behind her, pulling her legs out from under her and slamming her face into the snow. She cursed as she hung upside down, staring the vulgan right in the face as blood dripped over its teeth and down its mouth. The scent made her gag, and had she been anywhere else, she would have vomited right then.

It grabbed her other leg with its clawed hand, pulling at her legs. Pain soared through her. She was a ragdoll about to be torn apart just like she'd done to the blackbloods.

Desperate, Bo screamed, and shadows tore from her mouth into the vulgan's chest. The monster let go of her legs and dropped her into the soft snow. She could have cried from relief.

She righted herself mere feet from the monster. She narrowed her eyes, focusing all her magic on the vulgan before her, and more shadow tentacles pierced its head and neck at the same time.

Then more shadows. And more.

Until hundreds of tentacles pierced its entire body. Some wrapped around its legs, others around its neck. Countless more had speared it through the face, chest, and abdomen. It thrashed in her grip, but she was ready this time. She held fast as it screamed.

Interesting. It can't seem to disappear when my shadows hold onto it.

But what did she do with it now?

Finally, the vulgan stopped resisting, going still. Its mouth closed, returning its face to a smoky black sphere with no eyes or nose.

What's it doing?

A loud snap sounded, like bone breaking, then a tremble vibrated through its body. It twitched and fell limp, and she suspected it would have crashed to the ground if not held in place by all her shadowy arms.

Had she killed it? It looked dead but she would not be fooled. She had to be certain—

The vulgan shuddered, releasing a long, low moan that struck Bo like a physical force, blasting her to the ground. Her back struck something hard, knocking the air from her lungs. Panic pulled at the edges of her awareness, and she struggled to breathe. At last, she inhaled and sat up.

The vulgan had toppled to the ground, but its skin, though

usually gray and smoky, appeared paler. Flakes sloughed off the monster, drifting off in the breeze. Ash swirled as the beast's form collapsed in on itself, dissipating fully into ash and smoke.

Searing pain ignited in Bo's head. The scene around her darkened and then twisted.

An orb of brilliant light appeared before her as well as an orb of darkness. Although she didn't understand what she was seeing, she knew the two orbs were sentient, and that they were facing each other.

The light zipped forward, growing brighter, pushing back the darkness. A shriek like the sound of a dying animal pierced the air as the darkness shrunk back. The light grew brighter and brighter, blinding in its brilliance.

Bo shielded her eyes, a sense of awe filling her as she watched.

With one final, desperate scream, the darkness shattered into tiny specks, completely overwhelmed by the light. For several seconds, Bo basked in that light, feeling its warmth touch her soul. Tears sprang to her eyes as the light finally faded and a dull, glowing figure stepped toward her.

Bo observed her surroundings for the first time. Her companions were nowhere to be seen, and she no longer stood in a snowy forest. Instead, she was in some sort of ethereal garden. She felt soft grass underfoot, smelled sweet flowers on the air, and heard birdsong as warm light danced in brightly colored flowers.

The figure stopped in front of her, a young man with a slightly crooked nose and a cheeky grin. He was unsettlingly familiar.

Bo knew she should have felt fear, but in this man's presence, in this place, there was no room for fear. How was that possible?

"Who are you?" she dared ask.

The man dipped his head. "I believe I'm your great-great-great-great-great—I don't know how many greats—grandfather, Kieran the Unbreakable." He winked at her.

Bo's jaw dropped.

His gaze pierced her once more with that strange familiarity. Golden hair hung in ringlets at his shoulders, and there was a small scar on his chiseled jaw. If she'd tried to imagine what a Saint might look like, what a god might look like, he was the sort of heroic figure she would picture.

"Is that vulgan truly dead?" she asked, her voice escaping in a shuddering breath.

He nodded. "Only one of the Saints' Heirs can kill these creatures."

She stood there a moment, feeling strangely unsettled. She should have been happy, after all she'd killed a vulgan. So why did she feel so uneasy?

Then Bo recalled something David had told her long ago. The princess had killed one once. She remembered the feeling of it dying, that scraped out hole in her chest.

"That can't be true. The princess killed one."

"Injured it, yes. It was weakened near to death, but not all the way. Only a Saints' Heir can kill one. There are twelve vulgan, one for each Saint."

Bo's brain felt foggy. Was it the warmth she felt as she stood on the green grass, so at odds with the wintery terrain she'd been traversing? Or was it him, this godlike man who claimed to be her ancestor? She had trouble believing she could ever be related to someone like him.

"Where am I?" she asked at last, looking around. She swallowed hard, a sudden thought striking her. "Am I dead?" Why did the idea fill her with so much dread? Wasn't death supposed to be, well, peaceful?

Kieran shook his head, flashing a sad smile. "This is the space between life and death, a meeting place, if you will. But only briefly."

A space between life and death? Her chest caught. Would her mother be here? Could she see her?

"I'm afraid that's not how it works," he said.

"How what works?"

"I can see that look in your eyes. You are searching for your loved ones. But they have passed on. This space is reserved only for the likes of us." He paused, letting her absorb that information.

A sharp pain struck her in the gut. It was the hope of seeing her mother, and then just as quickly, that hope had been shattered.

"I'm afraid we do not have much longer, and I must relay some things to you."

She nodded numbly, staring past him at golden mountains in the distance. Or, not quite golden. One moment they radiated gold light, then the next, the light shifted, radiating a thousand colors she had never seen before. A prismatic rainbow of colors, ever shifting, ever growing, and expanding, beamed outward, as if darkness itself could not even come near such light.

Without thinking, she stepped forward, walking past Kieran.

Something struck her, solid but invisible. A barrier of some kind, between herself and those distant mountains.

"You cannot come. It is not yet your time." He cocked his head to the side.

"Then why are you here? Why aren't you in the afterlife?" she asked. Could he get past the barrier?

Kieran gave her a sad smile. "Only a Saints' Heir can open the veil between life and death, but there is a great cost."

"What does that mean?" Her gaze snapped back to the man.

The warm scene around Bo flickered, revealing a snow-laden landscape. Then just as quickly the warmth returned, as did Kieran.

"Quickly! Our time grows short. I cannot keep this tear open much longer!"

She nodded, keeping silent for once. She almost wished there were someone there to witness such an event.

"Malum's strength comes from those creatures. Without them, his power is limited. They were created with the darkness of his stolen magic, and that is where he draws his power."

She nodded, though she barely understood.

"We did not kill the vulgan, so we could only imprison Malum. We hoped we would have more time, but it seems the time we have is never enough."

The scene flickered out again, longer this time. The breeze that blew against Bo's back lingered even as the warmth of the garden returned.

"You must slay them. All of them!" he said, his voice growing urgent. "If you do not—"

But his form faded, along with the garden, leaving Bo standing up to her knees in snow. A bitter wind blew, kicking up snow and swirling it around her. Bodies lay strewn about, their blood and ash turning the snow a putrid black.

She had defeated one of the creatures that haunted her every moment for the last year and a half. She should have felt relieved, should have felt something other than the sheer dread now coursing through her veins.

Keiran the Unbreakable had not finished his words but she knew.

If they did not slay all the vulgan, they would never defeat Malum.

39

PETER

*P*eter buckled the straps of his bracers. Full armor would impede his movement too much, and he needed to be quick if he was to face the blackbloods head on. His fingers fumbled with the buckles, cold and numb and trembling with a fear that set his stomach tumbling.

Beside him Hasani and Ymira strapped on their own makeshift armor, forced to use what was on hand from the wolfmens' armory. They found little that fit Ymira, but Peter hoped his illusions could hold up and protect them well enough.

Shouts echoed from outside the keep, the vibration of launching ballistae rumbling through the rock. Dust fell overhead.

The battle had begun.

"What's our plan?" Peter asked. So far, they'd determined a siege ladder would be lowered for them in a discreet corner of the keep. Beyond that their plan was. . . undetermined. He was not particularly fond of such plans.

How *were* they supposed to save these children? It wasn't

that he didn't want to save them, only that he saw no way they could actually pull this off. He'd run enough cons over the years to know a gamble when he saw one.

And theirs was a losing wager.

"Your primary task is to keep an illusion up at all times," Hasani explained. "I'll see what I can do to separate any children from the ranks and get them to Ymira for healing."

"And how long will that take?" Peter asked.

The two looked between each other with pursed lips.

His breath hitched. "How long?" he demanded.

Ymira shook her head. "It depends. With Jill it hadn't taken long since she'd just been infected but—"

"But what?" *Saints alive.* How many children could they actually save? He had half a mind to march back up top and demand Jill reassign them.

"I don't know." Ymira refused to meet his gaze.

Heat seared his chest. "Dammit Ymira, what do you mean you don't know?" Panic edged its way into his voice as he stepped forward, reaching out to shake her.

A strong hand caught his wrist before he could do so. "You will keep your hands off her." Hasani's glare could have severed a man's head from its shoulders. Peter shook off his grip and stepped back.

Ymira looked small, her eyes wide as she stared at the ground, shrinking into herself.

"You two haven't ever fought before, have you?" Peter ground out. Of course this was his luck. Stuck on the frontlines with two rookies. It didn't matter if they had magic on their side, without battle experience, their task was doomed before it even began. Not that he had any battle experience, but he'd been in more fights than he could count.

"We'll figure it out," Hasani assured.

"Like hell you will! Do you understand what we're up

against? Do you understand that one wrong move and we're all dead?"

"We'll go without you if you're that afraid," Hasani said. "We can handle ourselves."

Peter huffed, trembling with fear and anger. It couldn't end this way. It couldn't. Not when he was so close to understanding how to save Liza. He had to make it back to her; he had to see her again. If she thought he'd abandoned her . . .

"You won't last five minutes out there without an illusion." His voice was a knife. "I'll go with you but *listen* to me. I've lived through enough fights to know my way around a battlefield."

Hasani stared at him, his polished onyx horns gleaming in the blue-fire torch light. He gave a reluctant nod.

"Ymira?"

The girl stared at the floor as if she hoped she might melt into it, her chest rising and falling rapidly.

"Ymira, you need to get it together." He knelt in front of her, forcing her to meet his eyes. "We will keep you safe. Just focus on healing whoever you can, all right?"

She nodded, though she still looked dazed.

Another explosion reverberated through the keep.

"Time to go."

Ten minutes later they were climbing down a rickety wooden ladder as a freezing wind pelted their backs. Peter kept the illusion in place as he descended, crafting it to look like the keep wall as it should have looked without three people climbing down a ladder. Essentially, they were invisible. In the middle was Ymira with Hasani following close behind. Unfortunately, only he could see the ladder, leaving them to feel their way down. A slow and grueling process.

Part of him wondered if he should have waited until they were at the bottom to put on the illusion, but he knew if anyone spotted them climbing down, even from where the ladder hid behind an outcropping of stone, their quest would fail.

"Volley!" a voice shouted above the wind.

The sound of a hundred bows snapping and the swish of a hundred arrows piercing the air screeched above them, followed by the muffled thuds of the shafts striking the decaying bodies before they hit the snow.

Peter surveyed the battlefield. Below them, the blackbloods continued marching forward, over the frozen forms of their former loved ones, their minds occupied only with reaching the keep. The blackbloods were only a hundred feet off from the base of the keep's wall. What exactly did they expect to do once they reached it?

He didn't have time to consider. A second later an unearthly howl shook the air around them. A vulgan materialized from shadows at the bottom of the ladder, smashing it out from below them.

Ymira screamed as they all fell.

4 0

DAVID

The blackbloods were nightmares come to life and now there was an army of them descending upon the keep. Their limbs were frostbitten and decayed; many were missing fingers and ears and even their noses. Stringy hair, if they had any, hung from their scalps, and their eyes were ringed in red. Inky black poison spiderwebbed through their veins. Behind them, the vulgan prodded them forward like sheepdogs herding a flock. Eleven total. How many had Bo said there were, twelve? But Jill had killed one in the Deadwood. So, all of them were here.

Ten volleys of flaming arrows had been fired, three rounds from the ballistae. They'd yet to hit a single vulgan, each one disappearing and rematerializing out of the way at the last second. He understood the princess's reasoning, but he worried they would run out of bolts before they'd struck down a single vulgan.

But the distance the vulgan kept made him most uneasy. They stood like sentinels behind the blackbloods as they lumbered forward. Watching. Waiting.

But why?

David fought back the bile in his throat. He fought the instinct that told him to run, to flee, to put as much distance between himself and those creatures as possible. Despite the panic blooming in his chest, he stood his ground, gripping his bow for comfort. It did little to soothe him.

There were so many of them. Hundreds of men, women, and children all turned into creatures of darkness by the vulgan. Could they be saved like Jill, or was it too late for that? Perhaps the more disturbing question, could he shoot an infected person, knowing they might be saved?

Could he end a life even if it meant saving so many more? Was it a mercy to kill them, or to let them live?

The questions troubled him and then he glanced at Jill issuing orders and leading without second thought. She'd almost become one of them. How close had she been to joining their ranks? If she'd turned completely, could he have ended her life to spare her this pain?

He watched the blackbloods as they swarmed the gates of the keep, pounding and clawing at the doors, crushing one another in their fury to beat down the doors.

They had to hold that gate, whatever the cost. How many families waited behind these walls? How many innocent lives would be taken if they did not win this battle here today?

Grimzy appeared at his side. "How are things over here?" Grimzy asked, his breath clouding the air in front of him. He'd been running between the ballistae, delivering orders and seeing to the archers. Though he didn't want to admit it, David had remained positioned close enough to the princess that he could get to her in time if necessary. If this turned south, he would grab her and flee, whether she wanted him to or not.

"The vulgan make no move, which worries me." David returned his attention to the battlefield. The snow had turned black with oily blood and ash. The stench wafted up toward them despite the wind, reeking of sulfur and rot. "What does the princess say?"

Behind them, the other soldiers reloaded another bolt and waited for his command.

"Continue firing arrows but hold off on the ballistae for now. Something feels off. It's like they're waiting for something."

David nodded, turning when screams pierced the silence. Wood splintered and crunched. Something like a battering ram slammed into his chest, sending him flying across the wall.

He somersaulted through the air, wind grasping at the breath in his lungs before he smashed into a wooden crate, pulverizing the box. Pain radiated through his back as he struggled to breathe, his vision tinged with red.

Bleeding Saints.

David lifted his head, his strength suddenly zapped from his body, cracks running up and down his back. He felt another on his head. Thankfully, they were already beginning to heal, but the pain nearly made him pass out.

On top of the keep was a vulgan—no, four vulgan—each one attacking a ballista. The creatures screeched as they swung their flailing limbs, sending men over the side of the keep wall to be devoured by the blackbloods below.

David inhaled, gathering his strength. He had no time to waste. He imagined locking away the pain he felt in a corner of his brain, and then he was up and running, launching himself at one of the vulgan's legs. David drew his blade, slicing at the creature. Grimzy charged at the same time, latching onto another leg. The creature jerked, taken by surprise at the mountain man's sudden attack, and it swayed.

"Archers! Fall back! Flaming arrows!" David called as his forehead began to crack.

The archers fled, some attempting to shoot the creature as they ran. The arrows bounced off the shadowy form, more like annoying splinters than deadly weapons.

Grimzy continued grappling the vulgan's leg while David tried to get beneath it. The creature thrashed and flailed but Grimzy held tight. Sweat slicked his back despite the snow falling from above them. Sticky black blood soon covered David. It reeked of rot and decay, death and nightmares. Still, he slashed at the beast, making sure to stay in its blind spots. Every time it tried to vanish, he stabbed its undersides which seemed to keep it in place. But nothing came close to killing the creature.

How had Jill managed to deliver a killing blow? What had she done differently? *Had* she killed it?

The creature suddenly vanished like smoke and Grimzy tipped forward, now clinging to nothing but air, and slammed into the ground. A bellow loosed from his lips as David whirled about, searching for the vulgan.

The monster materialized behind Grimzy intent on destroying the ballista. David surged forward, dodging and weaving between its legs, slashing its underside, doing everything to keep it distracted.

Out of the corner of his eye he saw Grimzy reach for a barrel full of bolts for the ballista and draw two.

And then the mountain man charged.

41

JILL

The princess of Erinya surrendered to the fight. Adrenaline pumped through her veins, and her blood coursed hot and swift. She was a tidal wave cresting against the shore. She was a battering ram smashing against a barricade. She was a fiery arrow loosed upon a golden summer field. She would blaze the world to the ground.

The vulgan had appeared atop the wall, four of them attacking each of the ballistae. Soldiers fought valiantly, but they were archers first and it showed. She didn't want to think about how many had been thrown over either side of the wall, or about how the ballista she'd guarded had been reduced to a pile of scrap wood. The other three remained, but this one was a lost cause.

One of the vulgan's legs nearly smashed into her and she ducked and rolled, ignoring the sound of a scream slowly lost to the wind as another soul disappeared over the wall. She prayed the soldier died on impact rather than being subjected to the terror of the blackbloods.

Jill jumped to her feet, snow and sweat and blood plastering her clothing to her skin. The tips of her fingers were numb from wielding her sword in the cold, but she pressed on. She swung at the back of the vulgan's leg, barely slicing through the hardened, yet smoky, skin. Black blood dribbled as the monster whirled to face her.

The battle around her seemed to still. Cries and screams dampened to a dull roar. The snow drifted lazily down. Her blood slowed to a rhythmic thrum. The vulgan, though it had no eyes she could see, seemed to stare at her, to single her out even as other soldiers attacked its flank. It paid them no heed.

It wanted *her*.

Like a strike of lightning the vulgan moved, lunging for her with those spindly claws. She barely had time to react as she threw up her sword to block. The vulgan easily knocked it away, throwing Jill off balance from the force of the hit. She stumbled back several steps before landing on the ground with a thud, barely catching herself in time. Pain shot up her wrist, but she refused to acknowledge it.

The vulgan struck again, and this time she was too slow. She leaned back, narrowly avoiding being decapitated by its razor-sharp claws, but they dragged across her neck, slicing into the soft skin there and drawing blood.

In any other situation, she would have been crippled by the pain that burst through her body. Instead, she rose, blood dripping down the front of her tunic. It was barely more than a scratch. Any deeper and she'd be dead. But she wasn't dead yet. She could still fight.

She swung her sword furiously, rivaling the speed of the wind that swirled snow around her. She was fast. She was strong. She was fury. And she would fight until her last breath.

She swung her sword at the creature, every impact on the

vulgan's shell-like exterior shuddering up her arms so violently she feared her bones would shatter. Adrenaline surged through her, forcing her to move faster. Her singing blood ignored the scent of death and rot on the wind; it ignored the screams of the dying; it ignored the overwhelming fear for her friends who fought on different parts of the battlefield.

She existed only in this moment. And then the next. And the next. The vulgan did not relent, increasing the speed of its attacks. It towered over her, lunging and snapping, swiping those claws, growling and shrieking like a hunting hound that could not capture its quarry.

But she was slowing and the vulgan was not. She didn't think her heart could possibly beat any harder. Her sweat dripped on the ash-colored snow melting beneath her boots. Another strike came at her. She was too slow and the vulgan's claws scraped her face and sent her hurtling to the ground.

Her vision went dark as pain seared through her. The scent of warm blood overwhelmed every other sense. It drowned her. It covered her eyes, her nose, her mouth. The taste made her want to gag, to vomit into the snow. But she was suddenly so tired.

She closed her eyes and waited for the end to come, letting the warmth of her own blood soothe her. It would be so much easier to sleep, to let everything go. Someone else could win this battle. Someone else could fight for these people. She'd been delusional anyway. What could an eighteen-year-old princess do against a four-hundred-year-old king with magic to control vile creatures like the vulgan and the blackbloods?

Let the real warriors, the real generals and commanders and soldiers take care of it. Let the Saints' Heirs with their powerful magic save Erinya from the darkness. She would sleep. Perhaps forever.

Then whispered words came to her. *Princess. Traitor. Usurper. Queen.*

Her eyes snapped open.

42

PETER

A scream rent from his chest, lungs burning in the cold. His stomach tumbled as he free fell, fear spiking through his body. He had only seconds before impact.

Then two things happened. Light flooded his vision. It radiated out from him and Hasani and Ymira, then spiraled toward Ymira's bracelets in a blaze that rivaled the sun. The second thing he became aware of was the slowing of his body. He should have landed in the snow already, but he hadn't.

Several more seconds passed, like a blink and a lifetime. Then he hit the powdery snow, sinking several feet deep as pain slammed into his back and reverberated through his entire body. He'd never felt anything more excruciating and yet, he knew he should be dead. His vision blurred as something above him blocked out the sun.

He did not know if his illusion was still in place, if it even mattered. Perhaps his illusions didn't fool these monsters and their dark magic. Was that why they'd been spotted almost immediately? Had they seen through his magic?

Light flashed as he opened his eyes and tried to sit up. Pain blinded him and he was forced back down. Ymira stood at a distance, glowing like some ancient goddess. The flame on her forehead burned white as she shot a beam of light at a vulgan. As the light struck the creature's foreleg, the vulgan released a deafening scream of pain as its flesh began to dissipate.

It tried to strike her, but she sent three more beams of light at it, each one searing some part of the monster's body. Peter clapped his hands over his ears as another scream sounded. Each spot where Ymira's magic struck the vulgan seemed to glow as its body evaporated into ash.

The vulgan screamed angrily at her once more before it melted completely into shadow and darkness.

Ymira stood frozen for a moment, stunned. Like she'd seen a ghost. Like she'd just killed a vulgan. Shivering, she shook herself out of the trance and headed for him, though still clearly disturbed by something.

Peter's body felt numb, in part from the cold but mostly from the fear that had turned his insides to liquid. How close had he come to being devoured? Or being turned into a monster himself?

Ymira appeared at his side, shaking but determined as she dropped to her knees, her hands glowing. Her glowing hands touched his face with the gentleness of a natural born healer as her assessing eyes looked him over before they closed.

Warmth flooded his chest, curling down into his stomach, his legs, and finally into his toes. The feeling reminded him of a bright summer's day on the banks of the Rose River as a child, the taste of blackberry pie, being wrapped in one of Liza's hugs. He felt stronger than he had in ages. He could fend off the entire army. He could do anything.

He tried to rise but a firm yet gentle hand pressed his shoulder down.

"Easy," Ymira said.

His vision cleared a bit. The warmth vanished, replaced with that bitter wind. He stared at the young healer before him.

"Your back was broken in the fall," she said. "Thankfully I was able to use the momentum from our fall to slow us and store up energy to heal us."

"Huh?" he said, the terrain around him still spinning slightly.

"My power uses kinetic energy to heal others. Not only was I able to slow our descent, but I also stored the energy in my bracelets to use for healing."

Peter nodded, pretending to understand what she meant as he became aware of the feeling returning to his legs, the muscles and skin and bones. He hadn't even realized he couldn't feel them until the sensations returned.

"Stay here while I heal Hasani. You took the brunt of the fall, I'm afraid."

He watched numbly as she found Hasani lying in the snow unconscious. Blood dripped from his forehead from where he'd struck it during the fall. Ymira's hands glowed and the light seeped from them into Hasani. He inhaled deeply and his eyes fluttered open.

Ymira released a breath, relief spreading across her face as she leaned down and wrapped her arms around him. The sight sent an ache through him as he thought of Liza, all alone, trapped in a cell he'd built to keep her from hurting anyone. He turned his eyes away from the couple and stood. His body felt lighter than before, but his heart was so much heavier.

He sensed Hasani and Ymira approach him from behind, staring out at the battlefield. He wondered about the first Saints. They had risen to defeat the dark power that now threatened the land once more. He knew much of their heroics, like many, but little of the people themselves. Were they ever as terrified as he felt staring out at the horde from the pits of hell? Or were they the brave, fearless heroes legend made them out to be? He wondered if Hasani and Ymira were thinking the same things, or if they were far braver than he was. After all, he'd been running his whole life.

Running from his family. From the memories that haunted him.

Hasani clapped a hand on his shoulder. "We must keep moving or we'll freeze."

Peter nodded, well aware Hasani was not referring to the cold. They stepped forward as one, making straight for the swarm of nightmares.

Peter crafted a new illusion to make them invisible as they drew closer to the blackbloods. Not one of the creatures looked in their direction, and unease swirled through him. They clawed against the keep gates, shoving into each other, pressing closer and getting more riled the more crowded the entrance became. It was like watching a pack of feral dogs fighting over scraps of food. They gnashed and clawed and growled, pushing and shoving.

"Jill wants us to run straight into that?" Peter asked.

"Do you question her?" Hasani asked with a raised brow.

Peter's only response was a muffled humph as he trudged forward, if only to keep his blood flowing. They drew closer, until they stood a mere ten feet away from the horde, not daring to go further until they were sure they spotted a child among the ranks.

The sound of snapping bones rang out and black gore squelched into the snow. Peter's stomach curdled. In this hellish mob, a child was likely to be crushed beneath the ranks of blackbloods.

They walked along the perimeter of the swarm, searching

for any small bodies among the frantic blackbloods. Peter had nearly begun to lose hope when Ymira stopped.

"There," she said, pointing into the swarm.

Sure enough, wedged deep inside he could just barely make out two small children, dirty and blue-fingered as they shuffled forward. He was surprised to see the pair holding hands, though the taller one held a bundle in their arms. From the distance and lack of discernible features, he couldn't make out their genders, but they were indeed children. And they were in the thick of it. If they didn't do something soon . . .

"What do we do?" Hasani asked.

Peter knew the gazelle man was waiting for his plan, but the only way to save those children was to cut down anyone who stood in their path.

"We fight our way through. I'll disguise us as blackbloods. Ymira, you grab the children and then we get the hell out of there."

Peter turned to Ymira who was paler than normal, eyes transfixed on the decaying horde.

"Ymira? Are you with us?" Peter asked, his voice hard.

The girl's eyes cut to him, her focus returning as their gazes locked. She hardened her features before nodding.

They dove into the fray. Peter ignored the sickening lurch of his stomach as he cut down one blackblood after another, inky gore spraying everywhere. He held the illusion as they shoved their way through. He prayed it would be enough, that the blackbloods were too far gone at this point to make sense of one of their own attacking them.

Peter cut his way forward while Hasani guarded them from behind, protecting Ymira with a fierceness that went beyond friendship. The children were only a few feet ahead, blocked by several large blackbloods who must have been fat nobles in their previous lives. Peter cut them down without a second thought, his blade slicing through them like they were made of butter.

"Hasani, grab them!" he shouted, fending off several blackbloods that lunged at them. The illusion held. Apparently, they were not above attacking one of their own.

Hasani rushed forward, lifting the children off their feet as they stared blankly ahead. It was a girl and a boy; Peter could see now. He guessed it was an older sister and her brother, given the way they held each other's hands. Such a human gesture. He prayed they could save the pair.

Peter spun and cut several more blackbloods down. They fell like stalks of grain at harvest. He began backing out of the ranks, still fending off any who might dare attack them until they reached the edge and nearly collapsed in the snow. Thankfully, no other blackbloods seemed to sense their presence and didn't pursue them.

Finally, they turned to examine the two children. Neither could have been older than six. The girl was a few inches taller than her brother, her hair falling out in patches. That inky black poison spiderwebbed through their veins, stark against their pale skin. Both of their fingers, noses, and ears were black with frostbite and their eyes held a hollow, unseeing look.

The bundle in the girl's arm moved, eliciting a small cry.

They all gasped. Ymira reached forward, gently pulling the bundle from the girl's arms. The girl let go without a fight.

It was a baby. Shivering, bony, covered in sores, and looking vaguely blue with black veins. *But alive.*

Rage twisted in Peter's chest. What kind of monster would do such a thing to innocent children?

"Ymira, can you do something?"

"I can try," she said, sounding exhausted but determined. She looked down at the baby in her arms, closing her eyes. She stroked the child's brow, light rising from her bracelets again, flowing into the child where her fingers brushed him. It was like watching a bud bloom into a spectacular flower. The poison in his veins began to lessen, evaporating like steam. His fingers turned from black, to blue, to a healthy white. And then the baby loosed a hearty, wailing cry. He was pink and plump and looked nothing like the monster child Ymira had held only moments before.

Peter heaved a sigh of relief but continued to stand guard, keeping his eye on the ever increasingly violent horde that continued pounding at the gates. Sooner or later, that gate would not be able to withstand the force, and it would come crashing down.

Keep your mind on your own mission. If he'd learned anything recently, it was that the princess wasn't nearly as incompetent as he'd initially thought.

She'll be okay. And with Grimzy and David up there, no harm will come to her.

The thought surprised him. He never imagined he'd care for any royalty, yet he found himself worried for her like he'd worry for a younger sister.

This is taking too long.

"Ymira, I know you're tired, but we have to keep going. You need to heal the other children," Peter ordered. They couldn't afford the time this was taking. Not if they hoped to do more.

Hasani stepped forward, taking the child from Ymira's arms as she turned to the young girl. The flame tattoo on her forehead flickered and burned bright. She took the girl's hands in her own, like a mother might. Her bracelets began to glow once more, the light flowing into her hands and then into the girl's. The girl's skin began to darken, no longer gaunt and pale. Her hair grew back, and the frostbitten fingers returned to their normal color. And then small horns began to sprout from her head, short but curled like Hasani's. He gasped audibly behind them.

At last, the light from Ymira's hands faded and the girl blinked rapidly, as if waking from a dream. She looked around at them, shivering in the rags that adorned her.

"Where am I?" Panic twisted her features as she realized where she was, on a battlefield likely farther from home than she'd ever been. She turned to her brother, monstrous as he stared at his older sister, showing no signs of recognition. The girl's chest heaved as she realized what was happening. "What happened? What did you do to my brother?"

"Ymira, can you put her to sleep?" Peter said, realizing the girl's panic was becoming dangerous.

Ymira nodded then grabbed the girl's hand. She fell asleep instantly and Peter caught her in his arms as Ymira took the boy's hands. Again, light rose from her bracelets and eased away the poison in his veins. His frostbite healed and, like his sister, short horns grew back on his head. The boy collapsed in her arms, his tiny body still skinny and frail despite the healing.

Peter looked between the three children, now healed of their infirmities. The baby looked nothing like the two older children, which he found odd, but he had no time to question it. He glanced at Ymira who looked ready to collapse herself.

"Hasani, get them to safety," Peter said, his voice unyielding. "Ymira . . ." He trailed off as he took note of the heavy bags beneath her eyes. Should he push her? Or should they consider these three children a win and return? Jill would likely be disheartened to learn they'd only been able to save three children. But it was still better than nothing.

Ymira rose to her feet without a single complaint. "Let's keep moving."

43

DAVID

Grimzy's battle cry split the air, shaking the entire keep as he ran at a full sprint straight toward the vulgan, wielding two six-foot bolts like they were little more than toys. Raw, unbridled fear coursed through David's veins at the sight of the furious mountain man.

Power seemed to radiate from Grimzy, flickering around him like lightning in a thundercloud, preparing to strike. David scrambled out of the way just as Grimzy launched himself at the creature, spearing the Vulgan on either side of its body with the bolts.

The creature wailed and screeched as it thrashed against Grimzy, who now stood on the vulgan's forelegs, driving the bolts deeper. Thick smoky blood oozed everywhere as the creature spun and reared back like a horse trying to throw its rider.

Still Grimzy did not let go, his answering bellows rivaling the cries of the dying vulgan. The creature spun one more time, even as its strength was fading, then it released a final ear-splitting cry before it crumpled to the ground.

Grimzy fell before it, his face ashen and covered in blood.

David rushed forward, kneeling before his friend. The man looked paler than David had ever seen him as they watched the vulgan's carcass slowly dissipate into ash and smoke.

"That was incredible," David said in awe. "Are you hurt?"

Grimzy remained frozen, staring at the remains of the creature, wide-eyed and silent.

"Grimzy?"

Still the mountain man remained silent and still. The wind seemed to blow colder, a gale carrying the whispers of death, icy and malevolent. David had never seen Grimzy afraid, could not even comprehend what could terrify such an unflappable fighter.

"Grimzy?" The words scratched against his throat.

"Only the heirs can kill them." Grimzy's voice was barely audible above the cries of battle, above the wind blowing harder now.

David's heart stilled, dread pooling in his stomach. "What?"

Grimzy's gaze turned on David, but the man's expression remained distant, as if he were not really seeing David. "Only the Saints' Heirs can kill the vulgan."

David shook his head, not understanding. "What do you mean? How do you know this?"

"I had a vision. My ancestor, Torryn the Gentle spoke to me. He told me only the Saints' Heirs can kill the vulgan."

"Grimzy, how is that possible? You've been here the entire time." David couldn't explain the fear coursing through his veins. What did this mean if it were true?

The mountain man shook his head, as if he didn't even understand. The prospect of Grimzy not knowing something was enough to make David tremble.

"I think they're still there, the Saints," he said, brows furrowed. "They're trying to communicate with us. When I killed the vulgan just now, it opened a gap between here and the Shadowlands for me to speak with Torryn the Gentle," he pondered aloud.

David's heart continued to hammer. He had no answers for his friend. He surveyed the battlements, watching as men fought valiantly against the creatures. The vulgan tore through the ranks effortlessly, snatching up soldiers and tossing them over the walls or crushing them in their massive claws. The thick and cloying scent of blood hung in the air. The bloodshed would only grow. If these creatures destroyed the gate, then everyone within Fenric's Keep would join the ranks of the blackbloods below or fall prey to their insatiable appetite.

Then something off in the distance caught his attention. Pure, cold terror bolted through his veins. A hundred feet away, Jill lay unconscious on the cold stone. Blood dripped down her face as a vulgan prowled over her, ready to make the devastating final blow.

David was at her side in an instant while Grimzy crashed into one of the vulgan's legs, startling it and sending it back a few feet. David slipped his arms beneath her, carrying her away from the fighting and helping her lean up against a wall. He quickly checked her vitals, ensuring that she was still breathing, despite the blood leaking down her neck. A deep scratch but nothing more, thank the Saints. He leaned forward and wrapped his arms around her as she began to stir.

David had never felt such terror in all his life. When he'd first laid eyes on Jill in the distance, when he'd seen her unmoving and covered in blood, he'd imagined the worst. Imagined the life leeching from her, ounce by bloody ounce. And in that moment, he'd known for certain.

He would fight for her. He would fight with her. And Saints be damned, he'd died with her if it came to that. But he would *not* live without her.

In the corner of his eye, David watched as the vulgan swung a leg at Grimzy, knocking the wind from his chest and disappearing before he could grab it again. It materialized in front of Jill and David. David jumped to his feet, blocking the strike aimed at Jill's head. David whirled and met the monster strike for strike despite its size and strength, forcing the vulgan back.

He felt his arms crack and fracture with every swing of his blade. They'd held together so far, but he could feel himself weakening. On the ground, Jill groaned.

Grimzy charged the beast again from behind, grabbing its back leg and gripping it with all the strength he could muster. Then he wrenched and twisted as hard as he could, ripping the leg free from the creature's body like one tears a leg from a crab.

The vulgan screeched like an animal caught in a trap. Grimzy tossed the leg away as it began smoking and dissolving to ash.

At last, the vulgan turned to him. David sensed the anger the creature felt, and that rage curled toward Grimzy like a physical entity. Solid shadow lunged at the mountain man, snapping its teeth at his exposed throat. Grimzy barely dodged in time, the vulgan's bite missing his neck by mere inches. The creature stilled with its back to the keep's edge, staring at the mountain man.

David glanced back at Jill.

I must protect her. No matter what.

The vulgan stepped toward Grimzy, bloody saliva dripping from its razor-sharp teeth. A second later Grimzy charged, tackling the vulgan over the side of the wall, hurtling toward the ground and the horde of blackbloods below.

That shook Jill from her daze, and she launched forward, a scream wrenching from her throat as their friend fell.

David watched in frozen terror. And he recalled his vision from the night in the Enchanted Wood. That feeling of freefall. The hitch in his breath. The surge of fear and adrenaline. The knowledge that he would hit the ground and shatter into a million pieces.

He remained still, his breathing quickening in panicked rasps as Jill ran to the edge of the wall, peering over the side. Images flashed through his mind, quicker than lightning. Running. Falling. Breaking. They repeated themselves, faster and faster.

Running. Falling. Breaking.

Running. Falling. Breaking.

"David!"

Her voice was like a siren's call, luring him out of his panic and self-despair. He blinked several times, his breathing still erratic, his heart still hammering faster than he ever thought possible. But his eyes locked with hers and the tightness in his chest began to ease. His muscles unclenched. He inhaled sharply, the cold burning his lungs in a way that reminded him he was alive. For now, at least.

He closed his eyes and forced himself to breathe deeply until his panic ebbed. It felt like a lifetime though it couldn't have been more than thirty seconds. At last, he opened his eyes and jogged forward, meeting Jill at the wall.

For the moment, the vulgan had retreated from the battlements, though every ballista but the one they now stood by had been demolished.

Somehow, whether because he was a mountain man, a Saints' Heir, or simply because he was Grimzy, their friend had survived the fall with hardly more than a few scratches. Now he stood, battling the vulgan with a ferocity that frightened even the surrounding blackbloods.

As David looked closer though, he saw smaller movements flitting around the creature's legs. *Animals*. Grimzy had summoned them to his cause and now they fought with him. As Grimzy fought head-on with the vulgan, the animals focused on attacking from the rear. A cougar attacked one leg as a wolf attacked another. Birds of prey swooped down and scraped at the creature with their massive talons. David didn't know where they'd come from, but he felt grateful his friend was not completely alone.

The vulgan's movements grew frenzied, panicked as the creature fielded attacks from every side. Still Grimzy pounded into its flesh with his massive fists, then wrapped his hands around the creature's throat as it thrashed against him.

But even from this distance David could tell Grimzy was flagging. He'd fought with the man enough times to know. And if he fell down there among all those creatures of darkness, that would be it for him. He would die.

Without another thought, David raced to the ballista, loading a bolt. A calculated risk, but a risk, nonetheless. Once the bolt was loaded and ready to fire, he took aim. It wasn't quite the same as archery, and he had only one shot. If he missed, he could hit Grimzy.

He inhaled sharply and released the trigger. With a whoosh through the cold air, the bolt sped toward the massive vulgan.

It struck the back of the creature's neck, penetrating it. The vulgan loosed a scream of pain, thrashing and wailing as it clawed at the bolt in its neck.

"We have to get down there," Jill said breathlessly.

"How are we supposed to do that? The gate is the only way in and out without ladders," David said.

"There's another way," a low voice said beside them.

They turned to see a wolfman soldier staring at them. It was one of the wolfmen who'd guarded the doors back in the mead hall, Ivan.

"How?" Jill asked, leveling the man with a suspicious glare.

"Come," he said, jogging off.

They followed close behind, David's anxiety growing with each step. He worried about Grimzy, about Jill. And about himself. The strikes from his fight with the vulgan earlier had cracked his forearms but nothing had broken. He could feel his body healing itself, scars taking the place of those cracks, the scar tissue knotting together into something grotesque, he was sure.

The wolfman led them through a doorway and down a stairwell. They hit the ground floor of the keep but the stairs continued spiraling deeper. David cast a glance at Jill.

He could see her energy waning, her eyes sunken and her face pale as blood ran from the wound in her neck. He wanted to say something to her, to encourage her to rest. He'd seen too many soldiers continue fighting with wounds that would not have been deadly, but combined with the strain of battle, eventually claimed their lives.

He kept picturing Jill sprawled on the stone. That image of her bleeding neck would haunt the rest of his days. How close had she come to dying?

At last, they reached the bottom of the stairwell, where tunnels branched off in several directions. Ivan forged ahead without a backward glance, choosing the corridor to the left. Slowly, their path began to wind back upward until they came to stand at an iron door set into a face of rock, barred with an iron rod.

The wolfman lifted the rod and a gust of wind swept in, bringing snow with it. They stood at the base of the mountain, the army of blackbloods off to the side. The gate was near to breaking. Honestly, he was amazed it had lasted this long. Any moment now and they would destroy it and flood the inner hold. And at the center was Grimzy, fighting them back single-handedly. The vulgan still screamed and thrashed, trying to pry the bolt from its neck.

David drew his sword and ran.

Jill and the wolfman followed, crashing into the blackbloods with blades swinging. While the pitiful creatures were numerous, they were weaker than he'd imagined. Their rotting bodies struggled in the snow and ice. He cut through them like they were made of water, each one collapsing to the ground with a heaving sigh, as if grateful to be relieved of duty.

He did not focus on the black blood that coated him. He ignored the scent and the faces of the innocent people he struck down. His only goal was to reach Grimzy.

It was a terrible battle strategy, he knew. To plunge into an army with just a handful of people, but the blackbloods had no ranks, no generals calling for order and lines. They had no weapons but their vicious claws that scratched at him, gliding across his hardened skin.

Still, David, Jill, and Ivan plunged deeper, getting closer to Grimzy with every step. He and Jill moved as though they had been fighting together for years. Rarely had he encountered a companion that he fought alongside so effortlessly. She seemed to read his mind, whirling and striking before a blackblood could reach him, and he did the same for her.

It was a dance of vile bloodshed. David could not look into the eyes of those he slayed, knowing what he'd find. He would see carpenters and hunters and mothers and fathers and ordinary people whose lives had been taken from them far too soon. He would see people from all races and stations and backgrounds who'd fallen victim to Malum's wicked schemes.

They fought on, slowly moving toward the center of the battlefield. His skin was cracked and aching, his lungs burned, and sweat bled down his face and neck, mixing with the blood splattered on him.

He noticed Jill's movements slowing. A dozen cuts and scratches covered her, each one seeping blood. Her determined expression was slowly fading, her fire likely giving way to exhaustion. But the horde surrounding them did not let up. They'd slain hundreds of blackbloods, but it wasn't enough. The battle raged on.

Jill slowed a bit, locking eyes with him amid the carnage. If something did not change, if some sort of help did not come, they would die here on this battlefield. David nodded just slightly, and she did as well. If they were to die here, they would do so together.

David swung his sword, slicing a blackblood across the chest, when the wind seemed to shift suddenly. A sudden vortex of air and snow swept past him, swirling toward Ivan. David paused, staring at the wolfman who stood in the middle of that vortex, ice and snow whipping around him, his face clenched in concentration. Then with an outward motion of his hands, the ice flew, freezing every blackblood within a hundred-foot radius of them. In an instant, the commotion surrounding them stopped.

The blackbloods stood like ice sculptures in a statuary, solid and unmoving. Jill's eyes were as wide as his felt. They both turned to Ivan, whose hands remained outstretched as his chest heaved.

"How?" Jill croaked, staring at the soldier.

The wolfman refused to meet her eyes. "I don't know."

Jill glanced back at David, that knowing look in her eyes. Another of the Saints' Heirs. They seemed to be falling into their laps. It felt too suspicious, too easy. After Kylian and the Order had searched for so long, why would so many appear just when they were needed most? Unless that was exactly the point.

He would have to ask Grimzy when he got the chance. The man seemed to know more than his fair share about the Saints' Heirs.

Grimzy.

He spun, searching for the mountain man. He was still a short way off, still fighting the vulgan, though he seemed to be wearing it down.

David, Jill, and the wolfman soldier sped through the frozen statues, racing toward the mountain man now covered in blood. Around him, animals lay dead, the wolf and the cougar bleeding out even as they continued fighting. Several of the smaller animals were smears of blood and fur in the snow.

Grimzy jumped toward the vulgan, grabbing onto the bolt still protruding from its neck. With visible effort, he yanked it out of its neck, leaving it half-decapitated. Smoke curled from its neck as it toppled to the ground. Its body heaved and shuddered. Grimzy dropped to his knees.

An explosion ripped through the air.

David's stomach dropped as he spun to the rear of the battlefield. He wasn't sure what he'd expected, but the sight made his jaw drop.

Bo stood at the back of the blackbloods' ranks, surrounded by a swirling mass of shadow that lifted her into the air, high above the battlefield. Despite the shadows that wrapped around her, her skin and eyes glowed with an otherworldly light.

To his side, Grimzy and Ivan both rose into the air, raised by some invisible force, their eyes and skin glowing as well. David scanned the battlefield, watching as several more figures rose into the air on pillars of glowing light that flowed beneath them like a waterfall, shimmering and sparkling in the darkness.

He sucked in an awed breath. He saw Peter and Hasani and Ymira. He saw Bo and Grimzy and Ivan and—incredibly—Lyra. All of them rising together as one, glowing with ethereal beauty.

It was like the magic of the Saints' Heirs was connecting somehow, coming together to launch an attack. Each of them shot toward a vulgan. Each one struck like they'd practiced years for this singular moment. Hasani dove for one of the creatures beside the wall while Ymira swept toward another. Bo surged forward, the only one surrounded by shadow instead of light as she fought a vulgan at the rear. Each Heir followed suit, fighting and diving and attacking the creatures.

The mass of blackbloods began to flee. They turned back, stumbling toward the forest, freed from whatever control the vulgan had over them. The vulgan batted at the Saints' Heirs like one might bat at flies.

Bo launched her shadows while Lyra seemed to be sending blasts of music. Hasani sent streams of green poison while Ymira sent bolts of light.

His stomach tumbled as the realization hit him. *Lyra's an heir.*

Then as one, the vulgan dissipated, vanishing into shadow and transporting themselves away.

And just like that, the battle was over. The blackbloods ignored David and Jill and everyone else on the battlefield as they fled. Some of the creatures collapsed, unmoving. Others were trampled in their attempts to flee.

Silence loomed, oppressive compared to the ringing in David's ears. His heart still pounded as he watched the remainders of Malum's army disappear into the tree line. His breathing was labored as he sank to the ground.

While he fought, he could withstand the stench of rot and decay. Now, as his heart slowed and chest eased, the scent became unbearable.

Jill dropped beside him, staring at the figures in the distance making their way toward them. He could see them all now.

Bo and Kylian. Lyra and Asif and Zyla. All of them were here.

Thundering footsteps sped past them as Ymira raced toward the group. The motion caught their attention and then Zyla rushed toward her sister. The sisters crashed into each other's arms, collapsing into the snow as tears flowed down their cheeks. Kylian and the others were close behind and soon they had all convened. Hugs and handshakes were exchanged all around as David watched with something like awe.

They were alive. They were alive and together. He rose to his feet and glanced at Jill, still sitting in the snow and staring at everyone with tears glistening in the corners of her eyes. Behind her stood Ivan, his face complacent as he watched everyone with keen eyes.

They had won this battle, but something didn't quite sit right with him. Yes, the vulgan and blackbloods retreated, but they weren't defeated, not by a long shot. They'd be back, likely stronger and more numerous than before. They had only delayed the inevitable.

David turned and offered a hand to Jill, but she refused it, shaking her head and climbing to her feet. He could tell her adrenaline was fading. Her face appeared gaunt and sharp, blood still leaking from the awful wound in her neck. She stumbled forward and David's heart lurched as he raced to catch her before she passed out in his arms.

"Ymira!" He called, panic grappling at his chest. Jill's eyes rolled back in her head, her body going limp in his arms.

Ymira was there in an instant, examining Jill with exhausted eyes. She placed a hand on the princess's neck. Pale light rose from her bracelets, faint and barely there. Still, the light bled into that cut, easing the skin closed.

"She'll be all right. But she's lost a lot of blood," Ymira said, looking nearly as fragile as Jill.

"Come," Grimzy's deep voice said. "Let us return to the keep. I suspect we all have much to discuss." He glanced at Jill, and lightly brushed a hand against her forehead, as tender as David had ever seen him.

"And what of the dead?" Hasani asked, gesturing to the fallen blackbloods all around them.

"We'll deal with them later," Peter said, and David was grateful despite his dislike of the con man. "I think Alpha Volkov will be very interested to learn about all the Saints' Heirs we possess." Peter gave a sidelong glance to the wolfman, who, to his credit, didn't react to Peter's words.

And so, cradling Jill in his cracked and aching arms, David returned to the keep with the others.

4 4

***

MILLIE

$\mathcal{M}$idnight came like a ghost. The large mahogany clock tucked in the corner of the king's room ticked ominously as Millie sat by the embers of a dying fire. She'd spent the last two weeks recovering from her time with the Ohans. For once, she was thankful for Malum's magic, which had sped up her healing with his elixir. Still, she mostly rested and tried to figure out who MG was and why they wanted to talk to her. Either way she determined to be ready.

In her lap she clutched a knife, the jeweled hilt catching the firelight and sending it dancing along the walls.

Soft footsteps sounded behind her, and she disintegrated into spiders, sending them skittering under furniture. She refused to be caught off guard.

"There's no need for that Millie," a familiar voice said. A cloaked woman stepped from the shadows of her room, materializing in the same fashion Malum often did.

She lowered the hood of her cloak, and Millie was suddenly transported back to a hut in the forest where she'd awoken months ago to find Jack threatening the woman before her.

Millie sent her spiders toward the woman, who stared at them unfazed. With her enhanced senses, Millie could smell the woman's emotions, and it was not fear that rolled off her but weariness. This ageless woman before her was tired.

Willing her spiders back together, Millie stood and faced the woman with her knife at her side. She'd once called herself Mother Goose, such a strange name, yet it somehow fit her.

"Why are you here?" Millie asked, glancing around. Would Malum be watching them now?

"He can't see us," Mother Goose said, reading her thoughts. "I have my own magic too."

Millie wasn't sure what she meant by that but filed the information away for later. "Why did you send that note?" Outside, the wind lashed snow against the window.

Mother Goose stepped forward, her face sagging as she slumped into a nearby chair. The embers cracked, echoing in the large room. Millie remained standing, uncertain if she should follow this woman's lead or not.

"Have you ever played rosepin, Millie?" Mother Goose asked, staring into the fire. It flickered against her face, painting it in haunting shadow and garish light. The woman looked leaner than when Millie had last seen her, her bones pressed against her skin and the hollows beneath her eyes deeper and darker.

"Rosepin?" Millie knew the game, but she'd never been good at it. It was a four-person game with four different corners on a board, each belonging to one of the players. The objective was simple—take all four corners of the board before your opponents did. Each player had twelve pins, not including the coveted rosepin, which stood at the center. Whoever retrieved the rosepin first was most likely to win. But it could be stolen by the other players, making the game more complex. Millie still recalled watching Doon play nearly a three-hour game with the other stable hands.

"Yes," Mother Goose said, "Have you ever played it?"

Millie wasn't sure what the woman hoped to gain by asking such a question. "I have a few times, but I never quite had the mind for it." In truth, she'd never won a single game. Once, her brother had beaten her in less than ten minutes. After that Millie vowed never to play again.

"Few do. Rosepin has many moving parts, requiring many tactics and strategies. Keeping track of it all can be a challenge." The old woman looked up at Millie. "Our kingdom has become a game of rosepin, with each opponent fighting for control of the land. But I fear there will be no winners."

Millie's blood pulsed beneath her skin and a shiver slid its cold finger down her spine.

"Why have you come here?" Millie asked again, more forcefully this time. She needed to know what threatened Erinya.

"Malum seeks revenge. Ohan-Jin seeks power. The princess seeks justice. What do you seek, Millie?" Mother Goose's gaze penetrated Millie, pinning her feet to the floor.

What did she seek? Once, the answer to that question would have been simple. She'd sought to free her brother. Then Jack came swooping in, looking like the most beautiful bad decision. He'd charmed her, saved her, and stolen her heart. But Malum had corrupted him, stealing his mind and body.

"In rosepin," Mother Goose continued, "people often move quickly, seeking to gain control as soon as possible, hoping a strong offense will win them the board. And sometimes that strategy works, if the other players are too timid to fight back. But I've often found that it is the calculated thinker, the patient player, the one who waits for others to make a mistake that often wins the game." Mother Goose rose to her feet again. "When players are not too afraid to fight back, when they fight together to overtake the oppressor, the aggressive opponent stands no chance."

Millie swallowed, staring at the woman. They were the same height, with similarly dark skin and yet they were so different.

"You think I should leave then?" Millie's voice cracked. Jack had given up so much for her, could she really abandon him to Malum? Surely, she could save him somehow, banish Malum back to the darkness where he came from. But she hadn't forgotten what Zillah had told her.

"I did not say that." Mother Goose gave her a sad smile and reached to cup her face. It was a strange sensation, the woman's calloused skin brushing against hers. Millie felt wet tears sliding down her face, though she wasn't sure when she'd started crying. "You have been so brave Millie. You have come such a long way from that timid girl who entered the tournament. This weight is heavy, and I wish it did not have to fall to you."

The words were an echo of what Zillah had told her.

"How can I just leave him?" Her voice was a shaking breath, a plea to some higher being that she would be spared from such a decision. That she would be spared from such heartbreak. "Everyone's left him. How can I do the same?"

Mother Goose gripped Millie's hands tightly in hers. "You're not the only one who has had to watch a loved one make horrible choices. Malum is my brother."

The floor tilted beneath her. She recalled a conversation long ago when Malum had called Mother Goose his sister. It was a memory blurred by feverish dreams and pain. How had she forgotten?

"So, Millie, I ask again, what do you seek?"

Millie inhaled, wiping the tears from her cheeks. She thought of Keyanna and her son. She thought of her brother and Master Ravala. She thought of all the families torn apart in Malum's quest for revenge.

But the princess is your ally, not your enemy. You must find her. Only together do you stand a chance.

Zillah's words were a phantom in her mind, a haunting cadence that dominated her thoughts. She had replayed them over and over since she'd been rescued.

"I seek peace." It was all she'd ever wanted. It was why she'd spent her life trying to remain quiet and unnoticed. But peace couldn't be achieved by standing still and allowing injustice. You had to fight for it. And she'd vowed to protect those who couldn't protect themselves. "And—" she swallowed. "The only way we will have peace is if Malum is gone for good."

Millie's heart shattered again as the words left her lips. Would it ever stop breaking? Would it ever stop hurting? Her chest ached like she'd been stabbed, and a fresh wave of tears rolled down her cheeks.

Mother Goose nodded. "I'd hoped you would say that. As we speak, rebels in the city lead people to safety outside the Citadel."

Millie thought of her vision from weeks ago, the one she surely must have imagined. How was that possible?

"The people have heard how you stepped in to save Keyanna, how you stood against the king's men. Already rumors spread of the rebellious paladin who's come to save us."

The heat drained from Millie's cheeks. "But I'm not—I'm not a hero."

"Maybe not yet," Mother Goose said with a smile. "But

you will be. So, Millie Muffet, will you help us? Will you help free the Citadel from Malum?"

Time seemed to slow around her, the heat from the fire suddenly became unbearable. Seconds stretched out before her and all she could hear was the hammering of her own heart slamming against her ribcage like it was trying to break free of her chest.

She blinked and everything slowed to normal speed. She would leave Jack and save the people. But she *would* come back for him.

"I'll do it."

"Wonderful," Mother Goose said. "Let's go."

PETER

They had managed to save thirteen children in total. Thirteen out of hundreds. The number felt far too small, and yet Peter could not imagine how they could've saved any more. Their plan had worked. With the help of his illusions, they'd located children among the ranks of blackbloods, pulled them out, and healed them. Whatever dark magic had turned these poor souls into creatures of the living dead, Ymira's magic could reverse it. He'd watched the process again and again, still unable to reconcile the monsters with the children she'd breathed new life into. Now if only he could find a way to get Ymira to see Liza.

A knot formed in his stomach as he thought of his wife. He'd hated putting her in that cell, leaving her alone in the dark. But he'd had no other choice. He could not lose her. Not after. . .

He shook his head, mind returning to the present issue. He, along with Grimzy and Hasani, led the children inside the keep after the battle, attempting to find a place for them to rest.

Many of them were confused, with holes in their

memories. A few were young enough that they could not recall their names or ages. Among them was the baby who'd belonged to the slain couple Jill and David knew. As despondent as David had been after the battle, he'd taken one look at the baby, Fyre, and told him the child's parents were dead, but he'd seemed relieved the child had not joined their dark fate.

Thirteen children. No more frostbitten fingertips, cuts, or bruises. No more hair falling out in clumps, or flesh rotting atop their bones. Not even bags under their eyes remained, though they were surely exhausted. All thanks to Ymira.

Yet he could see that strange, haunted look in their eyes. As they walked through the vast halls of Fenric's Keep, the children didn't laugh or cry or even whisper to each other. They followed directions without protest, plodding along as if they still marched within an infantry.

It was unnerving. He knew little of children. He had a brother nearly two decades younger than him but no children of his own. But he knew they were generally loud—full of energy and life and vigor. Sure, they had different personalities. All people did, no matter how young they might be. Some kids were brave and stubborn, some were shy and reserved, some were mean and told rumors, some made jokes and pulled pranks. He'd yet to meet a child who did as instructed the first time without protest.

But these children walked with near silent footsteps, eyes never straying from the path ahead. They may have been healed bodily, but something had clearly happened to their minds. Would they ever recover, or was it simply a matter of time? Did the length of time they were turned have any effect on how far gone their minds were? What would that mean for Liza? There were too many questions and no answers.

"These children will likely want to remain close to each

other," Grimzy said, interrupting his spiraling thoughts. "We'll want to find a room large enough to house all of them."

Peter only nodded, too tired for speech. Ahead he spotted Prince Tiernan, sword on his hip, striding toward them with wide eyes.

"Is everyone all right?" He glanced between them and the silent troupe of children.

"For now, yes." Grimzy's deep voice was calming and melodious. At the sound of it, several kids seemed shaken from their stupor and turned to him expectantly. For just a moment, the veil seemed lifted from their eyes, as if they finally realized where they stood.

"Where is the princess? I saw her enter the battlefield and I—" he swallowed, a look of concern and awe on his face. "Is she all right?"

Peter raised a brow at the young prince. Jill's betrothed. Such a strange turn of events.

"She's fine. Exhausted, and she lost a lot of blood, but she'll be all right," Peter explained. "Thanks to Ymira's healing."

"And who will care for Ymira?" Hasani asked, an edge to his voice.

"Many healers here will be able to aid her, though they do not possess the same magic," Grimzy rumbled, once again soothing everyone around him. "In fact, we should take these children there now to be inspected for further wounds."

Peter nodded but he wasn't sure healing existed for the types of wounds these children had endured.

"Peter, may I have a word?" Prince Tiernan asked as Grimzy and Hasani herded the children off to the hospital wing of the keep.

Peter resisted the urge to release a deep sigh. More than anything he wanted a strong drink and a long sleep. He wasn't sure he had it in him to make conversation with anyone now, let alone an upbeat, optimistic noble like Tiernan.

"Of course," he answered, unable to completely mask his fatigue. Maybe the elf man would take a hint. Where Tiernan had been during the battle he wasn't sure, but he seemed unscathed both physically and mentally, Peter wagered he hadn't seen much of the fighting up close.

Tiernan clapped a hand on his shoulder, sending an ache down Peter's arm. Right. The man was an elf. Stronger. Faster. More stamina. Perhaps he'd seen the battle, and it had barely winded him.

Peter followed him down a corridor, this one wider than many of the others in the keep, more formal than the rest, carpeted with thick red rugs and lined not with blue fire torches but lanterns that held strange orbs of glowing glass within. He'd seen them a few times in Carthesia and Welynn, their technology evolved beyond Erinya's more primitive ways.

Guards lined the corridor as well, broken up by the odd tapestry or out-of-place vase on a pedestal. Their pace slowed and Peter eyed the prince, whose face had turned thoughtful.

"Am I right in assuming that you and the princess are close?" Tiernan asked. His tone held no suspicion but the curiosity lingering in his voice pressed into Peter.

"I've known the princess no longer than a month and a half."

"But you are friends, are you not?" Tiernan asked, his voice a little more forceful this time.

"I suppose so. Though in truth she forced me into aiding her. Tied my hands really." The princess was far more capable than he'd first believed. When he'd met her that night in his pub he was underwhelmed, despite the stories he'd heard about her. In truth, he hadn't fully believed her story until he arrived in the Whitesaw Mountains. She'd been so unsure of herself then, timid and strange. So different from the woman he'd just witnessed charging into a battle of blackbloods with only two others at her side.

"She fought valiantly," Tiernan said, a lingering uncertainty in his voice. He stood there a moment, as if waiting for Peter to say something.

"She did."

Several more seconds of awkward silence passed between them. Peter crossed his arms, catching the sight of movement from behind the prince. David approached, his footsteps slowing as he spotted them.

"I'm sure you're aware of the arrangement between us," the prince said slowly.

"The knowledge has reached me." Peter had to work hard to keep the sarcasm from his voice and he still wasn't quite sure he'd managed it. He had little desire to stand around discussing arranged marriages with this man, least of all when David was within earshot.

Tiernan finally locked eyes with him. "Do you think, if I asked—properly asked her that is—that she would still agree to marry me?"

Behind him, David stiffened, then spun on his heel and walked away.

Peter crossed his arms. He really, *really*, didn't want to be having this conversation. "I honestly wouldn't know."

"But you're friends. Do you think—"

"I think you will have to ask her yourself. Despite your insinuations, I have no interest in the princess romantically. She is a strong woman, but certainly not my type." She wouldn't have been his type even if he weren't married. Nothing was wrong with Jill, but she wasn't Liza. But he didn't feel like explaining that to this stranger. "If you'll excuse me."

He gave a curt nod and strode off, eager to be free of the elf prince.

Ahead of him, David walked briskly, fists clenched. Peter strolled up beside the man, casually tucking his hands in his pockets. David barely spared him a glance.

"How is the princess?"

"Better now." David's tone was both harsh and strained.

"I bet you were worried."

"As worried about her as I was anyone else." He shrugged but it seemed little too forced.

"I'm sure."

"She's my comrade, my princess, and hopefully one day, my future queen. Of course I was worried about her."

"Of course," Peter said. He didn't look at David nor did he dare imply anything more. Much as he wanted to mess with the man, they'd been through too much that day. And yet . . . "Have you carried many comrades off the battlefield before?"

David's jaw tightened, the scars on his face bulging and whitening. "No."

Peter nodded but still, he didn't look at the man. Told himself he didn't care. But he saw the looks between Jill and David. Saw the hurt that flashed in her eyes when David ignored her, saw the way he remained stiff and formal around her. He was surprised a young woman as pretty as the princess would look past the ugliness of the scars adorning David's face. Just another thing that told him she wasn't nearly as shallow as he'd once thought.

"Well, it was kind of you."

David nodded absentmindedly. "I suppose." He paused midstride, then turned to Peter. Peter raised a brow and stopped. "I thought—" he cleared his throat, "Forgive me, I thought that you and her—but then back there you said you didn't—"

Peter was surprised to see the hunter at such a loss for words.

"Jill's been a good ally and friend. But frankly, I prefer my wife."

David's brows shot up. "Oh."

Peter smirked. "Yes. But even if I felt for her in that way, why would you care? After all, she's just a comrade."

David pursed his lips then continued walking forward. *Good,* thought Peter. *Let him stew.* He didn't have much desire to get in the middle of this, but he liked David, and he liked the princess, despite his initial instincts. Maybe he wanted to see them happy. Too bad Tiernan had just made his intentions crystal clear.

Saints he hated this sort of drama. But he'd be lying if there wasn't something mildly amusing about it.

"I messed up," he said, his voice barely above a whisper. "I don't know how she could ever forgive me."

"Maybe she won't," Peter said, shrugging. "But who knows."

JILL

Alpha Volkov and Prince Tiernan stared at Jill and Grimzy. David stood slightly behind her, leaving more space between them than she would have liked. Ivan, the wolfman they'd discovered was a Saints' Heir, stood beside them, head bowed to his Alpha in respect and subjugation. After their injuries and the children had been seen to, Alpha Volkov had immediately called a meeting, and though Jill could barely stand upright she'd acquiesced, although she remained covered in her own dried blood.

"You mean to tell me your group has among you six of the Saints' Heirs and one is among my own ranks?" Alpha Volkov said evenly. His jaw ticked and Jill was sure he was barely keeping hold of his temper.

Despite that, Jill's heart pounded sluggishly in her chest, as if her body no longer had enough blood to propel her to fear him. She nodded, too tired to speak.

Tiernan didn't look angry but thoughtful, one hand stroking his chin. "This changes things, Aleksandr," Tiernan said, glancing at Jill then the Alpha. She was surprised to hear the prince call the Alpha by his first name. She hadn't realized how close they must have been.

The Alpha leaned forward, pressing his hands into his desk. He started to speak, then his attention suddenly shifted to Ivan. To his credit, the young wolfman did not flinch beneath the Alpha's severe gaze.

"How long have you known about your magic?"

"It has only been a few months, Alpha." Ivan's head remained bowed.

"Have you told anyone of your gifts?"

"No, Alpha."

"And why not?"

Ivan visibly swallowed, the first sign he was not as fearless as he pretended to be. "I recalled the stories of the great apothecaries who were eliminated for fear of their magic. I did not wish to meet that same fate."

Several heavy seconds of silence filled the room. At last, the Alpha seemed to come to a decision in his mind. He stood up straight and folded his arms across his chest, turning his analyzing gaze on Jill once more before looking at Grimzy.

"Paladin Grimzy, you say your people have many tales of the rise of the new Saints, correct?"

Grimzy nodded. "Yes, Alpha."

"And you claim your brother is host to the ancient Black King Malum?" Alpha Volkov asked, his gaze returning to Jill.

"Yes." Her voice shook and her knees began to wobble. Sleep called to her, yet she saw no way out of this meeting.

Tiernan suddenly stepped around the desk toward her. Her legs finally gave out and the prince caught her before turning back to the Alpha. "Aleks, she can barely stand, can this discussion wait a day at least?"

Jill's face heated. She hadn't even known she was about to pass out until Tiernan's arm had slid around her waist, his grip firm and strong. She wanted to pull away, but she wasn't sure she could stand without his aid. Without meaning to, she glanced at David, whose entire body had gone stiff. He refused to meet her eyes.

The Alpha sighed heavily, but his gaze softened just slightly. "Ivan, bring the princess a chair. I don't need her passing out on me. And no, Tiernan, I'm afraid this cannot wait. Not if what she says about the King is true."

Ivan shuffled out and quickly returned with a chair, and Tiernan settled her into it as if he feared she might break. And maybe she would. It made her nauseous, but she didn't resist.

"Thank you," she said, forcing a small smile.

His returning smile was genuine. He was certainly handsome, but . . .

"So, these Saints' Heirs, they are meant to rise to fight Malum?" Alpha Volkov continued as if the interruption had not happened at all.

"Yes," Grimzy answered. "The first Saints arose after Malum stole the magic he now wields. Now that he's returned, they will rise again."

Alpha Volkov sank into the chair at his desk. His expression had turned from angry to pondering. Jill wasn't entirely sure what to make of the man. He was strict and severe, but she suspected it was rooted in a love and devotion to his people. She could respect that.

"Like many, I've heard of the tales of the Saints and the great Battle of Shadows against the Black King, but I'll be the first to admit my knowledge ends there. It was my belief that they defeated the Black King for good, yet you say he's returned. How is that possible?"

Jill sighed. "I'm not certain, but it seems the Black King was never truly destroyed, just imprisoned in between the realm of life and death. My brother Jack—" her voice cracked, suddenly filled with emotion. "He should have died in my mother's womb. But my mother used an apothecary to bring him back. That fractured his soul, and Malum took root within him." She knew it was a sign of weakness, but she could not halt the flow of tears sliding down her cheeks. After all this time, it was still so hard to think of her brother. She'd never gone so long without seeing him. When their world felt unstable, thanks to their father, Jack remained at her side. And yet, she could not help but feel that it may have indeed been better if he'd stayed dead. It was an awful thought.

"I can confirm this." Grimzy said. Saints, what would she do without him? "During the battle, after I slew one of the vulgan, I had a vision of my ancestor, Torryn the Gentle. He told me that only Saints' Heirs can kill the vulgan. The original Saints could not do so during their battle long ago and Malum lived. They could only imprison him. I'm not sure why."

Jill looked up and blinked. Tiernan had remained at her side. She'd seen him a little during the battle. He'd seemed keen to follow her orders and manned one of the ballistae. What did this all mean though? They were no longer engaged, or rather, Jill's father was not around to ensure their engagement.

The Alpha pursed his lips, deep in thought. "If what you say is true," he started slowly, "then we are all in greater danger than I first believed."

Jill tried not to show her annoyance. This was precisely what she'd tried to tell him when she'd first spoken to him.

"Princess, you mentioned the Ohans have terrible weapons. Could you elaborate?" The Alpha asked.

Considering she'd never seen one, let alone seen what they could do, she tried her best to describe them. But the Alpha seemed to understand despite the gaps in her knowledge. Even

Tiernan paled at their explanation. When she finished, they all sat in silence.

"It is possible," Alpha said, "That I've misjudged you, princess. I was curious to see how the battle would go today, and I was surprised how easily you took command. I'll admit, I was impressed. These weapons the Ohans have," he paused, again considering something. "Do you think they could be used against the blackbloods and vulgan?"

Jill swallowed hard. "It seems likely, yes." She felt a bit silly she hadn't considered the idea sooner.

"Then consider this a test, Your Highness. We will help you launch an assault on the Ohans, but we must get our hands on those weapons. They may be the only thing that saves us from Malum."

"And what of the Saints' Heirs?" Tiernan asked.

"Train them if you must. Take some of them with you, though Ivan will remain here. I won't have him risking his life for this mission. But if they couldn't slay the Black King long ago, then I doubt they can do so now." Alpha Volkov waved a hand as if to show just how inconsequential he thought them.

Irritation flared in Jill's chest at the sight of it, but she bit her tongue. She had just secured the very deal she'd hoped to make with the Alpha. She couldn't mess it up now.

"Thank you, Alpha Volkov."

"Don't thank me yet, princess. As I said, this is a test. Secure those weapons. If you do, we will see about a true alliance. If not . . ." He let the threat hang there. Jill couldn't possibly fathom what he might do to her or her friends if they failed, but she understood, nonetheless.

If she failed, her people would fall to Malum.

DAVID

*D*avid tossed and turned on the rickety cot he'd been given. Sleep evaded him as it always seemed to these days. After carrying Jill to the infirmary, he'd shuffled off to what he'd thought had been an abandoned corridor, only to overhear Prince Tiernan and Peter discussing the princess.

David rolled over to his other side as nausea twisted his stomach into knots. Nearby, Asif, Hasani, and Peter rested on similar cots. They'd been shoved into the nearest thing that passed for a room in this part of the keep, but it was closer to the size of a broom closet. Perfect for three grown men plus an adolescent boy. He couldn't complain though. He'd suffered far worse during his time in the army. At least he was dry.

He arched his back and rolled over again, rubbing at the scars on his forearms. They ached constantly what with the never ending fighting they seemed to be doing these days. And then he'd felt them crack even more as he'd carried Jill to safety. He shouldn't have pushed himself, should have let someone else help her. But he couldn't bring himself to let go of her. He'd wanted to hold her, to carry her, to feel the weight of her in his arms just once. Even now he could conjure the feeling of her head resting perfectly in the crook of his shoulder, the way she'd clung to him, as if even unconscious she yearned to be as close to him as he longed to be to her.

Something in his core ignited and he threw off the tattered blanket, rising from his cot. Sleep eluded him anyway. No point lying there yearning for feelings that would never be returned. And now that Prince Tiernan planned to propose . . .

David shoved on his boots and swept out of the room as swiftly and quietly as possible. He needed to clear his head.

The corridors were darker in this part of the keep, blue fire torches flickering every fifty feet or so. Small slits in the stone allowed slivers of light to shine in during the day, but after sunset only the blackness of night, along with a bitter chill, tumbled through them.

He wandered the halls until he found a more brightly lit area, closer to the mead hall as best he could tell. This place had proved to be quite the maze, teeming with endless hallways and corridors, barracks and armories, training areas and several different mead halls. Though at its center was the main hall where the Alpha met with his generals and diplomats. Where they would meet with him in the morning. Although he, Jill, and Grimzy had met with the Alpha earlier, it seemed that was just the beginning of many, many meetings.

David rounded another corner, and his breath caught. Somehow, he'd found a large room with a blazing hearth, where Jill sat wrapped in a blanket on an emerald settee. Her unbound auburn hair cascaded down her back. It had grown in the time they'd spent apart, and he couldn't help but notice how the red seemed to catch the firelight and dance around her head in a sort of angelic halo.

His fists clenched as something in his chest tightened. He should go. He shouldn't disturb her. She looked so peaceful and he, well, he couldn't stand the thought of looking into those eyes and seeing the hurt he'd caused.

He turned on his heel, but his boot scuffed against the ground.

"David?"

He froze even as his insides warmed. *Go,* his mind said. But his body refused to move.

He turned back to face her. "Sorry, Your Highness. I didn't mean to disturb you. I was just leaving."

Her face fell. "You don't have to," she said, her voice barely above a whisper.

"Well, I'd hate to keep you awake. You should be resting." David searched for an excuse even as he scanned her for injuries. She looked tired in a way he'd never seen before, as if the weight of the world rested on her shoulders. And in a way, he supposed it did.

She turned back to the fire, pulling the blanket tighter around her. "I know. But I can't."

David's palms started to sweat. He felt like a deer in the line of fire, unable to move even though he knew he should flee.

"Please stay," she said.

His body responded before he did, and he found himself sitting down beside her, carefully putting some distance between them even as he longed to close the gap.

For a while they sat in silence, watching the flames crackle and burn. Absent-mindedly, he rubbed at the scars on his forearms again, massaging the ridges of tissue that bulged and knotted into something resembling gnarled tree branches.

Every once in a while, he wondered how people saw him, the soldier covered in scars. He didn't often have access to a mirror, but when he did, he usually refused to look at himself. He wasn't a vain man, but the sight of his scars still made him cringe in shame. After nearly three years of this dreadful curse, he resembled a monster more than a man. Yet somehow, Jill saw past all of that.

Jill broke the silence as she nodded to his scars. "Do they hurt?"

He swallowed. "A bit." He dared not tell her that his forearms took much longer to heal after he carried her. At that moment, he hadn't cared. He still didn't. He would do it again. But he feared how it might make her feel to know she'd hurt him.

"I never said thank you," she said, turning back to the fire. "For coming back. For saving me from the blackbloods. And then again, during the battle."

"No thanks necessary," he said, then added, "Your Highness."

"You don't need to call me that," she said sharply, turning to meet his gaze.

Their eyes locked and his heart lurched. The light from the fire matched the burning in her gaze.

She didn't understand the sort of power she had over him, even now as rage threatened to boil over. Discreetly as he could, he inched away from her. Distance. He needed distance.

She caught the movement all the same and her head spun back to the fire, a stiffness replacing her relaxed position from a moment ago.

"Is this how it's to be between us then? You saving me, then avoiding me?"

David pursed his lips. "You know why it has to be this way." Did he know though? Did he understand why every instinct within him warred against his desires? At first, he'd been afraid to follow her, to fall in love with her because he knew she would lead him to his death. But now, given that she would soon be betrothed, it would be beyond improper. And he couldn't hurt her, no matter what they might feel for each other. What he might feel for her.

As much as it killed him, it was better this way.

"Why? Tell me, David. Why does it have to be this way?" she asked echoing his thoughts, her eyes growing brighter.

"Because."

"That's not a reason."

"Because you are a princess, and I am a soldier." He spoke more forcefully this time.

She rose to her feet, standing over him. He refused to meet her gaze. "That's an excuse and you and I both know it."

His blood began to pound faster beneath his skin. Funny how it could do that even when he could no longer bleed. "It is an answer. Your destiny is to become Queen of Erinya. Mine is to serve you loyally."

"And could you not serve at my side, instead of at my feet?"

Silence. Then he looked up at her. Longing struck him so forcefully that his fists began to crack as he clenched them in his lap. She had all but admitted how she felt for him in what she had just offered him—a place at her side. Somehow it was everything he'd ever wanted. And yet . . .

"That is not possible." He tore his gaze away from her, staring back at the fire.

"Why not? If I'm queen, can I not choose my king?"

Something snapped inside him, and he shot to his feet.

"We can't be together, Jill! I wasn't meant to be a king. I'm meant to be a soldier. Besides—" he stopped himself, his chest heaving as he was the one who now stared down at her. Close. They were so close. His mouth just inches from hers and yet he refused to close the distance, no matter how much he wanted to.

"Besides?" she probed, her face twisting with anger.

"Besides, Prince Tiernan plans to propose to you. Officially. The alliance would secure aid for Erinya in the approaching war."

The anger on her face gave way to surprise. "What?" she breathed, her eyes flicking back and forth as she tried to process this new information. "How do you know?"

"I overheard him discussing the matter with Peter."

"Peter doesn't know anything—"

"And he said as much. But Tiernan plans to propose all the same."

Jill sank back onto the settee, stunned and silent.

David swallowed the lump in his throat, knowing he would come to regret his next words. "You should accept his proposal."

Jill stared blankly into the fire, looking like a beautiful songbird trapped in a cage.

David warred within himself. He knew he was dooming her to a marriage of necessity, the very thing she'd fought so hard to free herself from. But if she was going to be queen, she needed every ally she could get, and he refused to stand in her way.

With Jack and the newfound threat of the Ohans, and no army at their disposal, they needed Tiernan's aide. Erinya *needed* this proposal. *Jill* needed this proposal.

"I will take your advice under consideration," Jill said, her voice stilted. A tear rolled down her cheek. The sight of it made him want to take everything back. Made him want to grab her and kiss her and say that he'd be her king if she wanted, that he'd do anything she wanted for as long as he lived.

But his fate was already sealed. Somewhere along the way he'd accepted that. He would die at her brother's hands. And she would claim her rightful place as queen, bringing peace to Erinya like none of her ancestors before her. And Tiernan would sit at her side, just lucky enough to share some of her light.

"Good," he said at last, his voice coming out gruffer than he'd intended.

Maybe she will. But who knows. Peter's words came back to him. No, he would not find forgiveness tonight. Probably never. And even if she forgave him, he wasn't sure he could forgive himself.

He took one last look at her, staring crestfallen at the fire that had died to smoldering coals, then he turned and left.

No, he would not be her king, but he would serve her until the day he died, however long that might be. Because that was another thing he'd come to accept. Once, he'd dedicated himself to serving Erinya even though he didn't care much for this broken kingdom. But Jill did, and she would be the one to fix it, he had no doubt. So, he would serve *her*. He would fight for *her*. He would dedicate himself to *her*. Even after she won this war and married Tiernan. Even after she bore Tiernan's children and grew old with him. It would all be for her.

He just prayed that someday she would understand.

4 8

MILLIE

"Go? You mean right now?" Millie stared at Mother Goose, her eyebrows broaching her hairline. It took Millie several seconds to process what the woman was telling her. They were fleeing. They were fleeing right now. A nagging sensation tugged at her core, even as her throat began to tighten. When she'd agreed to go with them, she hadn't meant right now. She thought she'd have more time. She thought—

"Yes. My note did tell you to be ready. Best not to vacillate too long. Make a decision and follow through." The woman leveled her with a fierce stare, daring Millie to challenge her.

"But my brother—and Keyanna and Master Ravala—"

"We can get them out. My people have already infiltrated the palace. We await your orders." At this the woman gave a sly smile. She'd known Millie would join her, had devised her entire plan on the assumption.

My orders. What did they really want from her?

The jarring scrape of rock and a following cacophony of clattering weapons shattered the serenity of the moment as a young man stumbled from a shadowed corner, a tapestry wrapped around him which was subsequently yanked off the walls before he fell in a heap on the floor.

Millie's weapon was already drawn but before she could do anything with it, Mother Goose swore so loudly and creatively that Millie blushed.

"I told you to wait for my signal!" the old woman hissed at the young man. "They're likely to send in a dozen guards after that racket!"

"I'm sorry," a deep voice mumbled.

Mother Goose huffed as Millie stared past the young man who remained hopelessly tangled in the tapestry at the ominous doorway beyond him. *A hidden tunnel.* It made perfect sense that it would be there, after all the royals would need a way to flee in the event of assassins or any other threats to their well-being. She swallowed, the darkened passageway like an open mouth, waiting to swallow her.

"What'll it be, Paladin? I'm afraid we don't have much time," Mother Goose said. "We must hurry if we wish to make it out of the Citadel by sunrise."

"My brother. I can't leave without him." Millie was once again surprised at the steel in her tone. It seemed several months of being a paladin had taught her how to speak with authority, or at least pretend she had authority. "If we leave without him, Malum will kill him." In fact, she could think of several people he might kill once he discovered she'd fled. Fled just like Jill.

No. No, she couldn't think like that. She'd done what she could for Jack, but she couldn't fix him. She couldn't save him, not while he held her captive at least. She shoved the thoughts away, forcing herself to focus on the problem at hand.

She looked again at the young man who'd managed to free himself from the tapestry. He was burly with tan skin and the beginning of a scraggly beard. With a start she recognized him as one of Doon's friends.

"Isaac?" Millie gave him a small smile. The boy had trained under Doon in the stables. He'd always been rather large for his age, but the horses loved him. Isaac reminded Millie of a puppy that did not understand how big and clumsy it was.

Isaac blushed then dropped into a stiff bow, bent in a perfect line at the waist. "Yes, Mi–Paladin."

She smiled at him, and his blush deepened. "You can call me Millie. And you don't need to bow to me."

"Oh—uh, right. Of course." His burly body shot back up, ramrod straight.

"What would you have us do?" The old woman asked, a gleam in her eyes.

"We have to rescue Doon, Keyanna, Ravala and any others who might be in the dungeon." Though her body felt weak, her voice remained strong, carrying authority. She looked from Mother Goose to Isaac. She need not challenge them. They would listen to her. She was a paladin.

She knew Madame Sorelle was down there, as was Paladin Willa, and although she knew neither woman well, she feared what Malum would do to them. Who knew how many others he held down there? Who knew how valuable they would be as allies?

Millie considered only a few seconds before making her decision. In this she could not waver. She turned to Mother Goose and Isaac.

"Last I heard Doon was in the infirmary. He should be there. Tell him I sent you."

"What if he doesn't believe us?" Mother Goose asked.

"Tell him he owes me one for the day he tripped me into

the horse trough." Millie almost smiled at the memory. "Isaac, you come with me."

Isaac nodded, a smirk dancing across his face though Millie couldn't imagine why. Until she recalled that Isaac may have actually been there the day Doon had tripped her. Once, she might have felt embarrassed but fleeing for one's life left little time to dwell on such things.

A knock came at the door and Millie froze, heartbeat pounding in her throat.

"Everything all right in there, Paladin?" a guard's husky voice asked.

Mother Goose shot a look at Isaac that would have chilled Millie to her bones, and it seemed to have a similar effect on the stable hand.

"I'm all right," Millie called, forcing a casual tone. "Just knocked tripped and knocked something over."

"Shall I—" the guard started to open the door.

"How dare you?" Millie shouted. "I'm indecent!"

The guard promptly shut the door as Mother Goose ushered her and Isaac into the tunnel. She hurried, praying her outburst bought them enough time. As her foot crossed the threshold she froze, glancing at the room behind her and the darkness looming before. She was leaving everything she'd ever known behind for a future that remained uncertain at best.

I'll come back for you Jack. It was a promise, an oath, a vow. She *would* return for him, even if it killed her.

She swallowed hard then dove into the darkness, pulling the scraping doorway closed behind her.

It took several moments for her eyes to adjust to the darkness as she took in their surroundings. They stood in one of the many stone corridors throughout the citadel, water dripping down the cold stone, a freezing draft blowing through. The only light came from a torch held by another man who looked older than Isaac, but thinner with pointed cat ears protruding from beneath a cap.

He introduced himself as Karam and then they were moving, racing down the narrow halls with a speed that made her leg ache. It had healed unnaturally fast thanks to Malum's elixir, but she knew it would still take time to recover the strength she'd lost in the days she'd laid about.

The corridor they were walking through split, one into a winding staircase that tunneled down while the other curved out of sight. Their group parted ways, Mother Goose and Karam taking the level hallway while Millie and Isaac took the ominous stairs leading deeper into the heart of the Citadel.

Millie had spent some time in the various tunnels as a child, playing games with the other servants' children and then eventually, as a maid herself. King Cole had preferred to keep his staff out of sight when they weren't needed, hence the secret labyrinthian corridors throughout the palace.

When she was younger, she couldn't understand why the king wouldn't want his servants close by. She hadn't understood many things as a child. Now she could see clearly. The servants were wanted to attend to his whims, but they weren't meant to be seen. They weren't meant to be heard. And they certainly weren't meant to enter tournaments and win.

But Jack had seen her. He'd seen her when she was nothing special at all. She wasn't yet a paladin or a Saints' Heir. She was just Millie.

I'll come back for you Jack.

The words were a mantra as she hurried down the staircase, conviction filling her chest, burrowing deeper, growing stronger. Malum had won this battle. But he would not win the war.

When they reached the bottom of the winding stairwell,

her legs burned from the long descent. She knew from sneaking into the prison to see Doon that they stood by the guardroom just outside the entrance. She slowed as she came to the doorway, listening for the telltale signs of guards chatting during their breaks.

All was silent.

That wasn't right. She'd known several of the guards assigned to this portion, and crass as they were, they were never quiet. She'd walked in on many foul discussions, games of cards, and even, on occasion, drinking on duty. But never quiet.

She motioned for Isaac to halt, and he politely obliged. She needed to be certain.

"Wait here," she mouthed. Before he could respond, she closed her eyes and melted into shadows.

Isaac's eyes bulged at the sight of her power, and he stepped back but fortunately remained quiet, if not a little disturbed.

Once, she might have felt shame at the sight of his fear. But something had shifted in the last several months. She was not one to laud power over others, yet she'd come to discover just how powerful she was. Before, her small stature and quiet demeanor had sentenced her to live a life overlooked and undervalued. Now, she was someone people feared, respected.

She sent a handful of small spiders scurrying under the door to the guardroom. She was always astounded by how large everything appeared from this vantage point. How did actual spiders feel about such vast spaces?

The sight that greeted her was not one she'd expected. Given the silence of the room, she would have thought the guards on duty were making their rotations, though one usually stayed back to intercept anyone who might wander down to the dungeons.

But now, three guards sat as still as statues at the table in the center of the room, staring at the empty space before them. She might have thought they were actually statues if not for small tells.

A blink here. A twitching finger there. The subtle rise and fall of their chests.

Something was very wrong indeed.

She recognized two of the guards. The first, Reynard, was an overweight boarman whose skin always seemed covered in a sheen of sweat. Despite his unfortunate looks, he was one of the guards she'd favored the most on her visits to Doon. Unlike many of the others, he was kind and chivalrous, refusing to engage in the bawdy jokes the other men made when she showed up.

The second man she recognized was, ironically, one of her least favorites. The exact opposite of Reynard in nearly every way, Thomas was an incredibly handsome young man, but the image was ruined by his crude sense of humor. He'd been known to make more than one of the maids cry and had a proclivity for putting his hands where they didn't belong.

It was for that precise reason why Millie sent her spiders scuttling up his pants leg, shifting and mutating as she went to form a single large spider. Nearly the size of the palm of his hand, she was surprised she went unnoticed as she crawled over his hip, up his chest, and out onto his arm which rested on the table. He didn't stir as her spider crept to the back of his hand, her fangs poised and ready.

She bit into the flesh of his hand, tasting his blood and feeling the tightening of his muscles in her mandibles. With barely a grunt, he flicked his wrist and shook her spider to the floor, blood dripping down his hand as he rested it back on the table.

She landed with a graceless plop, momentarily disoriented before coming to her senses.

Something was very wrong. Her wolf spider had a notoriously painful bite. With its long pinchers and stinging venom, it usually elicited shrill cries from even the toughest battle-hardened soldiers.

Malum had done something to them. She'd been suspicious of the guards for months now, but this went beyond even her worst fears. What had he done to them?

She called her spider back under the doorway and reformed before Isaac. Uncertainty swirled within her chest. She wasn't sure what her plan had been initially, only that these new guards presented a different sort of problem.

Isaac swallowed, refusing to meet her eyes. "What did you see?"

"I'm not entirely sure. Something's wrong with those soldiers."

To her surprise, Isaac nodded. "We've noticed the soldiers have changed. It's like—like they've been hypnotized or something."

Millie considered this. Five years ago, a traveling cirque had come to the Citadel, one of the booths boasting they could hypnotize anyone. She hadn't been braving enough to try it herself, but she recalled that in each case some signal could snap people out of their stupor.

But this wasn't the work of some traveling hypnotist eager for extra coin. This was the work of Malum. She doubted it would be quite so simple.

"Can you turn into any spider?" Isaac asked, pulling her from her thoughts.

She looked at him, his expression thoughtful. "To my knowledge, yes. Do you have any thoughts?" She prayed he wouldn't ask her to turn into anything deadly. These men, even one as vile as Thomas, didn't deserve to die for simply getting in her way.

Well, maybe Thomas could stand to learn a lesson.

"Have you heard of the nocturn spider? Its venom can cause severe drowsiness within minutes."

Millie didn't need to hear more. Although she knew some species of the spiders she could turn into, she didn't need to know everything about a spider to transform into it. The process, while difficult at first, had become rather intuitive for her thanks to Master Ravala's training.

She shifted again, willing herself to become a horde of nocturn spiders. They were smaller than she'd imagined, and she had the capacity to become even the smallest of house spiders.

She sent them scuttling back under the door, Isaac's voice following her, telling her that too many bites from these tiny spiders would kill the men.

Within the span of a few minutes, her spiders had found the supple skin of each of the three men, and she bit all three a handful of times. It was a wonder her pinchers could penetrate skin at all given how small they were. She made sure to bite Thomas a few extra times. Perhaps it was spiteful, but she was beyond caring.

It took longer than she would have liked—nearly ten full minutes—before the men's eyes began to droop. Another five minutes and all three were snoring with their heads on the table. She would have to remember that little trick.

Satisfied that they weren't waking up anytime soon, Millie reformed in the room and unlocked the door for Isaac.

"Thanks Isaac."

The young man nodded, a red blush coloring his cheeks.

Millie pulled the ring of keys off Thomas's belt and headed into the darkness of the dungeons.

The blue-fire torches provided little light and even less heat. Millie shivered as she wound further into the depths of the dungeon, Isaac trailing at her heels. With their hurried exit, she hadn't had a chance to grab her cloak, and she regretted it now as the cold made her skin prickle.

Her bare fingers trailed along the side of the walls, ice sapping them of the little warmth she had left. Her gut told her Malum had tucked away any who rebelled against his rule down here. She should have come sooner, but she'd been a coward.

She turned another corner and froze, a chill raising the hair on the back of her neck.

"I wondered if you'd come here," Malum said coolly. Wearing Jack's face in the half-light of the blue torches made him look like the villain she knew he was.

She remained silent, her heart rebelling against her with its traitorous thumping. Would it give away how terrified she was?

"I thought you'd at least say goodbye, Millie." The words were like the purr of a cat as he sauntered forward, hands in his pockets. She was frozen, she was—

She remembered the knife at her side.

Without a second thought she stepped forward and slammed the knife into his chest, shuddering at the sound of it pushing through bone and muscle. He didn't even seem fazed as he grabbed her and shoved her up against the wall, knocking the air from her lungs. His forearm crushed against her throat, expelling what little air she could manage to suck in.

His body shuddered, eye color flickering between black and green. His face twisted in rage but still he didn't let go of her.

"Jack—" She tried to speak but could only mouth the words. She was losing air fast.

His head snapped to look at her, his eyes turning green before going wide with horror. His grip finally loosened, and she pushed him away with all her strength, sending him stumbling backward. Only a few steps though.

For the first time, Millie heard the cries of the prisoners around her, watching from their cells. She stole a quick glance at Isaac, who had started cutting the locks off the cells with his sword. She was thankful he'd kept his wits about him at least.

Malum loomed over her, Jack gone for now.

He's still in there. He tried to save me.

"Will you leave me too?" Malum asked, fuming. "Will you leave *him*?"

Her knife still protruded from his chest, but instead of dripping blood, swirling shadow leaked from the wound. How did you kill a monster without flesh and blood? Even the Saints could only banish him to another realm, not kill him.

She opened her mouth to speak when a sword sheared through Malum's neck. She looked down at the sword in her hands. She did not remember drawing it, didn't even remember where it had come from.

Time stretched before her, silence cocooning her as she watched Jack's head fall from his shoulders and land on the floor with a thud, his body collapsing soon after. Smoke twisted out of the hole between his shoulders, out of his neck. Jack blinked, looking up at her in shock.

She heard screaming—her own—but she heard it as if she were underwater.

Isaac's arms wrapped around her, pulling her, dragging her. She fought against him, even as pain tugged her core. There were others now too, freed from the prison. She didn't know who. Didn't care.

Jack! No, no, no!

The scene before her blurred as tears spilled down her

cheeks. More shouts. More wrestling and fighting. She would not let them take her from him. She had to go to him. *Saints,* what had she done?

She was dragged upstairs. Dragged back through the guardroom, where those blasted guards still slept.

Her screams echoed as she was carried through more tunnels, led away like a child.

Because that's what she was. A child. How had she ever thought she could do this? How had she ever thought she could be strong enough? She was weak. She was a traitor.

She was ruined.

49

KYLIAN

ylian found himself in a library. It was in far better shape than he'd expected from the wolfmen, perhaps the nicest space in the entire keep. Oak shelves lined the walls of the cavernous space, rows of books spiraled in toward the center until they met a curving staircase that took him deeper into the library.

He wandered aimlessly, doing his best to avoid any social interactions. Fires burned in periodically placed hearths, giving the library a warm and cozy feel, a strange contrast to the rest of the keep. Reading nooks in corners interspersed the fires, filled with wolfmen scholars in blue robes, their spectacle-topped noses tucked into books.

A week or two ago he would have been thrilled to have stumbled across such a treasure trove of knowledge. He'd always had a fondness for books. But now he couldn't bring himself to even scan the shelves for interesting titles. So, he dragged through the never-ending labyrinth of books, allowing his mind to wander.

Nothing had gone according to his plans. Sure, they'd

discovered another Saints' Heir during the battle but that did little to comfort him. It still wasn't enough. *He* wasn't enough.

If he'd been given the power that Bo had—well perhaps there was a reason he hadn't. He'd already hurt too many people.

A rustle of fabric caught his attention, and he turned to see Zyla standing behind him, wearing a new gown of plain blue. She stared at her feet with her arms crossed and chewed on the corner of her lip.

Once he might have strolled up to her with confidence, brushed that strand of hair behind her ear, trailed a finger down the side of her cheek. But he couldn't bring himself to do such a thing, not anymore.

To a degree, he'd always known his confidence had been a farce, a mask to hide every doubt and insecurity. He just hadn't expected that with one run-in with the vulgan it would all come tumbling down.

"I came to see if you were all right. Are you?" Zyla still refused to meet his gaze.

He wanted to lie to her, to tell her that he was fine, that what had occurred had been but a brief lapse in judgment and no more.

The words evaded him.

Zyla took a few steps forward, dragging a finger along the bookshelves, scanning the titles. And Kylian saw her with fresh eyes. The way her hair tumbled and fell down her back and shoulders. The way her eyes brightened, and her head tilted as she pulled a book off the shelf. The way a hint of a smile graced her face. How had he not noticed *her* sooner?

"What did you find?" Kylian asked gruffly, ignoring her question. He worked up the courage to take a few steps toward her, interested in the title she'd grabbed.

"A very old story, one my mother read to Ymira and I when

we were children. It was one of my favorites." She stared down at the novel fondly, before turning a smirk on him. "You never answered my question."

Kylian shrugged then nodded to the book. "What's it about?"

"Answer my question first and I'll tell you." She turned to him, clutching the book against her chest.

Kylian's mouth went dry. He should apologize. He should beg her forgiveness. "Zyla, I'm so sorry." His voice cracked. He couldn't do this, not here, not now. Maybe not ever. This carefully crafted façade. It was cracking to reveal something so much darker inside him, something he'd pretended didn't exist.

"Kylian." Zyla took another step toward him. "You don't have to keep pretending."

He shook his head, looking to the ground. He couldn't meet her eyes. "I don't know anything else," he confessed. The words were a release, an exhale after holding his breath for so long.

"You do. You're not an idiot Kylian."

He glanced up at her to see that playful smile.

"How can you forgive me so easily? How can you keep going when you know what we're up against?"

Zyla pursed her lips. Then in answer, she held up the book.

"A book?"

She smiled, flipping the book open and thumbing through the pages with reverence. "The Owl and the Fox."

Kylian waited for her to say more until it became clear she wanted him to ask her. She wanted him to reach out to her. "What's it about?" His voice was gruffer than usual.

Her eyes sparkled as she glanced up at him. "The story is about two sisters who are cursed by a witch. One turns into an owl by night and a girl by day. The other is a fox by day and a girl at night. Together they go on all sorts of adventures. They stop bandits from terrorizing a little village, they hunt down the queen's stolen diadem, and they eventually find themselves as part of a traveling cirque where they discover the witch who cursed them is now nothing more than an unimpressive fortune teller. At first, they try to trick her into undoing her curse on them. When that doesn't work, they poison her, hoping she'll undo the curse if they promise to give her the antidote. But the witch is so old and frail and her magic so faint that she can't undo the curse, and she dies."

Kylian waited for her to say more. "And the curse was lifted after she died?"

Zyla shook her head. "No. They never broke the curse. They spent the rest of their days changing back and forth between human and animal."

Kylian frowned. "That's it?"

"Yep."

"You mean, after they were cursed, the girls were never both human at the same time again?"

"Uh-huh," Zyla replied, still smiling a bit as if there were some joke he was not privy to yet.

He frowned. "Why on earth would you like a story like that? It doesn't even have a happy ending. Why were they cursed in the first place? What was the witch's problem? And why did they have to kill her?" Kylian felt unsettled.

"It's a fairytale Kylian," Zyla said. "Mostly, my sister and I loved it because it also had two sisters in it."

"But they kill someone, and it doesn't even break their curse? What on earth does this have to do with forgiveness? Clearly, they didn't forgive the witch, and it didn't even matter. Is that what it means? That if they'd just asked nicely and forgiven the witch their curse would have been broken?"

The story felt like a riddle, a puzzle to solve. Surely, a kid's story could not be so dark and grim, right?

"Kylian," Zyla said, exasperated. "That's it. That's all there is to it. There is no secret moral or something to solve. It's just a children's story."

"It's a bit dark for children, don't you think?"

"Not any darker than the world we live in now."

Kylian contemplated that for a moment. She was right of course. The world they lived in was filled to the brim with darkness. Monsters and Saints and evil kings. But a darkness existed beyond the physical realm, a darkness that existed within the selfishness of man. It was a darkness where orphaned children were demonized, the scariest monsters were wicked men who exploited the poor and lowly, and where doing good was far more dangerous than doing evil.

"I suppose you're right," Kylian said slowly. "But what does such a story teach young children? That murdering old witches is okay?"

Zyla chuckled, "Not all stories teach something, you know. Some of them are simply entertaining."

Kylian tilted his head at her, still frowning. "And somehow all of this helps you forgive? Keep pressing forward? A dark children's story with no discernable morals whatsoever?"

Zyla turned from him, smirking as she shoved the book back into place. "Well, no—and yes."

Kylian crossed his arms and leaned up against the nearest bookshelf, some part of his confident charisma returning. "Care to explain?"

She pursed her lips. "Some think stories are little more than entertainment for children. And perhaps that's true, but all stories came from somewhere. Someone who imagined a world different from their own, who imagined people they'd never met. They cared enough to tell their stories and other people cared enough to listen. That's why I keep going, so that someday someone might tell my story, and for just a little while, people may grow to care about a world and a people not their own. And maybe they will feel just a bit less alone too."

A FEW HOURS later Kylian was herded into a large meeting hall to debrief the battle from days ago. Kylian had been privy to meetings like these daily, bartering and negotiating with nobles and governors and generals over various aspects of government and trade, but the wolfmen had an authoritarian government, so here the Alpha reigned supreme in both matters of military and state. Had the Alpha forbidden his troops to fight in the most recent battle and some disregarded his orders, it would have been akin to treason, and they would have been put to death.

Kylian suppressed a shudder. He already held such little love for the former king of Erinya, he could not imagine a world where the king held even more power. But he supposed that was exactly what the Black King had subjected this kingdom to. A reign of terror.

A sudden sense of panic overwhelmed him. His lungs felt like they were being squeezed by two giant fists. The room felt hot, so terribly hot. He stood ramrod straight as he waited for the feelings of panic and despair to pass, to flow through one part of his body and out another. A trick he'd learned long ago to master his body and facial expressions in scenarios just like these.

Instead, memories pummeled him. The fear on Lyra and Asif's faces as he'd exploded at them. The wailing and screeching of the battle they'd practically stumbled upon. A young woman snatching a baby from her bed. Him chasing after the woman with fire and fear in his veins, urging him faster and faster. To catch the woman who'd stolen his baby sister.

The memories came so fast he could hardly make sense of them. Flashing between decades and moments and years.

His thoughts swarmed him as well, berating him, chastising him, insulting him. If only he'd been faster. Braver. Stronger. Smarter. No matter the scenario, he'd never been enough. He would never be enough.

A hand gripped his elbow, yanking him from his spiraling thoughts. He turned in a daze to see the princess standing before him, a worried look plastered to her face.

"Doyle?" she asked, her voice low and quiet.

The room had filled nearly to capacity with all manner of people. Mostly wolfmen. But Grimzy and Jill were here, along with David, Luca, Hasani, Ymira, Aaira, and Bo, all of whom were finding seats toward the front of the room. Except for Grimzy who stood vigil close to Jill's side, making clear where his loyalties lay. Paladins swore an oath to serve their kings and queens no matter what. But technically his king was very far away.

"Your Highness," he said with a dip of his head.

"Is everything all right?" she asked.

He took a second to analyze her face. He'd made a habit of dissecting people's facial features to learn precisely what they were thinking, a habit that seemed to be wavering these days, for as he looked at her, he did not see the haughty, stuck-up princess he'd known back at the palace. Nor did he see a warrior hardened to stone by the difficulties she'd overcome. Rather he saw true concern etched into the lines of her face. Concern for him.

She'd never paid him any mind before. Clearly, they'd both changed.

"Of course, Your Highness." People were beginning to turn their gazes toward them. To watch as the princess and the king's former adviser chatted about Saints knew what. He realized instantly how uneasy it would make everyone else. The wolfmen didn't trust him or the princess, but they knew they would need the help of the future queen to survive what was lay ahead.

"Thank you," she said, "For coming, for helping in the battle, and for bringing Asif and Lyra here safely."

He dipped his head in respect, not trusting his own voice to keep from cracking. Regret and shame still consumed him, but he'd managed to push it to the back of his mind for now. But if he opened his mouth, if he confessed his shortcomings, well, his carefully constructed façade would crumble here in front of everyone. He wasn't ready for that. Didn't think he'd ever be ready.

The princess gave him another reassuring squeeze on his elbow, gentle but firm. Somehow, he knew it conveyed a very simple truth—they were in this together.

The meeting lasted hours, every high-ranking officer giving their debriefing and version of the events of the battle. Other personnel offered their timelines of the battle as well. And then there were the numbers. Numbers of the wounded. Numbers of the dead. Numbers of the artillery lost. Numbers of the weapons still at their disposal. Numbers of projected refugees that would arrive. Numbers of the days needed to make repairs, heal the injured, send out scouting missions.

Kylian couldn't say they weren't thorough. Indeed, he began to see why they were so successful in matters of military and state. He thought back to that library, vast and overwhelming and filled to the brim with scholars. Perhaps it was the marriage of military and scholarship that imbued them with such success. After all, he hadn't heard of a military loss by the wolfmen in the past two centuries.

After nearly six hours of droning on about which parts of the keep would need special repairs and the costs to do so, they finally decided to break for an evening meal.

Kylian rose from his seat, blood flowing back into his legs after sitting so long. Large sums danced around his head as he shuffled out into the long stone corridors along with everyone else.

"Hey."

Kylian sighed. He knew that voice and the thinly veiled animosity it held.

He turned, looking down at the young girl who was aged beyond her fifteen years. The girl who had endured so much.

"Bo," he said with a nod.

She peered up at him, leaning on her crutch and giving him the same assessing stare he used on others. He wasn't sure how he felt being on the other end of it. But perhaps that look was something they shared in common.

"Tell me you're sorry and we can go back to arguing with each other instead of not talking."

Kylian shook his head but couldn't hide the smirk. "You know I'm sorry."

"I know," she said, giving him the barest hint of a smile. "I just need to hear you say it."

"I'm sorry, Bo."

Her gaze narrowed but that tiny smile didn't fade. Not entirely. "I forgive you. But don't ever do it again."

"I wouldn't dream of it."

Bo finally, reluctantly smiled. "Good. I've missed fighting with you."

"Me too."

50

JACK

Jack knew only pain.

Writhing, twisting, stabbing pain.

His head had been severed from his body. But it was the heart ripped from his chest that hurt the most. Millie had abandoned him. Just like Jill. Just like Anna. Just like everyone it seemed.

He knew he should be happy for her. Happy that she'd freed herself from Malum's control and manipulation. But while his mind could see that, he could not say the same for the ache that filled his chest.

Slowly—so slowly he thought he'd go mad—his body knit itself back together. Even decapitation could not kill him. He wished it had. It would save all of Erinya such heartache and sorrow if Malum were gone. It would have saved Jack from feeling that heartache.

It will take more than that to kill me.

Trust me, I know. Resentment filled him as he thought of the bargain he'd made to save Millie's life. It had trapped him within his own mind and body. A prisoner subject to Malum's will.

Then as suddenly as if he had blinked, Jack stood in his study, looking out his window as the black churning waves of the Ataran Sea crashed upon the shore. Like a veil being lifted from his mind, he began to recall the details of how he'd arrived here.

Malum had healed his body, pulled himself from the floor and retreated to his chambers. He sensed his roiling anger, burning inside him with a constancy that worried Jack. Something big had happened, and Malum was not happy. It went beyond the decapitation, beyond Millie's abandonment. But he couldn't determine what. His consciousness was being pushed further and further back, making it difficult for Jack to latch on to anything. He no longer registered the passing of time. He could never be certain if it had been an hour since he'd last been present or several days. And was helpless to do a thing about it.

The scene before him shifted again. He sat in the throne room, watching as prisoners with hoods over their heads were led in. Light flooded the room from above, and Jack tried to piece together what was happening.

Another blink and he had returned to his chambers, sitting at his desk as he sipped on a goblet of scarlet wine. The room was dark.

What are you doing? What's going on?

Jack felt Malum smirk. ***I'm doing nothing. You are simply fading.***

If Jack were in control of his own body, he would have quivered with fear, cowering like a whipped dog hiding from its master. Instead, Malum's smooth, disarming calm swept through him, overpowering Jack's will. Overpowering everything.

What do you mean?

It seemed Millie was the final straw, your last breaking point. You fought valiantly, my prince, but I'm afraid your time grows short. Soon your consciousness will fade, and you will forget all that you were and all that you were meant to be.

Malum's tone dripped with pleasure. He'd done it. He'd crushed Jack's spirit once and for all. Hope slid from Jack's chest, melting like the last of winter's snow as it gave way to spring. But the sun wouldn't shine when Malum reigned.

And he would wear Jack's face as he ruined Erinya.

That was perhaps the most disturbing thing of all. People would not remember Prince Jack, lovable and charming. They would remember King Jack and his legacy of fear and bloodshed and violence. But it was not him.

Again, Jack wished he were in control of his body so he could weep the tears held back inside, so he could rage and scream and fight against the monster that had ruined him, ruined everything.

A strange pang of sadness that Jack could feel was not his own slipped through him.

I am sorry, Jack. I wish we could have seen eye to eye. We did not have to be enemies.

We were always meant to be enemies.

Malum shrugged, taking a long swig of wine as he sat in his chair. Jack could not taste it, could not feel anything aside from his own pain, scraping and clawing at him from somewhere deep inside.

Why are you doing this? If he had spoken the words aloud, his voice would have cracked with thick emotion, the words hoarse with unspent tears. *Why are you set on destroying my kingdom?*

It was my kingdom first. The words were an angry dagger. ***You were meant to die before you were ever born. You and I are in this position because of your foolish mother.***

Confusion twisted within him and Malum sensed it, releasing a dark chuckle that sent fear coursing through him.

You didn't know?

Jack remained silent. What could he say? Malum was in complete control, and they both knew it.

You died in your mother's womb. Your soul had gone on to whatever afterlife awaits us. But she dragged it back, tearing a hole in my prison.

Jack's heart would have thundered, his blood would have burned, his fists would have clenched, but he was trapped in a body that no longer belonged to him. He felt nothing.

I have been with you your entire life. I have watched you learn and grow. I have felt you fall in love and receive the beatings by your father's hand. I have seen the world through your eyes, and it must be remade—without the Saints' Heirs. Only then will my wife and daughter return to me.

Jack was silent. Exhausted. Utterly spent. What response could he give? He could do nothing to change Malum's mind. Now Millie was gone and Jill with her. If anything could be done, it was up to them.

An odd thought struck him then. If Jack had never been brought back to life, Jill would have been on the throne instead of him. Erinya could have been spared from so much violence if he'd never been born. Jill would have been a great queen.

No. She will *be a great queen.*

He could see it now. She would take the throne, wear the crown. Right his wrongs. He only wished he would live to see it. Because he knew now. To destroy Malum, he would have to destroy himself.

How uncharacteristically noble of you. But even if you destroy me, your sister will never be queen. She will die a traitor's death, if she hasn't already.

What have you done? The words, though not spoken aloud, were breathless, tight with fear.

Jack felt his face curl into a smile as Malum took another swig of wine, downing the rest of the glass. Jack's anger continued to mount, heat flaring inside him.

What. Have. You. Done? In his mind he flung himself against the cage Malum kept him in, screaming and prying at the bars.

At last, Malum answered. ***Two weeks ago, I sent an army to find your sister in the North. She had gone to Fenric's Keep of all places. But they were unprepared for an army like mine.***

Jack's emotions raged against Malum's callous calm, both fighting for control.

If you kill her, I'll—

You'll what? Malum stood and Jack imagined the two of them face-to-face, but Jack could only picture his own face twisted with that dark scowl, tainted by Malum's corruption. ***You are a coward, Jack. You always have been. You could not face your father, you could not face the woman you loved, and you cannot face me. You are powerless. It is why everyone in your life has abandoned you. So, I will kill your sister, and you will do nothing, because that is all you are capable of.***

Jack went completely numb. A roaring filled his ears until

all he saw and heard was darkness and silence. Malum had won. He would kill Jill and then he would kill Millie. It was over. Jack had lost. But then he sensed it, a sliver of uncertainty from Malum. He was hiding something from Jack. He was—

Darkness slammed down around him, blocking him out. He didn't know how long it lasted, perhaps days. Perhaps weeks. Malum had shut him out completely, not even allowing Jack access to his own senses. Just when he thought he might go mad from being consumed by overwhelming nothingness, light flooded in.

Moonlight sliced down from above, leading the way to a fortress. A night sky loomed over him as he walked up a massive staircase.

Where are we?

Look and see for yourself.

For a moment, it seemed Malum had allowed Jack to regain control of his body as he looked up. He was suddenly aware of so many sensations at once. The tightening of his throat. The slight quiver that rolled through his body. The freezing wind. Turrets and dark black stone and gargoyles loomed over him like oppressive beasts, ready to feast on his flesh.

He'd been here once as a boy and had vowed never to return.

He'd arrived at Ohans' fortress. And at the top of the stairs, like a prophet waiting for a pleading acolyte, stood Ohan-Jin, smiling at Jack.

51

JILL

*I*t had been nearly two weeks since the battle of Fenric's Keep, and it seemed word had traveled quickly that the princess led an army against the vulgan. Every day more freezing refugees arrived at the keep, begrudgingly welcomed by the wolfmen. The keep was massive, so the wolfmen's hesitant reception wasn't for lack of room but because the relations between her people and the wolfmen were tenuous at best. Although Alpha Volkov had agreed to aid her strike against the Ohans, clearly the past would not be packed away so simply.

Nor should it be. Evil had a way of haunting people generation after generation, and recovering from so many years of hostility would take time. Even so, Jill couldn't help but feel this was a step in the right direction, however small it might be.

A serving girl handed her a mug of steamed chocolate, a wolfman delicacy she'd come to enjoy during her time there. She took a deep pull from the drink, relishing the bitter sweetness on her tongue, the creamy feeling in her mouth. It was the perfect temperature to soothe her freezing fingers.

"The challenge at this time of year will be the western current," a gravelly voice said, drawing Jill's mind back to the issue at hand.

She stood in one of Volkov's personal meeting rooms with several admirals, attendants, and other military personnel to plan the attack on the Ohans. Prince Tiernan was there as well, leaving her feeling—well, she wasn't entirely sure what she felt about her former betrothed. Especially when Grimzy and David stood beside him. He hadn't proposed to her yet, but he'd been trying to spend more time with her while David seemed to avoid her at all costs.

The man currently speaking was Admiral Igor, a rougher looking wolfman whose dark face and hair seemed a stark contrast against the gray walls of the keep. "We have the capacity to row against it, but we will need to find a safe harbor for the fleet, otherwise the current will smash the ships against the rocks."

Jill set her mug down on the table, examining the map before her. She wished she had her brother's mind for strategy and diplomacy. But she had not been allowed in the meetings with generals to discuss battle strategy or with nobles to settle land disputes, petty squabbles, and arguments over useless titles. She hadn't quite figured out the delicate maneuvering required for such things.

It should have been so simple and straightforward. Do what you must, ask for help, and if they decline, ask someone else. But everyone seemed far too adept at employing this backhanded, manipulative, politically challenged motivation. She was quickly learning that people were rarely straightforward, releasing information only in a way that gave them power. Because that's all it was, a grab for power. It was beyond frustrating.

But power was what had led them all to this point.

Malum's greed for power had given rise to the first Saints. Her father's greed had pushed him to attack Carthesia for its resources, creating an enemy who once might have been an ally. And the Ohans' greed had left them all trying to figure out exactly how they were going to rescue hundreds of people from a fortified land with minimal casualties.

"Can we not bring the ships to this cleft in the rock here?" she asked, pointing to what seemed to be a sheltered place in the rock just east of the Ohans' territory.

Several low chuckles resounded throughout the room, and Jill fought back the heat climbing up her neck.

"That's the Siren's Wail," a wolfman named Artem explained. "She seems peaceful when the tide is low, but when she comes in, she—well, let's just say many a good sailor has fallen into her clutches."

Jill swallowed hard. She wasn't certain she completely understood, but she figured out enough to know it wouldn't be an option.

"Perhaps the princess has a point," Prince Tiernan said.

Jill's eyes flashed to him, an uncomfortable clench in her stomach. Should she be grateful for his intervention, or embarrassed that it was necessary?

"And what might that be?" Admiral Igor asked, raising a dark furry brow. Jill wasn't entirely sure where one brow ended and the other began.

She pursed her lips shut, resisting the urge to contradict the prince. She may not have completely understood the ins and outs of political conniving, but she'd learned rather quickly it was better to keep quiet. Better for others to think her a fool rather than confirm it by opening her mouth.

"The Siren's Wail has underwater caves, correct?" Tiernan's thick arms were crossed, one hand stroking his chin as he stared down at the map. He really was a handsome man.

"What exactly are you suggesting?" Alpha Volkov asked, his voice low. It reminded her of a wild dog's warning growl.

Whether truly oblivious or unafraid of the Alpha, Tiernan ignored him. "When the tide is low, several people can enter those caves—which lead straight into the Ohans' territory. It would be dangerous, a race against the clock, but if we could send an elite strike team in first, they could dismantle the Ohans' alarm system and let in more soldiers by another route" —he moved a finger across the map— "here. Then we could liberate the people and bring them aboard where the waters are safer."

Silence seemed to echo through the chamber, and Jill looked up to find David watching her before his eyes flicked away.

It felt like she'd been stabbed in the chest. On the battlefield they'd been a team, fighting alongside each other like they'd spent years training together. Now they were back to the tentative distance between them thanks to Tiernan's intentions.

Admiral Igor shook his head, drawing her attention away from the pain in her chest. "It's a suicide mission."

Jill resisted the urge to say that this entire operation was a suicide mission. Best not to have them backing out now. Not when she needed them.

"But it could work, couldn't it?" Tiernan asked, looking around the room before his gaze locked onto hers. She refused to look away despite the heat scorching her cheeks, the strange swirl knotting her stomach.

"Just because it's possible does not mean it's the wisest path," Alpha Volkov said. His knuckles pressed into the table, his face neutral as ever. "I would not risk my men on such a venture."

"How long would it take to travel through the caves?" Jill

asked out of curiosity. She wasn't sure she was on board with the idea either, but few options had emerged. They knew their only hope in an assault on the Ohans depended on stealth and secrecy. They couldn't hope to engage in an all-out battle on their turf, especially not with so many untrained citizens present. But if they could organize a swift and secret strike force to attack from inside, they just might be able to buy enough time to get the people out safely.

"It takes roughly an hour to traverse the caves, if you don't get turned around. At least, according to the very few accounts we have of anyone actually entering them and surviving," Artem explained.

"And how long will the tide stay out?" she asked, afraid of the potential ridicule she might face for such a question.

Artem gave her an unnerving smile. "Roughly an hour."

"And when the tide comes back in?" David asked quietly. All eyes turned to him, but he refused to look ashamed, bless him. She could have hugged him for being bold enough to ask the question she couldn't.

"There's a reason they call it the Siren's Wail." It was Tiernan who spoke, his gaze somewhat distant, as if recalling a specific memory. "When the tide pulls out, it looks like a safe, peaceful harbor. A shelter. But when the tide returns, the water begins to churn in a whirlpool. Like a mouth ready to devour its prey."

Ice slid along Jill's spine. She was ready to shake her head, to say they'd find another way, a safer way, when David spoke again.

"I'll go."

"What? No, you won't," Jill said, her eyes snapping to him.

David finally looked at her, his steely gaze boring into her. "I volunteer for this mission."

Jill fumed, struggling to hide the anger rising in her belly. She clenched her fists. "No, you will not. I won't allow it."

"With all due respect, you are not queen yet. I am offering to go on this deadly mission."

"And I am declining your offer. There are others—"

"What others?" he asked. "It's a suicide mission, like they said. Who else would go?"

"I'll go," she said.

David's eyes went wide. The room fell silent, tension pulling at them like a knot.

"Your Highness, I'm not sure it is wise for the future queen to undertake such a mission," Grimzy said. "These caves are a maze of death."

"Well then it's a good thing we have a mountain man who can navigate them." Jill didn't take her eyes off David, who now looked as she had moments before—face red, mouth twisting, fists balled. She turned to Grimzy who looked torn. It wasn't fair of her to ask him to come along, nor to put him in the middle of her and David but he was an advantage in this scenario. "These are my people. My father ignored and forgot them. I won't do the same."

At this, Grimzy nodded his assent.

"You cannot undo generations of harm." Alpha Volkov's growl shattered the tension in the room. "These people have only ever known slavery. To be rescued by their future monarch may seem heroic in your mind, but they may not see it that way. They may see it as a show of force, as a play for their loyalty."

At last Jill tore her gaze away from David, still seething.

She looked around, making eye contact with every person in the room. Everything about this mission was a gamble. But everything had been a gamble since she'd fled her brother that day so many months ago. At last, she locked eyes with the Alpha.

He looked more compassionate than she'd expected, as if he understood the weight that rested on her shoulders better than anyone. Afterall, people depended on him as well. He seemed a man accustomed to making hard choices that others didn't always agree with. That thought alone spurred her next words.

"You're right. Erinya is a broken, fractured kingdom. It has been for a very long time, but I was too blind to see it. Every clan, every tribe, every house is hostile toward one another. Once upon a time, all I wanted was to become a paladin. I dedicated my life to learning the sword, not to protect people but to win a tournament. Now I see how foolish I was. I see a path forward, one where we work together to forge a better Erinya. I know you all think me a silly, naïve princess. But if fighting for a better future for everyone makes me naïve, then so be it. I will go on this mission. I will risk my life if it comes to that. I will fight for my people, because they deserve better. We all deserve better."

Jill finished her speech, her breathing ragged and her blood pounding. She had to fight back tears. Never had she felt such love for this broken land, such love for her shattered people. She would do more than fight for them. She would die for them, if it came to that. She wished only for them to be free.

"I see there is no convincing you otherwise." The Alpha sounded unsurprised but, if she weren't mistaken, perhaps a little impressed as well.

One step at a time.

The Alpha was right. She could not undo generations of harm in a single moment. But she could take one step forward in the right direction. Change happened one step at a time.

An urgent knocking came at the door and Alpha Volkov

frowned before nodding to a nearby guard. It was rare to be interrupted during these meetings.

Jill glanced out the doorway and was surprised to see Kylian standing there, concern etched into the lines of his face as he whispered with the guard. Kylian, once a barely tolerated appendage of her old life in the palace, had become a friend in the time they'd been here. It was a tentative friendship as they learned who the other person had become in the time they'd been apart, but it was clear they were very different from the people they'd been. She'd been so shocked to see him here that first day, still more shocked to learn that he'd been seeking the Saints' Heirs for years, but she had come to trust him as an ally in a way she never had before.

The wolfman turned toward her. "Your Highness, this man wishes to speak with you. He says it's urgent."

Jill's heart immediately somersaulted inside her chest. What would it be now? What would have Kylian looking so worried?

"Let him in."

Kylian slid deftly around the wolfman, at her side in an instant, his tone hushed as he leaned toward her. "I'm sorry to interrupt. You know I wouldn't unless it were absolutely necessary."

"What is it?"

Kylian pursed his lips, looking nervous. Of the two of them, he was usually the more composed one. This only served to put her further over the edge.

"There's a young woman here to see you. She says she used to be your maid and that you'd likely want to see her. She's come a very long way."

Millie.

How had she escaped? How had she found her all the way out here? Never mind that. She did want to see her.

"Bring me to her." Jill turned back to the others. "I apologize, but something has come up. Can we resume our discussion at the same time tomorrow?"

The Alpha waved a hand and mere seconds later Jill followed Kylian through the halls, their footsteps echoing around them. They were headed to the mead hall, or so it seemed at first. Then at the last moment, Kylian led her away to the infirmary on the eastern side of the keep.

"When did she arrive?" Jill asked, gripping the pommel of her blade. She'd heard whispers of an uprising taking place in the Citadel. Could Millie have heard Jill was here and come? The timing didn't quite make sense, but the girl was a Saint's Heir and Jill knew they were not to be underestimated.

"She arrived only hours ago. When she ran into me, she asked to see you."

They arrived at a room just off the side of the mead hall. Hasani and Peter stood outside looking grimmer than usual.

"She's in there?" Jill made for the door.

Hasani nodded. "Ymira and Zyla are with her. They're checking her now."

"Was she injured?"

Saints. If something happened to Millie because she'd come all this way to find her, she'd never forgive herself. The girl had been through so much, and enough trouble had come from Jill's own hand. She couldn't imagine what Malum must have done to Millie for helping her escape that day.

The three men looked between each other, an uneasy tension filling the silence.

"You'll see." Kylian refused to meet her eyes.

Jill threw open the door and entered to find a private surgeon's room. There was a low bench covered in a white cloth and a table in the back covered with bandages, medicines, and surgeon's tools.

Ymira and Zyla stood facing the bench, their backs to Jill so that she couldn't get a good look at the young woman sitting before them.

She stepped forward and Ymira and Zyla spun toward her. The door shut behind Jill quickly and she found herself, yet again, wondering what could have made everyone so nervous and jumpy.

"Mill—" the name died on her lips as Zyla stepped out of the way to reveal a young woman who was not, in fact, Millie.

For a moment, Jill stood there, trying to place the girl's familiar face.

Former maid. Inkwell. Red hair.

"Anna?"

It was indeed her former maid, the maid she'd had *before* Millie. The girl who'd left suddenly because she'd fallen ill nearly eight months ago.

Jill sucked in a breath. Anna sat up to reveal a belly swollen with child. Her eyes were rimmed with red; her face was ashen, and her freckles were pale. The girl stared at the ground, either unwilling or unable to meet Jill's gaze.

Anna was pregnant. Very pregnant. And Jill was frozen to the spot.

"Your highness, I—I—" Anna choked on her words.

Jill collapsed to her knees before the girl. How on earth had she traveled this far north in her condition? What horrors had she suffered? How was this even possible? This world was not particularly kind to unwed mothers.

"It's all right," Jill said, grasping the girl's frozen hand in her own. She could think of nothing more to say. The words wouldn't form. *Saints.* It couldn't be, could it? This changed everything. Or did it? She wasn't sure of anything anymore.

"I should have found you sooner," Anna whispered, a tear sliding down her face. "But you—you—"

"I know." Did she though? Did she know anything? Her head spun and her stomach threatened to heave.

"I was afraid."

Jill nodded. She needed to ask. She needed to know for certain. "The child. Is it—" she swallowed, her mouth devoid of moisture. "Is it Jack's?"

Anna shuddered, a fresh bout of tears rolling down her cheeks. "It is."

5 2

MALUM

Malum was reluctant to admit how much he liked the Ohans' fortress. Its black stone seemed to suck the light from every source, bathing the long hallways in an unearthly glow. Gargoyles lined the corridors, hideous and terrifyingly beautiful—like fallen angels. They loomed between tapestries of gruesome battles, the colors so vivid he frequently found himself touching the fabric to see if they were truly splattered with blood.

This darkness held a beauty he did not expect many to understand. Once, in his youth, he might have found such a thing barbaric and horrific. He still did. But he could appreciate darkness for what it was. Darkness was the comfort of a closely held secret. Darkness was a womb from which all life had come. Darkness was the night sky, granting reprieve from the harsh light and burning heat of the day.

Yes, darkness had its own special beauty, and the Ohans saw what Jack had not. If only Malum could have convinced Jack to join him, truly join him. They would have been unstoppable.

Not that Malum wasn't already. But having Jack lurking in the back of his mind gave him quite the headache some days. He could still feel him there—like a candle barely flickering—holding on to life, to consciousness. But he no longer spoke to Malum, no longer fought him. Millie had broken his will where Malum could not.

And still Jack clung to life. To hope.

Foolish, really. But he had to commend the young man for his dedication, even if he was not cognizant of it in his current state.

Ohan-Jin had quickly recognized him for who he really was, the Black King Malum. How he'd learned this, Malum couldn't be certain, but he saw no use in lying to the man. Not when doing so no longer served his purposes.

He'd come to the Ohans to establish a treaty. Although they'd captured and tortured Millie—and he had not forgiven them for such an atrocity—he was willing to negotiate with the man. For they had weapons at their disposal that rivaled his magic, his vulgan even.

He'd spent nearly a week with the Ohans, and each day he and Ohan-Jin negotiated over a game of rosepin. A game that had lasted the entire week. Of course, Malum could have won the game anytime, but he had to let Ohan-Jin believe he had a chance of winning, of besting the Black King.

It was all a careful balancing act. And he relished every moment of it.

Malum sat in the plush, blood-red velvet chair, taking in the game board in front of him as Ohan-Jin watched him. Malum stroked a finger across his chin, feigning a thoughtful look. Ohan-Jin had left himself vulnerable to an obvious attack, too obvious. Malum of course knew this and knew that in three quick moves he could have ended the game then and there. But rosepin was a game of feigned missteps and furtive moves. Much like ruling a kingdom. One must be able to see everything from above and calculate when and how the pieces would fall into place.

"So, Jin," Malum said, for they'd quickly established a first name basis with each other, "What shall we discuss today?" He did not lift his gaze from the board as he moved a quartz piece two spaces to the left, pretending to advance on Jin's vulnerable defense. If the man moved his onyx piece three spaces forward, Malum could capture his piece and hold it hostage until Jin's jade piece made its way to the center. But of course, he knew the vulnerable defense had been a trap left by the reptile man, one he was only too eager to release as an ivory piece swooped forward and captured Malum's quartz piece.

Ohan-Jin pocketed the piece with a smile before rising and strolling over to a cart filled with bottles of the darkest liquor. Some looked to be as old as Malum himself. The reptile man poured the drink into two skull-shaped glasses.

Malum chuckled darkly as the man offered him the drink. He really did appreciate the reptile clan's macabre sense of style. It suited them. Or it suited Ohan-Jin at least. Surely not everyone in the reptile clan was as beastly as the man before him.

"Perhaps we skip talk of treaties and alliances today and instead discuss what we shall do when that *princess* arrives on these shores." Ohan-Jin sounded every bit the snake he was as he hissed about the princess and her pathetic new allies, the wolfmen. "My sources tell me they plan to be here in less than a week."

Malum swirled the liquor in his glass. It was a dark ruby color, made from crushed chasteberries he believed, then left to ferment in barrels of a clear alcohol for twenty years. It was among the most potent of drinks in the five kingdoms. It reminded him of blood. He chugged the entire drink then set it on the table beside the rosepin board.

"A week? How very brave of them, to sail the seas this time of year. Do we know precisely when they will strike?" Malum did not look up at Jin, focused solely on the game. Although his quartz piece had been captured, he'd intended for that to happen. Sometimes sacrifices were necessary to win the war. And there was nothing Malum would not sacrifice. He smiled to himself. But he kept pretending not to see the winning move, staring at the board, pretending to flounder.

Jin took a sip of his drink, his jaw clenching and fingers tightening around the rim. "We do not have exact times. But a week should give us plenty of time to prepare. They have clearly learned about the weapons we possess."

Malum nodded, no longer thinking about the game but about seeing Jill again. Last time he'd seen the princess, Jack still had considerable control of himself, and she'd betrayed him. Malum almost felt grateful to the princess for that, as it had allowed him to dig his claws further into the prince's mind. To twist Jack's pain into anger and vengeance. For what was anger but fear to a heightened degree?

"I'm curious, Jin, how would the princess have learned of these weapons? Do you have a traitor among your people?" Malum delivered the line with such casual coolness that he could see the moment the words wedged themselves under Ohan-Jin's skin.

His thin lips grew even thinner, and the glass began to crack. It seemed Ohan-Jin was not always as controlled as he would have everyone else believe. It was a sloppy mistake on his part. For it was clear he knew precisely how the information had found its way to the princess.

"He is not among us, I'm afraid," Ohan-Jin admitted. "But he's a traitor nonetheless."

Malum leaned back in his chair, studying the reptile man carefully. His rigid posture, the slight twitch in his eye. "What is his name?"

"The smuggler who brought the weapons to us in the first place. Peter." Jin spat his name with as much venom as when Malum spoke of the princess.

Malum picked up the empty glass he'd set down, staring at the hollow eyes of the glass skull, the wheels in his head turning. "Peter, Peter." He said absentmindedly. "Why would a smuggler join the company of the royal princess?" He'd heard whispers of this smuggler, this man who'd become a hushed legend.

Ohan-Jin slumped down in the seat across from him in a rare display of defeat, and Malum sensed the man was not feigning or acting but displaying genuine displeasure. "I've not the slightest idea. As long as I've known him, he's hated royals and everything to do with the nobility unless they're buying from him. But the princess has no money, and barely any promises she could actually keep, so I can't imagine why he'd help her. A man like that is selfish down to his core. It's why I hired him in the first place. You can always trust a selfish man to be selfish."

"Something must have changed then," Malum whispered, half to himself. Again, he stared at the game board without really seeing it. "Does he have any family? A wife or children perhaps?"

Ohan-Jin jerked almost imperceptibly, his eyes clearing. "He has a wife, though I don't know her name. Her identity and whereabouts are his most closely guarded secret. In fact, most people don't even know he has a wife."

Malum closed his eyes. In the last month his magic had gone from tenuous to strong, and he could extend his consciousness to his monsters, the prey they turned, and the soldiers under his hold. Thanks to his power, he could travel further as well.

Malum's essence dissolved to shadow, much like Millie's would dissolve into spiders, and suddenly he stood before a little pub over a hundred miles away. *Peter's Pumpkin Alehouse.* The perfect cover for a smuggler. He watched and listened from the shadows as patrons came and went. Time moved differently, hours passing by in mere seconds, or so it seemed to him. Time was irrelevant to a creature like Malum. Four hundred years in the Shadowlands had taught him as much.

Soon the darkness grew and the lights in the pub burned out, a trickle of smoke whispering out the chimney the only evidence anyone had been there at all. A young woman exited the building, pulling the hood of a long cloak over her head, so he couldn't make out her appearance.

Could this be the smuggler's wife?

The young woman looked all around, as if worried someone might see her. As if someone lurked in the shadows. Stepping out into the snow, she hurried down a path that led into the woods, footsteps crunching lightly. Malum followed close behind, bleeding into the shadows like a wraith.

The girl walked only a few minutes before she approached an old woodshed. Except the shed was barred as if it caged some powerful beast.

The young woman approached with a basket in her hands. A smile crept over Malum's face. It couldn't be, could it? It was too simple, too easy.

From the basket, the girl pulled out several rolls and shoved them through the slats in the window as quickly as she could before jumping away.

"I'm sorry, Liza. Peter will be back soon," she said in a hushed whisper so quiet Malum almost couldn't hear it.

A ravenous shriek sounded from the other side as another young woman reached through the bars and clawed on the outside of the door. Her hair had completely fallen out and scars and scabs crusted her entire face.

One of his vulgan's creations. The monster he'd created pounded and clawed at the door, continuing to shriek like a wraith, like some terror that belonged in the Underworld.

This was the great smuggler's wife. An unspeakable monster locked away in a woodshed. Because, despite Peter's hate for the royals and everyone else, he must have loved this woman. Why keep her locked away where she couldn't harm anyone else? It was the act of a man who hoped. Hoped that she could be returned to her human state.

And Malum could do exactly that.

The Black King entered the young woman's mind. It was a terrifying place, fraught with an unquenchable desire to kill and hurt and maim. And she would hurt anything, including herself.

But as Malum entered Liza's mind, he stilled all those thoughts, bringing her comfort and peace for just a moment.

"Liza? Is that you?" The girl outside stepped toward that barred window, hope appearing on her face as she looked at Liza. "Liza?" she pleaded again.

Malum struck then, launching Liza's body forward and giving her extra strength. She burst through the door, the locks snapping and bone crunching as she tackled the other woman into the snow.

Blood splattered and Malum whisked Liza away on his shadows, carrying her back to Ohan-Jin's study.

When he returned, he held the young woman in his arms, her decaying flesh covered in blood as she lay there fast asleep. Like she was a small child and not a brutal monster.

"Ohan-Jin, may I present to you, Peter's wife."

Malum sent his power flowing through her. Her skin went from pale and gaunt to the color of burnished bronze. Her hair grew back and the scars and scabs on her face disappeared entirely until she sat up before them looking like a maiden from a fairytale waking from a long sleep.

"Where am I? Who are you?" Fear and distrust twisted her features, but Malum just placed a hand atop hers.

"I've saved you," Malum said softly.

The reptile man smiled, again looking every bit the serpent he was. Malum smiled back at him. "As you said earlier, you can always count on a selfish man to be selfish."

53

JILL

$\mathcal{A}$nother week passed as Jill spent day after day, meeting after meeting, configuring plans for the raid on the Ohans' territory. The minutiae of such a plan were becoming exhausting. Every plan had a backup plan. Every day, hour, and minute was accounted for. Plans were made in the event of storms. Plans were made in case the Siren's Wail prevented them from docking altogether. Plans were made if they could not rescue as many people as they'd hoped.

Saints, it was all so much. In a way, she couldn't wait for the day of the assault to arrive, if only so she didn't have to sit through another meeting of logistics. Or sitting beside Prince Tiernan. He'd been nothing short of a gentleman, saving her a seat at each meeting, bringing her a warm drink when she was visibly shivering, speaking up on her behalf. He remained close, but didn't lurk or prowl. He was kind and friendly and seemed to smile no matter how bleak the topic of conversation. In any other world, she might have learned to love him.

But then her gaze would catch on David. David who did not save her a seat as he lingered at the back of the room, who made no effort to bring her anything she did not ask for, who barely spoke to her.

And yet, every now and then she would catch his eye, and the world around her would still. The voices would turn to murky background rumblings, her heart the only thing unaffected by the stillness as it galloped inside her ribcage as if it might burst out of her chest and race across the room to him.

Then he would tear his gaze away, disinterested, and she would struggle to catch up with the conversation around her.

Despite Tiernan's friendliness, the elf man made no move to propose. She wondered if he was waiting for the proper moment or waiting until after the assault or if David had been grossly misinformed.

Prince Tiernan was a good man. He seemed to be on a first name basis with nearly everyone, remembering every guard's name, which shift they worked, and which areas they patrolled. He was well-liked too, had been known to make even the Alpha smile on occasion, a feat she hadn't seen accomplished by anyone else. She knew what she *should* feel for him, but she'd come to realize she didn't want to feel that way about him.

Then there was the matter of Jack's child. *Saints.* She was going to be an aunt, to have a niece or nephew. When she thought of the child, her heart nearly burst. She didn't know it was possible to love someone you'd never met so much, someone you hadn't even known existed just a week ago. And the child wasn't even her own.

Yet there was a very real fear for Anna and the child as well. Anna had been showing signs of what Ymira called preeclampsia, which brought risks to both her and the baby. It was only because Ymira herself cared for the girl that Jill felt any sort of relief, otherwise she wasn't sure she could've stomached leaving Anna alone for even a minute.

At last, the day they were to set sail arrived, the date and time chosen so precisely it had taken three days to come to an agreement with everyone. They would take a fleet of twenty longships, almost every ship the wolfmen had, to carry back as many people and as many supplies as they could. The trip there would take a few days with the winds behind them. Although they'd fight the wind on the return trip, they would have extra manpower to row the oars—in theory at least.

It had been decided that Hasani, Ymira, and Zyla would remain behind to care for Asif, Lyra, and Anna. Tiernan would stay as well, though he wasn't pleased with this. Grimzy, Kylian, Bo, Peter, Aaira, Luca, and David would be going with her on the raid along with the wolfmen who would man the ships and launch an attack from the shores.

As she walked through the long stone corridors of Fenric's Keep, she rehearsed the plans again. People were bustling about everywhere, preparing for the journey. Zyla and Ymira oversaw the medical supplies, ensuring every possible injury or illness from the rescued people could be tended to. Hasani had discovered his poisons could be extracted and bottled and had set to work on creating several different combinations they could use to their advantage in a fight. Ivan, the wolfman and Saints' Heir who'd come to her and David's aid in the battle, had been charged with ensuring enough weapons, armor, and explosives had been loaded onto the boats. Grimzy headed up most everything else, the Alpha deferring to his judgment, though the wolfmen would oversee everything to do with preparing the ships themselves.

Long and sleek with a wolf's head carved into the prow, the longships were things of ornate beauty. She'd watched them preparing the day before and the sight was enough to take her breath away. She'd never been on a ship before—never had any reason. Her father traveled on only a handful of diplomatic trips when she was a child and then no more. And, of course, she'd never been allowed to go with him. As she watched those billowing sails filled with icy wind, she could see why her brother had always felt drawn to the ocean, had always longed to see the world and travel the seas.

But while everyone else prepared to set sail, Jill found herself pacing back and forth in the armory. Soft voices of those who'd be accompanying them on the raid bounced around the cavernous space. Jill inhaled, packing away her bracers and examining her sword. How many months had it been since she'd lost the sword's twin? Since she'd lost her own twin? Or rather, since her twin had been taken from her.

She tried not to think of Jack these days, not any more than she had to. Thoughts of him broke her heart all over again. And thinking of what she would have to do before the end— she couldn't bear the idea of their next meeting. Was he still in there, fighting against Malum? Or had he vanished, lost to the depths of his own mind?

Saints, she didn't know what she hoped for. She couldn't stand to think he might still be alive, somehow trapped within the darkness of Malum's mind. But to imagine that he might be gone forever . . .

No. She couldn't do it.

Quickly, she wiped down her sword with oil and sheathed it, giving no more thought to its twin or her own.

A breeze whispered through the armory, and she sensed him behind her before she saw him, his presence as familiar as her own skin. He was a warm fire on a bitter-cold night, bright and constant against the dark.

She turned to see David standing behind her, his black armor tight against his muscles. It was a special design Peter and Grimzy had dreamed up with interlocking metal scales and an inner lining that should protect him from breaking or cracking too much. They'd spent countless days in the training arena perfecting the design.

Now he stood in front of her, silent and grim. Sweat broke out on her palms at the task before them. At the man before *her*.

"Grimzy wants to know if you're ready. It's almost time."

Jill inhaled but her lungs couldn't seem to drag in enough air. The what-ifs tumbled through her head like a splash of coins down a busy city street, rolling into and away from each other until they were scattered everywhere.

What if it wasn't enough? What if they failed? What if people died?

The last thought was the most foolish. Of course, people would die. People died, especially in times of war. A mission like this was no exception. If anything, this mission was destined for failure. And yet, that had not stopped volunteers from offering their services. Ivan and Tiernan and even the Alpha himself had offered their aid and support so they might save her people, and she might become queen.

It was all too much.

"I can't do this," Jill whispered, barely breathing the words. She wiped her sweaty palms against her pants. She didn't understand why she was so frightened. She had battled many times now, but this was different. She was coming to liberate her people, but it would also be the start of a dangerous war against the Ohans. She started to pace again.

"Jill." David's voice was so soft, so tender. Almost like it had been the night they'd sat beside the fire together. The night she'd dared to dream they might be something more, and he'd shattered those illusions as if they were made of the same glass he was.

She paused her pacing and looked up at him, examining the scars along his face. It had been so long since David had said her name without the title *Princess* in front of it. She hadn't realized how much she'd missed it, hearing her name on his lips.

"If this doesn't work—"

"It will," he cut her off. "It's a good plan. I'll be by your side the entire time." He stared at her, his gaze filled with pain. "I won't leave you."

Jill's stomach clenched. "You've said that before."

A commotion broke out on the other side of the armory, a sudden clattering of armor and weapons sending up shouts and yells before it died down again.

Jill was growing tired of the keep, tired of hiding from Malum like a beetle who feared the light. Too long she'd been standing still, waiting for something to happen. She'd vowed to take the throne, yet she felt no closer to doing so than she had when she first spoke that vow.

"I know," David said, lowering his head.

They stood there in silence louder than the racket they'd just heard, the gap between them growing wider by the second. How she longed for the easiness that had once existed between them. How she longed to say something that would change things, change the hand destiny had dealt them. Could he not see that she didn't want Tiernan?

"I'm sorry. I never should have left you the way I did. I just —" he stopped, running his fingers through his hair in agitation. "I was just afraid." He took a step toward her.

She gritted her teeth, blood suddenly pounding through her. "*You* were afraid? How do you think I felt? One second you were promising to stay by my side and the next you abandoned me in a magical forest for people you'd just met?" Pain and anger sharpened her words.

David winced. "Jill, you don't understand—"

"What don't I understand?" She cut him off. Her skin

flushed and her breath quickened. There were too many things she wanted to say and yet all she could do was lash out. "Is there a reason you keep pulling away? I'd love to know why you just left me on that hill—"

"I didn't want to leave you that day!" he shouted, silencing her. Then he swallowed and took another step forward. "I didn't want to leave you at all." This time he looked at her, really looked at her, his warm brown eyes gazing at her in a way that sent flutters rushing through her chest even as the anger waged war against it.

Jill didn't dare hope. They were different people than when they'd met, when she was just a spoiled princess and he a simple hunter and soldier.

"I didn't mean to hurt you," he said, his voice cracking.

"Then why did you?" she demanded, tears springing to her eyes. "Why did you leave me David?" Her voice cracked this time as she looked up at him, begging for an answer she feared would never come.

"Because if I didn't leave then, I never would have left your side. Ever."

Time froze as the world around them melted away. Blood rushed to Jill's face and her hands shook.

"Do you understand what you do to me?" he asked.

Jill shook her head, daring a step toward him. The gap was shrinking, but the distance still felt too far.

"Why'd you leave me, David?" She asked again. "I needed someone. I needed you." A tear finally slid down her cheek. The confession terrified her. How long had she believed he didn't care for her? Did he know just how alone she'd been? She'd lost everyone. Her mother, her father, her brother, Will. And then him.

A warm finger brushed the tear away, his skin so soft despite how brittle it was. It shouldn't have been possible.

Gently, he lifted her chin to look up at him and she was reminded of that day back in the Oasis.

"Jill, you will be the death of me." David smirked, a dimple appearing through the dark stubble on his face. "But if you were an ocean, I would drown for you. If you were a storm, I would chase you down. And if you asked me to follow you to the gates of the Underworld, I would hold your hand until death took us both. Jill, where you go, I'll go too. I won't leave you again."

Lightning exploded in her chest. "Prove it."

He finally closed the gap between them, pressing his lips to hers. The kiss was both soft and hungry. The ache in her chest faded away as she reached up to wrap her arms around his neck. Seconds twisted into eternity and back again and then all too soon he was pulling away, resting his forehead against hers, holding her in a way she'd never been held before, as if she were the most precious thing he'd ever held before. As if he loved her.

"Tell me this isn't a dream," she whispered, her eyes fluttering.

"It isn't." He pressed another kiss to her forehead, and she could feel him smiling. "I love you," he murmured. "And I know I told you to marry Tiernan, but I can't stay away from you. You haunt my dreams, and my every waking thought belongs to you."

The thrill those words sent through her chest. Just the sound of them made her giddy. After Will, she never thought she'd fall in love again, let alone that someone might love her in return. But now, marred and broken as it might be, she gave her heart to him freely.

"I love y—"

Someone's throat cleared. "Your Highness?"

They jumped and spun to see Kylian Doyle standing

before them, looking genuinely apologetic. Too quickly, David stepped away from her, stiff and formal. The feeling of him lingered on her skin as she swallowed and nodded at Doyle.

"Yes?"

"It's time."

5 4

DAVID

With the whipping winds and the western current, it had taken exactly three days to sail to the Siren's Wail, just as they'd planned. David should have been overjoyed that all had gone to plan so far, but there was still time for things to go wrong. He knew that better than anyone.

In that time, David had discovered he did not care for sailing. The way the ship bobbed and rolled over the waves, undulating like a serpent, made him nauseous. The freezing wind and snow that pelted his skin was also a nuisance, like being struck by frozen needles. Thankfully, it didn't cause his skin to crack.

He stood at the port side of the ship, staring out at the choppy gray seas. White foam lapped against the hull as the white sails billowed behind him. A wave smashed against the side of the ship, spraying him with icy salt water.

Saints, he was ready to be off this boat. Even if it meant traveling through the tunnels in the Siren's Wail. At least then he'd be doing something productive. On the ship he was less than helpful, forced to watch as trained sailors hustled about. More often than not, he was simply in the way, a frustrating feeling.

Jill sidled up next to him, her presence quiet and unwavering. She grabbed his hand, twining their fingers together. Her fingers were as icy and stiff as his, but she was here, at his side. Holding his hand. He smiled, turning to look at her and pulling her closer until his arms wrapped around her and his chin rested atop her head.

He didn't care who saw them, nor did she. He wanted only this moment with her in his arms.

"Are you just using me to keep warm?" Jill asked.

"Maybe." He tipped his head and smiled down at her.

It all felt like a dream, like soon he might wake, and she would vanish like sea mist. How long had he fought these feelings for her? Fought against every instinct that drew them together.

Too soon she was pulling away, a mischievous smile lighting up her face in a way that sent his heart galloping. Only then did he notice what she was wearing. Instead of the thick coat and pants designed to stave off frostbite, she now wore her leather armor, her sword and a knife strapped to her side.

"We'll reach the Siren's Wail in an hour, so be ready. You know how short our time is."

At that his smile faded but he nodded, a soldier receiving orders.

One hour. They had a single hour to row across the bay, reach the caves, and travel all the way through them before the hour was up. They had no chance of rowing across the bay at high tide, so every second counted. Once they exited the caves, their group would split up. Grimzy would cause a disturbance in the labor camps that would begin the evacuation. Meanwhile, Jill, David, Luca, and Peter would infiltrate the Ohans' fortress while Kylian, Bo, and Aaira extracted the Order of the Saints. They believed the high-ranking members of the Order were kept in the dungeons below the fortress while the lower members were held in the Convent. They had contingency plans in place just in case. With no time to scout ahead, and not wanting to risk tipping off the Ohans, they'd agreed this was the best course of action.

David made his way below deck and began fastening on his armor. The soft inner lining was made of wool, the exterior metal scales locked together in a fashion that had been inspired by the Komodo dragons' reptilian armor.

When he finished, he joined the rest of the crew on deck where several wolfmen were dropping two boats over the side. Currently the tide was still in, and they would have to be ready the instant it began pulling back out. They loaded up the two boats, Grimzy and Peter in one and the rest of them in the other. Two wolfmen would row them there, drop them off in the caves, and then row back so the longships could travel to the shores beside the labor camps. From there the wolfmen would storm the beach and help rescue the people.

They waited in silence, watching as the tide ebbed. In the center of the bay, water shot up, the sound like a thousand cymbals crashing against each other. The sea churned and swirled, foaming and frothing.

"Welcome to the Siren's Wail," one of the wolfmen said, giving them all a grim smirk. He stared at the water shooting upward. It screeched and shrieked like a wraith, like a siren.

"We're rowing across that?" Bo looked unnerved.

"Yes," said Jill. "Anyone who doesn't wish to come doesn't have to. But I'm going, even if I go alone." The princess didn't look at any of them but stared across the bay at the tunnels that would lead them into the Ohans' territory. David knew she meant what she said. She would go alone if it meant she could save her people.

His love for her grew in that moment, and it was one he was sure he'd never forget. That image of her standing before the railing of the ship, gripping the hilt of her blade. Her hair was braided back but the wind tugged strands from the plait and whipped them around her face. She rolled her shoulders back and turned to them, more determined than he'd ever seen her. It was as if the very world around them held its breath and stilled. She leveled each of them with that fierce, hard gaze and he wondered for the first time if perhaps she wasn't one of the Saints' Heirs herself, wielding a power that would shake the world to its very core.

Not a soul rescinded their offer or dared back out. They would follow her. Even the wolfmen standing nearby straightened, looking to her in a way they never had before. A way he'd only seen them looking at their Alpha. They all recognized power and authority, and Jill commanded their attention now. She commanded them all.

Grimzy was the first to kneel before her. "I will follow my queen, wherever she goes."

David knelt a second later. Then Kylian, Bo, Luca, and Aaira. And then they watched in awe as the wolfmen followed suit one by one. Peter was the last one, giving the princess a slight nod before joining them. Each soul on board soon knelt at Jill's feet.

Jill did not balk or shy away from the devotion, instead holding her head high. But David could see the tiniest crinkle between her eyebrows, that seed of doubt that asked whether she was doing the right thing. Whether she would make a good queen.

David met her eyes and gave her the slightest of nods.

You will be a good queen. As if the thought could travel on the wind, that crinkle smoothed, and she nodded at her subjects to rise.

~

THE BOAT RIDE WAS SWIFT, the water choppy and rough even as the skilled wolfmen rowed across the bay. David had underestimated their strength and speed, and they reached the caves in less than ten minutes. The cave they chose did not have much in the way of a shore but something more like a ledge they'd have to scale before they could reach a tunnel that wasn't a dead end.

Since Aaira was familiar with many of the tunnels in and around the Convent, she'd been chosen to guide them through the caves, Grimzy helping where necessary. They had less than fifty minutes to exit the caves before the tide came back in and flooded the tunnels.

One at a time they climbed up the ledge as the boats rocked unsteadily beneath their feet. Up first was Peter, then the rest of them followed. David stared down at Grimzy, who was sitting in a boat far too small to hold him, and Bo, who gripped her crutch so hard her knuckles turned white as ice.

Grimzy had offered to carry Bo through the tunnels so they could move swiftly. Reluctantly, Bo had agreed, though David sensed it was humbling for her to accept his help. She was so capable he often forgot she still had challenges to overcome. He berated himself inwardly. He didn't want to baby her or assume she was weak. But he didn't want to pretend he didn't see her differences either. He just wanted to see her for who she was.

Grimzy lifted the girl, who looked preposterously small in the large man's arms, and hoisted her up to the top of the ledge where they all stood. Then in one step he settled himself on top of the ledge. He helped Bo climb on his back and then they were off through the tunnels.

Aaira lit the torch she'd brought with her and led the way, her steps certain and sure even as they wound about in nonsensical patterns. Sometimes the tunnel curved up, then led them downward. Sometimes they were forced to climb up or slide through smaller tunnels on their bellies.

Minutes passed in relative silence, the only sounds were their heavy breathing and grunting and the swish of leather and weapons bumping along the walls. They had no way to know exactly how much time had passed since they'd left the boat, but he suspected they were approaching the one-hour mark.

As if responding to that very thought, a low gurgling sound filled the tunnels.

The tide was coming in.

"We need to hurry," Peter said.

"I'm well aware of that," Aaira said as she took a left at the next intersection. They all picked up speed, racing against the gurgling rushing up behind them. David's heart pounded as they found themselves faced with another tunnel only a few feet high.

Aaira was already crawling through, Jill following right behind her. One by one, they got down and crawled, slowed by their weapons. Grimzy hummed as they moved forward, doing his best to widen the tunnel, mostly for himself.

David followed Luca, who crawled faster than everyone else. The damp cavern floor did little to reassure him as he continued moving forward and the tunnel grew narrower. Would Grimzy even fit? Was his power waning? Why wasn't the tunnel widening?

The rushing sound filled his ears and a second later, icy water flowed past his fingertips. David kept moving, refusing to think about what would happen if they got stuck in this tunnel and it filled with water. A strange thought struck him then, unbidden and rather unwelcome. Could he drown? His skin could crack and break and heal, but what if he inhaled water? Were his lungs made of glass? Surely not. He still needed to breathe. He would definitely die if this tunnel flooded with him in it. He didn't want to find out one way or the other.

David started to panic, his breathing coming in ragged gasps as the water rose higher around him. His fingers were numb with cold. The water rose past his knuckles, swishing around his wrists as he continued to crawl. His breaths came faster, and his heart raced like he was fighting in battle, not crawling through a tunnel.

The tunnel narrowed, conforming around him like a glove. He froze, the walls around him closing in, tightening, squeezing him. He couldn't move. He was stuck. Where was Grimzy?

The water rose higher. It flowed up past his wrists, drenching his forearms, then coming up to his shoulders, inches from his face. Soon the water would cover it, and he would drown.

"Grimzy!" he shouted, unable to hide the panic in his voice. "Jill!" He was stuck in the darkness as the water rose, trapped in the tunnel.

He was about to find out if he could drown or not. He flailed then, despite his instincts telling him to keep calm.

A deep rumbling shook the earth beneath him, the water sloshing about, splashing his face. Then the tunnel around him opened and widened, light appearing before him as someone grabbed his arms, pulling him out of the tunnel and into a cavern larger than any they'd come across so far. He was pulled to his feet, water dripping from him as he looked up at Luca, then at the rest of the group, their eyes wide with fear.

Grimzy crawled through a second after, Bo clinging to his back, her breathing nearly as ragged as David's. He rose to his full height, towering over all of them. Water continued pouring in through the opening they'd come from, now larger thanks to Grimzy. The cavern they stood in had no other outlets. They were trapped.

The water was nearing their knees, rising higher and higher, the cold almost unbearable.

"We need to climb," Jill said, running to the wall. She climbed up a few feet then stopped where the cavern curved up and in, making it impossible to climb any higher. She dropped to the ground, her chest heaving. She turned to face David, panic lacing every feature.

Then Grimzy set Bo down gently, and the young girl again gripped her crutch as if it were the only thing holding her together. As if it were more than an aid to help her walk, as if it were a lifeline. Perhaps it was.

Grimzy closed his eyes, his voice dropping lower than David had ever heard it. The ground beneath their feet thundered as his rhythm and humming grew louder. Strange melodies struck the air as if not one man hummed but a hundred, the sound like a hive of bees but with warbling harmonies alongside the melodies. The notes twisted and spun, the earth around them shifting and turning with Grimzy's humming as a small opening in the walls widened, boring a tunnel before them up toward the surface.

At last, Grimzy stopped, but the music continued echoing through the cavern, as if the sound itself was widening and growing until it tapered off into silence. The silence was bizarre after the melodious music they'd just heard. But the water was up to their hips now and they had to move.

They all hurried forward, Jill at the front. Stars appeared within their line of sight, the icy water lapping at their heels, chasing them upward as they fought through the tide, their movements painfully slow. Behind them, Bo hurried along, her crutch sloshing through the water while Grimzy held up the rear.

They broke into the cool night air, out of the caves and into a clearing at the top of a hill. David heaved a sigh of relief but was surprised by how exposed he suddenly felt without the cover of the caves. He shivered as a freezing wind blew against his wet clothing. Although it was winter here as well, the Ohans' territory was prone to biting wind and rain rather than snow.

A mile off stood the Ohans' fortress, vast and dark. Black towers twisted upward, bulwarks and parapets wrapping around the massive structure, fires blazing periodically along the wall as guards made their rounds, on the lookout for miscreants and invaders. On the lookout for them.

Further off was the Convent, the building out of place in such a dark place. Where the fortress stood dark and foreboding, the Convent seemed to exude light, even in the night. The surface shone as if constructed from moonbeams. While the fortress was all jagged edges and gargoyles, the Convent was curves and swooping verandas with golden parapets dulled by dirt and time. David could tell the structure had once been magnificent, breathtaking to behold.

What had it been like before the Ohans had taken over this part of the kingdom?

Even further off lay the mines and labor camps. The smell struck him first, pungent even from so far off. The scent of unwashed bodies, of sulfur and excrement, of blood and decay. Large gates surrounded camps, shutting the people in. Staring at that was more foreboding than the fortress. To see the dilapidated barracks the guards shoved hundreds of people into, to hear the crack of that whip . . .

Cold anger seared its way through David's veins, threatening to undo him until he felt a hand grip his own. He glanced over to see Jill beside him, staring in the same direction, her gaze burning with the same fierce anger.

"This is why we're here," she whispered, loud enough for all of them to hear. "This is why we fight."

David squeezed her hand. He did not need to say a word to know she understood.

"It's time," Kylian said, coming up beside them. "We part ways here. But I expect to see every last one of you at the extraction point. No dying allowed." Kylian flashed them all a lighthearted smile, as if unaffected by the sight before them. But he knew the man well enough now to know that his own heart burned with the same anger, the same desire to free these people.

They parted ways with little fanfare. They couldn't afford to waste time on pleasant goodbyes. But perhaps more importantly, they couldn't afford to think about the possibility of more permanent goodbyes.

Grimzy began making his way to the labor camps, where he would disable their alarm systems, letting the wolfmen in and beginning the exodus of the miners to the boats. Likewise, Kylian and Bo followed Aaira as she led them toward the Convent.

David glanced at his crew and then again at the Ohans' fortress as panic trickled into his veins. Staring up at those dark towers, he jolted as flashes of memory accosted him. Images of running down dark hallways, climbing stairs, of Jack kicking him off a high tower.

David sucked in a breath and squeezed his eyes shut, blocking out the memories. No, not memories. Visions. Visions of what was to come. It had been inevitable from the moment he'd been cursed. But now to see it there in front of him, to know what was coming, could he face it?

He was stuck in the caves again, his lungs squeezing as he tried to force his breaths to slow. They only became more erratic. His blood thundered like one of Grimzy's songs, roaring past his ears with the fury of a tidal wave come to swallow him whole, to drag him under the surface and—

"Is everything all right?" Jill whispered.

He looked over at her, as if seeing her for the first time, and he was reminded of fighting by her side in that tavern so long ago now. And he realized she'd had his heart from that moment. He'd laid eyes on her and something in him had stirred, drawn to her like a moth to flame. How true that statement was now more than ever.

He tamped down his fear. David could do this for her. He'd stay by her side, no matter what came. He'd told her he would follow her to the gates of the Underworld itself. Little did she know that it hadn't been a metaphor.

"Everything's fine," he said with a forced smile. "Let's get going."

Sing a song of sixpence,
A pocketful of rye,
Four and twenty blackbirds
Baked in a pie.

When the pie was opened,
The birds began to sing—
Wasn't that a dainty dish
To set before the king?

MILLIE

For the third time in less than a month, Millie woke to surroundings she did not recognize. She lay on a thick bear skin rug, several blankets piled on top of her. A canvas tent fluttered around her, followed by the sounds of a camp—muffled voices, the crackle of fires and clanging of pots, the pounding of footsteps and rattle of weapons.

She tried to recall how she'd come to be here, to leaf through her memories, but they were darky and murky, like some half-remembered dream. Only the feelings remained. A deep silence yawned inside her like a pit of darkness, waiting to consume her. Flashes struck her then, of the Mother Goose's arrival and her escape. Of Jack's head as she severed it from his body.

A fresh wave of tears threatened to spill over, to seize control of her and send her retreating into sleep. Sleep welcomed her with its warm embrace, whispering gently to fall back into its clutches, to succumb to the heavy weight in her chest.

And she longed to, oh how she longed to lean back and

curl up under the blankets, hiding from everyone and everything. That unbearable ache dug its claws into her chest. Sleep could free her, could ease that pain, if only for a little bit.

Someone pushed the entrance to the tent open and stepped inside.

"Millie you're awake!" Doon rushed to her side, wrapping his arms around her.

That was when she finally broke.

Tears spilled down her face as she buried it in her big brother's shirt, sobbing until she could hardly breathe. She clung to him, gripping his shirt as he rocked her, holding her as if she were a small child and not just two years younger than him.

He let her weep. He did not say a word, only held her as she soaked his shirt, her chest heaving with the effort. His fingers threaded through her hair as his arms tightened around her, as if to say, *I've got you.*

Her tears finally, slowly, receded until she was practically gasping for air. Until the ache in her chest had eased just a little bit. She could not even pinpoint the source of her grief, for there were too many. She grieved for Jack. She grieved for herself. For all that she had lost and all that he had lost. Mostly she grieved for a future they might have had together, had Malum not ruined everything.

She pulled away from Doon, rubbing away the tears from her swollen face, puffy from her crying. She sucked in another shuddering breath, fighting to calm herself, to breathe normally.

And through every moment, Doon waited silently. He did not urge her to dry her tears, nor force her to be quiet or try to rush her back into joy. He simply let her be sad, offering his silent presence to her without judgment, and for that she was more grateful than she'd ever find the words to express.

"Millie, I'm so sorry," he said at last, his voice cracking.

She looked up at him, his eye watering. "I thought—I thought—" Her words cut off as she choked back more tears. She didn't even understand how she had any tears left.

"I know," he whispered. He didn't gloat—didn't need to. He'd warned her what would happen if she continued serving Jack, serving Malum.

"Thank you," she said, swallowing back the lump in her throat. She wanted to hide that weakness, those feelings of pain and grief and loss, deep inside where no one would ever see that part of her again. But she could not do so with Doon. Her brother would always encourage her to be honest with herself, a task that proved far more difficult than being honest with anyone else.

As if reading her thoughts he said, "Don't shy away from the pain you feel. Wear it proudly, and you will encourage others to do so also."

She forced a half smile. It was all she could manage.

"Where are we?" she asked, finally able to face whatever new reality awaited her. She could grieve more later. But right now, she needed answers.

"We're camped outside the Southern Marshes. We've been traveling for the last few days, but between everything that happened in the Citadel and your injuries, you've been pretty out of it," he explained.

"Master Ravala? Keyanna?" she asked.

Doon nodded. "They're here. And Ravala's okay, though he doesn't trust these people at all."

Her heart skipped. "And who exactly are we with?" Mother Goose had come to rescue her along with several other people, but that didn't mean Millie knew what she'd gotten herself into.

Doon pursed his lips, clearly hesitating. "They call themselves the Blackbirds."

Millie arched a brow. "What's wrong?"

Her brother was incredibly thoughtful and generally had good intuition, so if these Blackbirds made him nervous, she hated to think what they might've gotten themselves wrapped up in. "Millie," he said carefully, his single eye piercing her with twice the ferocity, as if making up for the one he was missing. "They're a resistance group."

"A resistance group?" She blinked.

"Yes. They're planning to assassinate King Jack."

Millie stilled. So much hung unsaid in those words. And with it came the uncertainty that had plagued her for months now. Aside from Mother Goose, they didn't know the monster they sought to kill wasn't Jack, but Malum. They couldn't possibly understand what they were truly up against. Even Millie herself didn't know, not truly. In her heart, she knew Jack would recover from the blow he'd been dealt and that his head would reattach itself, a thought almost as disturbing as severing it in the first place.

"There's more," Doon said, dropping his voice even lower.

"What?" she asked, the air twisting out of her chest.

"They want you to lead them. To be the one to"—he swallowed— "the one to end him."

Millie's entire world fell silent as death. Her stomach threatened to rebel against her, to heave up its measly contents. Sweat coated her palms and the back of her neck as her vision began to swim again. She'd already cut off his head, and it had been the single worst experience of her life. She'd vowed to save Jack, but not like this.

"Why me?" The bite in her own words, the venom laced in those two syllables, surprised her.

Doon shook his head, running a hand through his hair. "I don't know. But if you come with me, you can talk to them, make them see reason."

"Me?" Millie choked, feeling her eyes widen at the prospect. She'd become a paladin sure, had been kidnapped and tortured for information but that didn't mean she knew how to talk to people like these, people who wanted to murder the man she—

She stopped the thought from going any further. She wouldn't say those words, not even to herself.

"Yes, you." That single eye stared at her again, boring into her with such strength she could only hold his gaze a few seconds before looking away. "You've always been braver than you believed, Millie. Talk to them."

"And if I can't?"

"You can."

Doon was so certain, so matter-of-fact that she could argue with him no further. Did not even want to.

"Fine," she agreed, "Take me to them."

Doon rose to his feet, stretching out his arm to her. She accepted the help greatly, groaning at the soreness in her muscles. She'd just reached a point in her training with Master Ravala where her workouts with him no longer resulted in such extreme muscle soreness that she limped and winced everywhere she went. Then she'd been tasked with hunting down Jill and waylaid by injuries. Now she felt as if she were starting all over.

She followed Doon out of the tent and into the small camp that had been assembled in what looked to be an ancient, overgrown orchard. Massive trees soared skyward, rich with plump fruits she couldn't identify. The camp was small, perhaps only twenty people roamed around. A small resistance then. More tents crowded around a main gathering area, though no fire burned in its center. Horses were tied to a tree nearby, and everything was so neat and organized she got the sense the camp was designed to be taken down and packed up at a moment's notice.

They walked toward one of the larger tents, and the camp around them grew quiet as everyone turned to stare at her. Some wore expressions of awe and pride, others of suspicion and vague distrust.

She was reminded of the first time she'd entered the ballroom after the Paladin's Tournament, when every eye had been fixed on her, every subtle whisper had echoed her name. She'd been more terrified then than during the tournament itself.

But something in her had changed since then. Instead of cowering, she reminded herself of Jill. She reminded herself of Jack's words to her that day.

People will always talk, no matter what we do, so we may as well do what we want.

So, Millie rolled her shoulders back and held her head high, ignoring every gawking face and suspicious sneer.

Then a familiar face caught her attention, one that sent her heart pounding and blood boiling. The short gazelle man locked eyes with her, then glanced away quickly. Before she knew what had overtaken her, she marched up to the young man, grabbed the front of his shirt, and shoved him up against a nearby tree. Still, he refused to meet her gaze.

"You." She spat the words. "What are you doing here?"

The gazelle man—Esmeray—was so timid and so short, only a few inches taller than her. The gazelles were a tall, willowy people. She'd never seen one who wasn't at least a foot taller than her. Even his horns were shorter, likely a source of shame for the boy. For that's all he was. A boy. Probably around Millie's age.

"I fled the Ohans," he said, giving a timid shrug, still refusing to meet her gaze. "Came here."

"Why?" She didn't trust him for a single second. He could be a spy for all she knew.

"Where else could I go?" he said in a broken, desperate way.

"Millie," Doon's soothing voice said from behind her.

She released the boy's shirt but made no move to step back. Sure, he'd helped mend her wounds, but only after Ohan-Jin had tortured her. He'd watched from the corner, unable or unwilling to do anything.

In her mind, she knew her hatred for him wasn't fair. He'd likely been as trapped as she was, forced into aiding Ohan-Jin. That didn't mean she wanted him here.

"How'd you find us?"

"I found him, actually," a familiar voice said.

Millie turned toward Mother Goose who stood, watching her with a cool, assessing expression. Her hands were clasped in front of her.

"And you brought him here?" she asked, barely containing the hold on her rage. So rarely did she allow such anger to take control of her. But she was so tired of holding it all together. It felt good to release it all for once, to let her displeasure show.

"I did. He's not so different from you Millie," she said, giving her a meaningful look.

Millie inhaled as she looked back at him. He sighed before the air around him warped and fuzzed, and then ethereal light shot from his face, his hands, his entire body until he was glowing. His appearance warped and shifted, until she looked back at an identical copy of herself.

Her jaw dropped. The air around him shifted again and

the light faded away, his head bowed, and before her was the gazelle man once more, though he looked far more ashamed than he had before.

"This is Esmeray, heir of Amari the Eternal."

Millie's mouth felt dry. Her anger had lessened, but she did not know what to make of that. He was a Saints' Heir, like she was. Yet he'd helped Ohan-Jin torture her.

He helped heal you actually, she reminded herself. But that did little to soothe her mind about the entire ordeal.

"The Ohans threatened to kill me if I didn't help them," Esmeray explained.

Millie resisted the urge to tell him that perhaps it would have been better if he'd been killed, but even she wasn't that cruel, though part of her longed to be. A strange sort of exhaustion came with being gracious to others so often. Sometimes she longed to dissolve into the petty, vengeful monster that Malum had tried to make her.

"Millie, let us discuss these matters in privacy, why don't we?" Mother Goose must have read the expression on Millie's face, the thinly veiled anger that threatened to burst through.

"Fine," she said. "But I'd keep an eye on him if I were you. If he can take anyone's face, who's to say he isn't spying for the Ohans."

She stomped away, ignoring the stares that followed her. Good. Let them stare. Let them see she wasn't the cowering child she'd once been.

They ducked into a nearby tent, and she was shocked to find how stark and empty it was. A sleeping mat lay on the ground in one corner and a few people sat in a circle on the ground in the middle. There was nothing else. No war maps, no trinkets or weapons, no tables laden with food. When had she grown so accustomed to the benefits of being a paladin?

It disturbed her more than she cared to admit.

Only three people sat in the center of the tent, all of whom she recognized. Mother Goose sat down, listening as Isaac relayed information from some sort of scouting mission. Beside him sat two other ladies Millie recognized. Madame Sorelle and Paladin Willa.

It was such a strange sight, having so many people from different parts of her life all together. Particularly strange was seeing Madame Sorelle sit cross legged on the ground, dirtying her torn skirts. Millie had been terrified of this woman for the larger part of her life but her sitting there looking old and frail was by far one of the more disturbing things Millie had witnessed recently. The night in the dungeons, after she'd decapitated Jack, remained somewhat blurry, but clearly Isaac had managed to free these two. No doubt, Paladin Willa had taken charge when Millie had become a liability herself.

"Welcome, Paladin Millie," Madame Sorelle said, nodding her head in a sign of respect.

Millie swallowed hard but returned the nod.

Mother Goose gestured to a spot beside Paladin Willa, "Take a seat."

Millie did so, though her stiff muscles protested the simple movement. Saints, had she been this out of shape her entire life?

Doon sat beside her, solemn and sturdy as a tower behind her. He said nothing but somehow made his presence both known and felt. He'd never been that way before, but it might have something to do with the eye patch he now wore.

Millie glanced over at Paladin Willa, a woman nearly ten years her senior, ragged blonde hair nearly brown with the dirt and grime in it. She'd been one of the first thrown in the dungeon when she'd refused to swear fealty to Malum.

The young woman gave her an assessing gaze, as if sizing

her up. Millie straightened out of habit, reminded somehow of the princess in that look.

"Did you know," Paladin Willa started, "that in the hundred years the Paladin Tournament has been held, only four women have ever won it? And two of them are sitting in this very tent."

Millie wasn't sure what to make of this, but the woman gave her a slight smile, her eyes alight with something mischievous.

"I suppose that's quite the feat for both of us then," Millie responded, not sure what else to say. Had the paladin thrown her a life rope by making the comment? Or was she simply making small talk? Somehow the latter option seemed unlikely for a woman of her character, but she'd never talked to the woman before.

"I thought the princess would win the tournament. But then you revealed your dark side."

Millie's blood ran cold. Her body stiffened as she recalled that day, recalled transforming and torturing her mistress with fear. She'd been that fear. It was like the signal of a trapped animal doing everything in its power to escape.

Because that's what Jill had been. Trapped. As Millie had once been. In many ways she and the princess could not have been more different, but in others she felt as though she knew Jill better than she knew herself.

"My dark side, yes," Millie said sharply, making it clear that line of conversation would go no further. "Keyanna, is she here?"

"We got Keyanna and her son out, yes. She's safe with the others who left the Citadel."

Millie's stomach tightened. "Where are they?"

"Hidden. I have more of my Blackbirds caring for and

guarding the refugees who fled with us. The boarmen have agreed to take care of them in the Southern Marshes."

She said nothing. At least the people were safe. But where did that leave them? Why weren't they with this group?

She turned to Mother Goose. "Tell me why you rescued me, why you've brought me here. What exactly do you hope to accomplish?"

Mother Goose cracked a smile. "I'm sure your brother filled you in on several things, did he not?"

"He did," she said evenly. Her heart gathered speed, but she did her best to inhale deeply, to seize control of her facial expressions. "He said you're a resistance group intent on assassinating Malum."

"That's true."

Millie pursed her lips, waging an internal battle. She wanted Malum dead, and this group would help her accomplish such a task. But could she kill Malum and save Jack? Did they want to save Jack?

"It won't be easy," she said, choosing each word with care. "He's not some mortal man."

"You're right. Jack is no mortal man. He never has been. Not since he returned from the dead inside his mother's womb." She paused and Millie felt her eyes go wide, but she remained silent. "Malum has been pulling the strings long before Jack even knew he was there."

Millie didn't think her heart could break any more than it already had. And yet she felt another wringing, that twisting feeling so strong it was almost painful. It made her want to break into sobs again. To wail and scream and shout at the gods or the Saints or whoever would listen that it was all unfair. It was all too much.

Instead, she said, "I wonder who Jack might have been had none of this ever happened."

Mother Goose gave her a sad smile. Millie's heart suddenly twisted in a new direction. If Malum had not intervened, Jack wouldn't be here at all. And so, for just a slice of a moment, she dared to dream who Jack might have become. She allowed herself to grieve the what-ifs and the might-have-beens. She allowed herself to imagine what he might have done if he had not been possessed by Malum. Of the king he could have been, of the brother he might have been. She imagined he would have been more confident but not arrogant. Foolhardy at times perhaps but honest and hardworking. He would have fought for his sister, for his kingdom. He would have fought for Millie. Because she knew it now. That everything he had done, every sacrifice he'd made, it had all been for her.

Because he had loved her. No, he loved her still.

And she loved him. Even as she sat here plotting with a resistance to end his life, she loved him. Had loved him from the moment he'd bumped into her in the hallway and smiled at her. She felt more grief than she could have ever dreamed for a future she would never see.

For she knew she must end Malum no matter what, even if it killed Jack too.

"It seems you've come to a decision." Mother Goose's eyes gleamed, as if she had listened into Millie's thoughts, as if she knew exactly how hard it was to come to this decision. And Millie supposed she did.

"I have," she said, glancing over at her brother. Doon. He'd been so solid through all of this, standing by her side no matter what. And he'd paid the price dearly. She swallowed hard, her resolve strengthening. "I will kill Malum."

PETER

David was hiding something, of that Peter was sure. He watched the scarred young man's face change as soon as he saw the fortress, beholding it in all its gothic glory. But something else lingered in his features as he forced a smile at Jill, as he reassured her that he was fine. Peter was no stranger to those lies, the lies told to loved ones before something terrible was about to happen.

But he didn't say a word as they picked their way down a forested hill with only the light of the moon and stars to guide them. They had three hours to sneak into the fortress, rescue the matron and others, then find the vault with the cache of weapons. Peter knew from his visits that the Ohans' vault was up high, making it virtually impossible to sneak past the dozens of guards posted, let alone break into the vault itself and sneak contraband back down seven flights of stairs. However, they had no intention of carrying the cache back down the stairs. All they needed to do was destroy the weapons the Ohans had while collecting one or two of their guns for the wolfmen to study and model new weapons after. And then—well, they'd use the length of ropes slung over their shoulders to rappel down the side of a tower.

They continued down the hill and through the trees until they reached the edge of a road. These were the roads the Ohans' visitors traveled down. Peter, having been far more than a visitor, had taken the back roads used solely by the Ohans' men and partners. Those roads would be far more occupied, but the road for visitors was far more open and could be seen from the fortress from nearly a mile off. The fortress was designed with a clearing at its front and massive iron gates circling the perimeter. At its back was the forest, designed for discreet comings and goings. That would be their entry point.

They would make their way along the backroads, Peter's illusions giving them the appearance of the Ohans' lackeys if they were caught. He didn't want to use too much magic if he could avoid it, not yet at least. He'd need every drop for the grand illusion he had planned.

They wound their way through the trees until Peter found the specific road he was looking for. Their progress was slower than he would have liked, the emphasis on stealth during this part of the mission. Soon stealth wouldn't matter at all, but until then, their part had to be done quietly.

As if responding to his thoughts, the clanking of weapons and armor sounded on the road. Each of them froze. Peter used their surroundings to construct his illusion, fashioning it to look exactly as it would have appeared had they not been there.

The soldiers, if they could be called that, were coming down the road away from the fortress, likely making their rounds on horseback. Or they were up to other nefarious deeds. There were only two of them, and their horses cantered along slowly as they chatted loudly about many things Peter would rather not have known.

The men drew closer to their hiding spot, and Peter motioned for all of them to remain still. It was far easier to hold an illusion of a still image than one that moved. He'd explained this to them all beforehand. He just prayed they remembered and didn't panic.

Peter's back was pressed against a tree as he looked over at the approaching soldiers. Considering their pace, he'd wager they were slacking off. His old Nanny could walk faster than these horses were being prodded along.

Something snapped behind him, sending a spike of fear and alarm through him. He resisted the urge to whip his head around at the culprit though, instead maintaining his stillness.

The horses snagged to a stop. In an instant, these men had gone from slacking lackeys to trained mercenaries. Without a word between the two, the one closest to them hopped off his horse. But instead of bearing a sword or axe, the man carried a pistol.

Peter's stomach churned. This certainly changed things. They'd upped their production to the point where they could give even the lowest on the rung a gun. Even if they destroyed most of the guns, they clearly had a way to make more of them, and quickly. Not to mention, they wouldn't have a way to take every lackey's gun from them.

One problem at a time.

The first problem was the man marching toward them, pulling that same pistol from his pocket. But instead of stepping into the tree line he stopped, raising the pistol up with one hand and closing the wrong eye. His form was so awful Peter wanted to rip his hair out. But the scary truth was, it only made the man more dangerous.

He pointed to where the sound had been, and slowly

Peter turned his head to see Jill's eyes wide with fear. He motioned for her to get out of the way when the shot rang out.

Jill pressed a hand to her mouth, as she looked up to see a hole in the tree above her head. The bark had splintered apart and smoked around the edges.

"Must have been a squirrel or something," the other lackey said.

The man's eyes scanned the trees, looking unconvinced. But at that moment a distant screech pierced the air, quickly followed by the peal of a loud bell, echoing through the woods.

An alarm.

The man with the pistol climbed back on his horse and then they both turned their mounts back the way they'd come, trotting off before Peter had time to process everything that had just happened. He dropped the illusion and stepped out of the trees into the road, his gaze following the men who'd left them behind.

Grimzy was supposed to disarm the alarm bells around the guard stations, but there must have been another one near the Convent where Kylian, Bo, and Aaira were. He did some quick calculations then spun back toward the group where they all stood dumbstruck. David and Luca stared at the hole in the tree.

"You could have died," David breathed.

Right. He'd forgotten they'd never actually seen a gun used before. It was alarming and disconcerting, especially if it was aimed at you. But they didn't have time for this. Their plan had just lost at least an hour. Now every guard from here on out would be on alert.

"We don't have time to gawk, but now you know why an entire army equipped with these weapons would be bad."

Jill still looked a bit dazed but nodded, her instincts kicking in.

"Move now, process later," he said. "I don't know why the alarm was triggered, but we have to keep moving."

They said nothing as he took the lead. So much for stealth. Now they'd have to rely on his illusions. He didn't bother hiding his annoyance.

They ran down the road now, Peter throwing up an illusion of two men on horses, looking similar to the two men they'd just encountered. Unfortunately, his illusions couldn't mimic or cover sound, so no sounds of trotting horses accompanied them, but it would have to do for now.

The road was a straight shot to the fortress. They slowed as they heard a ruckus of shouted orders and distribution of weapons ahead. This was where they stopped.

"Jill, do you have a vial?"

The princess nodded and pulled off her pack, pulling a small vial from it. An inky black and purple substance swirled around inside. They had two dozen of them, but they'd go fast given all that lay before them.

"Luca, think you can drop this into the center of those men?"

The feline man smiled as if he'd been waiting for the task. He snatched the vial and dashed off on near-silent feet. They hid in the shadows and watched as Luca climbed a tree then jumped from branch to branch to get as close to the center as he could before he threw the vial onto the ground.

It shattered, releasing the black and purple substance in a cloud. Those closest to the vial were struck down first, coughing and gagging as pox and sores erupted all over their bodies. They dropped to the ground in fits. The substance rolled across the group, each row collapsing as they were struck with the malady Hasani had dreamed up for this very purpose.

One of the new poisons he'd crafted with his magic would cause immediate pox and leave their enemies in too much pain to stand, let alone fight against them. It wouldn't kill them, but all these men would be bedridden for weeks after. Which would also keep the men from following and hunting them down.

When every last man had fallen and only moans of pain filled the air, Peter darted through the center toward the back entrance to the fortress. He ignored the looming monstrosity as he jogged over to the large oak doors.

This was the only entrance he'd ever used. They stepped over the threshold and into an open training yard that was blissfully empty, most reinforcements having already migrated outside when they'd launched their first poison assault. They tore through the training yard to a side door Peter knew led to the kitchen. There would be women down there, slaving away in the heat to feed the Ohans' men. And indeed, as they all crashed through the doors, they were met with the startled screams of women of all ages hovering over steaming pots, kneading dough, pounding meat with mallets, and spooning food into wooden bowls and plates.

The women startled but made no move to stop them as they dashed through the massive kitchen to the doors, which he knew led to a corridor adjacent to the great hall. Under normal circumstances, the hall would be filled with soldiers eating their evening meal, but after the alarm, they would've been summoned to each of their captains for orders. Peter took a left ahead, and they flew past the black stone walls, illuminated in eerie blue light from the torches.

An informal meeting room lay ahead, one that was rarely occupied. From there they'd part ways. Peter would use his illusions to find the keys to the vault. Jill, David, and Luca would head to the dungeons, disarming men with Hasani's poisons along the way.

And all the while Peter would endeavor to weave the most complex illusion he'd ever attempted. He tried not to let his heart shudder at the thought of what might happen if he couldn't hold it, if his abilities weren't up to the task.

Focus.

They reached the meeting room and slowed. This hallway, being one mostly frequented by servants, was empty—for now at least. He swiveled toward his crew. No, not his crew. This wasn't any sort of con or heist, not in the traditional sense. And they weren't his to command, but that didn't stop him as he said, "This is where I leave you. You remember how to get to the dungeons?" They'd gone over the map and layout of the fortress extensively, so he already knew the answer.

The trio nodded, Jill and David slightly winded. Luca appeared completely unaffected by their sprint.

"Good," Peter said. "I'll meet you at the vault. You have less than an hour at this point. Disarm anyone you come across."

"We know," David said flatly.

"I know you know," Peter said, "But our time frame's moved up."

"Will you be able to hold the illusion?" Jill stared at him with an arched brow. Her tone held no challenge, just genuine curiosity.

Peter gave a curt nod. "I'll be fine. Now go."

Without another word the three of them ran down the hall, all attempts of stealth gone as they plunged deeper into the fortress, working their way down to the dungeons.

Now it was Peter's turn. He couldn't let them see his doubt even as it threatened to suffocate him. Truthfully, he wasn't sure he could do this. But he couldn't let himself linger on those thoughts. He'd practiced extensively beforehand to maintain two different illusions in two different places. He hadn't mastered it by any means, but he had to try. No, not just try. He had to succeed. There was no room for failure.

Peter closed his eyes. He'd start with the easiest illusion first. Disguising himself as Ohan-Jin. He pictured the man's tall stature, the black scales on his face. The narrow, distrustful gaze. When he opened his eyes he sensed the illusion in place, the magic like a wall around him. It was a simple illusion, one that coated his skin and would easily move with him. Again, the drawback was that he couldn't make himself sound like Ohan-Jin, so he had to hope he didn't come across anybody who wished to speak with him. Or the real Ohan-Jin.

He began strolling down the hall, confident to the point of arrogance. This was *his* fortress. These were *his* soldiers running around.

As he walked toward the man's study he imagined the next illusion. The complexity made him want to stop and close his eyes, but they couldn't waste any time, not to mention how quickly he'd be caught if someone found him standing in the hallway with his eyes shut like an idiot. He had to keep moving.

First, he pictured the front of the fortress, the open space outside of it. He imagined the black iron gates, ornate and deadly. And then he imagined the gate flying open as thousands of blackbloods shoved their way through. He recalled the vision he'd seen that day upon the walls of Fenric's Keep, the decaying bodies stumbling forward, pushing and trampling over one another. He pictured the hair falling from their heads, the black blood oozing from the sores on their bodies, the sickly blue tint to their skin.

He pictured as many details as he could recall, sending

them up and casting them out to the gates. He pictured an army coming to attack the Ohans.

He knew it was working when screams and shouts began to echo through the corridors. When more alarms sounded, calling all the soldiers to the front. He sensed the chaos that would follow. He began to imagine soldiers running toward the chaos, deliberately leading the real soldiers away from his friends and toward the imaginary army.

He paused suddenly. *His friends.* Was that what these people had become?

He kept walking, thankful he had an illusion to cover the face he must surely be making to himself. He'd never really had friends before, aside from Liza. He'd had crews, men he commanded who he expected obedience from. But friends he could trust who also trusted him? None.

Until now that was.

Friends. He liked Jill—David too for that matter. He liked what they fought for, even if they were overly idealistic about how much the kingdom would change after Jill took the throne. He had no doubt she would now. He'd seen that look in her eyes on the boat. It had shaken him to his bones. It was a look of such ferocity he knew she would do whatever it took to save her people—her kingdom—from Malum. And though he'd never loved a royal in his life, when those around him had knelt before her, his body would not let him resist. He'd taken a knee, determined to follow her lead as well, to follow her rule.

Approaching soldiers snapped him out of his thoughts and he swore internally. He'd let himself become distracted, a deadly mistake.

Three soldiers approached. Their weapons clanked against their armor as they ran, hurrying toward the direction he'd come from.

"Commander," one said, giving a slight bow as they stopped in front of him. "What are your orders?"

Peter glanced out a nearby window, the first time he'd gotten a good look at the illusion he'd cast. It was impressive, and that was being modest. Thousands of blackbloods milled about, standing outside as if waiting for orders to attack. They rocked on their feet, swaying. They pulled out their hair, scratched at scabs and sores, and growled at each other. They were incredibly realistic, and he couldn't help the smug smile that rose to his face.

Peter imagined how Ohan-Jin would react to such a situation. He wouldn't be frightened, he was too arrogant for fear, even when he should have been afraid. The reptile man would be angry, taking it out on those around him. He'd seen it often enough before.

"Gather at the base of the fortress, but don't attack. I want to see what they do." Peter imitated Ohan-Jin's voice as best he could, giving it a deep raspy sound like the hiss of a snake, since that's what the man was after all. And not just because he was of the reptile clan.

Two of the men nodded, but one in the back's brows furrowed in confusion. And suspicion. Was the voice off? He'd never been great at imitating voices. Perhaps he would remain confused but scurry off with the other two. Peter only needed to convince them a few more minutes, just until he could make it to Ohan-Jin's study.

"Yes, sir," the man at the front said, preparing to leave.

"I thought you were in a meeting with King Jack, Commander?" the one in the back said.

Peter almost let all his illusions slip. *A meeting with King Jack?* Several curse words nearly slipped past his lips.

"The meeting ended a while ago." It was a terrible lie, but he was still reeling with this new knowledge.

The king was here.

"But you said—"

"Stop wasting my time!" Peter snapped, "And questioning my orders. Go!"

The man still looked suspicious but reluctantly ran down the corridor after the other two men. Peter needed to hurry. Another run in with anyone might have them questioning his orders.

He needed to figure out why the king was here and what exactly he had planned. Sweat beaded on Peter's forehead as he picked up his pace. He was still another ten minutes or so from the study, thanks to the vast fortress. He knew the way and prayed he wouldn't be slowed by any other encounters.

To his surprise, he wasn't. The men running by did not bother to stop or acknowledge him beyond slight nods of respect as they hurried off to wherever their orders bade them. Alarms still rang; chaos still lured everyone out of the fortress.

But he knew sooner or later they'd realize the arrivals standing at their gates made no move to attack, but also made no sounds. Once the Ohans' discovered it was all an illusion, well, they had to be gone before then. Hopefully Grimzy had signaled the wolfmen to come ashore already. That was their army. Those were the forces they needed if they wanted to rescue people and get the supplies they needed.

At last, he could see the doors to the study, a set of oak double doors, painted such a deep green they were almost black. They were impressive compared to the rest of the massive fortress. Instead of blue-fire torches in this part of the fortress, gas lamps in sconces adorned the walls, interspersed between the mounted taxidermized heads of animals.

He'd always hated hunting trophies, found it distasteful. He understood the intention behind it, but to him it hardly seemed impressive. An animal had no weapons with which to defend itself, so why should it be considered such a bragging right to kill one for fun? He knew David was a hunter but a humble one. It was a way for him to feed his family, something Peter could respect. But killing an animal just because . . .

Well, he'd never understood it.

But he wasn't being paid to philosophize over the tastefulness of hunting animals for sport. Well, technically, he wasn't being paid at all. Another unthinkable decision for him.

Two guards stood sentry outside the study, maintaining their position no matter the orders given to the other soldiers. This was the trickiest part of the entire charade. If he tried to enter the study but Ohan-Jin was already in there, he'd be discovered immediately. If Peter made it past the guards and entered the study but Ohan-Jin arrived while he was still in there, he would be discovered as well. If anything was off even slightly, the guards at the door would know and the game would be over.

But he couldn't get in there without looking like Ohan-Jin. The guards wouldn't let him enter and would probably haul him off to the dungeons.

His mind worked furiously as a plan came to him. It would be tricky, trying to pull off so many illusions at the same time. He still felt the tug of the army of blackbloods outside, felt the weight of it on his shoulders, bearing down on him like a physical burden. He couldn't afford to let it slip, not even for a second.

Peter conjured a duplicate of himself, disguised as Ohan-Jin, and made it walk toward the guards with purpose.

"Halt!" the one on the right said.

"It's me, you imbecile," Peter said, throwing his voice across the room; it was the one thing his illusions with sound could do.

"Ohan-Jin is in a meeting already and hasn't come out yet."

The man stepped toward the illusion. "You must be an imposter."

"And how do you know the imposter isn't already inside?" Peter said, motioning to the door. His confidence seemed to give both men pause. They traded glances with each other, but did not relax.

"We'll ask him then and see." The second man turned to raise a fist and knock but before he could, Peter let the Ohan-Jin illusion shift to look like himself and sent it running down the hall.

The first man took off after it, surprisingly quick despite his large size and heavy armor. That took care of one of them. But now he needed the other gone, and he needed the real Ohan-Jin *out*.

Peter felt the illusion of himself running deeper into the fortress and was certain the guard followed close behind. He just had to keep him busy long enough.

The strain was almost too much as he conjured yet another illusion, this time of one of the soldiers he'd first met in the corridors, the one who'd questioned Peter's identity.

Peter made the illusion run up to the second guard, panting and heaving.

"You need to alert the Commander, we're under attack and we believe an imposter of him has been sighted in the left wing."

"The left wing?" the man said, brows furrowing. "We just caught one imposter heading to the right wing."

"There must be more than one," Peter said through the man. "Do you know for certain the man inside is the real commander?"

"I—" the guard's mouth opened then hung there a second before snapping shut. "I don't know for certain."

"We need to be certain."

The guard nodded then turned to knock on the door, the sound reverberating through the space. All of this Peter watched from a distance. Watched as the door opened and the guard poked his head in, watched as Ohan-Jin strolled out the double doors, watched as King Jack—Malum—followed.

As the two men explained the situation to Ohan-Jin, a smile eased its way up the reptile man's face. A smile that made Peter's blood run cold. This man was not afraid, nor was he angry. He was delighted. Ohan-Jin was not a man delighted by anything other than victory.

Peter had half a mind to turn on his heels and run, to get out and leave and make sure he never crossed paths with this man again. But he had to stay. He'd promised Jill. He'd promised his friends.

Ohan-Jin looked between the two men, the real one and the illusion, his eyes sliding back and forth. There must have been some tell, some wrong detail, because Ohan-Jin turned to Peter's illusion and swiped a hand through it. It vanished to mist, Peter's grip on the different illusions finally slipping.

"I know you're here, Peter," Ohan-Jin called to him. Peter remained hidden behind the head of a large elk, considering his options.

He could run, but he wouldn't make it far. The weight of holding the illusions was growing so heavy, more sweat dripped down his forehead. He could try another illusion to get him out of this mess, but he didn't trust it, not with his weakening hold and Ohan-Jin's senses.

"I know what's going through your head Peter, you're debating your next move. Should you run or hide or fight?" The reptile man's voice was warm, almost inviting. "But may I suggest another option? Come out and give yourself up. It will do you no good to resist. You will lose this battle and every battle after this. Your pathetic princess is no match for our armies."

Peter's breath caught. *Our armies.*

Not his. Ours. His and Malum's. They were doomed. Even if Jill saved everyone here, destroyed every last weapon of the Ohans', and gathered the supplies needed to last through winter, she had started a war. Not just against the Ohans but against Malum too. Their odds weren't great against one of those forces, but both of them? They would lose. Malum's vulgan and blackbloods would roll through the kingdom, devouring everything in their path. Ohan-Jin's weapons would aid them. Together, they could conquer not just Erinya but all five of the great kingdoms.

Was that it? Was that what Malum wanted? Ohan-Jin? Surely, they would turn on each other eventually. But until then . . .

Peter swallowed hard, debating. He should run. He should—

"Oh, and there is someone who's been dying to see you. What are you doing Peter, locking your pretty little wife in a cell?"

The floor beneath his feet tilted, his heart screeching to a painful halt. He stormed from the shadows without a second thought, driven by anger and fear and longing. If Ohan-Jin had hurt her—

"So nice to see you again, Peter." Ohan-Jin smiled as Peter fumed in front of him, chest heaving.

"What have you done with her?" he demanded, throwing every ounce of force into his voice.

"Come and see for yourself." The man's eyes twinkled. Behind him, King Jack hovered, assessing him, as if dissecting Peter with that cold gaze of his.

"Peter, is that you?" Her voice was like the parting of

clouds on a stormy day to reveal sunshine glistening across dew-laden grass. It tinkled and sparkled like the diamonds he was so fond of stealing.

Liza was here. Not only that—she appeared at the door of the study, looking completely unharmed and absolutely ravishing. Her hair had grown back into its luscious dark waves, her gazella horns twisting elegantly upward. Her skin had returned to its beautiful bronze glow instead of sickly gray and covered in bleeding scratches and sores. A red dress hugged her curves, highlighting every feature he loved about her.

She ran to him and he to her, collapsing at her feet, as a sob wrenched from his chest. He didn't understand even as he clung to her, burying his face in the folds of her dress. She dropped to her knees, pulling his face up to look at her. Concern and worry etched itself into her beautiful face. He wanted to wipe that look away, to steal her from this place and never return. How many nights had he dreamed of her? How many times had he imagined her alive and well and in his arms, just like this? How many times had he all but given up hope of seeing her returned to this state?

He kissed her then, not caring where he was or who watched or the danger that haunted every corner around them. He kissed her, not knowing when, or if, it might end. If she might be taken from him again. Saints, he hoped not. She was not an illusion. She was flesh and blood and here with him, and Saints he hoped this never ended.

"How?" he said, breathless, looking into her dark brown eyes. "How are you here?"

She smiled then, so bright and beautiful and damn near blinding in her joy. "The king saved me."

Peter's stomach sank to his toes, the smile sliding from his face. "No," he breathed, looking up at the two most dangerous men in Erinya. It was Malum's turn to smile.

"You are going to help us capture the princess," Malum said, "Or you will say goodbye to your wife for good."

Peter swallowed. This. This was why he didn't have friends. He was far too selfish for them, which was why he found himself easily saying, "Deal."

BO

*B*o had hated the journey on the sea, had hated clinging to Grimzy's back like a child, had hated those terrifying caves with water spewing upward, threatening to drown them all. But more than any of that, she hated that Kylian and Aaira continually had to slow their pace for her.

She was used to leaning on her crutch, used to the bite of it in the crook of her armpit, and used to the way it rubbed her skin raw. She was even used to uneven terrain and putting weight on her foot when necessary. But she wasn't used to a pace so fast she struggled to keep up, even as she knew they couldn't afford to waste time.

Kylian looked like he wanted to offer to carry her but was holding the words back. Instead, they slowed, never saying a word as she trudged through the darkness toward the Convent. It loomed in the distance, silvery and bright, in such stark contrast to the dark fortress of the Ohans. She suppressed a shudder. She still recalled the damp, decaying smell of the Ohans' dungeons, still recalled the hopelessness she'd felt before Zyla had rescued her. Not just by breaking her out but by giving her hope that perhaps something could change.

Since Bo had arrived at Fenric's Keep, she'd felt strangely untethered from the action around her. Kylian had been in near-constant meetings with the princess. Hasani and Ymira spent their free hours together, and Zyla seemed unafraid of being the odd man out with the blushing couple. Even Asif had Lyra and had avoided her at all costs. Once again, she wondered where she fit in all of this.

And she still wasn't even sure how she'd convinced Kylian and Jill to let her come. They had been uncertain about the decision not because of her leg but because she had no other real fighting skills aside from her magic.

Now as she hobbled through the forest, she felt like deadweight. She'd slowed them down in the caves and she slowed them down now. She'd never been self-conscious of her foot before—it was just part of who she was. But in that moment, she wished she were just a bit faster.

"Just a little further," Aaira whispered. The feline girl crept through the undergrowth on near silent feet, her feline ears flicking at every sound. She drew to a halt in front of them, lifting a hand to stop them. They did so as her ears continued to flick around, picking up on some sound neither she nor Kylian could hear.

It really was a wonder humans survived at all. They were so feeble and unimpressive compared to the other races.

What does that make me then?

The disturbing thought struck her out of the blue, but she quickly shook it away. Now wasn't the time to ponder her own shortcomings. She'd done that enough already.

Bo glanced up at Kylian to find him already looking down at her, a muscle feathering in his jaw.

"What?" she said under her breath.

Aaira whirled on her, eyes blazing with a warning to stop talking. Bo pressed her lips shut, ignoring the young man's gaze on her.

Kylian had been like that more and more recently, quiet and withdrawn, refusing to tease her or argue with her. She hadn't realized how much she'd missed it until she'd been all alone, wandering around the keep, searching for something to do. Someone to talk to.

She hadn't realized how much she'd talked to him until he'd stopped talking to her.

She opened her mouth to speak again, but Aaira waved them over and they obeyed promptly. Aaira pointed to something through the trees. A path illuminated by moonlight that led to a side door in the Convent. But it was half a mile beyond the tree line, and they would be spotted the instant they stepped out of the safety of the woods.

"I don't see any guards," Aaira said, "But that makes me even more suspicious. Why keep this door unguarded?"

"Do they know of it?" Kylian asked, his gaze trained on the door ahead.

Stepping forward, Bo saw the path wound through what must have once been a garden, lined with dead rose bushes and dried up fountains. There was a scattering of ponds filled with nothing but scum, and the branches of a few dead trees dotting the landscape reached out like gnarled fingers grasping at the air.

The skeletal garden haunted her more than the sight of the fortress. For this was something that had once been beautiful, cared for, but in time had been left to rot. She tore her gaze away, shaking off the feeling of spiderwebs coating her skin.

"Why is the Convent of the Saints falling apart? Is it because of the Ohans?" Bo asked, though she wasn't entirely sure why. "I thought people worshiped the Saints?"

Aaira let out a low scoff. "The Saints aren't meant to be worshiped. Revered? Remembered? Certainly. But they were still human, granted power by the great Deity. Power they were supposed to use for good against the Black King. The Order of the Saints was established not as a place of worship but as a place to raise up new warriors dedicated to the good of Erinya. Only the nameless Deity should be worshiped."

Kylian's brow furrowed. "I didn't know that."

Aaira's lips thinned as she side-eyed him. "Most people don't. The Deity is the one who gifted the Saints with their magic, choosing the bloodlines best suited for the task."

Kylian shifted uncomfortably and Bo was about to ask what was going through his mind when Aaira held up her hand again, gesturing for silence.

Movement caught her eye as a ghostly white figure fluttered into existence. One second nothing had been there, the next a translucent figure floated through the air.

Aaira inhaled sharply, her eyes going wide.

Bo felt it too, that strange intangible sense of fear that cooled her blood and left her frozen to her spot. The figure loosely resembled a woman wearing flowing robes. Long silver hair hung to her thighs, the strands floating and dancing around her like she was underwater.

The ghostly woman floated around in a circle, bobbing up and down like a light on the ocean. Then she disappeared.

"A wraith," Aaira said, her voice tight with fear. "They've captured a wraith."

"How?" Kylian asked, looking just as terrified as Bo felt.

Bo knew little of wraiths. They were ghost stories, not meant to actually exist. Souls that could not pass into the afterlife, they were trapped here. Unlike ghosts, wraiths had committed some heinous act before their deaths, damaging their souls beyond repair. And so, they searched for a soul that would allow them into the afterlife, sucking it from a person's body until they left nothing but a frozen husk behind. And then they would scream. Scream because they could not capture the soul, because they were forever barred from the afterlife.

And the scream would ring out for miles. Or so the stories claimed. Even during her time in the Harrow Forest she'd never come across one.

"Mirrors," Aaira said, pointing. Sure enough, where the wraith walked in a circle, Bo saw the ring of mirrors at the center of the decaying garden.

"Where did they even find a wraith?" Kylian asked.

Aaira shook her head, clearly perplexed. "These are dark times. It wouldn't surprise me if this is not the first dark thing to awaken, nor will it be the last."

Bo chose to ignore that ominous prediction for the time being. "What do we do?" She asked. "We have to get to that door." She glanced at Kylian who looked to Aaira. Of the three of them, she seemed to know the most about these creatures.

"I know they fear water, and that they can't stand the sight of their own reflection. But I'm not sure that helps us at all." She spoke aloud but had clearly retreated into her mind with the problem, her ears twitching slightly as she puzzled over it.

Bo glanced at the ghostly apparition again then inhaled slightly, an idea striking her. "What if we released it?"

Kylian and Aaira's gaze snapped to hers.

"Release it? Are you insane?" Aaira said.

"Let her speak," Kylian said curtly. Aaira shot him a look of disdain but shut her mouth.

"What if we released it and let it roam? Do you think it would chase us instead of pursuing freedom?"

"It's difficult to say," Aaira mused, chewing on the corner of her lip, "Due to their nature, nobody really knows how aware wraiths are. Some legends claim they could speak, be reasoned with. Others claim they were monsters driven by rage and an unquenchable desire for violence."

Lovely. "So somewhere in the middle then," Bo said absentmindedly.

"What do you mean?"

Bo hadn't realized she was staring again at the creature until she forced herself to look at a confused Aaira and Kylian. "I just mean the truth is somewhere in the middle of the stories. It usually is anyway." She shrugged. "I heard the stories about the girl in the woods. Some claimed she was an orphan, too afraid to join society. Others claimed she was a witch with dark magic who would feast on people's souls then give their bodies to her monsters." She swallowed, taken aback by the sudden wave of emotions coursing through her. "But the truth was that I was a scared orphan with a dark power I didn't want." Her throat grew tighter, and she found herself unable to speak any further on the matter, blindsided by it as she was. "Perhaps, we can speak with the wraith and bargain with her— it—whatever."

Bo's heart hammered in her chest, and not from the nearness of the wraith or the danger that lurked on all sides. It was painful to think of the terrified girl she'd been, to think of the days and years wasting away all alone. She'd never asked for any of that, an existence away from people who might have cared for her. But after her mother died, she just didn't know what to do, especially shackled to the vulgan as she was.

"Alternatively, we run around it and ignore it altogether," Kylian voiced.

"If it sees us though, it will scream," Aaira said, shaking her head. "And I'm sure guard posts trained to listen for that are stationed nearby. Getting caught now would jeopardize the entire mission. We can't risk it."

"Can we go around?" Bo asked, her gaze still drawn back to the figure, floating around in circles.

"We don't have enough time," Kylian said tightly.

"On my own I could probably sneak past it but . . ." She trailed off, not bothering to say the obvious, that Bo and Kylian were not skilled enough in the art of sneaking.

In the distance, the wraith stilled, even while its hair and robes continued to blow around in some absent breeze. It turned, slowly, until it stared in their direction. But it did not scream, only watched them.

Bo stepped out of the tree line before she knew what she was doing. Kylian grabbed at the back of her shirt, but she shook him off wordlessly, drawn to this creature by something she did not fully understand. She walked down the path, the only sound her crutch scraping against the ground. To her surprise neither Kylian nor Aaira stopped her, nor did they emerge from the trees to follow her.

It was only Bo and this creature. As she stepped close, she could see the wraith's features more defined, though the wraith seemed blurry, like a separate image existed over the top of itself but offset from one another. The wraith's eyes were completely white and for a split second she was reminded of the guardian at the well whose eyes had been completely black. Despite the lack of any pupil or iris, Bo knew the creature watched only her.

A few feet from the edge of the mirrors she stopped, watching the wraith as it watched her.

A monster. That's what Bo had been called her entire life, and she knew the same was true for this creature as well. Maybe it couldn't help what it was but neither could she. She'd been born different, from her club foot to the magic in her veins to the monsters that had obeyed her every command. But she wasn't a monster.

The wraith cocked its head, such a strange humanly action. And then it spoke. "I know you." Its voice was the rasping of a hundred voices, ethereal and otherworldly.

"How?" Bo breathed, not daring to move.

The woman shook her head. "I do not know. But something about you feels—I know you."

Bo swallowed. She hadn't expected that and yet she knew the wraith spoke the truth, for she felt it herself. Her heart continued to pound, though not with fear. No, it was excitement that pounded through her now, as if she were on the cusp of some great discovery. But she didn't know what it was nor why she felt that way.

"I don't know you." Bo risked a small step forward, entranced by the young woman. "Who are you?"

A ghostly tear slid down the woman's cheek before dissolving like smoke. "I do not know who I am anymore. Only that I am lost."

The words struck Bo with such force she nearly lost her breath. A sudden ache struck her chest, an unmet yearning for something she could not identify. Something she'd not been able to identify since the day her monsters had been torn from her. She'd hated them, yet who was she after they were gone? She was not the orphan in the woods or the witch with monsters. So, who remained after everything she'd known to be true about herself had been torn away? Who was she when all was said and done? Even on this mission she'd become a barely tolerated appendage.

"I don't know who I am either," Bo whispered, a tear slithering its way down her cheek as well.

"I keep searching for her, but I fear she is gone. That she is no longer part of this world," the wraith said, blinking away more ethereal tears. "I do not understand what I've become.

What happened to us . . ." The woman trailed off. Her tears had stopped but confusion remained.

Bo wanted to ask her who *us* was, what she meant when she said she didn't understand what she'd become. But she knew they were running out of time. She hoped Kylian and Aaira were sneaking through the garden as they spoke.

"Who were you before?" She had to know what drew her to this woman displaced by time.

The woman, still floating in the air, pinched her eyes shut, as if recalling some painful memory she'd rather not. Her head twitched, then her entire body. It twisted and contorted as if some great force were moving her about like a doll.

Bo's fear spiked.

"Split," the woman's voice deepened like a roll of thunder, "The guardian said it would happen. Severed. Torn." Her eyes shot open, and although still wholly white, Bo knew she'd angered the wraith. "We did this for you!" She hissed like she was in pain. Bo stepped back and the leash on the wraith's sanity seemed to snap.

She threw her arms back and screamed.

The scream was otherworldly, unlike anything Bo had ever heard before. It was a bolt of lightning inside her head, knives jammed into her ears. It was glass shattering over and over. It was bones snapping and breaking with a single voice. It was pure, unbridled anger and terror and pain consuming her as she dropped to the ground, paralyzed and deafened.

Bo could not move, could not breathe, could not think. Why was she here? Who was she? Was she about to become a wraith herself?

She didn't know. She heard only that scream that could shatter glass, that wail that feasted upon her eardrums.

Someone grabbed her and she was grateful. She might never stand again, might never know another sane thought, might forever hear the echo of that scream ringing in her ears, haunting her to the end of her days. It would follow her. Somehow, she knew this. The wraith's scream would linger in her bones, would sing to her in the quiet moments, trying to wrench her soul from her body just as the legends claimed.

The person holding her ran, the scream growing louder even though she moved further from it. She glanced back at the creature, stuck in its prison of mirrors. It continued to scream, and the toll of warning bells followed. But it had turned, its gaze following her. Bo didn't miss the flood of tears pouring down the creature's face, as if it could not help what it had done and hated itself for that.

A door opened and slammed shut, the scream growing only slightly quieter behind the safety of solid wood.

Kylian held Bo and she hadn't realized how she'd clung to him until he went to set her down. Reflexively she continued to grip him, even as he pulled away. He stiffened. Then Bo stiffened, finally regaining control of herself.

A headache pounded behind her eyelids, a furious beating that sent a wave of nausea rolling through her. Still, that scream outside did not relent.

"I'm sorry, Bo. We have to keep moving." Kylian spoke but his voice was warbled, slipping in and out of her brain like oil. She barely grasped what he was saying before he hauled her to her feet and handed her a crutch.

Her legs threatened to collapse beneath her, and she'd never been more grateful for her crutch. She moved forward in a daze, hardly comprehending her surroundings or the route they took through the Convent. Her vision blurred and she felt an arm wrap around her waist, simultaneously holding her up while also hurrying her along. It was Aaira, and if it had been any other circumstance she would have shoved the girl away.

But Bo could barely walk a straight line, let alone walk down the stairs of the Convent.

At last, they stopped, and Bo leaned up against the cool wall before sliding to the ground. The ringing in her ears had abated, though distantly she could still hear the wraith's shrieking. Or perhaps that was in her head. She couldn't be sure. Her vision finally cleared, though her head still ached like she'd been struck on the head with a hammer. She swallowed, her mouth dry as dirt.

They stood in a long hallway with doors lining either side. A few blue-fire torches burned but they were scant and waned in the darkness of the hall, as if some magic kept them from burning fully. Bo focused on one, the blue flames burning but not consuming the wood. Another wave of nausea rolled through her.

Split. Severed. Torn. The wraith's words echoed in her head, repeating themselves over and over. What had she meant? Was she referring to her own soul being severed from the afterlife? She was sure it meant something, but she couldn't figure out what, especially in her addled state.

A new alarm bell rang out, coming from the Convent itself. The ringing pounded against her head, but she was grateful for the reminder that they had to hurry. She shook herself out of her stupor and forced herself to her feet, leaning heavily on her crutch. Somehow Aaira had found the keys and began unlocking doors, letting out an assortment of men and women. She recognized a few of them from the meeting she'd attended so long ago, but she didn't know any of their names. After only a few minutes, all the doors had been opened and nearly fifty people stood in the hall, all eyes on Kylian.

Bo glanced around. Where were the guards? Why did this all feel too easy?

"We don't have much time," Kylian said, his voice strong

and comforting all at once. "We've launched an assault on the Ohans, and our best hope is to get out as quickly as we can. Ships wait for us along the shore. Aaira will lead you there."

They all listened to him in earnest, relying on his leadership. Because that was who he was—a leader. He always had been. And though she'd thought him a pompous prig when they'd first met, she now saw how much respect these people had for him. The façade melted away, revealing a man who acted with honesty and integrity. A man driven by a cause he believed in with his whole heart.

"What will you do?" someone asked.

"Bo and I have other tasks to complete before this is all done," he answered simply.

Eyes swung in her direction, and she felt the temperature drop from the ice in their glares. She was the reason they'd been locked away by the Ohans. She was the one who'd betrayed them.

The guilt threatened to knock her to the ground. She wilted under those stares of accusation, of feral animosity. Chief among them was one girl Bo recognized clearly. The girl who had served in the Ohans' household, whom she'd thrown a bucket of urine on and locked in the dungeons in her place. It had been a terrible thing to do, but she'd been desperate.

"How can we trust her?" the girl sneered. There were nods of agreement and Bo's face flushed red with shame.

She looked at Kylian, his face caught between the desire to reassure people and fear of what might happen if he did. If they didn't trust him, they could ruin this entire plan. They'd already had too many things go wrong. They couldn't afford for these people to doubt him. Kylian, brilliant as he was, knew he walked a dangerous line. They needed these people's loyalty, not their wrath.

Suddenly, he smiled. It was his charming, persuasive smile,

the one Bo had grown accustomed to seeing. Something stabbed at her chest at the sight of it. Only thirty seconds ago he'd been relaxed, open, honest. But honesty would do them no good where Bo was concerned. So, he'd donned his mask of shrewdness.

All because of her.

"Bo was being trailed, yes, but didn't understand what she was doing. These last several months, she has more than proven herself trustworthy. Afterall, she came back to save you all, even knowing you might not forgive her." He paused, perhaps for dramatic effect as he often liked to do. "Aside from that, she is one of the Saints' Heirs. Do you believe the magic would choose wrong?"

"It might," the girl from earlier spat. She seemed dead set on rejecting Bo.

Kylian waved a hand dismissively. "The Saints' magic chose her. It does not choose wrong." A sudden tightness clung to his words, one that Bo couldn't place. Why was this topic difficult for him? "Regardless, we have little time to waste. We can bring Bo to trial later—"

A door slammed and two dozen guards flooded the hall.

"Follow me!" Aaira called out, and despite the tension from a moment earlier, everyone obeyed and raced to the other end of the corridor.

Bo and Kylian remained, blocking the path so the others could flee. The guards rush toward them.

"You should go," Kylian said suddenly, looking at her.

"What? No. I'm not leaving you," she said.

Why? She asked herself. She'd fled months ago without a thought of those left behind. Why did she stand her ground now?

Because I've changed. She didn't want to be a coward. She didn't want to just survive for the sake of survival. She wanted a life, a life with friends and . . . family. And she'd fight to protect that.

Kylian's throat bobbed, as if he wanted to force her to go but couldn't make himself.

"Besides, there's no way you're taking these guards down without my help," she said with a smirk.

She called forth the shadows that lingered inside her, the ones she realized had always been there, waiting to be released. They curled out of her palms then shot forward at her unspoken orders. Wielding this power of hers was becoming easier. The shadows grew, swirling in the hallway like dark storm clouds. They obscured the lights, drowning them all in darkness. But somehow, Bo knew exactly where each guard was, as if her shadows granted her sight despite their darkness.

The shadows grabbed at the men's weapons, most of them various kinds of guns, whipping them up into the air like they'd been carried away on a breeze. One of the shadows grabbed hold of a guard's knife and slashed it through the back of each man's ankles, dropping them to the ground one after another.

She let go of the shadows and instantly the hall was lit again, each man on the ground groaning and gripping their feet as blood dripped out of them. She hadn't wanted to kill them, but they couldn't be allowed to follow either. Perhaps this way they'd all be down for a while.

Kylian blinked at the sudden, blinding light, then stared at the collapsed men.

"Let's go," she said, turning on her crutch and hurrying down the hall.

5 8

KYLIAN

Together, Kylian and Bo raced down a winding set of stairs, Bo swinging her crutch to each next step with expert precision. He'd been prepared to help her, but she didn't need it. He shouldn't assume she needed help all the time.

She'd taken down all those guards in mere seconds. He'd known she was powerful but still he'd told her to run. Because he couldn't bear the thought of something, anything, happening to her. To his little sister. It had been harder and harder to think of her as anything other than his sister lately.

He knew he should tell her about that day so long ago, about their relationship. But fear held his tongue. He'd known for so long now, and the longer he waited to tell her, the angrier she'd be when she found out.

Which is why he'd written her a letter. Just in case. He needed her to know who he was. Who she was to him, and why he'd cared for her.

He'd stumbled when his former friends had turned on her, accusing her of betrayal. He should have defended her quicker, but he'd hesitated. And she'd noticed. He'd seen the light fade in her eyes when he hadn't come to her defense, like a candle flickering out.

They hit the bottom of the stairwell, sweat slicking his skin. His legs were jelly from all the stairs, but adrenaline pressed him forward. All they had to do was—

A deafening bang sounded as something struck him in the shoulder. Pain exploded through his body, and he crashed to the ground. He blinked back tears as he struggled to make sense of his surroundings. More guards appeared, five in total. Four charged at them, while a fifth hung back, a gun raised and aimed at him.

Hot blood seeped down his shoulder and his vision threatened to darken completely.

Bo screamed, her shadows coming to their defense when a thick, gravelly voice said, "Stop."

Kylian pressed a hand to his shoulder, struggling to stand. The burning, aching wound hurt unlike anything he'd ever experienced. Blood seeped through his fingers.

Bo stilled, her face twisted in absolute rage, and Kylian knew she would shred them apart. These men wouldn't simply have their tendons severed. She would kill them.

"Stop, or I shoot him again." The reptile man who spoke, the one who still had his gun pointed at Kylian spoke in a calm voice, unperturbed by the chaos around him. The guards slowed, coming to stand in front of them. At their back was the stairwell, but with his new injury they'd never make it.

Bo called her shadows back, but they swirled around her wrists and hands, in check, but not absent altogether. A warning. Just like the man's gun was.

Kylian's breaths came faster, and the room began to spin around him.

Stay upright. Do not let them see weakness.

If ever a negotiation depended on his wits, it was this one. Regardless of what happened to him, he had to get Bo out. Get her to safety.

The man stalked forward. Kylian felt uncharacteristically disarmed. He was different from the other reptile men Kylian had seen around the fortress. Green scales flecked his cheeks and black hair hung to his shoulders, disheveled compared to the other guards whose hair was closely shaved to their heads. This man dressed differently as well. While the guards bore the uniforms and insignia of the Ohans, this man wore a nice shirt with rolled up sleeves and a vest. Trousers were tucked into low cut boots. He didn't look like he was from Erinya at all, let alone from the Ohans.

"What are you doing here?" he asked, eyes flicking between the two of them.

They didn't answer, Bo out of defiance and Kylian because he wasn't sure he could speak without blacking out.

"Quiet, I see." The man's voice carried a deadly softness.

A spike of warning flared in Kylian's chest. Instinct told him this was the most dangerous man they'd find in the Ohans' territory, save for perhaps Ohan-Jin himself.

"You don't have to answer me now. We'll see if your lips become a little looser after some quality time together." He didn't smile as he spoke.

The guards moved forward to grab the two of them.

"Wait!" Kylian said. Another stab of pain washed over him. The guards stilled for a second then kept moving forward. "Wait!" he said again through gritted teeth.

The well-dressed man held up a hand, motioning for the guards to stop. They obeyed but were still far closer than Kylian would have liked.

"Take me, let the girl go."

Bo's head swung to Kylian, fear and anger mixing on her face.

"Why would we do that?" he drawled, tilting his head a bit to study Kylian.

Kylian inhaled a few quick breaths, trying to clear his head. "Because—" he said, struggling to come up with any reason they should let her go, "she doesn't know anything. She's worthless."

At this the man finally smiled faintly. "Liar. You think I don't know one of the Saints' Heirs when I see one?" His gaze flicked to Bo, studying her. Bo bared her teeth in response. In any other situation, Kylian might have rolled his eyes at her childness.

His blood was dripping on the ground, however, and his thinking was far too slow and muddled to come up with a proper response. They'd never take him over her. Not unless . . .

"A party trick," he said. "An illusion. Crafted by another Saints' Heir. You've heard of him, right?"

The reptile man's eye twitched, all the confirmation Kylian needed. He'd indeed heard of Peter and must have known about the man's power.

"He's not with you, though. Which makes me think you're just trying to get this girl out of here." He studied Kylian, examining him with eyes that saw far too much. "Why?"

Lie! His instincts screamed at him. Don't tell him—

"Because she's my sister," Kylian confessed.

Bo's mouth dropped open, whether shocked at the revelation or shocked by his presumed lie, he wasn't sure. It was the worst kind of risk, because it relied entirely on the desperate truth. He prayed that somehow the man would have pity on him, and not use it against him instead. But he didn't have much time to dwell on his own foolishness. His body was growing weaker, and he fought to keep his legs from wobbling. The darkness pushed in at the edges of his vision.

"Just let her go," he begged. "Take me. I was close to the princess. I know their plans. I know all the Saints' Heirs. Where they are, what their powers are. She's nothing. Nobody."

The man took a step forward, lowering his gun before putting it in something akin to a sheath. Kylian couldn't be sure. Everything was growing fuzzy.

"Please," he said again, though he wasn't sure the words actually made it out of his mouth. His heart thudded dully inside his chest, pumping his blood out of the wound in his shoulder. Was this to be a slow death then?

"You're telling the truth." The man lowered his weapon slightly, and Kylian sensed Bo take a step back. He cast a glance in her direction, shock and betrayal pulling at her features as tears slicked down her cheeks.

"Kylian," she said, her voice low. "What do you mean?"

He heaved a sigh. "It's the truth Bo. When you return, there's a letter for you in my quarters. It explains everything—"

"A letter?" Bo snapped, "You knew—"

"Enough." The man's words were quiet but firm, as if he knew he did not have to raise his voice to be terrifying. "You're friends with the illusionist?"

Kylian swallowed, unsure how to answer. This man was unreadable, yet Kylian sensed the reptile man could read everyone more easily than even he could. Kylian gave one quick nod.

He scowled slightly, then shook his head. "I owe Peter a favor. Consider it paid. Let the girl go."

"What? No—" Bo started.

"Shut up!" The man's jaw clenched, and he adjusted his grip on the gun, nodding slightly to Kylian. "You'll come with us. I'm sure my father would love to speak with you about the princess."

The guards surged forward, grabbing Kylian with such force he let out a cry of pain.

"Stop! You're hurting him!" Bo cried, as Kylian was dragged away. The man turned back to face her.

"Run little girl," he said, "Run and don't look back. If you do, I'll kill him. That's a promise."

Kylian glanced back at her, his eyes becoming blurry once more, not from pain but from the tears clouding his vision.

"I'm so sorry." The apology was barely a whisper, hissed through the pain.

She stood there, dumbfounded.

"Go!" He yelled at her.

She shook her head and called forth her shadows, but Kylian shook his head. "Get out of here, Bo. Now!"

For a moment, he thought she'd disobey him, thought she'd release her shadows and kill them all. But then she turned and ran.

He watched her go, grateful she'd listened to him. Yet part of him was devastated she hadn't fought for him.

The guards dragged him through the tunnel, and pain lanced through him again. He pinched his eyes shut, trying to block out everything. But the pain was too constant, too overwhelming.

"You're a lucky man," the reptile man said, Ohan-Jin's son. He remembered hearing about him once, a long time ago now, Ohan-Jin's only son who'd fled Erinya as a young man, bringing dishonor on his family. What had his name been? What was he doing back here?

Kin.

"Lucky?" he spat. It didn't have quite the vehemence he'd hoped for though, not in his current state.

"Lucky my father didn't get his hands on that girl again," Kin said, staring straight ahead as they made their way outside.

Kylian pursed his lips shut. He didn't know what relationship Kin and Peter had, nor the favor owed him, but he thanked the Saints that Bo had made it out alive. Even if it meant he'd probably never see her again.

JILL

ill, David, and Luca fell into a rhythm as they tore across wide corridors, narrow hallways, through rooms, and down twisting staircases. Peter's illusion was doing its job well. Hardly any soldiers were left in the fortress, all of them called to the front where an army of blackbloods supposedly stood. She'd glanced out the window several times now and had shivered each time at the authenticity of the illusion. They were as horrifying as she recalled, things borne of nightmares. It was the perfect distraction really. Peter just had to make sure it lasted long enough to get in and get out.

As they entered what appeared to be a small, unused ballroom, several of the Ohans' men greeted them, running the direction they'd just come from. Running toward them. Surprised by the trio's sudden appearance, one of the men reached for his blade rather than the gun holstered at his side.

Thank the Saints.

They couldn't fight against those weapons, but swords and steel? That they could fight. Jill drew her sword, launching toward the man before he swung his blade. Luca drew another vial from the pack, preparing to send it hurtling at the soldiers. The glass exploded at Jill's feet and immediately billowed up and out, as if eager to poison its victims. At that moment, Jill was incredibly thankful Ymira and Hasani had thought to give them a special elixir beforehand that would protect them from the airborne poison.

The three men dropped to the ground, sores erupting all over their bodies as they coughed and gagged. Their bodies spasmed and all of them began moaning in pain.

David and Luca were about to leave when a thought occurred to Jill, and she reached down to grab one of the men's guns along with the holster that held it. David and Luca followed suit. She didn't know how to use it and neither did Luca or David, but having it gave her the sense of evening the odds by just a bit. Not that she was sure she could stomach actually using it on someone.

Was it any different from a sword though?

She'd have to ponder that sometime but not now. Not while their time was waning and they still had to make it to the dungeons to free the prisoners held there and then make it back to the very top of the fortress. The thought of all they still had to do and the time they had to do it was enough to make her nauseous.

The thought of falling behind pushed her to run faster as they sped down yet another winding staircase. Peter had been relentless in teaching the three of them the layout of the fortress, and she was grateful for it now, though she'd been annoyed at the time. Thanks to Peter, she knew this staircase would take them to the first door leading to the dungeons. They'd have to get past the guards there since they'd be exempt from the orders calling everyone else to the front.

Again, this would be easily done thanks to Hasani's

poisons. In fact, aside from some minor setbacks, all of this felt a bit too easy. That should have reassured Jill. Instead, a slow dread dripped into her stomach. Surely, other guards would have learned the fortress had been infiltrated, but the soldiers they'd come across in the ballroom had seemed surprised to see them. She knew the illusion of blackbloods was good, but somebody should have sounded an alarm to be on the lookout for intruders.

Jill's pace eased as she drew closer to the bottom of the staircase. Behind her David and Luca slowed to a stop, the former placing a gentle hand on the small of her back. If they'd been anywhere else, Jill would have leaned into that touch, into the feel of him behind her—

Focus.

For Saints sake, they were in the middle of a deadly mission and the touch of his fingertips threatened to make her dizzy. She was acting like some silly schoolgirl. Yet she cast a quick glance at David only to find him already looking at her, his chest heaving from their run, mirroring her own heavy breaths.

"Really?" Luca hissed under his breath. "This is hardly the time—"

His comment was lost as the ring of gunshots nearly deafened all three of them. Instinctively, Jill dropped to the ground, covering her head and neck as the stone stairs dug into her body. A warm body covered hers. David. He was protecting her from the shot, wrapping himself around her to keep her safe.

Would a gunshot kill him? Or just crack his skin like everything else? She still didn't understand his curse. Nor did she have time to consider it before another shot rang out. Thankfully, the shots were wild, but the echo reverberated through her body.

"Luca!" David shouted. He didn't need to say anything else.

Luca chucked a vial down the stairs, the sound of glass breaking quickly followed by gasps and wheezes and thuds as bodies hit the stone floor.

Jill was tempted to feel bad for the men they made ill. But she ignored it. They were on opposite sides. It was no one's fault, but they were in her way, and she would do whatever it took to free the people in these dungeons.

They scurried down the last few stairs, stepping over the two men who'd joined the ranks of Hasani's victims. David swiped the keys from one of the guard's belts and quickly began inserting each of the keys into the door to the dungeon. The fourth one was a success, and they pushed it open, the metal groaning.

Several more steps greeted them, along with a stench so foul, Jill slapped a hand over her mouth and nose as soon as they crossed the threshold. It was the scent of rancid sweat and rotten blood and bodily excrement. It was the scent of death.

She and David exchanged a look, as if they both were preparing themselves for the worst-case scenario. Jill knew from experience how brutal the Ohans could be, as Ohan-Jin once nearly beat his servants to a pulp in front of her. And Jack had told her of his own trip to this very fortress as a boy. When she'd pressed him for details, he'd been too haunted to speak of what he'd seen here. Years later all he'd described was the way death clung to this fortress, like some evil spirit lurked in every stone, drenching the place in an omnipresent darkness that went far beyond the black decor.

In their haste to accomplish their task and reach the dungeons, she'd pushed past the weight of that feeling, the weight of that darkness. But as she entered the stench of decay and stepped away from the feeble attempts at light, she felt it.

It hovered at her back, reminding her of Malum's monsters lurking in the shadows.

David reached for her hand, as if he could sense that presence too, that despair that seeped into her bones, her soul. It smothered her, as if whispering to her that she would not make it out of this dungeon alive, as if whispering to give up hope.

Had Jack seen these dungeons? Is that what had left him so haunted he'd been unable to speak of his time here for years after? Her heart fractured just a little at the thought.

Oh, Jack. He'd been chased by darkness all his life. She could see that now. Malum had always been there, lingering at the back of Jack's mind, just waiting for Jack to succumb to it, to him. Yet Jack had fought back, refusing to relinquish his light, his joy, his love of life. A great big world existed beyond the Citadel's walls, and he'd wanted to see it all. She'd thought him silly, thought the entire notion silly while she trained every day to become paladin. To become *his* paladin. Not her father's—Jack's. They were a team, brother and sister, and now she wished more than anything in the world that she hadn't looked down on his dreams, hadn't looked down on him for his joy and hope despite everything.

Because now he was trapped in that darkness for good.

"This place does things to your mind," a voice rasped out, and Jill started.

Like she'd been in a trance, she shook her head and realized she'd stepped into a hall lined by cells, standing there as her thoughts weighed heavy on her. Beside her David and Luca looked equally shaken, and they all spun toward the voice.

In the first cell at the base of the stairs, an old woman sat hunched on the ground. In the darkness it was difficult to make out her features, but Jill inched closer despite the reek coming off her. How long had she been in here? How long had she been subjected to the kinds of thoughts Jill had just endured?

"Are you the Matron of the Order of the Saints?" Jill had seen the woman at the tournament, but that was months ago now. She barely recognized the woman before her.

"I am. Or I was." She sounded tired, and if aches and pains could voice themselves, she imagined they would sound much like this woman's voice. Heavy, gaunt, hopeless. A few words had communicated so much.

"We're here to rescue you," Jill said, stepping closer to the cell before gripping the bars.

"Then you've wasted your time," the old woman said bitterly. A sudden fit of coughs wracked her body, the hacking lasting for a full minute before she said, "My days are numbered child. You should've saved someone else."

David stepped forward. "We're with Kylian, Hasani and Ymira. They told us the Order was still here, so we came to help."

"How kind of them," a new voice spat. They spun to see a young man in another cell, approaching the bars.

Jill sucked in a breath. Clearly, he'd been tortured. Repeatedly. He was covered in cuts and bruises, his nose was twisted and broken, one of his ears was completely gone along with all his fingernails. Burn marks traced up and down his arms over what had once been the beautiful tattoos belonging to an inkwell. But the worst was the dead look in his eyes, and Jill knew it was one that would haunt her nightmares for the rest of her life.

"We helped them escape Orion," the Matron spoke to the young man, "We knew what would happen to us."

Orion's dead eyes rolled from the Matron back to Jill,

surveying her with a look of disgust. "You're the princess, aren't you? Kylian told us about you." He sneered. "He told us all you care about is yourself, that you're obsessed with becoming a paladin, or you were, and you'd crush anyone who got in your way. He told us you're a stuck up bi—"

"Enough," the Matron said, her voice authoritative despite its breathiness. "This place has made you forget yourself, Orion."

Jill's heart hammered, her hands suddenly slick with sweat. Beside her, David had grown still and quiet, but a muscle in his cheek twitched. He was seconds away from adding more bruises to the man's broken body.

"I haven't forgotten anything," Orion said. "I just no longer care."

Jill had expected many things during this mission, had planned for things to go wrong. But she hadn't planned for the prisoners to attack her verbally and possibly refuse to leave altogether. She knew things had been going too smoothly.

"We're here to get you guys out," Jill explained again, refusing to even acknowledge Orion's insults. Unfortunately, she knew they had to take him, otherwise she'd have been tempted to leave him in his cell. He was a Saints' Heir, and they needed him on their side. She'd deal with him later, preferably after Ymira had him healed so she could pound him in the training yard.

"How?" Orion asked, still dead-eyed.

"I'll escort you out." Luca stepped forward. Luca had a calming presence, and Jill was grateful for that now more than ever. "We're to meet Kylian, Aaira, and Bo outside the labor camps. And then we'll get you on board a boat to have your injuries treated."

"A boat?" Orion's hostility disappeared for a second as confusion overcame him instead. "Where did you get a boat?"

"The wolfmen lent us a fleet." Jill met Orion's bewildered look with a steely stare.

"The wolfmen?" His face shifted from bewildered to shocked.

"We promise we'll explain." David's voice was stern as he eyed the young man. "But we have to go now."

"Go, Orion," the Matron said, her voice shaky. "Leave me behind. I'll only slow you guys down."

"With all due respect, we won't let that happen," Luca said. David flipped through the key ring and found the key to her cell, inserting it in the lock before she could protest further. Luca walked in and picked up the old woman with ease.

David opened Orion's cell. The door flung open and for a moment, Orion stared at them, as if unsure this was actually happening, as if he'd dreamed of freedom for so long, he believed it could only ever be a dream.

"We need to hurry," Luca said. "Are there any others with you?"

Orion shook his head, "Because I'm a Saints' Heir and she's the Matron, they only wanted us close by. Everyone else is locked away in the Convent."

As they'd suspected. Still, they'd believed a few more people would be in the Ohans' dungeons. That meant Kylian, Bo, and Aaira would have their work cut out for them to get everyone else out on their end.

Orion limped out of his cell. He had no shoes and Jill saw that, in addition to his other injuries, he was also missing one of his big toes. She wasn't sure why, but it was that detail that broke something inside of her.

A tear slid down her cheek. But it was not one purely of sadness. It was one of anger. She did not know Orion, had never met him before today, but what the Ohans had done to him—what Ohan-Jin had done to him, was horrific and unacceptable. It was the action of a man who was evil to his core, a man who would use anyone—hurt anyone—to further his twisted plans. He needed to be stopped at any cost.

So she vowed then and there. She would make Ohan-Jin pay.

60

DAVID

avid and Jill followed Luca as he scrambled up the stairs with the Matron on his back, Orion limping behind him. Peter had told them about another set of tunnels leading out of the fortress where they could avoid the bulk of the guards and servants and anyone else who might try and stop them. Jill and David would take a different route through the fortress and do their best to cause enough chaos on their way up to the vault to buy them time.

He sure hoped Peter had managed to snag the keys to the vault by now. If he hadn't well—

Focus, David chided himself. It wouldn't do any good if he worried about everyone else's tasks instead of focusing on his own. It was the most basic of principles of military leadership. Delegate well and trust everyone to do their jobs. A captain who tried to do it all himself was not a captain for very long— and usually wound up dead.

David glanced at Jill, her face slicked with sweat, dirt, and grime, but it was only a reminder of all they'd been through together. After all, love was not the sunny, perfect days everyone dreamed it to be. It was the effort and the grit of facing every challenge together. It was the sacrifice of laying down yourself for the other person. It was messy and beautiful, just like she was.

And what if these are your last moments with her?

The thought was so brief, but it was world-shattering as he imagined life without her, as he imagined her trudging on without *him*. He owed her an explanation, or a parting word. Something.

"Jill—"

"We gotta go," she said, cutting him off. They parted ways with Luca, and she started toward the next set of stairs.

He jogged after her. *Later.* He would tell her everything later. They didn't have time for him to say everything he wanted to say to her. They'd never have enough time for all he wanted to tell her. She was right to hurry.

He *would* tell her. Perhaps nothing would happen. Perhaps the visions he'd seen in the Enchanted Wood really were the forest playing tricks on him, just as the vision of his mother had been. Those woods were riddled with nightmares, so it made sense the vision of falling to his death was nothing more than that.

He followed Jill closely, their breathing growing more labored as they climbed the stairs and sprinted down more gloomy halls. They ran down a wide corridor, thankfully bereft of guards or anyone else. He knew the turns they would have to take, had memorized the map and been forced to recite the path to the vault forward and backward.

Anxiety threatened to swallow him as they ran, the lush carpet under their feet dampening their thunderous steps. The halls were steeped in darkness. Hideous paintings lined the walls, gothic chandeliers with dripping candle wax hung above them, and gruesome weapons were mounted to the walls, some of which still bore stains. All of it was enough to make David yearn for light, for a reprieve from such darkness.

They had just neared the end of the corridor when footsteps approached ahead of them, a single set from the sound of it. Jill slowed, starting to reach for another vial when her hand stilled. Instead, she drew her sword as the reptile man rounded the corner and faced them. He was prepared and launched himself at her, wielding a massive, spiked club. Not everyone had guns it seemed.

He swung and Jill barely dodged the blow to her head. She ducked out of the way, but not before it struck her shoulder. Her scream ripped through the corridor, a sound of terror and pain so haunting and terror-stricken that David's arrow was nocked and drawn before he knew what he was doing. Half a second later the arrow released and hit its mark, the arrowhead protruding six inches out the back of the man's neck. The man gagged and squelched, dropped his club, and grabbed at his neck, panic blazing in his eyes. Then he dropped to the ground.

What happened to him after that, David didn't know. He was at Jill's side as she writhed on the floor, blood dripping down her broken arm. Tears ran down her cheeks as her body twisted in agony. Watching the woman he loved in such pain was a torture unlike anything he'd ever experienced. How was it that she'd sustained yet another injury?

"Jill. Jill, look at me." He grabbed her head in his hands, ignoring the tears that ran down his cheeks as well. Her eyes were hazy with pain, but she tried her best to look at him. Her body shuddered in his grip.

"Can you hear me?" he asked, trying to calm the rising panic in his voice. *She'll be okay.* He knew it. For he recalled now how she'd been injured in his vision, that same arm bleeding. She'd been okay though. *She* will *be okay.* If he believed it with enough conviction, then surely, he could make it so.

Her breathing was coming in quick gasps, the pain likely crippling her. He began digging through Jill's pack. Hasani had worked with Ymira to make a vial of pain reducer. It wouldn't heal her, not by a long shot, but it would numb the pain so they could keep moving and get out of here.

How will she rappel down the tower? That was their plan after all, to use the ropes they had to climb down.

One step at a time, he told himself. They needed to get to the vault first. But before they could do that, they had to get her pain under control. He snatched the vial and forced it down her throat. He didn't know how much would do so he made her drink all of it. She coughed and gagged but managed to swallow most of it.

He stayed by her side, waited for her breathing to calm and the blood to slow. He tore the ruined fabric at her shoulder to examine the wound. It wasn't as bad as he'd imagined, but it still wasn't good. The skin was a shredded mess, thanks to the spikes on the club that tore through her flesh. The clavicle was broken in several places near the shoulder and would likely never heal quite right if Ymira didn't see to it soon. He could only hope they could get out of here and back home before the injury began to mend itself.

At last Jill's eyes fluttered open, groggy but clearer than they'd been. Her breathing was no longer erratic, even as she forced herself to a sitting position. A grimace was the only sign that some pain remained, but she said nothing.

"How are you?" David stared at her, unable to hide the relief that washed over him.

"Feel like I got struck with a club," she said, attempting a weak half smile.

He brushed the hair out of her eyes and behind her ears so

he could see her face better. He lingered, cupping his hand behind her neck, his thumb brushing the line of her jaw. She looked so tired, so fragile. For everyone else she was the future Queen of Erinya, but for him she was just Jill. It was something he could get used to, seeing her guard down, seeing her for who she really was.

"Promise we stay together, all right?" David said, pressing his forehead against hers. She leaned into his touch.

"I promise," she whispered.

Tell her. Tell her. Tell her.

But they were out of time. Peter was likely waiting for them already.

"I'm so sorry, but we've got to keep moving," David said, pulling away and standing to his feet. He grabbed her uninjured arm and hauled her to her feet. Blood oozed everywhere, dripping down her arm onto the ground. David tore a long strip of cloth from his tunic and bandaged her shoulder. It was a lousy bandage, and he'd been trained to do far better on the battlefield, but he didn't have the supplies they needed. Not yet anyway. This would have to do for now.

Their pace had slowed to a jog as they followed the path to the vault. The stairs proved the hardest for her, winding her and making her dizzy. Several times they had to stop so she could catch her breath, and David wished it had been him who'd been struck instead of her. The pain would have been incredible, but he could be fixed, put back together—for the most part at least. And although the pain would have lingered, it would not have been nearly as bad for him as it was for her. Even as they finished the last of the stairs, blood seeped through the bandage. Her face was pale and covered in a sheen of sweat.

"We're almost there," he said. They ascended the last few stairs, their progress slow compared to what it had been. They took a left down one hallway, a right at another, and they would be there.

Jill tried to jog, her face steeled against the pain. Any other time he would've forced her to walk, but they didn't have that luxury. She'd have to keep pushing through, and he hated himself for it.

They rounded the next corner and relief flooded through David to see the vault ahead. A single large iron door stood at the center of the hall; a series of complex locks bordered its edge. Blazing torches flickered on either side of it but there were no guards. Strange. They drew closer, their steps slowing as they searched for any sign of Peter. David halted, his senses prickling.

Something wasn't right. Peter should be here by now. Had something happened to him?

The vault shimmered and three figures flickered into life before them. The first was Ohan-Jin, looking smug. The second was Malum. And beside them was Peter.

David's veins turned to ice.

Guards materialized behind them. They were trapped. He glanced at Peter, the man grim and silent as he stared at them.

"Peter?" Jill asked hesitantly. "What are you doing here?"

Peter's lips thinned, but his face remained expressionless. "I told you I'd meet you at the vault. Here I am."

A wicked grin slid up Malum's face, confirming what David had suspected the moment he'd laid eyes on the trio. Peter had betrayed them.

"Welcome, princess, to my humble home," Ohan-Jin gestured around them with two claw-tipped hands. "What do you think of it?"

Jill's face turned to loathing, pure hatred emanating from her. "Your home is a den of nightmares," she quipped.

"Excellent!" Ohan-Jin said, clapping his hands. "The

perfect place for a little family reunion."

"That thing is not my brother," she hissed through gritted teeth.

"Hello to you too, sister," Malum said, striding forward to stand directly in front of her. "I see you're keeping to your habit of choosing poor, untitled men to be your lovers."

A loud crack rang out as Jill slapped him across the cheek. Malum's head snapped back, and he smiled again as blood dripped from his lip. He dabbed a finger against it, admiring the drop of blood there before saying, "Nice one. Do you feel better now?"

Jill's chest heaved but she said nothing, choosing instead to glare at him. He doubted she had the strength to do much more as she began to shake. David glanced between the siblings, fear curling in his stomach. She shouldn't have slapped him. To risk Malum's wrath was dangerous and stupid, even if she had come to his defense.

"What are you doing here, *Jack?*" Her gaze never left Malum's.

Instead of answering her he reached up and plucked a strand of her hair, examining it in the torchlight. David stiffened. "Your hair has grown out," he observed. "I always thought it looked better longer."

"Why are you here?" Jill asked again, her words more forceful this time. David could see the blazing look in her eyes, so distant from the fearful, pained expression he'd seen only ten minutes ago. He wasn't sure which he preferred in this moment.

Malum dropped the lock of hair and stepped back. "I'm here for you. We've known you were coming for weeks. How and when though, we couldn't be sure. I must say, Ohan-Jin and I are both very impressed with you. How exactly did you manage to sneak into Ohan territory unseen?"

A muscle ticked in Jill's jaw, but she didn't answer even as he bent over to look her straight in the eye as if she were a child. The image made David take a step toward her. He wouldn't let her be treated as such.

Malum's head swiveled to face him. "Aw, the little glass soldier, come to defend his princess. You know, I'd almost forgotten about you. Millie told me she had a little run in with you, but Jill was nowhere to be found. I was almost convinced you didn't care for her." His words held no mirth, just calculated banter. He leaned in closer until his face was inches from David's. "Almost."

"Your Majesty," Peter said, his voice sounding bored, "My reward?"

"Reward?" David snarled, his anger finally breaking free. "You turned us in for a reward? After we fought together? After everything we've been through? We trusted you, Peter."

Peter looked unfazed, that red hair of his shining in the torchlight. He shrugged, the action so casual and nonchalant. "Your first mistake was believing a con man like me could ever be trusted."

A growl loosed from David's throat, but he held his tongue. Not when the anger surging through him was as much at himself as anyone else. Because for the love of the Saints, Peter was right. They should never have trusted a man like him. He was a smuggler, a con artist. Even if he was a Saints' Heir.

"What do you want, Malum? I know you didn't come all this way just to catch up," Jill said, turning the conversation away from Peter.

David watched as Ohan-Jin lingered toward the back, content to watch everything unfold. He didn't buy for a second that he and Malum had allied themselves together, not truly. The man was far too ambitious to watch someone else take Erinya's throne.

"We've had enough dancing around the point I see," Malum said, chuckling darkly, "I guess I just wanted to know how far you've come since the day you abandoned me." Jack's smile vanished, his black eyes turning green for just a second, so quickly David almost didn't catch it.

"You left me long before I ever left you, Jack." Sadness tinged Jill's voice.

The siblings stared at each other, closer than they'd been in months and yet David sensed the gap between them had never been wider.

Jack's eyes flashed green again, his face twisting with grief, and then they shifted back to black, and his face contorted into a sneer. "You will hand yourself over for execution, Jill. Or I will kill the man you love."

David stilled. Jill froze.

"Jack, please—"

Her pleads died in her throat as Malum raised a gun he'd been holding and pointed it at David's head. David's eyes locked on Jill's, terror pooling in them.

"Please, Jack—Malum, please don't do this!" Her voice was breathless, terrified. The sound of it broke his heart.

"Jill," David said, "You can't die. You must live—"

"No! I won't leave you! I won't let you die for me."

David smiled at her, tears pricking his own eyes. "Jill, I have always been willing to die for you."

She shook her head, no noise coming out.

"Let me do this—"

"I surrender!" Jill said, falling to her knees, raising her right hand up, unable to lift the other one. "I surrender. Take me, but please, let him live."

"No!" David roared. "Jill—" All the reasons bombarded him why she could not die. They needed her. The kingdom needed her. *He* needed her. He didn't want to live in a world without her, and if that meant taking her place, he would gladly do it.

Malum lowered the gun and marched forward, signaling to the guards who pulled chains from their belts.

David's mind turned frantic. This wasn't how this was supposed to go. He was sure of his vision. His eyes darted to the door off to the side of the corridor. It led up to the tower, the one they were meant to escape by. He could still get her out, still save her.

"Where's Millie, Malum?" It was the first thing he could think of as he scanned the room. She'd always been close by, staying at his side regardless of the monster he'd turned into. But she wasn't here. Malum was all alone in the home of his enemy.

Malum froze. His icy glare turned on David.

"Where is she?" he dared ask again. "Why isn't she here?"

Malum's mouth morphed into a snarl. "She left."

"You let her go?" David was treading dangerous waters, and he knew it. But he'd remembered the gun at his belt. He didn't know exactly how to use it, but he had a pretty good idea.

"Jack let her go, even as it broke him," Malum said, his eye twitching. "She abandoned him, just like everyone else in his pathetic life. If it weren't for me, he'd have crumbled under the weight of it all."

David inhaled, a sudden realization striking him. "You fell for her too, didn't you?" Malum remained silent, his gaze burning into David. "You both loved her."

Malum didn't bother to deny it, and David knew what he had to do.

"And she left you anyway."

Malum surged forward, propelled by anger, but David drew

his gun and fired. The shot was deafening as it echoed through the hall, the sudden pain knocking Malum to the ground. A second later, Jill's sword was drawn, and she swiped at Ohan-Jin before spinning toward the door. Unsurprisingly, Peter had managed to sneak away at some point during their conversation. *Coward.* If he ever came across the smuggler again, he would—well, he supposed he wasn't likely to ever meet him again. But he'd hate him for the rest of his life, however long it might be.

They bolted for the door, flinging it open and running up the last few stairs. Adrenaline must have propelled Jill forward as all thoughts of her injury seemed to fade. David followed close behind and they burst through the door at the top of the steps and out into the night air.

Footsteps thundered behind them, but they kept moving until they stood on battlements that felt far too familiar to David.

Jill ran for the edge of the tower, where they were supposed to rappel down. David's breathing quickened and he reached for her wrist, pulling her around to face him.

"Jill, I just need to tell you, I love—"

Malum burst through the door, striding toward them with purpose. They backed away from him, only a few steps from the edge of the battlements.

David knew what came next. Had seen it so many times in his nightmares. Jill gripped her shoulder, the bleeding increasing now. Malum's eyes were mottled green and black, twisted in rage. A bullet hole ripped through his chest, but it only smoked, wisps of black shadow oozing from it instead of blood.

"How could you Jill?" he screamed, his eyes wild and wide. David knew now what he was asking. How could she leave him? How could she abandon him again?

David took a step forward, "Jack—" he tried to reason but was cut off.

"King Jack!" he bellowed. He turned his attention to Jill. "You would take everything from me? You would betray me like this?"

"Jack," Jill said in a broken voice, clutching her arm. "Please, you're not yourself."

David grabbed Jill's hand. He glanced at her, taking in the tears running down her cheeks, the blood seeping down her arm, her hair falling from its braid. Could he still change this? Or had this always been his future?

"No," Malum said, "I'm not."

Malum marched forward. David shoved Jill out of the way right as Malum lifted his leg and kicked David in the chest so hard he felt it crack straight down the center. He couldn't breathe as he stumbled back, trying desperately to regain his balance. But he felt himself slam against the wall of the battlements, felt himself lose his balance. Then gravity pulled him down, clawing at him with hunger.

The sensation of falling was so much worse than he'd imagined. He heard Jill's scream, and he felt a new sort of ache. He had been the cause of that scream, that pain.

And as he fell, he thought of that woman's strange little poem.

> *Humpty Dumpty sat on a wall,*
> *Humpty Dumpty had a great fall;*
> *All the queen's horses and all the queen's men,*
> *Couldn't put Humpty together again.*

"Goodbye, Jill," he whispered.

Then he struck the ground and shattered.

61

———

JILL

The sound was glass in her eardrums, ringing and cracking and breaking over and over and over. Jill ignored the pain in her shoulder. The pain in her chest wrenching her ribs apart was far worse. She ran to the edge of the wall and peered down, ignoring Malum.

The world was silent as she stared down at the broken man at the base of the tower. She was reminded of shattered porcelain, the pieces scattered everywhere.

She turned back to face her brother, numb with cold. Eyes blurred, ears deaf.

His eyes were wide and green. So green. He almost looked like himself at that moment. This was it though, the end of David. The end of her.

Jack made no move toward her, his face only contorting more. His eyes flashed between green and black, the green finally winning.

"Go, Jill," he said, his voice husky from struggling. "Run while you still have a chance."

Jack turned on his heels, walking back through the door

they'd come. Jill rushed to loop her rope around an iron sconce secured to the tower. Then she wound it around her waist and wrapped the rope around itself several times, making a sort of seat for herself. She only had one good arm, so she prayed it worked.

And if it didn't, perhaps she'd see David again soon after all.

She climbed over the edge of the wall, gripping the rope in her good hand, legs pushing against the tower bricks.

Move now, grieve later.

She launched herself off the battlement and descended, the rope sliding through her hand. It burned, but she barely felt it as she dropped several feet at a time, lowering herself to the ground.

It was grueling. Her muscles ached, and her good arm strained. The pain was returning, and she was growing dizzier by the minute. But she had to keep moving. She had to get to him.

She could put him back together.

Tears dropped from her cheeks, sliding down her neck. She barely felt them, barely felt the aching of her entire body even as it shuddered from the strain. She was close to the ground now. So close.

Her feet hit the earth, and she was running. Running to that broken glass. So many pieces, thousands, tens of thousands. But if it took her entire life, she would find a way to put him back together.

Her fingers found two small pieces and she pressed them against each other, but they didn't fit. She grabbed another piece, frantic, desperate. No luck there either.

Another piece. And another. And another. None of them fit together.

"David, please!" A sob wrenched out of her, her voice breaking. "Please don't leave me. You promised, remember?"

The sound of an explosion ripped through the night. And another. She cupped her ears as the ground beneath her shook. The wolfmen had launched their assault. It seemed Bo and Kylian had been successful. If all was going according to plan, they were escorting the rescued people to the ships.

Rain began to fall, then pour, fat drops landing on her, soaking her within minutes. Still, she sat there, drenched in water and blood and tears, trying to put the pieces back together. Her fingertips were sliced to ribbons, blood getting on everything as she continued trying, and failing, to put David together.

"No one is too broken to be loved, David," she cried, "not even you. Please."

Another slice to her fingertips and she collapsed to the ground, burying her face in the dirt.

"David, please," she whispered, begging. "You promised." Her voice was cracked and broken. She knew she couldn't stay, yet she couldn't bring herself to leave.

Thunder sounded in the distance, or maybe it was another explosion. She didn't care. None of it mattered without David.

"Princess?" Grimzy's deep voice rumbled through her bones.

She sat up to see the mountain man staring between her and the pile of shattered glass. And then Grimzy collapsed beside her, falling to his knees as his entire countenance changed. She'd never known the man to be shocked or afraid of anything. But as he stared down at David's shattered form . . .

They sat there in silence for several, dreadful minutes, until at last he spoke. "Jill, we have to go." His voice was a whisper, even as a tear slid down his face.

She shook her head, unable to speak, to breathe. She couldn't leave him. She wouldn't.

"I'm sorry. He always knew this was a possibility."

"I won't leave him!"

"I know," Grimzy said. Then he lifted her off the ground, carrying her like a rag doll, and began to run.

Another explosion sounded, but it might have been a whisper for the scream that tore from her throat. She pounded her fist against Grimzy. She fought and screamed, but he held her tight.

You promised. You promised. You promised.

"They need you to be their queen," he said softly. "They need your strength."

Jill said nothing, felt nothing.

His pace slowed until eventually he set her on her feet. Jill was aware she was standing, but some part of her barely understood where she was, what she was doing. She wasn't strong. She was just a stupid princess who'd been insane enough to think she could somehow change things. Somehow save her kingdom. But she was nothing.

"Grimzy," her voice was weak. The pain in her arm had resurfaced, making her head spin. "I can't do this. I don't have any strength left to give."

"You can," he said, "You have more than you know."

You promised.

Jill trudged forward, her legs limp as adrenaline drained out of her. She was bloody and dirty and drenched as they walked to the labor camps. The assault in this area at least had been successful. People were making their way to the boats.

But did they have the supplies? They certainly hadn't destroyed any of the weapons. If they didn't get the supplies as well, they'd have extra mouths to feed and nothing else to show for it.

Raindrops skittered down her back as they passed through the gates to the labor camps. The stench of refuse smacked her in the face even through the rain dumping on them. Wolfmen and reptile men fought all around them while others escorted the people toward the ships. Jill felt like time stood still around her. Her body would not move, her mind would not think, and her heart was nothing more than a dull ache in her chest.

He can't actually be gone, can he?

They didn't have much longer before they had to retreat.

"Where's Kylian?" she asked Grimzy, still numb as they fell in behind the shuffling laborers. Although some moved fast, many were malnourished or injured and couldn't move any faster.

"We haven't heard from Bo or Kylian, though Aaira and Luca both showed up with the freed prisoners. They've already boarded the boats."

Once, Jill might have been worried, might have insisted on going to find them. But she couldn't feel anything aside from the hollowness of her own chest. She followed the crowd, her boots slushing through the mud, rain falling around her.

You promised.

She hadn't even had the time to gather David up, to give him the burial he deserved. Would the pieces of him remain there forever? Would someone scoop them up and toss them out? The ache in her chest constricted, and a fresh wave of tears threatened to consume her, to wash her away in grief.

First Will and now David. Was everyone who loved her cursed to die by her brother's hands?

How did one keep moving forward when all that welcomed them was more heartbreak? How did one keep breathing when every breath felt like inhaling water? How did one keep from standing still and letting grief consume them?

She followed the crowd and boarded a rowboat and then a

ship, silent. Someone came and examined her shoulder, poking and prodding, and still she barely felt it. She watched the shoreline, watched as the last of the stragglers were rowed to the safety of the ships, watched as wolfmen loaded the liberated supplies on the largest boat in the fleet.

And as they set sail, Jill gazed at that tower in the distance, its cruelty sharp against the dark sky.

"Goodbye, David," she whispered. The tears started falling.

6 2

JACK

The look on Jill's face would haunt him until the day he died. In his anger he'd killed her first lover and now he'd killed this one as well.

Perhaps it had been Malum, but something had snapped inside him, some leash tethering him to his sanity. He didn't understand how he'd become this angry, vengeful person. Malum had influenced him, but the anger that coursed through him was all his.

All because David had mentioned Millie. And if he couldn't be with his love, then Jill shouldn't either. Except that look of pure horror, of fear, a fear of *him*—he wanted to forget that he'd seen it on his sister's face, forget that it had been directed at him.

Perhaps that was why, before he'd left the Ohans' fortress, he'd ordered one of his men to find all the pieces of the broken young man. Perhaps that was why, as he stood in a dank cellar back in the Citadel, Malum strangely silent, he found himself staring at all the broken pieces this young man had become.

Perhaps that was why he picked up two pieces and fitted them together.

And they held fast.

63

BO

The voyage back to Fenric's Keep was even worse than the voyage to the Ohans' territory. In part because of the riotous waves that sloshed them around constantly, making Bo heave her guts up day and night. And in part because Kylian was not there to distract her.

From the moment they'd met, he'd been there. When he'd been sharp with everyone else, he'd been gentle and kind to her, well for the most part anyway. He had teased her and pushed her and comforted her. He'd been the first person to see her for who she truly was and not shy away from the darkness inside her.

But he'd lied to her.

How long had he known they were—

Bo couldn't bring herself to think the word. She'd wondered if she might have a family out there somewhere, maybe a part of her always had wondered that. But she never could have guessed that Kylian was her—

She squeezed her eyes shut, forcing down the wave of nausea. Bo spent most of the journey back tucked away in a dark, dank corner below decks, hiding from the cold and the wet and the light. She didn't deserve to live in the light, not after abandoning him.

He told you to run, she chided herself. But only ten minutes earlier she'd been telling him she wouldn't leave him. Then she'd fled like the coward she was. She'd fled the day the Ohans had attacked the Convent, and she'd fled while her own brother was taken captive.

Brother.

This time she couldn't stop the wave of nausea and vomited into the bucket she always kept close by these days.

She and Kylian were supposed to sabotage the Ohans further, setting fire at certain points, releasing the horses in their stables while Aaira met up with Luca and escorted the freed prisoners back to the boat. But after Kylian had been taken, all reason and logic had fled her, and she hurried back through the chaos to find the first rowboat back to the ship that she could. Because she was a coward. A bleeding, Saints-forsaken coward.

She'd informed someone, one of the wolfmen captains, that Kylian had been captured, and then she'd crawled into the first hiding spot she could find, like some sort of beetle afraid of the light. Bo *was* afraid of the light, far more afraid of it than she'd ever been of the dark. The light revealed things, like the grimy, twisted parts of her she'd never shown anyone before. They were parts she scarcely wanted to admit having at all.

So, she sat in the darkness, heaving and crying and somehow drowning all at once. She knew what they'd do to Kylian, what he'd all but confessed he would do. He would give them information, but she was sure it would be false. Once they learned that though, they'd torture him. Bo knew better than anyone what Ohan-Jin was capable of. She still recalled that potion of his that made her relive her past with horrifying accuracy and immersion. And Ohan-Jin could see it all.

She inhaled sharply at the thought. They *could* get real information out of him, force him to relive those meetings with confidential information. Everything would be compromised.

She would have to tell Jill, though she didn't relish the thought. David had lost his life on this mission, and she knew the girl was devastated. Sometimes Bo forgot the princess was only a few years older than she was. They had lived such completely different lives, she and the princess.

Bo had been aboveboard a few times, only to find Jill staring out at the ocean, a shell of herself. Though it was different, Bo somehow knew what she was feeling. She'd also felt that pang of sadness when she'd learned of David's death. He too had been kind to her.

They reached the keep the next day, and Bo could hardly move fast enough to get off the boat, her crutch slipping on the wet docks as she hurried to the keep. Kylian had left a letter for her, and she needed to read it, needed to know what it all meant. Needed to know why he hadn't told her sooner.

Anger spurred her on as she stepped off the dock onto solid ground—well, as solid as it could be with several inches of snow. The sudden absence of rocking beneath her feet made her legs buckle just a bit.

"That'll take some getting used to," said a wolfman nearby. "Sea legs and all."

Bo stared at him, but he gave no further explanation as he went back to wrapping long, thick ropes around a pillar. She ignored him and looked up toward the keep. It was a ten-minute walk through the snow to a side entrance in the mountains off the coast. Bo hadn't even realized it was there until the day they'd cast off. The wolfmen kept a bevy of guards stationed here at all times—one set to watch the boats, another to guard the entrance that few knew about.

But it wouldn't stay that way for long as the refugees piled off the boats, heading for the doors that would take them into the safety of the keep. Bo intended to beat them there. She urged herself faster, her sole focus on finding Kylian's quarters and getting answers.

Inside, she relished the warmth that greeted her. The cold, wet voyage had really done a number on her if she thought the keep was warm. She headed straight for Kylian's quarters then froze as a familiar face greeted her with a brilliant smile.

Zyla.

Bo nearly lost her stomach again as the girl ran to her, wrapping her in a hug before looking around, eyes still searching. Searching for him.

They locked eyes and Zyla's smile slid off her face.

"What happened?" She was trembling, Bo could feel it as the girl gripped her arms. "Where is he?"

So Bo told her everything. She told Zyla about the wraith, and the prisoners, the guards that ambushed them. About how Kylian had been shot and had bargained his life to save Bo's. By the time she'd finished recounting everything Zyla had collapsed into Bo, tears streaming down her face.

Why Kylian?

She wanted to blame him, but she was the one who'd run. Who'd fled instead of taking out the men who'd captured him. Why hadn't she used her power? Why hadn't she saved him?

Because he lied to me.

The realization struck her like an arrow to the chest and it left her breathless and filled with shame, but she could not change her feelings. And she couldn't change the past.

~

SHE WAS STILL cold and wet when she found Kylian's quarters. Because of his relationship with the princess, he'd eventually been given his own private room with a cot and a desk, though it was still quite small and simple. The wolfmen were a practical lot, something Bo begrudgingly admired.

Heart pounding, she made her way to the desk and yanked open the top drawer. There it was. The parchment was neatly folded, the handwriting on the front crisp and clean, just as Kylian had always been.

She reached for it, then curled her fingers into a fist, anger suddenly pulsing through her. What gave him the right to tell all of this to her in a letter? Why couldn't he have told her face-to-face? Why hide this from her?

For a second, she was tempted to slam the drawer shut and storm out of there, leaving the letter untouched. She knew the truth now. What more could she learn?

Maybe cowardice runs in the family, she thought grimly.

Then heaving a sigh, she collapsed in the chair. She still felt like she was on a boat, felt the phantom waves jostling her around, and thought she might vomit again even though she felt the cool stone beneath her feet.

She reached for the letter again, lifting it from its place. It felt wrong to remove it, like a violation somehow. But the front of the letter read plainly:

For Bolynn, in the event of my untimely absence.

She held it in her hands, the letter both so heavy and so light. She felt like she stood on the edge of some great precipice, preparing to jump, because after this moment everything would change.

She tore the letter open without another thought and then stared at it, blinking away tears.

My dearest Bo,

She nearly stopped reading it right there, cringing at Kylian's language. Some habits would never die it seemed, like his ridiculous formality in every situation. She forced herself to keep reading.

If you are reading this letter, it seems the worst has happened, though selfishly, I do hope you never have to read it. But that cannot be, for you must know the truth.

You are my sister, and I am your brother.

I suppose you have many questions, so I shall do my best to answer as many as possible within this letter. First off, I am sorry I did not have the courage to tell you all of this sooner. I may pretend to know everything, to be confident and in control, but in this one area of my life, I confess I'm a coward. I suspected you were my sister from the moment we met. Only when you told me stories of your "mother" were my suspicions confirmed.

So, I shall begin with a story. It is a sad one, I fear. Many years ago, when I was ten, my mother gave birth to the most adorable baby girl—Addison Jane, or Addie Jane, as we called her. We all loved her so dearly, me most of all. My parents, or rather, our parents, had struggled for a decade to have more children after I was born. You were everything we all longed for. Your foot was twisted from birth, but we did not care in the slightest. We knew you were special. Little did any of us dream that you'd become a powerful Saints' Heir.

But one night, when you were only a year or so old, a strange woman broke into our house in the middle of the night. I was there in the bedroom with you and woke to your screams and cries as this woman pulled you from your crib then climbed out the window into the night. I screamed for father and climbed out after you. But the woman was fast, unnaturally so, like a dark magic carried her away. From what I know now, it probably did.

Father and I ran after you, following the sound of your cries. They broke my heart, and yet I could do nothing to save you, to bring you home to us. We searched all night but found no trace of the woman.

Bo, we searched for years. We all did. Mother and Father and I traveled far and wide searching for you. But then the money ran out, and Mother got sick. After she passed, Father was quick to go as well. Both of them asked for you on their deathbeds, having forgotten that you'd been taken from them long ago.

After they were gone, I nearly lost hope of ever finding you. Yet something inside me urged me to the Citadel. I thought perhaps if I could work my way up, if I could gain some sort of power or wealth, I could use it to find you.

I excelled in every job, working my way up from a minor clerk to a loan officer, to head servant of the king's household, eventually to the king's adviser. I had so many duties to perform, and King Cole kept me busy. It was only by chance that I met the Matron of the Order of the Saints. From there I was drawn into a new cause as I learned of the Saints' Heirs and the threat that loomed over Erinya.

And in that time, I began to forget about you. I forgot about the promise I'd made to find you and bring you home. I was so wrapped up in my own problems, my own beliefs and schemes, that I compromised the very thing that had brought me to the citadel in the first place—my search for you.

So, when you stumbled out of the forest with David that day, looking like our mother and leaning on a crutch because of your foot, I was shocked. I thought I must be getting my hopes up. Surely, my sister of fourteen years lost had not just *fallen into my lap after all this time. And yet, the more I learned, the more I grew certain of your identity.*

I knew I should tell you, but you were so lost and volatile. I feared what would happen if I added to your burdens. I feared you would hate me or even renounce me because of the love you had for your mother. But mostly, I feared telling you because I'd forgotten about you and I did not believe myself worthy of being a brother to you, not after so much time was lost between us.

Then it seemed we were swept away on an adventure, if you could call it that, and no time felt like a good time to tell you. You hated me, and I felt I deserved it. I deserved to be hated for giving up on you.

But Bo, please believe me when I say I never stopped hoping you were out there somewhere. You are every bit the feisty, funny, wonderful young woman I always imagined you'd be. And so, I am grateful for the time we had, however short it might have been. I am grateful I found my way back to you.

With love,
Your big brother, Kylian Doyle

Bo did not know how long she sat there and wept, but it wasn't until the room began to grow dark that her tears finally subsided a bit. She reread the letter again and again and again. Something cracked inside her, opening wider and wider with every reread.

Her mother—the false mother who'd raised her—had once told her stories of ancient beasts formed inside the rocks. These rocks existed far below the surface of the ground, pressure and time hardening the rocks and the beasts inside them. After great pressure, they would be drawn from the earth and men would hammer away at them. Slowly, so slowly that sometimes it took years, the rocks would begin to crack and open. And then the beast would come raging forth, free yet formed by the heaviest of pressures.

She felt like that now. Something had been hammering away at her from the moment she'd met Kylian. No, even before that. Everything in her had resisted, shying away from the light, away from the warmth of people who cared about her.

But Kylian's words . . .

She'd been loved. Wanted. Yearned for. Long before she was even born, her family had wanted her. And after she'd been taken from them, they had searched for her, had never stopped searching for her. Kylian had loved her so much he'd taken her place back at the Convent, saving her from the torture that would have followed. He'd taken all of that on himself.

"You fool, Kylian," she whispered into the darkness. "Why did you leave me?"

Why did I leave him?

She wiped away the tears that continued to leak down her cheeks, finally rising to her feet. She'd sat there so long she was completely dry from her journey, though still quite dirty.

Bo clutched the letter to her chest as she left Kylian's quarters, both heavier and lighter than she'd felt in days. She wished she could tell someone, anyone—

"Nice to have you back, Bo," a voice said suddenly.

She turned to see Asif standing across the hall, a smirk on his face.

She opened her mouth to say something snarky, but instead she found herself saying, "It's not Bo. Not anymore." She swallowed the lump in her throat, a smile easing onto her lips despite the pit in her stomach. "Call me Addie—Addie Jane."

JILL

They'd failed to destroy the Ohans' weapons, Kylian had been captured, Peter had betrayed them, and David had died. And as Jill stood on the docks while Ymira healed her shoulder, watching the wolfmen unload the stolen supplies, she knew it wouldn't be enough. The wolfmen had managed to launch an assault, and Peter's illusion had kept many of the Ohans distracted, giving them time to haul away carts of dried goods and provisions and whatever else they stored by the labor camps. But Jill could tell it would not be enough.

Word had gotten to her that Grimzy's father struggled to maintain peace within the Whitesaw Mountains as supplies grew scarce. Getting these new supplies to him with winter coming provided an extra challenge. But the refugees in the mountains would not risk the journey to come here. So that left a treacherous journey to bring them supplies that would last a week at best.

Not enough.

The words swirled in her head. They had risked

everything for this assault, and while they'd freed the people from the Ohans tyrannical grip, they had less to show for it than ever. How long before fighting broke out within the keep? How long before people were calling for her to accept responsibility and pay the price?

Little did they know she'd already paid the ultimate price. Her body was here, but her heart had been left behind, shattered along with David.

"Your Highness," Grimzy said, rousing her from her thoughts.

"Yes?" she said, doing her best to hide the fatigue and her red eyes. She'd hardly slept on the journey back, unable to keep from dreaming about that moment over and over.

"The Alpha and his council would like to see you. As would Prince Tiernan."

Jill licked her chapped lips and nodded a thank you to Ymira. She rolled her shoulder a bit and while there was some residual pain, it felt better than it had in days. There would likely be some scarring, because she'd not been able to have Ymira heal it any sooner. But she was okay with scars. She always had been.

She followed after Grimzy while eyes followed her as they made their way off the docks and through the crowds, some of the rescued people even bowing to her as she passed. She wanted to tell them not to, to tell them not to put her on a pedestal, that she had rescued them from one prison only to take them somewhere far more dangerous. But instead, she held her head high, giving small smiles when someone met her gaze.

It was exhausting, but Grimzy told her the people needed her, needed her strength. So, she would give it to them, however false it might be.

As she passed an older feline man, one of the first Jill had seen among the new refugees, she noticed the man kiss the tips of his fingers then press them to his forehead before raising them out to her.

Jill stopped, eyeing the man. He was short but strong for his age, probably why he'd lived so long in the labor camps. The tips of his catlike ears were covered in graying, orange fur, and his eyes were a bright shining green. The folds of his skin were deep and covered in ash and dirt, but he wore a smile all the same.

"What does that mean?" she asked, unable to quell her curiosity.

He smiled broader, revealing missing teeth. "It is a feline blessing. It means, 'my words and mind will honor thee,' " he said.

"My words and mind will honor thee," she repeated, almost to herself. Around her, several others made the motion as well, though no others were feline. "Thank you," she said, dipping her head to the man. "You have honored me as well."

She wasn't really sure if it was the right thing to say, but the man continued to smile at her and made the gesture again as she began walking off. From there the path opened before her as everyone stepped back, making the same blessing gesture. She nodded at them, walking slower despite the urgency she sensed from Grimzy.

It couldn't be good if Grimzy felt the need to hurry. But soon they were out of the cold and inside the walls of the keep once more. Jill wasn't sure she preferred it to the rocking ship where she'd spent the last week and a half. The keep felt far more oppressive as she walked the halls, and more people turned to stare at her.

Her heart pounded faster as Grimzy led her to the meeting room where they'd discussed all of their plans before the assault. Except this time, when they entered, there were only a handful of people in there.

The Alpha stood at the head of the room, giving her a slight bow of respect when she entered. Beside him stood his right-hand man, the Beta whose name she could never remember. Prince Tiernan was also present, along with several other stuffy looking men she'd never seen before.

Every eye was trained on her as she entered, the expressions of the three men beside Tiernan especially sharp. Only his gaze was friendly as he smiled at her. He'd wanted to join the assault and had told her many times despite the Alpha's protests, but eventually someone had argued that if he were spotted attacking the Ohans, it was as good as a declaration of war from Welynn. So reluctantly, he had stayed.

"Your Highness," the Alpha said. "I'm glad to see you back safely."

"Thank you," she said, her voice sounding hollow even to her ears. She'd remained safe, but others had given their lives for this mission. A mission she'd spearheaded. She inhaled, turning her gaze from the Alpha's back to Tiernan's.

You promised.

The thought struck her, and she had to flutter her eyes to blink back the sudden tears that threatened to fall. "Forgive me," she said, her voice quavering slightly. "It was a difficult journey back."

"There's nothing to forgive," Tiernan said, stepping forward.

A thin man beside Tiernan cleared his throat. He wore spectacles, and his face looked stuck in a permanent scowl. The tips of his ears were pointed slightly, telling her everything she needed to know. This man—elf—was from Welynn. And he didn't look particularly happy to be here.

"Miss Jillianna," the man said, his voice squeezed thin like he had a head cold, "I am Prince Gaylor's Head of State, Lord Beezlebum Hingam." The name was unfortunate, mostly because it fit the Lord so well.

She caught sight of Tiernan pressing his lips together tightly, as if to keep himself from laughing. Apparently, she wasn't the only one who found the name amusing.

The man launched into some spiel that she'd immediately tuned out thanks to Tiernan's expression, but she raised a hand to stop him.

"It's Your Highness," she corrected, "not Miss Jillianna."

Once, she would have been indignant. And at another time, she wouldn't have bothered to correct such a silly man. But she'd lost everything recently, she would not lose her self-respect too.

The man sneered but continued, barely hiding his disdain for her. "As I was saying, as Prince Gaylor's Head of State, I have come here to bear witness to the proposition of marriage between you and him. Now if you'll just—"

"What?" she said, shock washing over her like the icy ocean waves. "Proposition of marriage?" Her head swung between Grimzy who looked displeased, Tiernan who looked almost sheepish, and the Alpha who looked unamused by the entire affair.

Tiernan stepped forward, "Jill, wait, I'm so sorry. I didn't mean for it to be like this," he ran a hand through his blonde hair. "I had to get permission from the heads of the princedom before I could officially propose, but they simply came straight here and then you were gone and—" he stopped, noticing the look of shock on her face. "Jill, will you marry me?"

Jill could barely breathe, barely think. She stood in a room, surrounded by men, each one there to—what? Decide her fate? Did they think she couldn't be queen on her own?

To her surprise it was the Alpha who broke the uncomfortable silence. "Your Highness, with all due respect, you didn't really think you could come into my home and take up residence and not expect something of this nature?"

"I had hoped," she said cooly, "That we'd moved past our differences."

The Alpha gave a wan smile that didn't reach his eyes. "We have taken a single step forward in mending relations. But it is not enough. Now you come back with more mouths to feed and less to show for it than you promised. You did at least destroy the Ohans' cache of weapons, did you not?"

Jill wilted.

"I see. So Erinya is lost then. And yet I know you'd expect us to continue supporting you—"

"It's more complicated than that," she interjected, finally finding her voice.

"Is it?" the Alpha said, a dangerous edge to his tone. He was not a man one interrupted. "Did you or did you not destroy the Ohans' weapons cache?"

Jill's palms slicked with sweat. "We did not. But we found three guns and brought them back for your people to study."

The Alpha's steely gaze told her that this would not be enough. "Then I have no reason to let you remain here. The smart thing for me to do would be to turn you over to your brother and humble myself to the Ohans. Perhaps then they will only kill half of my people instead of all of them when they come."

Jill's throat tightened. She could make no defense, no argument. She'd failed. They'd angered the Ohans and had not even been able to give themselves a fighting chance by destroying the weapons.

Not enough.

"I fail to see what this has to do with Prince Tiernan's

proposition." The proposition that made her sick to her stomach.

"Simple. Prince Tiernan has offered to pay me to let you stay here. He's even offered to send extra supplies to those within the Whitesaw mountains. And you will accept his proposal, or you will find yourself at the king's mercy." He paused, staring at her with those intense eyes. "I warned you, princess, this mission was a test. And you have failed. I will protect my people, even if it means sacrificing you."

Jill's eyes welled with tears again. She'd been a fool, an absolute fool to think she could do this. To think she could escape her fate and take the throne from her brother.

She had failed. Failed her people, failed her brother, failed David. How poetic that her fate would lead her back to a man like her father, controlling who she would marry.

"I'm so sorry, Jill," Tiernan said again, "I didn't want it to be this way." She could tell he was earnest, that he meant every word he said. But it wasn't enough. He might care for her, but she could never reciprocate his feelings. But he would offer an alliance, an alliance that might help them fight back against Malum and Ohan-Jin and the destruction they would cause.

"I suggest you make a decision swiftly, princess," the Alpha said.

She had no choice. She would do this, for her people. After all, David was gone. He wasn't coming back.

"I accept your proposal," she said, nearly choking on the words.

Tiernan smiled and walked forward, pulling a ring from his pocket and sliding it on her finger. She barely felt it. Barely felt anything as she signed papers and treaties and whatever else the weasel of a man Lord Hingam made her sign to make the proposal official.

Once, she would have resisted with every fiber of her being. But that part of her had died on the tower.

Hours later, she was freed from the suffocating room and nearly ran all the way to her quarters, her head spinning, her stomach lurching, her heart threatening to burst.

When she finally reached her rooms, ready to collapse in a puddle of tears she heard someone shouting her name. She spun to find Zyla racing toward her, concern etched in every line on her face and, she noticed, her eyes ringed in red.

Jill wanted to shake her head at the girl, to tell her, "No, I can't handle any more bad news today. Let me fall apart in peace."

But she didn't have that luxury.

"What's the matter?" she asked.

"I'm so sorry, Your Highness," Zyla said, nearly out of breath, "But it's Anna. She's in labor, has been for several days."

Jill froze, a new fear gripping her.

"It's too early," Jill said, numbly.

"I know, which is why you should come. Ymira is doing everything she can but—" The girl halted herself, swallowing hard.

"But what?" Jill forced herself to ask.

"The baby is stuck."

No. No. No.

This could not be happening. This was not real. She was having another horrific nightmare she would wake up from any minute now.

"We should hurry," Zyla whispered.

And so, they did. As they hurried through the halls, Jill

wondered if someone could reach a limit for the grief they could hold. As she ran toward what she feared might be more heartbreak, she felt hollow and numb, as if her own body could not handle the pain it carried.

They arrived at the birthing suite what felt like only seconds later. And Anna—poor Anna—was gasping in pain. Blood and tears ran freely, and Jill felt sick to her stomach. The girl sat with fists and knees pressed into the mattress, covered in a sheen of sweat. She wore a light gown that was stained with far too much red.

Ymira sat beside her, whispering soothing words and using her healing powers, pressing her hands on different parts of Anna's body. But Jill didn't miss the stubborn wrinkle in Ymira's brow that told her something was wrong.

"Thank goodness you're here, Jill." Ymira never too her eyes off Anna. "Anna, look who's here?"

The girl tried to look up at Jill but let out another gasp of pain, and her breathing turned raspy and heavy.

"Just breathe," Ymira said. "Push your belly out as you inhale. We have to get the baby out now, okay. You'll have to push."

"I can't," Anna rasped, tears squeezing from her eyes.

The scene was almost too much for Jill to bear. She'd never spent much time around pregnant women, let alone witnessed the birth of a child. But she knew enough.

"Should I really be here?" Her mouth had gone dry. She was accustomed to blood, yes, but not like this. Nothing like this.

"She needs you," Ymira said. "You are the closest thing she has to family, and this baby is your niece or nephew."

Well, when she put it like that.

"Okay, Anna, it's time to push. Just get as comfortable as you can, listen to your body—"

"My body is screaming at me," Anna snapped. And despite the direness of the situation, Jill laughed just a little. Perhaps she and Anna could have been friends had their titles not gotten in the way.

"Come to her side," Ymira ordered Jill, unfazed by Anna's outburst. "Comfort her."

Jill did as instructed, though she wasn't entirely sure how to give comfort. She settled for placing a hand on Anna's shoulders. The girl grabbed Jill's hand with a sudden fierceness and squeezed so hard Jill nearly gasped.

"It's okay," Jill squeaked out. "I'm right here."

Anna grunted, still clinging to her. Jill let her, not wanting to pull away. She didn't know how long they stood there while Anna breathed and pushed and moaned in pain. It felt like a long time to her, though she was certain it felt longer for Anna.

"One more time, Anna," Ymira said, pressing a damp cloth to the girl's forehead. "You're almost there."

Anna whimpered as she gasped for breath. Jill's hand had gone numb, but she no longer cared. The young woman gave another push, and the wailing cries of a tiny infant filled the room.

"It's a girl." Ymira smiled as she gathered the baby into her arms.

Anna collapsed, rolling to her back as Ymira handed the screaming babe to her, wiping it down even as Anna clutched the tiny creature to her chest.

Jill hadn't even realized she was crying until the tears started running down her neck. She stared down at her former maid, at her niece, all pink and wrinkly and covered in tiny tattoos like those of her mother's people. They were adorable and—

Anna inhaled at the same time Jill did, the two of them staring down at the child.

"What's the matter?" Ymira was at Anna's side in an instant, and then she saw it too.

The Inkwells were born with tattoos that prophesied their lives, who or what they would become.

And Jill's niece had been born with the tattoo of a crown upon her head.

MILLIE

Millie found herself standing in a dark room, shadows curling at the corners, giving the room a hazy feel. She wasn't certain how she'd come to be here, yet she sensed the importance of her presence in this place.

A door opened somewhere outside her line of sight, and twelve figures appeared as if out of thin air. One by one they entered her field of vision and then sat at chairs that materialized in a circle. A table was next to materialize.

I'm dreaming, she realized.

She glanced around at the figures who sat in the circle. She recognized them all immediately. The Saints. They did not seem to see her though, as if she were nothing more than a ghost haunting the shadows.

A young man with blonde hair, Kieran, leaned back in his chair as shadows twirled between his fingers. Beside him sat a young inkwell woman who wore glowing bracelets. Uri the Bright. Uri eyed Kieran with something like distaste, as if she disapproved of his shadows. Beside the two of them sat two gazelles, one female and one male. They spoke in hushed voices, and each bore a strong resemblance to the other. Inerys and Amari, the twin Saints.

Looking around the circle, Millie identified each of the Saints with ease, as if aided by some supernatural knowledge. Felix the Trickster. Briar the Cunning. Cairn the Strong. Torryn the Gentle with a small furry creature sitting on his shoulders. Once again, she was struck by how ordinary they looked. None of them looked as they were portrayed in the books and in statues and carvings. They didn't even look like warriors.

At last, her gaze came to rest on a face she'd seen before. Zillah the Vengeful, or rather, Zillah the Avenger. Her own ancestor. The woman's gaze was the only one that met Millie's, as if she alone could see Millie. She looked younger now than when Millie had first spoken with her, and Millie realized then that this must be some sort of memory.

Millie swallowed, and their gazes locked. Zillah said nothing but nodded, as if she knew precisely why Millie was here even if Millie did not.

Zillah stood then, turning her gaze back on the group. At once everyone hushed, eyes turning to the young woman. It was clear now that she led these warriors, these Saints.

"Thank you for coming," Zillah said, looking around the circle. "I know many of you would rather be off fighting than stuck in a meeting like this."

"It's not as if we had much choice," Kieran said, shadows still winding between his fingers. The action reminded Millie of the boys in the stable who were always flipping coins across their knuckles.

"Knock it off, Kieran. You're the only one who doesn't want to be here," Uri said, frowning at the young man. Kieran shrugged, not bothering to deny it.

Zillah eyed the two of them but continued. "I think we can

all agree that Malum has grown too strong. Ever since he drained the land of its magic, Erinya has been fading. Now he has these creatures, these vulgan, with horrific powers. I fear if we don't stop him soon, we won't be able to."

"What are our options?" a melodic voice asked. Millie turned to see that Nadia the Peacemaker had asked, her feline eyes wide and beautiful. Kieran seemed to straighten as she spoke, his attention focused on her.

Zillah gripped the back of her chair, knuckles going white. "We must destroy those creatures before they consume the rest of the magic Erinya has."

"And this is all because he wants to bring back his wife and child?" a new voice asked. A man who looked older than the rest of them, perhaps in his thirties, though he still had a youthfulness about him. His shoulder-length hair was a deep red, his eyes greener than any Millie had ever seen. Felix the Trickster. She could see how he'd earned that name. There was something . . . unsettling about the man.

Zillah released her hold on the chair, running a hand through her dark hair. "I believe it started that way. But this stolen magic has corrupted him. He wants vengeance. The only way he can raise them is with access to the well, and since that's under our control, he will do anything to destroy us. Including harming the innocent people of Erinya."

Silence hung over the room, and everyone stilled. Even Kieran stopped fiddling with his shadows.

"What do we do then?" Kieran asked, the only one it seemed who was brave enough to ask that harrowing question.

At this Zillah inhaled deeply, as if preparing to give bad news. "I've consulted the guardian at the well—"

Immediately the room burst into chaos, several groaning and others outright angry, Kieran being the loudest of all of them.

"Hush!" Nadia's voice sliced through the sudden cacophony. "Let's hear her out."

"Don't use your magic on us, Nadia," Kieran spat, his interest from earlier suddenly gone.

The feline girl glared at him as if daring him to object further. He opened his mouth as if to do such a thing, then snapped it shut, turning back to Zillah.

"Why did you go to the guardian? She's the reason we're in this mess in the first place. If she hadn't given Malum everything—"

"You forget she is the one who pleaded with the Deity to give us our magic, *Kieran*. We wouldn't be here now if it weren't for her."

Kieran rose to his feet, ready to argue with her but was quickly cut off.

"What did the guardian say?" A low voice rumbled through the room. Torryn the Gentle, a Whitesaw mountain man who loomed over all of them.

"She said if Malum gains more power we may not be able to defeat him at all. But—" Zillah stopped, looking rather pale. Everyone sat on the edges of their seats, waiting. "There may be another way. We could imprison him in the realm between life and death."

Again, silence hung over the room and slowly, Kieran sat back in his seat, looking troubled. "There's more, isn't there?" he asked, eyeing Zillah with suspicion.

Zillah's jaw clenched and she nodded. "Yes."

Millie, despite being trapped in a dream, felt her heart ramp up in speed, hammering inside her chest so loudly she would have feared they could hear it if she didn't know better.

"To open this veil requires a great amount of magic and sacrifice. We must combine all our magic to open it and imprison him. And," Zillah paused, looking away from all of them, "we will be trapped as well."

Millie gasped, though no one could hear her. *What did this mean?*

"So, you expect us to sacrifice our freedom to trap Malum?" a quiet voice asked. Millie looked to see a figure she'd only glanced over earlier. A reptile man with black scales along his cheekbones. Jin the Resilient.

"I believe it's the only way," Zillah said sadly.

Jin nodded.

"Will it be enough to stop him?" Nadia asked.

"The guardian believes it will be. But before we do, we must choose heirs to receive our magic once we're—" Zillah stopped, then continued. "Once we're imprisoned as well. Some of you have children already. That should be enough. But those without must choose heirs to accept our magic once we're gone."

"Why do we need heirs if Malum will be imprisoned?" Kieran asked.

Zillah sighed and Millie could see how tired the young woman was. Millie understood that feeling all too well. "Because it is a temporary solution. One day, Malum may be able to free himself. We must take precautions to prepare for that event."

"Then why do any of this at all?" Kieran said, throwing his hands in the air.

"Because I don't know what else we can do!" Zillah shouted back at him. Her chest heaved with frustration, and Millie wished she could step forward and hug the girl. But she may as well have been a ghost. "We cannot defeat Malum. Our only hope is to imprison him and pray that our heirs are successful where we were not."

"You would lay that burden on a future generation?" Torryn stared at her, brows raised.

"I fear we have no choice," Zillah said.

Kieran's face twisted with anger, and he stood again, running a hand through his hair. "Why us? Why did the Deity choose us?"

Zillah shook her head. "I don't know, Kieran."

Kieran crossed his arms, turning about, huffing and grumbling. Then at last he faced Zillah as if coming to some conclusion. "Fine. If this is the only way, then so be it. Let's imprison this bastard and end this once and for all."

"I will help as well," Jin said, nodding with quiet acceptance.

Nadia and Torryn were the next to agree. Then the twins. Then Uri. One by one, each of the Saints agreed to help imprison Malum.

Millie's heart twisted. They had given up everything to save Erinya.

They went all the way around the circle until it came back to Zillah. She did not need to voice her acceptance. It seemed she'd accepted her fate long ago.

The scene before Millie began to fade, the figures turning misty and the shadows growing darker until only one figure remained.

Zillah stood before Millie, despair etched into every line of her face. Despite the young woman's sadness, Millie felt a spark of anger. She had indeed pushed this problem onto a future generation. Onto her.

"Why show me all of this?" Millie asked, unable to hide her animosity toward Zillah.

"Because you needed to know," Zillah said. "You needed to understand what happened that day. We could not kill Malum then, but I believe *you* can."

Millie shook her head. "Zillah, he's even stronger now. He doesn't just have the vulgan anymore, he has the blackbloods. People the vulgan have turned into monsters to do Malum's bidding. How on earth are we supposed to defeat him now?"

If the Saints hadn't been able to defeat him then . . .

"You forget that we've been imprisoned *with him* for the last four hundred years, Millie. We know more than we did then. And you will not be alone."

A thought struck Millie, one she hadn't considered before. "How are you showing me all of this? If you're trapped in that realm, how are you contacting me now? How do I know any of this is real?"

"Because Millie, you nearly died yourself. Malum's power pulled you back just before your soul entered the afterlife. Like Jack's, your soul has cracks now. For that reason, I can speak to you from our prison. You and anyone else who has killed a vulgan."

Millie collapsed. She felt numb. She felt no anger, no fear, no sadness. Just . . . a coldness. It was all too much.

"The princess," Zillah urged. "You must find her. Together, the two of you must return to the well. Only then can the wrongs of the past be righted."

Zillah's form faded completely, and Millie's eyes fluttered open. It was still dark, and she could barely make out the tent above her.

She knew in her heart that Zillah was right. All of this had started with the well. Suddenly, Millie knew with utmost certainty—everything would end at the well too.

JILL

*A*nna struggled for several months after her daughter, Elyse, was born. Jill had been surprised but touched that the young woman had named her daughter after Jack and Jill's mother. Ymira watched over her day and night, protective as a mother hen. Or a mother bear. Rarely had Jill seen Ymira so riled. She ordered the young woman to stay in bed, consume warm foods, and focus on her baby. Ymira barely let Jill in to see Anna, and when she was finally permitted to visit Anna and Elyse, Anna seemed grateful for the company.

They didn't talk much. Mostly Jill held a sleeping Elyse while Anna rested. She was fine with that though. She preferred if far more than meetings or any interactions she might have had with Tiernan.

She glanced down at her hand, at the finger which held an obscenely large emerald on it. The ring was beautiful, but it represented everything she'd been trying so hard to flee. It had been two months since his proposal. As he'd promised, his princedom had sent extra supplies to the Whitesaw mountains. According to Tiernan, there were secret tunnels from Welynn into those mountains, something that had conveniently never been mentioned before. She suspected the Whitesaw people had plans to split from Erinya and join the kingdom of Welynn. But that was another issue for another time.

Winter was nearing its end, and she hadn't heard a whisper of retaliation from either her brother or the Ohans. Certainly, the snows had prevented any armies from coming north but it was of little comfort. They were planning something. Something big.

A small cry drew her attention from her dark thoughts. Baby Elyse arched her back, stretching adorably in her little blanket sack with embroidered snowflakes on it. Jill smiled down at her. She was beautiful. It felt too early to say who she looked like, but her coloring was dark like Jack's.

Oh Jack.

Nothing made her heart ache for her brother like holding his child, knowing he had no idea she even existed. Jill wanted to be angry with Anna for hiding it from Jack. After all, he deserved to know about his own child. But Anna had left because she feared King Cole, and Jill knew she was right to do so. Their father had been cruel. If he'd known Jack had sired an illegitimate heir, he'd likely have had Anna and the baby killed, not because he'd cared much about what Jack had done but because another heir might threaten his throne someday.

Glancing down at the girl's tattooed crown, Jill thought the fear may have been well placed.

The tattoo had given her much to think about the last few months. Jill had instructed Anna, Ymira, and Zyla to tell no one, and the baby hadn't left her mother's side since she'd been born, so that had been easy to conceal at least. For now. But sooner or later she would have to tell someone what it meant.

Grimzy would be the first to know, because, well, it was

Grimzy. She'd likely never find someone as loyal as he was, though they'd still yet to discuss his identity as a Saints' Heir. With everything else going on, it never felt like the right time to bring the matter up.

"How is she?" a soft voice asked. Anna sat up in her bed, yawning but gazing lovingly at the bundle in Jill's arms.

"Perfect," she said, stroking Elyse's cheek. She hadn't known it was possible to feel so much love for such a tiny little thing, especially as her world seemed to crumble all around her. But she would do anything for her niece. She would fight the kingdom for her. She would win back the throne for *her*.

"You've changed you know," Anna said.

Jill looked up at her, taken aback. She wasn't entirely sure if Anna meant it as a compliment or if it was simply an observation.

"A lot has happened," she said. "Anybody would change."

"I don't think so," Anna said, shaking her head. "I think the more things change, the more people want to stay the same. It's easier to stay frozen than it is to accept things might never go back to the way they were."

She had a point. But did Jill really want to go back to the way things were six months ago? With her tyrannical father forcing her into a marriage, Jack wrestling with the voice in his head in secret, and Millie hiding her powers? She'd wanted to be a paladin, but that dream felt silly compared to the weight on her shoulders now.

"I didn't ask for any of this, and yet, if I had to do it over, I don't think I'd change anything," she said, astonished by her own honesty. Except David. She would change that.

Elyse started to squirm and fuss, so Jill handed the baby over to her mother to nurse.

"I know what you mean," Anna said, looking down at her

daughter. "I wouldn't change anything if it meant not bringing her into the world."

She stared at Anna and Elyse, watching as the mere presence of her mother soothed Elyse to sleep. Anna smiled down at her, glowing from within. Glowing with love. Distantly, Jill was aware of some tiny spark inside her catching, whispering, breathing life into her after all that had happened.

It was hope.

Jill had lost everything, but she *had* saved her people.

A knock sounded at the door and somehow Jill knew it was Grimzy. She gave Anna a squeeze and kissed her niece on the head then strode to the door, feeling lighter than she had in days. Not all hope was lost, not as long as life remained.

She flung open the door, staring up at Grimzy. He nodded briefly to Anna inside before motioning for Jill to follow him.

"Come."

Her nerves were immediately set on fire, palms sweating and heart pounding as they walked down the corridor. "Is everything all right?"

"No, it's not."

Her steps slowed, panic crushing her lungs. Only moments ago, she'd felt peaceful and serene despite everything around her. Then she'd stepped back into the real world.

"What happened?"

"We just got word," he hedged. "It seems more refugees have fled the Citadel, heading south." There had been reports of refugees fleeing south for months. Though where exactly they were going, and who offered protection no one had been certain.

"Okay," she said slowly. She felt guilty that her first thought was how grateful she was they weren't coming here. They'd pushed the Alpha's generosity to its limits already. And even with the new influx of funds from Tiernan thanks to their alliance, she knew the Alpha was ready to have her gone. "Is there more?"

"Yes, I'm afraid," he said. "It seems Malum is displeased they've left. So, he's sending twenty thousand troops after them, including the blackbloods."

Jill sucked in a breath. How did he even have that many troops? The Citadel was big—but twenty thousand troops? And to send them after civilians? Terror and anger burned through her.

This was what he was planning. He'd waited not for an opportunity to attack her, but to attack innocent people he knew she would come to save.

"There's more."

She shut her eyes. "Just tell me everything."

"Carthesia is invading from the South. And the Ohans are sending troops our way."

Jill struggled to keep her breathing under control. Their enemies attacked from all sides, deliberately penning them in to keep her from sending aid to the refugees in the South. Saints, those people were about to be completely surrounded.

"What can we do?" she asked weakly.

Grimzy heaved a sigh, one that shook the walls around them. Then he knelt in front of her. Even when he knelt, she had to look up at him.

"Do you remember what I told you long ago, about how the stars and the earth spoke of a queen unlike any other who'd come before?"

She nodded, though doubt niggled at her chest.

"I do."

"She would bear no magic, yet she would right the wrongs of the past, magic coming to her aid." He spoke words she'd never heard before, and Jill wondered briefly if he was making it all up to comfort her, to encourage her. "I believe you are that queen. On your own, you have no hope of winning this war. But you have what no other army does."

"What's that?" she said weakly, forcing back tears.

"The Saints' Heirs. They will rise when darkness comes to aid Erinya and restore its power to its rightful place."

She shook her head, "I don't know what that means, Grimzy. All I know is I've led these people to their doom. They trusted me, and I've failed them all." She knew she should keep her voice down, that someone might hear her, but she didn't care.

You promised.

Maybe she could have faced this with David by her side, but without him, she didn't know how she would ever face anything again.

It's easier to stay frozen than it is to accept things might never go back to the way they were. How true those words felt.

"There's something you should see," he said, rising to his feet. She followed him down another corridor and then into the large mead hall they'd entered when they first arrived at the keep. The doors swung open to reveal several hundred people huddling inside, as if waiting for something. They all turned toward her, looking hopeful and expectant.

Jill's stomach lurched.

A young woman stepped forward, looking thin and unnaturally pale despite her dark skin, gazelle horns cresting on her head. One of them had been sheared down, an act she heard was incredibly painful for the gazelle people.

"Thank you, Your Highness," she said, stooping low. "The day you rescued us from the Ohans, you saved me from a fate far worse than you know." The young woman looked up at her, and Jill knew this beautiful woman had experienced cruelty beyond anything Jill had ever been subjected to.

It made her angry. And one day Ohan-Jin would feel her wrath.

More people came forward, thanking her, bowing to her, giving the feline blessing to her. She didn't know how to feel about it. She'd helped save them, yes, but she was not a savior. These people needed something more than to put their hopes in a fallible human being.

She eyed the front of the room where a little dais had been raised, only a few feet taller than everyone else. On it stood Ivan, Hasani, Orion, Lyra, Ymira, and Bo—or rather, Addie.

The Saints' Heirs. Or the ones that were here anyway. Who knew where Peter was. She shoved the thought of that traitor away.

The path in front of her opened, people stepping out of her way as she ascended the dais. Grimzy stayed on the ground yet still loomed over her.

Hundreds of expectant eyes turned to face her, each one filled with hope and admiration.

Hope.

Hope still lived. The odds were not good, but she'd made a vow to protect these people, to protect all her people. Even if it cost her her life.

"Tell them," Grimzy prompted.

She almost said no and walked right out. How could she look them in the eyes and tell them the truth?

She turned to them, rolled back her shoulders, and held her head high. Finally, she had a plan.

"It is no secret who I am and what I've done. My name is Jillianna, princess of Erinya. Months ago, I fled the tyranny of my brother Jack, with a plan to take back the throne and bring peace to Erinya once and for all."

She saw some nods of assent and heard sighs of relief at the words. But they needed to know everything.

"However, my brother seeks to execute me. Ohan-Jin will likely do the same. They've both sent troops to attack us." Gasps and cries of despair filled the room, but Jill forged on. "But we are not as helpless as they believe. We have something they do not. The Saints' Heirs, wielding magic unlike anything we've ever seen." She gestured to her friends, who nodded. "I will train them. And together we will fight and bring peace to Erinya, once and for all."

A wave of people dropped to their knees, bowing before her. Then the chanting began.

"Long live the Queen."

EPILOGUE

Quiet followed Ohan-Jin like a wraith as he entered his study. A silent rage echoed through his bones even as he closed the door behind him, leaving his guards outside. He stood there for three seconds, examining the splattered blood on his scaled hands. He was covered in it.

Blood soaked his tunic and his sleeves. He felt the crust of it drying on his face. None of it was his. No, he did not bleed.

But he would make the princess bleed.

At last, his temper snapped. He reached for the nearest glass bottle and hurled it into the empty fireplace. The glass shattered, the amber liquid inside spraying the stone. He picked up another jar and threw that one as well, watched as it hurtled through the air before exploding in the fireplace, the two liquids combusting on contact.

Ohan-Jin forced his heart to slow, his blood to cool. He would make that Saints-cursed princess pay for what she'd done, for the slaves she'd taken from him. But he couldn't do that if he let his anger feast on the blood in his veins. He would have to be cunning.

Stepping behind his desk, Ohan-Jin sat, soothed by the familiar feel of his chair beneath him, of his papers blotted with ink, of the metal disk that sat in the center of his desk. He could feel its call and knew exactly what it was made of and how much it weighed.

Ohan-Jin smiled to himself as he pulled out a piece of parchment and quill, dipping it once, twice, into the blood-red ink bottle beside him.

He may have lost this battle, but he still had several tricks up his sleeve.

The letter was brief but clear. He would not bother with codes or ciphers, not this time, not when he wanted them to know exactly what his plan was.

Send the battalions. Order the infantry to pass through the countryside and tell them they may slaughter any who stand in their way. The war has begun. Let us finish this once and for all.

Ohan-Jin leaned back in his chair. Let the princess gather her precious Saints' Heirs. Let the king gather his vulgan and army of monsters. They would be useless against him.

He folded the parchment and slipped it into a yellowed envelope before letting hot wax drip on the front. He pressed his seal into the silver wax until it cooled.

He lifted his fingers into the air, feeling that beautiful humming course through his body. The silver disk on his desk melted into a puddle then rose into the air as well. The liquid metal floated in the air like a fish in water, weightless.

He called the metal to himself, watching in awe as it broke apart and tipped each one of his fingernails, forging them into tiny blades sharp enough to cut through steel. He closed his eyes, drinking in the power. He felt every piece of metal in his study, from the large shield that hung over the fireplace to the smallest ring of silver tucked away inside the desk drawer.

In another breath the metal pieces in his study lifted into the air as well. The shield, the candle holders, the letter opener, the knife at his belt, all of it rose as one, floating in the center of the room. As he formed a fist, the pieces converged together, melting and melding until a large mass of molten metal floated before him.

With ease he called it toward himself, letting it coat his entire body like a second skin. It was lighter than any armor he'd worn, but he knew it was stronger too, thanks to the impendium shield and sword.

Oh yes, he had many tricks left up his sleeve, for now he knew for certain.

He was Ohan-Jin, heir of Saint Jin the Resilient, and he was going to enjoy shredding the princess apart, piece by piece.

ACKNOWLEDGMENTS

Truth be told, I'd had every intention of writing acknowledgments for my first book, Broken Crown, but then at the last minute, I panicked and chickened out. I was terrified of forgetting someone, and with the pressure of everything else, I figured it would be fine without them. But then I realized there are so many people that without whom, this book would not exist. I swore this time around I would not make the same mistake! So without further ado, here it goes.

First and foremost, I want to thank God for bringing me to this point. All I do is because of Him, and without Him, my passion and ability to write would be for nothing. Thank you, Lord.

To my husband, Alton, who has supported and encouraged me throughout this entire journey. You'd think being a writer that I could put into words how grateful I am to have you in my life and express how much I love you, but there's not nearly enough time in the world for that. So I will keep it simple; thank you. Thank you for encouraging me to "push past my limits" and keep grinding away. Thank you for the Fridays at Starbucks to work alone while you hold down the fort. Thank you for being nearly as passionate about my book as I am. Thank you for not giving up on me and my dream even when I want to. This book would not be here without everything you have done for me. I love you.

To my children, who while they have not made writing

this book easier—quite the opposite actually—they have been my inspiration for these stories. To my sons, I hope you grow up to become men of honor like David, who do the right thing even in the hardest of circumstances. To my own feisty red-headed daughter, I hope you grow up to have the courage and strength of Jill and the humility and kindness of Millie. I love all three of you with my entire heart. You three are the reason I keep going.

To my parents, who taught me to fall in love with reading from a young age and have helped in any way they can since then. To my mom, who probably loves Jack even more than I do and wants so badly to "Pray for Jack" haha! I love and thank you for all you've done for me. To my dad, who is the reason I fell in love with fantasy. You've battled your own metaphorical dragons in recent years, and your perseverance and love for me and your family are the kind they write stories about. Thank you, dad! Words could not truly capture how incredible it is that you've not only supported me but also this dream of becoming a published author. You guys never doubted me (or at least you never told me if you did, haha), so thank you both!

To my sister, Lindsay, my first friend—and enemy, my partner in crime, my critique partner, my reel dealer, my writing buddy, my first fangirl, and everything else. Truthfully, as a kid, I was so annoyed that you wanted to be a writer like me. I wanted to have something that belonged solely to me. Boy, am I glad that was not the case. I'm not sure where I'd be without your writing expertise—though I'm loath to admit it—and I know I'm a stronger writer and better person because of you. The sibling bonds within these pages are inspired by you. So thank you, sis. Once again, words can't truly capture how I feel about you. Love you!

To my editor, Stephanie Cross. Not only did you whip this book into shape and make it so much better, but you have become a sweet, dear friend, and I look forward to working on many more projects together in the future. Thank you for loving Ruined Reign and these characters as much as I do and for helping execute my vision for the story. We are all the better for it!

To my book club, which is conveniently filled with my sister and cousins who are also fantasy lovers. Mikayla, Merritt, Robyn, and Lindsay (again,) you guys are the best, enough said.

To my in-laws, Brett and Laurie, and my brothers and sisters-in-law, almost none of whom are fantasy lovers but have loved and supported me and my books regardless. Elaine, Haley, and Corrie, I realize we share a last name and are kind of stuck together; I scored the lottery when it comes to you guys, and I thank you for being the bonus sisters that you are and being excited for me and my dreams no matter what.

To the rest of my family, who have not only purchased my books and shared them with others but have been my family. I love you all dearly.

To my friends, Joe and Ellen Miner, and Shelly and Cory Ottre, thank you for doing this crazy life with us.

To the other authors who've inspired my work and writing from the beginning, and whose endings gave me enough trauma that I had to end my own books with crazy cliffhangers just to get back at you all. Rick Riordan, Marissa Meyer, Leigh Bardugo, Sabaa Tahir, and many others. I realize you'll likely never read my books, but just in case. This ending was inspired by the heartbreaks caused by you all.

To my Instagram writing and book community and the endless friends I've made there who've helped my book succeed. Your love for my story and these characters is mind-boggling, and it's amazing that I not only have an opportunity to share my books with the world but that people actually read them and liked them and shared them even more! I'm floored by every message I receive and review you guys leave. Seriously, you guys are the reason I keep going and keep writing even when the negative reviews and comments get me down. You guys are amazing!

To my Kickstarter backers who were so excited about Ruined Reign, they contributed financially and helped bring this book into the world. You guys are amazing. Thank you Dawn, Hannah Pennington, Joey Speten, Samantha Newberry, Estee Gray, Shelly, KJ Benson, Sierra Fairclough, Reagan Taylor, Mikayla Hansen, Zoe Zeman, Gee Rothfuss, Izi Miller, Amanda Balter, the Munjar family, Andrea Gibson, Cortney Babcock, Liza Clarke, Elaine Lozier, Kayla Ann, Haven Arthur Russel, Makenna Zornes, Elaine Talbott, Leigh G, Deana, Jessie Wilkerson, Dani Warren, Megan Trahan, Isabel K., Jacqi Tracy, Nancy Newman, Jamie Spalding, Natalie Colburn, Patrice Wallace, Robyn Payne, and a person that loves books and helping. Thank you all so much! I'm so deeply moved by your love for me and my story.

Lastly, I want to thank my husband yet again. Thank you for being my best friend, my rock, my love, and everything in between. Alton, I don't know where I'd be without you. Thank you for inspiring the love story within these pages, even if you aren't much of a romantic yourself. I love you.

ALSO BY SABRINA LOZIER

The Broken Crown Trilogy

Broken Crown

ABOUT THE AUTHOR

SABRINA LOZIER is the author of the young adult novels, *Broken Crown* and *Ruined Reign*. A lover of all things fantasy, it was only a matter of time before she wrote her own stories. She resides in the PNW with her husband, children, and their annoying cat.

Find Her At
Sabrinalozier.com
@Sabrinalozierwrites on Instagram

www.ingramcontent.com/pod-product-compliance
Lightning Source LLC
Chambersburg PA
CBHW022009300726
48970CB00003B/813